Boomer War
(Losing Faith in God and
Country)
BY
Robbie Appenzeller

They march in cadence against the
blood drenched sky
Towards the distant thunder
Seeped in slaughter
Dripping with death
Nourished by timeless words
Spewed by hypocrites and the well
meaning
They march alone
Their waters mingled
The sweat of fear
The tears of loneliness
Endless
The chill is upon them
A cry in the darkness
Distant but distinct
Across the darkness of time
Disperse! Disperse!
Break your ranks
Step into the golden sunlight of
love
Bathe in the quiet water of wisdom
Laugh as children
With warm hearts of compassion
Sleep my sons
Gently
Dreamlessly
In the sweet repose of peace
They march in cadence against the
blood drenched sky
Towards the distant thunder
Forever
Forever
Forever

W.B. Appenzeller 1968

April, 2015
Pattaya, Thailand.

The moment had finally arrived. My laptop was between my legs and I felt comfortable on the purple cushioned lounge chair with an old faded Budweiser towel keeping my thighs from sticking to the naugahyde. I looked out at the sea some twenty feet in front of me noticing that last night's rain had muddied the waters. I glanced back at the empty white space on my computer and wondered *how am I going to start this thing?*

Though I had put off starting this story for forty-five years, I had lots of practice getting it ready because I told it to almost every person I met. If I had an hour or two, I would get lost in this story, which was by far the most significant event in my life.

Following my retirement in 2003, writing down the story became my main goal in life. But, by 2005, I found myself in Bocas del Toro, a tropical island in the Caribbean, where I rediscovered the joy of surfing and that became my passion. I also met a talented singer, Vicky Rosas, and we traveled to Brazil, Ecuador, Mexico, Central America and Peru. I had seen much of America, but when I realized I was going to be seventy in a year, I knew that if I didn't start writing my story soon, I never would.

So there I was in Thailand as far away from everyone as I could get with the laptop between my legs wearing my San Diego

Padres ball cap, my blue eyes staring at the tropical clouds, my mind wondering how the hell to write a story that took place forty-five years ago. I realized right away that it was not going to be a memoir or history book. Too much time had passed. It was an oral history that evolved into what was clearly fiction. It was a novel about a Catholic school trained California surfer who found himself in the middle of Vietnam with training and skills that led to his getting advancement and a degree of power and freedom. At the same time he learns the real reasons the United States is fighting the war and the complicity of the religion he was raised to believe. It is a transformational story of intellectual and spiritual growth.

Blue Balls

Long Bihn Post,
Outside Saigon
South Vietnam
Summer 1968

We loaded the footlocker filled with weapons onto my truck, then, after covering it with truck parts, returned to the motor pool, and hid the footlocker behind the 448 bay. After parking the truck, we walked back to my room.

"Damn, J.R.! You ate twenty-two of those tacos. That's got to be a record," I said as we entered the hooch, wobbly after the five shots of Chivas Regal at the club

"Just doing my job for God and country," said the big Russian, laughing as he threw his hat onto my Hollywood bunk bed freeing his curly blonde hair, "Turn on that air conditioner, Applefuck. It's hot in here."

"Hold your shit, Romanasky, I have to do everything around here." I said also laughing while turning on the air conditioner full blast. Then went over to my built in cabinet to put my fatigue shirt on a hanger and my hat on a hook. I glanced at myself in the foot long mirror and couldn't help admiring my neat new brown mustache and longer slightly curly brown hair. I looked into my eyes and was reminded of my mom, whose eyes were just like mine. I looked over at J.R. his hulking six foot two, tight end body, looking suddenly tense.

"Well, we are fucking committed now, Apple. I didn't really think we could pull off getting a footlocker full of captured weapons from the 25th infantry. It seemed like a cool idea when we were planning it, but now, dude, we could be fucked if the Army finds out."

"Yeah, in the back of my head I know we have made a huge commitment that could get us in deep shit, but I think we got it covered. After TET the Army has way more to worry about than us. But, yes, the idea of trading stuff for guns goes against everything I believe in, but we can trade for some important shit with those guns, JR, and you have to admit, it's about the coolest thing anyone has done here."

"For sure Apple, but what the hell was that with Sergeant Major Wellington in the club? I thought he was going to bust our asses for the shit we got going. He looked like he was reading you the riot act. You must have talked to him for twenty minutes," Romanasky reached for the Jack Daniels on the shelf above my little refrigerator. I placed two glasses on the counter, then offered him a cigarette from my pack of Tareytons.

"I'll tell you later, J.R. He knows what's going on. He just wants his cut. He was pissed off that we weren't making any money. He couldn't believe we were providing meat just because we wanted to be the kings of the club. I didn't tell him about our other business with the guns and shit," I said, snapping open my lighter.

"You know that son of a bitch is the highest ranking non commissioned officer in the entire army. He has power, Apple. He can fuck with us."

"I let him know we're cool. He gave me a lecture about the real reason we're in Vietnam. I listened. I gave him my best Eddie Haskell. What was I going to do? Argue with him? Are you kidding me? I know who that motherfucker is. I know the racket he has going. So, don't sweat it, you Russkie. I got the shit covered."

"I hope so, Applefuck. We got a good thing going here. I don't want to screw it up."

"It's covered, J.R. Don't sweat it."

"You got any oysters left? I want to fry some in this Jack Daniels," he said, laughing. He took a swig from the bottle, opened the refrigerator, and looked in.

"Goddamn, J.R., how can you be hungry after twenty-two tacos?"

"They're tiny little suckers, only two bites to each taco. Why do you care, Applefuck? It's free! Everything is free for us. We're the Kings of Long Bien!" We slapped hands, sliding our hands back to back, then bumped fists, laughing at our exploits.

The door opened. A head appeared from around the corner. In a perfect imitation of Walter Cronkite, the head said, "Good evening, welcome to CBS Evening News. This is the news of the day."

"No, shit, it's the Secretary," Romanasky said, as the door swung open and Tom McNamara from South Boston bounced into the room smiling his straight toothed smiled, his blue eyes gleaming. Behind him, looking up at the bottles on the shelf, stood the Secretary's sidekick Larry Dunphy from deep in Arkansas completely the opposite of McNamara with a crooked nose, small off center black eyes deep in his freckled down right ugly face.

"What have we got here? Mind if I have a shot, J.R.?" When Dunphy flashed his toothless grin we started laughing.

"Goddamn it, Dunphy, I'll give you anything to get you to turn that ugly head away from me. How much ugliness can one man take in a single day? Where are your fucking choppers?" Romanasky asked, laughing and handing him the bottle.

"I left 'em in the truck. I ain't got no more Polident. And you ain't so good lookin' yo'self," Dunphy drawled, grabbing the bottle.

Romanasky drew back his fist like he was going to knock Dunphy across the room.

"Wait a minute," McNamara said, in the perfect voice of NBC News Anchor Chet Huntley. "News just in! The ugliest man in the history of mankind has just been declared. On Long Bien Post, outside of Saigon, a creature beyond description has been discovered. They call it a Dunphy--some long-time descendant of the Neanderthals." We rolled over laughing. Romanasky falling on the lower bunk, grabbed his stomach.

"That ain't so funny," Dunphy mumbled.

The funny looking all-gum smile afterward made us lose it again. Then

Dunphy started sucking his lips inside his mouth, his nose nearly touching his chin, which looked like half his face went into his mouth. Then he blew out his lips, which fluttered like a horse's. That was his signature move and drove us crazy with laughing.

"Don't fucking look at me, Dunphy, I can't take it anymore. I'm going to bust a gut," Romanasky screamed. When Dunphy smiled revealing his two rows of pink gums, it made us hysterical again.

The door opened and my roommate Freddy Chaves stepped into the room with his fresh fatigues, newly grown thin mustache and dark glassy eyes. "What the hell is so funny?" he asked. We were so out of control that we could only point to Dunphy, who grinned, sucking his lips in and out. While laughing hard, Chaves asked, "Where are his teeth?"

"He used up his fucking Polident," Romanasky yelled, pounding the bed with his fist.

"I got some Raleighs," Chaves said with his South Florida accent. "Anyone want to take a hit?"

The weed around Long Bihn came in repacked cigarette packs that you could trade for a carton of Salem Cigarettes. There were three kinds, a pack of Winston's, a menthol flavored Paxton and a

Raleigh that was dipped in opium. We called that a "three day weekend."

"Goddamn it, Chaves, how the hell do you even walk around after smoking one of those opium soaked things?" I asked, catching my breath, trying not to look at Dunphy. "I told you to lay off that shit. You got a job to do, man. You can't be fucked up all the time!"

"Why not?" He looked at me, dumb-founded.

Taking another swig from the Jack Daniels, Dunphy chimed in, "I gots ta say, I agree wid him, Apple." His toothless grin set us off again.

"Get out of here, Dunphy," Romanasky screamed, holding his gut. "You're killing me. I can't look at that face."

McNamara, interrupted in his deep Walter Cronkite voice, "And that's the way it is, a day like all days, filled with those events that alter and illuminate our time. A day that saw the first death by ugliness in recorded history. John Romanasky from Sacramento, California died laughing today due to the absolute ugliness of his comrade Larry Dunphy."

We just about passed out when the Secretary finished.

"Damn, you're good," Chaves yelled. "I swear to God, you're as good as Rich Little."

McNamara, now doing Johnny Carson, said, "Well, thanks, Chaves. Tonight our guests are Jonathan Winters, Charo and the hilarious Rich Little." He hummed the "Tonight Show" music. We hummed along or laughed. Just as he was starting on his Jonathan Winters, we heard a loud knock on the door.

When the door swung open, there stood our company clerk North. "Attention!" he yelled, sharply and stood stiff as a board.

In walked a young man in a freshly starched uniform with silver bars on his lapels. We jumped to attention, eyes forward, hands to our sides, fingers slightly curled, heels locked, feet at an angle, eyes straight ahead, focused on an imaginary object in front of us.

"At ease!" the lieutenant said in a commanding voice. We continued to look straight ahead, separating our legs, placing our hands behind our backs. "I mean it, men, be at ease," said the officer, his accent betraying his Southern roots.

A little shorter than me, about five foot seven or so, he wore black horn-rimmed glasses and had a clean-shaven baby face. "What's going on here, men?"

We'd heard rumors about a new commanding officer. This had to be the third or fourth since I arrived six months ago.

"Letting off a little steam after a long day's work, sir," I said, noticing the name Weber in black above his pocket.

"And who are you, Soldier?"

"I'm Specialist Fifth Class Appenzeller, sir."

"What do you do, Specialist?"

"He runs the motor pool, sir," chimed in North.

"Oh, so you're the colonel's golden boy?"

I shrugged.

"Is this your room, specialist?" he asked, while looking around, focusing on each thing in my room.

By now I had accumulated a little stove, a refrigerator, a shelf with bottles of good alcohol on his left. My color TV sat on top of the refrigerator. Another shelf had a turntable and receiver connected to two large speakers in the corners. Album covers were behind the turntable, featuring Cream, the Doors, and Jimi Hendrix. What we called Hollywood bunk beds were in front of him with built-in cabinets on the wall to his right. The air conditioner was in the only window.

Six of us were crammed into this eight by eight foot space. North remained outside the door. The room now seemed quiet after the ruckus of the last few minutes, the loud whirr of the air conditioner making the only sound.

"I have a room this large, Specialist, with a bunk, a wall locker and a footlocker, he said slowly, still pondering each object in the room. "How did you get all of this?"

"Trade, sir."

"What's that?"

"We trade for things, sir. If you have something valuable to trade, then you can get things. You can buy some of it from the PX, but most of it came through a trade."

Silently mulling over my words, he looked at me.

"Is there something that the lieutenant would like to trade for? In my position in the motor pool I have access to almost anything."

After another long silence. "Well, I would like an air conditioner to start with, was that Appenzeller?"

"Yes, sir, Appenzeller," I paused then shrugged. "Air conditioners are difficult to get, sir." Then inspiration hit me like a thunderbolt that involved surfing and my beautiful wife Alexandra. "But I might be able to get one, if the lieutenant has something to trade for it."

"What do you mean, Appenzeller? What would I have to trade for an air conditioner?"

"Well, there's one thing that you can do for me that would be of equal value to an air conditioner."

"And what could that possibly be?" he asked, eyebrows arched.

"A seven-day emergency leave, sir."

His eyes widened, startled. "I can't do that, Soldier. What's your emergency?"

I waited a few seconds, finally saying, "A bad case of blue balls, sir."

"What did you say?"

"Blue balls, sir. I'm married, and I haven't been with the wife since I took my R&R to Hawaii. I have a bad case of blue balls."

"Soldier, you are being impertinent!"

"No, sir, the lieutenant asked what he could trade. I said he could trade an emergency leave, he asked why, and the fact is, I have blue balls."

"But I can't possibly get you an emergency leave."

"I believe you can, sir. Specialist North, our company clerk, can explain how."

North stared at me, his eyes like daggers.

"Is that true, North?" Lieutenant Weber, turned to him. "You know how to get this emergency leave?"

North moved his glare from me to the lieutenant, his eyes softening. "I believe I can, sir. It's been done in the past."

I knew this because North had gone to the Philippines twice on an emergency leave.

"Do we have a deal, sir?" I asked.

"Maybe, Specialist, I'll look into it." He paused, his eyes fixed on me, then said. "Carry on, men."

He started to walk out, then stopped, looking back at me. "Appenzeller, I'll check on this emergency leave business."

"When you do, sir, it would be my privilege to get you that air conditioner."

Lieutenant Weber turned sharply, then marched out of the room. North, frowned at me with squinted eyes, then pulled the door closed behind him, and went into the barracks.

"Attention!" North barked to the soldiers on their bunks. We heard the men scrambling to attention.

I put my hands up, palms outward, to prevent the inevitable eruption. McNamara opened the door, stuck his head out, then looking back at us, announced in his best David Brinkley voice, "The lieutenant has left the building."

Everybody practically fell down laughing. "Blue balls!" shouted Romanasky, "Blue balls, Applefuck, that's a classic!"

"You ain't just got blue balls, Apple, you got big 'uns, too." Dunphy said with a big toothless grin that made us erupt in laughter.

"I'm going surfing again, you bastards! And I might never come back!" I yelled.

Romanasky, slapping my back so hard I almost fell over, said, "You're a motherfucker, Applefuck. Man, you're a cool-ass motherfucker."

While we stood by the beds laughing, we looked back at the other three, each had a bottle in his hands. When they raised the bottles high, the Secretary, in his Tom McNamara voice said. "Hail to the King of the REMFs."

As I turned to Romanaski, his light blue eyes shining, we clinked glasses and it hit me just how cool this day was and wondered how in the middle of a horrible war I managed to put my self into this amazingly funny and happy place. I looked at the smiling faces of my comrades while an overwhelming thrill swelled in me knowing I had money and soon would see my beautiful Alexandra again and I'd be riding Hawaiian waves. I glanced around my room at my laughing friends and wondered, *how the hell did I get here.*

PART ONE
Drafted

Chapter 1
The CAMFs

Fall 1966
Ventura, California

The dream was familiar. I'm walking around the college campus suddenly realizing I had forgotten to go to a class the entire semester. *How could I have done this?* My heart is racing, blood pounding my head, hot guilt flashing. So intense are the feelings, that I move quickly from the dream state to consciousness, trying to count how many times this dream had invaded my sleep since starting college. Finally, looking around the small room in our one-bedroom apartment, I sensed Alexandra's eyes on me, and knew those eyes, so usually filled with love, now narrowed in deep concern.

"Repeat for me what you said last night before you passed out."

Even with her dark brown pageboy hair in disarray, her even darker eyes glaring at me, she was beautiful.

Trying to recall what I told her, I swallowed, suddenly remembering. "Oh, yeah," I started, then hesitated before getting the nerve to continue. "At the poker game last night Joey Cohen and I put this plan together to join the Army on the buddy system."

She stared even harder at me then slowly asked, "And when would you and your, *buddy,* Joey Cohen want to do this joining?" Again she narrowed her eyes as if she knew a correct answer was dubious.

"This week?" I answered, apprehensively, fearing her response.

"This week, this week!" she repeated louder. "And you're going to leave me with this apartment to clean, quit your job, then just take off?"

"Well, I guess so." I cleared my throat. "Not a good idea?"

She glared at me. "About as good an idea as you quitting college to watch the World Series."

I had, in fact, quit school to watch the World Series after betting fifty bucks on the Dodgers. How the hell would I know the Dodgers would only get two runs in the whole series? The Orioles in a four-game sweep. Who would have guessed that?

"But the Dodgers had Drysdale and Koufax," I muttered.

"I don't care who they had. It wasn't a good idea to quit school. It's also not a good idea for you to abandon me here while you go off with your "buddy," Joey Cohen!"

"Okay, bad idea." I looked away. "So what is a good idea?"

Her voice softened, "Robbie, sweetheart, let's stick with our plan. You give notice at work. We tell the owner about the apartment, and in a month or so you enlist. I know this is frightening for you, and you don't want to do this alone, but I will be there for you. You know that, right?"

"Of course, Babe, I am sorry, my life just seems so out of control right now. I can't believe I'm actually going to be in the Army, and that Army is fighting in a war. I just don't know what to do. I know quitting school was stupid, but I already had my draft notice. I felt like I couldn't concentrate on school."

"That's over now, Robbie, we have to look to the future." She kissed me softly on the lips, and gave my hand a tender squeeze before getting up to go into the bathroom. I glanced at my nine-two Dewey Weber in the corner and knew I would feel better if I went for a surf session at Ventura Point.

That was the second time I had quit college. The first time I did so with five of my fellow CAMF brothers, led by my lifelong friend Tom Golden.

Tom's dad owned Matt's Liquor Store, the biggest liquor store in Oxnard, California. Tom and I had been friends since kindergarten at Santa Clara Catholic School. Throughout elementary school Tom had been the quarterback, and I was a running back.

In high school Tom went to Loyola High in Los Angeles. We were both the oldest sons of large families - mine with ten, and Tom's, eight. Tom came back to Santa Clara for his senior year. We were on the baseball team where he played second base, while I took shortstop. We were a hell of a double-play combination. I made All League and All CIF. I could hit. Tom couldn't.

Tom went to Marquette University after scoring high on the SATs, while I scored so low colleges that originally wanted me to play either football or baseball, pulled their scholarships off the table. The local junior college wasn't so picky.

The Ventura Pirates wanted me to play football, but I wanted to concentrate on baseball. The football season started. My friends on the team kept pestering me, so I went to football practice for one day, but when my one hundred-fifty-five pounds on a five-foot-nine frame got knocked around by the men that played for the Pirates, I didn't show up the next day.

One of the assistant coaches for the football team was the head baseball coach. I didn't get in the pre-baseball P.E. class he ran. When I asked to get in, the coach indicated he didn't want me. He thought I was a quitter. He might have been right.

I identified myself as an athlete throughout high school, avoiding places where there was alcohol, but not by design. Practicing and playing football and baseball along with surfing took up most of my time. If I had free time I wanted to ride the waves or be with my girlfriend. Alcohol wasn't involved, but hugging, kissing and touching became my favorite extracurricular activity. Unfortunately, I lost that girlfriend and was no longer on a team. What was I to do?

I saw Tom Golden during the summer. He was asked not to return to Marquette, but never explained why. He said he was going to Ventura College and suggested we find a place to room together. We looked around Ventura and found an old Victorian style house for sale as a business. On one side of the property was the five-story Bell Telephone Company; on the other a couple of women operated a hair salon. Tom went to the real estate agent and pleaded with him to let us live in the place until it sold. He even bargained him down to a hundred and twenty-five bucks a month. When we got a key to the place we were stoked. It had a living room, dining room, kitchen, bedroom and a bathroom downstairs, and upstairs, four big bedrooms and a bathroom. The large front porch faced the one-square block of the lovely downtown Ventura Park.
"This is perfect," Tom said. "It'll make a great frat house." Not having gone to a four-year college I

wasn't sure what a frat house was. "And I know the perfect name for it." He had a gleam in his blue eyes, a big smile on his face.

"Yeah? And what would that be?"

"We're gonna be the Cool-Ass Motherfuckers," Tom said, laughing. "It's going to be the CAMF house. We'll sell monthly memberships. Ten guys can stay here for a hundred each. Man, this will be the coolest thing to hit this town ever." I started to realize why Tom might have been kicked out of Marquette.

The CAMF house did become popular at Ventura College - there was no competition. We cut off the membership at a hundred and had parties almost every night. Tom had access to his dad's liquor supply, so our bar was well stocked. Tom developed a relationship with the police. When a party got out of control, Tom would call the cops, and they would arrive acting like they were breaking it up. Tom gave the cops bottles of whiskey as a thank-you gift. We didn't bother anybody living around us because the businesses were closed by six. The CAMF house was the coolest thing going.

Tom was president of the CAMF, and I became secretary-treasurer. Eight inch letters on a crossbar above the porch said CAMF HOUSE. We had a dance area in the living room, a folk section in the dining room, where I sang and played *Blowin' in the Wind, Don't Think Twice,* my favorite *Greenback Dollar* and several others.

Eight other friends from Santa Clara High lived in the house. A poker game started at midnight, and an exclusive group called the "Sun Up Club" toasted the dawn with a Tom Collins every morning.

On Saturdays my fellow CAMF men and I buried bits of meat under the grass across from us in Ventura Park. We sat on the porch with a Tom Collins laughing when people trying to train their dogs at a class held there each week, yanked the leashes and smacked their dogs, when they went nuts trying to get at the meat.

It was at the CAMF house that I met Alexandra - tall, dark haired, olive skinned, high cheek bones with the body of a model. We really fell for each other, and it wasn't long before we became a couple. She went to Ventura and got good grades. I was in the Sun Up Club and laid down about six in the morning. I'd ask someone to wake me for my first class at eight, but Alexandra usually woke me about three or four in the afternoon. This went on for about a month.

We knew we were all going to get Fs in our classes unless we withdrew and received Ws instead. We had a CAMF meeting led by Tom. "Okay, CAMF men.

Tomorrow we go from class to class making our teachers give us our Ws. We'll tell them we're joining the Air Force." We nodded in agreement.

The next day we marched into each class like heroes demanding our Ws. We drove to downtown Oxnard to talk with the Air Force recruiter. He told us our options. We took a few tests and said we'd be back the next day to sign the papers.

That night, Alexandra and I spent the night together. I woke up thinking one thing, *Six years! Joining the Air Force would be a six-year active-duty commitment. Six years! Enlisting in the Army was three years; if drafted it would only be two.* The next day I didn't go see the recruiter to sign any papers.

When we saw Tom at the CAMF house that afternoon he was pissed off. "Where the fuck were you guys?" Apparently Tom was the only guy to sign on the bottom line.

All of us said the same thing: "Six years, Tom, six years!"

"Holy shit," Tom shouted. "Six fucking years!"

Chapter 2
Drafted

A month after we'd ceremoniously received our Ws, I got a call from my mom. "Robbie, I have an important-looking letter from the government addressed to you. Honey, it looks like it could be a draft notice. You didn't quit school, did you?"

I gulped. *Holy shit. Only a month after the Ws and the Army was calling? What was I going to do?* I kind of knew there was a war. There were a few long-haired weirdos at Ventura College protesting something, but I was a preppy, and they were weirdos. We didn't have a TV in the CAMF house, and if we did, I wouldn't have watched the news. The front of my mind didn't know what was going on. The back of my mind did. It knew there was a war. It knew my dad was anti-war.

Willard Butt Appenzeller junior was the first in the family to graduate from college. Raised in Portsmouth, Virginia, my dad became a baseball and track star in high school, earned a scholarship to the College of William and Mary, was elected the president of his fraternity, and graduated near the top of his class. The year he graduated the Japanese bombed Pearl Harbor. He enlisted in the Navy, and was sent to midshipman school in Chicago. After being a first mate, he got his own ship, a sub chaser, at age twenty-two. He served in the South Pacific, and came away from that experience hating both the military and war.

While on temporary duty in Santa Barbara, he met a beautiful nineteen year old from Texas who happened to be the lead singer with a jazz band playing at the Biltmore Hotel. Mitch Smith was vivacious, and he knew it. Captivated, he pursued her after his return from the South Pacific. They married and had me, the first product of the marriage.

I dreaded telling my Dad that I had quit school, exposing myself to the draft. He was a kind man and my friends loved him. I loved him. He was the head counselor at Oxnard High School, and was a follower of the Carl Rogers school of psychology, which emphasized empathy. He learned that empathy led to understanding, and that understanding led to sharing, the outcome being a loving relationship. He understood what I felt. I knew he was proud of my athletic accomplishments in high school, and had high hopes for me, but was understanding when I didn't do so well on my SATs. I dreaded he wouldn't understand my being drafted. How could I disappoint both him and my mom?

"Robert," my mom said, after a long pause on the phone. She only called me Robert when she was worried about something or angry at me.

"Mom," I said slowly. "Send that letter back to the government. Tell them you don't know where I am."

Silence. "But, Robert, I do know where you are. I can't lie to the government."

"I know that, Mom, but, in an hour, I won't know where I am."

"Robert, what are you planning to do?"

"I don't know, Mom, I don't know, but I know I won't be here." I paused again and thought about the wondering troubadours I admired like Hoyt Axton and Bob Dylan who hit the road and went from town to town, singing. Then suddenly inspired, I announced, "Mom, I'm going on the road. I don't know where."

"Robert, honey, please tell me what you're going to do."

"I really don't know, Mom. Just send the letter back. I'll tell you when I get to wherever I'm going."

"But where, Robert? Honey, where are you going?"

"I don't know, Mom, I just gotta go. I love you, Mom."

When I hung up, shaking and terrified at what I was about to do, I went to my room looking around for a suitcase. Seeing none, I asked my surf bud

Rick, who was studying, if I could borrow his. He looked up from his book.

"Sure, it's under my bed."

I knelt down and pulled it out.

"Where're you going?" He looked puzzled with his eyebrows raised, his eyes wide open.

"I don't know."

Rick's dad, a commander in the Navy, taught him discipline. He had a plan and signed up for the Navy Reserves. He'd be leaving at the end of the semester.

I stuffed my clothes into the suitcase, put my guitar into its case, and counted my money - fifty bucks. I checked my self out in the mirror and thought I looked pretty cool in my blue long sleeve button down shirt with tailored tan slacks and penny loafers. I combed my brown wavy hair into place so it looked preppy. Looking at my dark blue eyes, I thought of my mom whose eyes were exactly the same. Carrying my suitcase and guitar, I walked out the door, crossed through the park, headed down the street to the on-ramp at Highway 101, and there, like Bob Dylan and Hoyt Axton, I put my thumb out to hitchhike for the first time in my life.

While car after car rushed by, no one looked closely at me as I stood there, which gave me time to ponder my situation. I had a positive sense of self in high school. My football and baseball coach held me in high regard and gave me a chance. I did well and our teams did well. I received awards that heightened my self esteem and had several girl friends who gave me affection. I was also a surfer, which was the latest and coolest trend. It pissed off the bikers, but their girlfriends loved me. Now a year and a half out of high school, without the constant appreciation, I was floundering, drinking every day, staying up all night, doing nothing to better myself. Now I was drafted. The military was definitely not the career path I had in mind. What that career path was, I didn't know, but I had heard enough from my father to realize that being in the Army was dead last on the list.

After a half hour a guy stopped. He stuck his crew cut head out the window. "Where ya headed?" he asked in a Southern drawl.

"I don't know. Where are you headed?"

"I'm going to El Paso, Texas."

Realizing my mom had relatives in El Paso, this was serendipity. "El Paso, Texas is exactly where I want to go." I grabbed the handle of the passenger door, threw my stuff into the back seat, and slammed the door shut.

We drove non-stop to El Paso. Billy, the driver, dressed in a Pendleton shirt and jeans, was kind enough to find a phone booth, so I could call my mom to tell her I was in El Paso.

"Thank God, Robbie. Your father and I have been so worried."

"I know, Mom. I'm sorry to make you worry. Do you know where either of your Cousins Kenneth or Bob are located?"

"I have Kenneth's number, Robbie. I'll call him and tell him you're in El Paso."

"Give me his number, Mom. I'll ask him where he lives. The guy I'm with is nice. He'll take me there."

She gave me Cousin Kenneth's number, so I called him, gave the phone to Billy, and after he wrote down directions, he gave me a ride to Cousin Kenneth's house. I thanked him, shook hands, and he wished me well before driving off.

Kenneth was cool, and gave me a big hug when I arrived. We hadn't seen each other since 1956 when I was 10. He reintroduced me to his wife, Alice, who had a blonde bouffant hair do and their two children. They moved the boy out of his room and gave me his bed.

Kenneth had been the athletic director at Texas Western College. He quit that job, and was supposed to be studying to be an insurance agent. Every day we would leave for the library to study. At least that's what he told Alice. Instead, we headed straight for Juarez, Mexico where he bet on East

Coast horse races. We had eggs with shots of tequila and were both drunk by noon.

Drunk or not, we would drive across two borders to Sunland Park in New Mexico in the afternoon where his mom, my rich Aunt Dovie, had a box seat. We bet on horses, and I won some and lost some, but eventually lost my fifty bucks.

After five days of this, Alice figured out what we were doing, and told Cousin Kenneth that I had to go. "Where ya wanna go, Robbie?" Cousin Kenneth asked.

"I guess I'll head to Virginia, where I was born."

"Well, why don't I drop you off at this truck stop I know."

"Cool with me."

He dropped me off at a truck stop at the edge of town, gave me five bucks and said, "I envy you. You can go anywhere in the world right now. I have a wife and kids. I'm stuck here for life."

I didn't feel sorry for him. I was back on the road with no particular place to go.

I could talk Texas talk by then, and knew about "Dandy" Don Meredith and the Dallas Cowboys. I met a tall thin trucker with a black leather vest and black jeans sitting at the counter who was heading to Houston. My saying, "How 'bout them Cowboys?" got Jim Bob's attention. He was glad to give me a ride to Houston. There, he introduced me to another leather clad trucker with a long beard going all the way to Atlanta. I felt like I was lucky.

I had only been in the South once before, when my dad, mom, and the family drove back to Virginia in our Chevy station wagon the summer of '56. I remembered being startled by the discrimination I saw then and was curious about how it was now after the passage of the 1964 Civil Rights Act and the just passed Voting Rights Act.

The first trucker, Jim Bob, asked me to play the guitar and sing him a few tunes. He stopped me in the middle of *Blowing in the Wind*. "Son, is that the kinda stuff you gonna play in the South? That shit ain't gonna work. You know anything by Buck Owens or Jimmy Dean?" I nodded no. "Well, if they ask ya to play, you tell um you got busted strings. They're gonna wonder about you if they hear that Bob Dylan shit. Now where'd you say you was from?"

"I was born in Virginia, but my dad and mom moved with me to California when I was a year and a half."

"Well, shit. Don't tell anyone down south that you're from California. They'll think you're weird or something. You were born in Virginia, right?" I nodded. "Well, tell them you're from Virginia. That way they'll think you're a good ole boy and won't treat you like shit. We got freedom riders invading the South right now. If they think you're a freedom rider, they'll beat the holy shit outta ya."

From that moment on I was from Virginia. If asked where I'd been, I said, "Texas." If asked where I was going, I said, "Back to Virginia." If asked what I was doing, I'd say, "I'm going back to join the Army."

It worked like a charm. When we went through the Deep South, at truck stops I'd give that army line to the waitress. She would sigh saying, "Honey, whatever you want to eat is on the house." One waitress in Biloxi, Mississippi, after putting a plate of food in front of me, smiled and took a picture off the wall to show me. It was a picture of her father and grandfather standing with a bunch of white men next to some poor black guy who had been lynched. She showed it like you would show pictures of your relatives next to a deer they had shot. I gulped, looked away, trying to hide my repulsion.

In Atlanta I ran out of truckers and was stuck on the back roads. I was told that they were arresting anyone hitchhiking near the freeways. I hadn't slept in days and wore the same clothes I'd worn in Texas. It was early December and cold. Every ride was for less than ten miles. I met all kinds of people. Some I couldn't understand; they were speaking English, but it could have been Pig Latin. Two guys near the Georgia, South Carolina border wanted to take me on a "nigger hunt." I declined, telling them that the next stop was mine. Another was a preacher who talked at me for half of one night. He knew his Bible, able to quote passage after passage. I realized that even though I was raised Catholic, and attended Catholic schools for twelve years, I didn't know anything about the Bible. Consequently, I just had to listen, and couldn't counter his arguments, which made me wonder about my Catholic School upbringing.

When I got back on the road, a middle aged pudgy guy picked me up. I gave him my Southern boy going home to join the army line. He started talking and said he had been in World War II. He described his tour of duty in Italy. With little or no sleep for the last few days, I began nodding off, my head leaning on the window but could still hear him talking. He was telling me about the boys he had met in Italy. I wasn't paying close attention, but that changed when I felt his hand on my leg.

I shook my head trying to grasp what he was saying and doing. He leaned toward me so he could caress my leg, his eyes glancing from me to the road. Perspiration formed on his forehead and under his eyes. He seemed to be breathing heavily.

"What are you doing!" I asked, shaking my head back to full consciousness. It dawned on me. He was talking about the boys in Italy, and he thought I was one of those boys. I pushed his hand away. "What's wrong with you?" I asked looking at him.

He now looked frightened and started apologizing. "I'm so sorry, I thought you were one of those boys I had met. I miss them so much."

Oh my God, I thought, *he was* "queer." *He liked boys, not girls.* I had heard rumors that there were men that felt that way, but I didn't think it was true. It wasn't a myth. Here was one right here on the back roads of South Carolina. "Pull over and let me out!"

He did so quickly. Perspiration now covered his face, his pathetic frightened eyes stared at me. I grabbed the handle, reached into the back seat for my luggage and guitar case, then hopped out. He looked relieved that I did't try to hurt him, but also sad that I wasn't one of those boys.

After another day of no sleep, I desperately threw rocks at cars that wouldn't pick me up, hoping they would come back, believing I could talk them into a ride. Realizing that I was close to a freeway, I walked across some fields, venturing onto the four-lane road, sticking out my thumb waiting to be arrested. At least I would have a place to sleep.

A guy with horn rimmed glasses and a mustache pulled over right away to warn me that hitchhiking was illegal on the freeway. When I asked where he was going, he said Norfolk, Virginia. I told him my grandpa lived not far away in Portsmouth. He felt sorry for me, and said he would give me a ride. "Thank you, Jesus," I said like the preacher I had met a day or so earlier.

He took me to my grandfather's house. My grandfather was Willard Butt senior, but the family called him Pappy and my grandmother Anna was Mammy. They didn't know I was coming, and barely believed I was who I said I was. He called my dad who confirmed that I was his oldest son. They gave me the up-stairs apartment filled with crab cages. Pappy was retired from the Naval shipping yards, and was now a crabber. After finding the bed, I slept long and hard.

When I recovered, Pappy invited my godfather, Robert Grandon, over for a visit. I was named after him and my dad's brother, Uncle Bob. A big black guy carried Grandon into Pappy's par-lor. Grandon was a tiny little man with a high voice who had had polio as a child. I was told my dad used to carry him on his back from class to class in high school and college. Now he was rich, because he invested in property and became a slumlord.

He ranted and raved all night about how he would kill the members of the Supreme Court for having started the end of segregation with Brown vs. the Board of Education. "I'd shoot that nigger-loving Earl Warren myself if I had the chance," Grandon growled. Pappy and Uncle Bob seemed to agree.

I couldn't help but protest. "Dad never allows us to use the "n" word. He's proud that the president of the student body of Oxnard High is a Negro. I have a black kid in our class at Santa Clara, Bob Zander, who plays on our basketball team, and I consider him a cool guy and a friend."

Robert Grandon looked at me like I was a traitor, and called me, "A nigger-lover from California." Now I knew why my mom and dad moved me out of Virginia when I was a toddler. I had never heard such hatred. Standing quietly in the back of the room was the tall black man who had carried Robert Grandon, and carefully set him in a chair. I wondered what he thought about the conversation.

I lived in the apartment above Mammy and Pappy for a couple of weeks and found a job selling shoes at J. C. Penney. I wrote long letters to Alexandra telling her how much I loved her. She wrote back that she felt the same.

I proposed marriage in one of the letters, leaving it to her to tell her father, retired Commander David Johnson, who would be concerned to hear that his beautiful, oldest daughter, a good student, would be marrying an unemployed college dropout. In typical Robbie Appenzeller fashion, I left it up to Alexandra to tell him the good news. Alexandra had gumption. I knew she wouldn't back down.

I took a long bus ride back to Oxnard from Portsmouth, knowing Alexandra was waiting for me. We drove directly to the secret lemon grove, where we parked her blue VW bug, and fogged up the windows, as we somehow made steamy, passionate love in the passenger seat. I had five orgasms, relief for my first bad bout of blue balls.

We got married at Santa Clara Church with a high mass in Latin by Father O'Sullivan who was my confessor and my dad's good friend. It was a big wedding. Alexandra looked fabulous in an embroidered white dress with a middle eastern looking head dress and a long veil. The reception was at the Officers Club at the Port Hueneme Seabee Base with a sit down dinner and a big band. The band called up my mom to sing and she wowed the crowd with her renditions of *Won't You Come Home Bill Bailey*. She snapped her fingers and smiled her radiant smile and then brought my dad, Bill, on stage to sing *Just My*

Bill to him directly. There wasn't a dry eye in the room.

After the wedding, we drove Alexandra's VW bug to Las Vegas for our honeymoon. I don't think we ever left our room.

We got a little apartment. Alexandra continued at Ventura College working at Colonel Sanders' KFC. I got a job at a fancy restaurant called the Trade Winds as a bus boy and re-enrolled at Ventura College once again. Then came the World Series, the hitless Dodgers and Brooks-Fucking-Robinson makes MVP.

Chapter 3
Applefuck

Eating a steady diet of Col. Sanders' Kentucky Fried Chicken and sweet and sour shrimp at the Trade Winds added several pounds to my body the first few months after Alexandra and I were married.

I had an uncle who lived with my family after his father died. Dick, whom we called Stubby, was five foot six, but weighed about three hundred pounds. Though overweight, it didn't stop him from playing sports. We had a basketball court in the alley behind our house on G Street in Oxnard. The alley was flat, but raised up for the garage behind us. Stubby and I could beat anybody in Oxnard on that court. I could shoot over a much taller guy from the raised section; Stubby could block out a seven-footer. He moved his big body between the tall guy and the basket, and if I didn't make the shot from the outside, he'd get the rebound, and toss the ball underhanded onto the backboard into the net.

Before I quit school the second time the draft notice came to our apartment, I thought being married would keep me out of the army, but found out we had to have a kid. We didn't, and none was on the way. It looked like I was doomed, unless I could find another avenue out of the army. Stubby was the only guy I knew who was beating the draft. The government called him every six months. He would go to L.A., get on the scales, and they'd send him home.

Since I was already pretty overweight myself, I went on a banana cream pie and brownie diet, eating as much fattening foods as possible. Days before my physical I tipped the scale at nearly two hundred pounds. I looked like the Pillsbury dough boy, but didn't care. This was my ticket out of the army.

I hugged and kissed Alexandra, and said goodbye to my friends before leaving on a bus to L.A. confident my weight would keep me out. "Don't worry," I assured everyone, "I'll be back soon."

When we went through the physical with my friend, the Fire Chief's son, Davey Manfrino, one of the funniest guys I had ever met, he purposely forgot to wipe his butt when he took his last crap before the physical. When the doctor stuck his finger up his ass, he said, "God how disgusting!"

"What did you expect? Candy?" Davey said.

Those of us standing around in our boxers couldn't stop laughing.

I couldn't wait to get on the scales, get weighed and sent home. When my turn came to step onto the scales, I leaned down as hard as I could. The sergeant adjusting the scales, frowned at me and shook his head in disgust at my belly protruding between my boxers and my tee shirt.

"God, you're fat," he snarled.

"Thank you," I said proudly, thinking my plan had worked.

"But not fat enough! FATBOY, YOU'RE IN THE UNITED STATES ARMY!"

Oh, shit!

Later, I found myself in a room with a bunch of other losers with my hand in the air repeating whatever the sergeant in front of me was saying. When we finished, he said, "You are in the Army of the United States of America. You'll gather your things and get on a bus outside. By tomorrow morning you'll be in Fort Ord to do your basic training. NOW GET THE FUCK OUT OF HERE!"

We were allowed to use the phone, and I called Alexandra.

"Babe, I wasn't fat enough. They swore me in. I'm a soldier in the United States Army. In an hour I will be on a bus to Fort Ord."

"Oh, Robbie, I'm so sad. I'll tell your folks, I know they'll be worried. I'll visit you as soon as I can. You be strong, my love."

When we arrived at Fort Ord, a small wiry Filipino sergeant yelled at us to get out of the bus. After we exited, he stood in front of us screaming. I looked to my left and right. No one knew what the hell he was saying, but we soon realized he was ordering us to go to a building to get our uniforms. I got a size large everything. They took away our civilian stuff, which we put into boxes to send home. One idiot brought a bowling ball. The sergeants went nuts laughing at that guy, showing it to everybody as if it was the craziest thing they had every seen.

The Filipino sergeant ordered us to run to the next place where we had to get our hair cut. The barber asked how I would like it cut. "A little on the sides," I said, like a dope.

"Okay," he smirked, and skinned off all my hair in less than a minute. On the way out I glanced in a mirror and noticed my bald head seemed kind of pointed. I looked like a pinhead in the freak circus, and remembered my mom said I was in the birth canal for twenty-seven hours. I had befriended a few guys before we went into the barber shop, but couldn't recognize anyone when I got out. Everyone looked the same with their green uniforms and white bald heads.

We marched to a building where we took tests, and answered some questions about our interests. I said I didn't like to walk, I didn't like to shoot, I didn't like anything that might get me into the infantry. I had joined the army at the last minute, adding an extra year to my commitment. The recruiter said I would go to something called "computer" school, and would be sent to Germany; however, the sergeants at Fort Ord said, "Forget all that. The army will decide where, when, and how you will serve."

We got assigned a barracks, which were two-story wooden buildings that were similar to those I had seen at Port Hueneme Sea Bee Base, or in World War Two films. I found a bottom bunk. The guy in the top bunk had been in the navy. When he took off his shirt, I saw he had several tattoos. The most prominent looked like Mickey Mouse, but when I looked closer, I realized that Mickey had a penis for a nose. *What the fuck is that?* I thought. *Who would put that on their arm for the rest of their lives?* It was clear to me that I was meeting a whole other class of people.

For the next couple of days we learned a few tips from a tall skinny guy with black horn rimmed glasses waiting to go to officer training school. He showed us how to stand at attention, do left and right face, how to march, and how to keep in step. He wasn't a bad guy.

On the third day the officer training guy came into the barracks with a sad look. He stuck a piece of paper onto the bulletin board that announced our drill sergeant. He turned to us and with a grim expression said. "You guys are in deep shit, I got some bad news."

We glanced at each other, gulped and waited to hear about this bad news.

"You've been assigned to the B11, led by the meanest son of a bitch in the army, Staff Sergeant Hostetler. He's a killer, boys. An expert in hand-to-hand combat. Some of you won't make it. I'll give you a heads up, he hates two kinds of people, college guys, because he thinks they're smart alecks, and fat guys because he thinks they're lazy. So, good luck, boys, you're going to need it."

We had our names on our shirts by this time. Everyone in the platoon took a glimpse my way. I'd talked to several, who knew I'd gone to college, and in my size large uniform, they could see I was fat. Now I was a two time loser - a college drop-out fat boy. Grinding my teeth hard, my front tooth popped out. "Oh shit," I yelled, and caught it before it hit the ground.

I'd lost that tooth in the big April swell of '63. Against the wishes of my baseball coach, I'd gone surfing with my friends at a place called La Conchita. We hadn't surfed it before, but this swell was lining up great there. We jumped a fence onto the pier, threw our boards into the water, and dived in after them.

By mid-day, a group of Southers, guys from L.A., were on the inside down from us. We were on the point by the pier. I took off on a set wave, cruising down the face. Seeing two Southers taking off in front of me, I yelled, got by one, while the other went over the falls. His board came flying out of the water without my seeing it, hitting me directly under my chin. The next thing I remember, I was dreaming about drowning. When I opened my eyes, I realized I was lying on the bottom of the ocean. I thrust myself to the surface to get a gulp of air. Through my wet hair I saw another wave crashing toward me. I dove under that one, caught the next, and bodysurfed it into shallow water. When I stumbled to the jetty, my teeth felt like I had popcorn in several of my molars. Reaching back with my tongue to push the grit out, blood and several bits of teeth splashed into the water.

My mom took me to the dentist, who worked on my back teeth for days. When he put gold in the holes, he thought he was finished. I asked him about my loose front one. He reached in. Out it came. I was in the chair for another three days due to that front tooth. The tooth got loose at significant moments;

before the senior prom, before graduation, before my wedding day, now it was
loose again.

"Oh shit, boys, here he comes,"
said one of the guys looking out the
window. Hostetler walked slowly toward
the barracks with a Smokey-the-Bear hat
hiding his eyes. When I saw his mouth,
it seemed to have no lips - just a line
near the bottom of his square head. He
didn't walk, he marched as if each step
had a purpose. He made a square turn,
and climbed the steps of our barracks.

We scrambled back to be next to
our bunks. Hostetler made another
square turn into the barracks, then
looked through squinting dark eyes just
below his Smokey-the-Bear hat. He
screamed something intended to get us
out of the barracks, and we ran out,
none of us wanting to be last.

We lined up like the officer-in-
training had told us. "DRESS RIGHT
DRESS!" he screamed. We knew to put out
our left arms. I stood in the second
row. "A-TEN-HUT!" he screamed. We came
to attention: chests out, arms straight
down by our sides, hands slightly
curled, legs and heels tightly together, feet at forty-five-degree angles,
eyes staring straight ahead at an imaginary figure.

He started down the line looking
at each name on our uniforms. He had
something to say about everyone - none
of it good. He came to me, looked at my

name, saw the APP, but couldn't see further.

"APPLEFUCK! YOU ARE ONE FAT BAS-TARD! I'M GONNA MAKE YOU RUN UNTIL YOU DROP! I'LL HAVE NO FAT BOYS IN MY OUT-FIT! DO YOU UNDERSTAND, PRIVATE!"

I didn't know if I was supposed to say yes or no.

"I SAID, DO YOU UNDERSTAND THAT, FAT BOY!"

"Yes, sir."

"DO I LOOK LIKE I HAVE SOME SHIT ON MY LAPEL, SOLDIER?"

I didn't know if I was supposed to look at him or not, but did.

"DON'T YOU EYEBALL ME, APPLEFUCK! I'M A SERGEANT IN THE ARMY OF THE UNIT-ED STATES OF AMERICA. YOU WILL ADDRESS ME AS SERGEANT! DO YOU UNDERSTAND THAT, FATBOY?"

"YES, SERGEANT!" I yelled as loud as I could.

"DOES EVERYBODY UNDERSTAND THAT?"

"YES, SERGEANT!" Everyone yelled

He moved on to the guy next to me. *That wasn't so bad*, I thought. I wasn't dead. I'd had a football coach who yelled a lot. I could deal with this.

Hostetler moved along the line yelling at each soldier. Bored at standing at attention, I began playing with my tooth, pushing it in and out with my tongue. Suddenly, I felt him coming, and locked into place. He stood in front of me.

"DID I SEE YOU CHEWING GUM IN MY FORMATION, PRIVATE?"

"No, Sergeant."

"YOU'RE A GODDAMN LIAR, APPLEFUCK! I SAW YOU CHEW ON SOMETHING!"

"It was my tooth, sir, I mean, Sergeant!"

"ARE YOU FUCKING WITH ME, PRIVATE? YOU CAN'T BE CHEWING ON YOUR TOOTH!"

I opened my mouth, pushed my tooth a little, until it popped out, resting on top of my tongue.

"THAT IS THE UGLIEST THING I HAVE EVER SEEN! APPLEFUCK, PUT THAT GODDAMN TOOTH BACK IN PLACE BEFORE I PUKE!"

I wedged it back in with my tongue and shut my mouth.

"NOW WHERE IN THE FUCK WAS I?"

When he finished with everyone, he stood in front of the outfit. "YOU'RE THE SORRIEST BUNCH OF RECRUITS I'VE EVER SEEN! WE'RE IN A GODDAMN WAR. DOES EVERYONE UNDERSTAND THAT?"

"YES, SERGEANT!"

"YOU'VE GOT TO GET INTO SHAPE TO BE ABLE TO DEFEAT THE COMMUNISTS IN VIETNAM! DO YOU UNDERSTAND THAT?"

"YES, SERGEANT!"

"WELL, WHAT THE FUCK ARE YOU WAIT-ING FOR? LET'S GET GOING! RIGHT FACE! FORWARD, MARCH! DOUBLE TIME, MARCH!"

We started running in unison from our barracks to the asphalt parade ground. Sergeant Hostetler ran next to me. "I BETTER NOT SEE YOU SLOW THIS PLA-

TOON DOWN, APPLEFUCK, YOU KEEP UP, GOD-
DAMN IT!"

I was keeping up, but this was the
most weight my body had ever carried.
Quickly winded, I started breathing
heavily through my mouth. All of a sud-
den my tooth jumped between my lips
onto the parade ground. When I stopped
to pick it up, Sergeant Hostetler raced
toward me.

"WHAT THE FUCK ARE YOU DOING, AP-
PLEFUCK? YOU ARE SCREWING UP MY FORMA-
TION! GET YOUR FAT ASS BACK UP AND
START RUNNING! DO YOU HEAR ME?"

I jumped back up running with the
rest of the outfit, leaving my four-
hundred-dollar tooth lying on the parade ground.

When we stopped, I tried catching
my breath with the others. "A-TEN-HUT!"
the sergeant screamed. I snapped to attention with everyone else.

"DRESS RIGHT, DRESS!"

We threw out our left arms. My
mouth hung open as I gasped for breath.
My eyes stared straight ahead. Suddenly, Sergeant Hostetler stood in front
of me.

"PRIVATE APPLEFUCK, OPEN THAT GOD-
DAMN MOUTH!"

I did as ordered.

"PRIVATE APPLEFUCK, WHERE IS YOUR
GODDAMN TOOTH?"

"On the parade ground, Sergeant!"

"YOU MEAN TO TELL ME THAT YOU LOST
YOUR GODDAMN TOOTH?"

"Yes, Sergeant!"

"I HAVE TO LOOK AT THAT UGLY HOLE IN YOUR HEAD FOR THE REST OF THE TIME YOU ARE IN BASIC TRAINING?"

"I guess so, Sergeant!"

"WELL, HERE IS YOUR FIRST ORDER PRIVATE! YOU WILL KEEP THAT UGLY MOUTH CLOSED FOR THE ENTIRE TIME YOU ARE IN FRONT OF MY FACE! DO YOU UNDERSTAND THAT?"

"Yes, Sergeant!"

"GOOD! NOW SHUT IT, AND SHUT IT FOR GOOD!"

Chapter 4
Hostetler

"IT'S 4:30, LADIES! LET'S NOT SLEEP THE DAY AWAY!" BAM, BAM, BAM went his drill cane on the trash can lid. Whatever dream occupied my brain was gone in a flash. I swung down quickly, and started to make my bed. "I BETTER BE ABLE TO BOUNCE A QUARTER ON THAT BUNK, APPLEFUCK!"

Cringing at his words, I folded the corners as instructed, pulled the blanket taut, and made sure no wrinkles were on the bed. I checked my footlocker. Everything was in place. My bedding had been thrown on the floor once, along with my footlocker. That was not going to happen again.

"WE'RE GOING TO RUN BEFORE BREAKFAST, SWEETHEARTS, BECAUSE YOU'RE STILL THE SORRIEST RECRUITS I HAVE EVER SEEN! BE READY FOR INSPECTION IN THREE MINUTES!"

I was ready in two, standing at attention. A minute later Sergeant Hostetler walked up and down the row of bunks. "GODDAMN IT, DUNBAR! WHY CAN'T YOU GET YOUR FOOTLOCKER SOP?" Dunbar's footlocker went flying through the air. "YOU HAVE EXACTLY ONE MINUTE TO FOLD YOUR DRAWERS AND SOCKS AND GET THAT DAMN FOOTLOCKER IN ORDER OR YOU'LL BE RUNNING FROM DAWN TILL DUSK! THE REST

OF YOU IDIOTS, IN FORMATION IN TWO MIN-
UTES OR YOU'LL RUN 'TILL YOU DIE!"

It was Week Two of our ten weeks
of basic training - the most humiliating two weeks of my life. Day One was
basic marching training. That was relatively easy. Hostetler kept looking at
me, as if daring me to open my mouth.
It remained closed like I had lockjaw.

Day Three we took our first Physical Training Test. Five measures of
physical training. Four out of the five
were beyond my capacity. We started
with the low crawl. Hostetler insisted
we crawl on the ground for twenty-five
yards in less than a minute to pass. My
start was good, but when Hostetler
thought my butt was too high, he started riding me like a pony. I stopped before the finish line. "THAT'S A BOLO,
APPLEFUCK! WHY AM I NOT SURPRISED?"

The next measure was the monkey
bars. I had gone my entire life without
ever doing monkey bars. We didn't have
them at Santa Clara. About a third of
our outfit were from Guam. They must
have been born on monkey bars. They
went through them back and forth like
they were walking with their
hands. When it was my turn, I stood on
the top rung hanging onto the first
bar. I stepped off the rung frantically
reaching for the second bar, but
couldn't grab it for what seemed like
minutes, my left arm stretching, my

right arm inches away from the second bar. Unable to reach it, I fell into the sandbox.

"HOLY SHIT, APPLEFUCK! YOU CAN'T DO ONE BAR! THAT'S THE MOST PATHETIC EFFORT I'VE EVER SEEN!"

The third test was the obstacle course. I had never done anything like that before. The first obstacle included a rope climb up a wooden wall. I had never climbed a rope or a wall. My failing to get over the first obstacle almost caused Hostetler to have a heart attack.

The fourth test was the only easy one. We had to throw three fake grenades at a tire that had three rings around it, each ring about four feet from the next. I hit the tire once getting inside the rings each time. Impressed, Hosteler said, "WELL, I'LL BE DAMNED, THERE IS SOMETHING YOU CAN DO, APPLEFUCK! PRAISE THE LORD!"

The last test was the mile run. To max it we had to run under six minutes in our combat boots. I did it in just over a half hour. The only recruit who did worse than me overall was a guy named Dunbar. He threw the grenade like he had never thrown anything in his life. It barely got out of his hand. Hostetler was apoplectic. He took us aside.

"YOU TWO ARE THE WORST RECRUITS IN THE HISTORY OF THIS MAN'S ARMY! I'VE NEVER HAD A RECRUIT FAIL TO PASS BASIC

TRAINING AND YOU WON'T BREAK MY RECORD!
APPLEFUCK, AT LEAST YOU KNOW HOW TO
THROW, SO YOU BETTER TEACH THIS LADY
HOW TO THROW BY THE FINAL P.T. TEST OR
I'LL FAIL YOU BOTH!"

We were supposed to eat three
times a day. To get into the mess hall
we had to do the monkey bars. If we
didn't get to the end, we had to do
twenty push-ups, then go back to the
end of the line to try again. After my
third try, I would finally be allowed
to eat. Hostetler stood right next to
me. "DON'T YOU DARE TOUCH THAT GODDAMN
POTATO, APPLEFUCK, YOU LOAD UP ON THOSE
PEAS. YOU CAN EAT THE MEAT, BUT IF YOU
GET NEAR THE DESSERT I'LL BE ON YOU
LIKE A BULLDOG! NOT EVEN THE JELL-O!"

After two weeks of basic training,
twenty pounds of fat evaporated from my
frame. My uniform didn't fit; my pants
were twisted around my waist. At night
extra sets of sit-ups and push-ups
toned muscles that had deteriorated after high school. Over time I got the
rhythm of the monkey bars, and could
eat without doing push-ups. On Sunday
afternoons I practiced climbing ropes
and walls with Dunbar. Proving to
Hostetler that I wasn't his worst recruit became a goal.

Another humiliating experience oc-
curred at the end of the first week
when three of us had to meet our commanding officer. He had files on his

desk, and was going through our records and P.E. scores. He saw that the other two guys had passed the P.T. test, but I had the second lowest score in the outfit. He glanced at our accomplishments in high school; one of the two flunked out, the other was on the bowling team. He shook his head when he read mine.

"It says here that you were All-League and honorable mention All-Southern California in football, All-League three years and first-team All-Southern California in baseball? How can that be, Appenzeller?" I almost didn't recognize my name after the week with Hostetler. Looking at his surprised face caused me to smile. The big gap in my front teeth only added to the doubts of the officer.

"Well, sir, I have never done monkey bars or climbed a rope. I was fat when I joined the Army, but I guarantee that I'll pass that P.T." I hadn't learned how to pronounce words well with my missing tooth; pass came out "path," monkey bars "monkey barth."

"That doesn't seem possible, Soldier. Dismissed!" I knew then that not only would I pass, I would be near the top of my class, or die trying.

By Week Four I was back to my high school weight, and passed the next P.T. test with flying colors. I learned while playing football at Santa Clara High School to go as hard as I could, hit hard and stay low. Get attention by your positive attitude. Become the person you knew the coach wanted to see. It worked well in high school; it also worked well in the army.

Alexandra got off work and school for one weekend. She drove from Oxnard to Fort Ord. Hostetler yelled down the hallway, "Mrs. Applefuck to see you, Private!" Was what I expected him to say. In reality he was kind and called her "Mrs. Appenzeller."

I was embarrassed to see her. I must have looked awful with that hole in the middle of my face, my pinhead, and size extra large uniform on a size medium body, but, Alexandra smiled sweetly, squeezed my hand, and kissed me gently on my lips and cheek. I couldn't believe how sexy she looked with her brown hair in a lovely tan scarf tied Indian style that fell halfway down her back. The guys were at the window gawking at us outside walking hand in hand. Even Hostetler seemed impressed and afterward looked at me differently.

We missed each other so much, and were so happy when we found a little private space between the barracks under a tree to hug and kiss passionately.

My heart melted when she said, "I'm giving notice at work so that wherever they send you, I will be there."

Hearing that, I felt more in love with Alexandra than ever. While holding her, I told her how awful the Army treated people. We knew there was nothing we could do, but sigh, and look at each other. We had three long years to do.

I kept working with Dunbar on his throwing technique to no avail. He couldn't throw that fake grenade farther than five feet. On the day we had to qualify with a real grenade we were hyped, and Dunbar was frightened.

The grenade area was four cement blocks about ten-foot square with a three-foot by two-foot ditch surrounding it. A soldier had to throw the grenade over an eight-foot fence into the field beyond. He received a high score if he tossed the grenade onto the hill in back. I knew this would be my best event. I could throw a guy out from deep shortstop in high school. My arm was in shape after throwing every day with Dunbar.

I went onto the cement block with Hostetler. Being now eight weeks in, he no longer yelled at us. "Are you ready, Soldier?" he asked as he handed me the grenade. "Grab the ring with your left pointer. Keep hold of the safety as you hold it in your right hand. When you throw it, the safety will come off, it'll blow up in less than eight-seconds. If you want to throw it far, let the safety fly off, then throw it. Don't let it fall out of your hands. If you do, I'll kick it into the ditch, while you and I dive to the other side. You understand?"

"Yes, sergeant!"

He gave me the grenade. It felt similar to the one I practiced with. I pulled the pin, held it, looked him in the eye, loosened my grip around the safety, and was a bit startled when it flew off. I took a skip-step forward like an outfielder, drew my arm back, and let that son of a bitch fly. It hit halfway up the hill. So high that we saw it explode over the eight-foot wall.

"Damn, App! That looks like a top score," Hostetler said almost in awe. It was the first time he didn't call me Applefuck.

There was a big cement wall for the rest of the platoon to stay behind for safety. When Dunbar inched his way over to the cement blocks, everyone scrambled behind that wall. There were four thick windows where we could look at the throwers. No one went out to the other blocks with Dunbar. We knew there was no way in hell he would be able to toss that grenade over that eight-foot wall. After working with him for eight weeks, he had never come close to that distance.

"Get over here, Private Dunbar. You have to throw this grenade to pass basic training,"

Dunbar got in the middle of the cement. Hostetler told him what to do.

"I don't think I can throw it over the fence, Sergeant,"

"You will, soldier." He gave him the grenade. "Now pull that pin, Private Dunbar, and throw that grenade."

"I can't, Sergeant."

Hostetler reached over. He pulled the pin. "Let go of the safety, Private. Let that thing fly." The safety flew off. We pressed our faces to the glass. Dunbar took two steps closer to the wall, and threw the grenade as hard as he could. It cleared the fence by a foot, blowing up just on the other side. Hostetler pounded him on the back. We ran around the wall clapping. "Goddamn it, boy! You're going to make it!"

On the next-to-last day of basic training we had to take our final P.T. test. Now, in the best shape of my life, only one person in our platoon was better, the Guamanian Andrade who Hostetler had chosen as our platoon leader after the first two weeks. The Guamanians hung together. I didn't know Andrade well, but he was a great athlete. Easily the best in almost every section of the P.T. test.

The first event was the twenty-five-yard low crawl. My time was a second under the max time giving me a 100. Andrade beat me by two-seconds. The work with Dunbar on the obstacle course earned me another max time. I came in second. Andrade was first. Three shots on the tire earned me the highest score in the platoon. Andrade hit the tire twice; his third landed in the first ring. He scored 90 out of 100. I was in the lead. I had never done seventy-six monkey bars in under a minute which was what we had to do to get a perfect score of 100. I got them done in a minute and a half for an 80 out of 100. Andrade maxed again. Now he was in the lead.

Running the mile under six minutes seemed like an impossible task. Andrade had done it twice. No one else had. The whole battalion ran the mile together. I started out quickly, keeping up with Andrade for the first three laps. We were in front of everyone else. Andrade started pulling away halfway through the last lap. We were lapping some of the men. With a second wind I caught up with him. It was neck and neck to the finish line. Only a foot or so separated us at the end. I had never run that long and fast in my life. We both were under six minutes. Andrade scored a 490. I got the second highest score of 480. Hostetler and our company commander were there to congratulate us. With that last effort, we had earned the outstanding platoon award.

Hostetler called me into his office that evening. We were getting our dress blues ready for graduation. "Private Appenzeller, only ten people in this platoon have earned the rank of E2. You're one of them. Congratulations! Only two will get the company commander's and my recommendation for Officer Training School. Andrade has accepted. I am also recommending you." I hadn't thought about being an officer. From what I'd heard, they added two more years to your commitment, more important, infantry officers were the most likely to not survive in Vietnam.

"I'm honored that the sergeant has made this recommendation. May I have some time to think about it?"

"Permission granted. We need to know by tomorrow after graduation." He paused. "You have turned into an excellent soldier, Appenzeller. I know I was tough on you, but you responded to that toughness. You should think hard about that officer training."

I paused, making a quick and important decision. "Sergeant, I appreciate what you did for me. I had a coach in high school who did the same thing. He believed in me, then I believed in myself. Sergeant, I don't really need to think about it. I respectfully decline the company commander's and your offer. I'll serve out my time. I'll do my duty for God and country, but as an enlisted man not as an officer." He stuck out his hand. I reached out and grabbed it. He damn near crushed it. My face didn't grimace.

"You'll find out your next assignment tomorrow!"

For all of basic training, the guys who had been drafted made fun of the few of us who had joined. "You have to take this shit for an extra year," Carl-fucking-T. Baker told me every day.

On the final day I got the last laugh. Sergeant Hostetler read off the names with the assignment. Every drafted guy heard the same thing; "Private Baker, Advanced Infantry Training, Fort Polk, Louisiana; next stop, Vietnam." When he read my name, it came out differently, "Private E2 Appenzeller, Supply Training School, Fort Lee, Virginia? Goddamn it, App, you're going to be a REMF."

"What's that, Sergeant?" I asked.

"A Rear Echelon Motherfucker, what a waste of a good soldier!"

Private Dunbar, who had barely passed, was going to Fort Polk. He whispered to me. "You lucky son of a bitch!"

Chapter 5
The List

Alexandra, Mom, Dad, and Alexandra's parents came to my graduation from basic training and watched us march on the parade grounds under the hot sun. It was no big deal. The big deal was me with Alexandra in the hotel room afterward. We barely made it to dinner and rushed back to the room right after. I couldn't get enough of her.

For the first time in my life I flew in an airplane. When the plane took off, my throat tightened, my hands clutched in a fist, my heart thumped madly, but five hours later the flight attendant woke me for the landing. I'd slept through the whole thing. Alexandra drove her dark blue VW Bug across the country with my sister Tina to meet me at Pappy's house in Portsmouth.

A bus from the airport took me to Fort Lee. The supply school was so full that I was assigned classes from 8:00 in the evening to 6:00 in the morning. It angered and embarrassed me that Pappy wasn't excited about having nigger-lovers from California staying up-stairs, so Alexandra, Tina, and I looked for a place close to Fort Lee. We found a small trailer in a trailer park that cost more than our place in

California. Obviously, Some people were glad there was a war.

We were poor because I wasn't receiving my marriage allotment, and Alexandra and Tina couldn't find jobs. We acted like it was Easter Sunday if we put a hot dog into the macaroni and cheese we ate most nights. Fort Lee was a training center for mess-hall cooks. Sometimes I'd sneak food inside my shirt to bring home. In the afternoon Tina and I practiced the two Beatles songs we knew, *Yesterday and In My life.* Then, we'd have dinner before I had my class at night. Going to bed each morning with Alexandra after a night of classes seemed strange, but a wonderful way to fall asleep.

The classes weren't difficult; however, after the instructor completed an easy lesson, invariably someone raised a hand and asked the instructor to slow down. Bored, I drew pictures of girls from snapshots the guys gave me and sold them for a couple of bucks each.

I asked our first sergeant about "computer" school. He acted like he'd never heard of it. He said he'd check, but he never got back to me.

After ten weeks I knew enough about how the army wanted its supplies handled and graduated second in the class. That wasn't saying much since the rest could barely read. The day after graduation the Army gave me orders for Fort Sill Oklahoma.

Alexandra and Tina drove the VW across the country. Tina hopped onto a bus to California from Oklahoma City. Alexandra waited for me in Lawton, the town outside the base. The Army flew me to Dallas, Texas, then sent me on a bus to Fort Sill. The mission there was to train soldiers to shoot long-range conventional weapons.

I went to the hospital where I was assigned. They said they didn't need my Military Occupational Status, or MOS. I wandered around the base looking for an outfit that might need my training. A 105 Howitzer outfit put me in the motor pool.

I worked with the parts manager, a cool guy from Minnesota named Tom Burt. He showed me how a motor pool could be run efficiently, and demonstrated how to order parts and organize the parts room. He knew shortcuts and ways to please the army with enough paperwork for them to think he was doing everything according to Standard Operational Procedure, or SOP, but he knew the mission was to keep the vehicles running.

He had a secret stash of parts in a container next to the bay where the mechanics fixed the vehicles. They used them most of the time. He had them fill out orders about five times a day. If they had enough paperwork with wrapped parts filling the bins, the inspectors would be happy. If the vehicles were running, the colonel would be happy. Everyone was happy with Tom Burt.

Tom had worked out a system of parts collection that looked like he was working all afternoon collecting parts. In reality we could get the parts in an hour or two. We spent the rest of the afternoon playing golf or hanging out at the Non-Commissioned Officers' club. We weren't NCOs, but Alexandra got a job at the club as a lifeguard, which gave us access to the club. Life was good at Fort Sill.

Alexandra and I looked around for an apartment. The first one we found was pretty clean and cheap, but turned out to be ten feet from the railroad tracks. The first time we heard that engine coming, we thought we were going to be run over. The house shook like an earthquake every time it went by. Three came every night after midnight. We stayed two days.

We found another. The landlady showing the place told us how happy she was that there was a war. She said she had been forced to rent to "niggers," and even worse, "Indians." "Glad yer white," she said, but took me aside and asked about Alexandra. Dotty, Alexandra's mom, was Greek and Alexandra inherited Dotty's beautiful, high cheekbones and olive skin. When the landlady asked "She ain't an Indian, is she?" I assured her she was a genuine white American.

We had a great time at Fort Sill. Alexandra loved her job. Tom and I loved that Alexandra had that job. A month's pass at Fort Sill's golf course went for ten bucks. I bought some old clubs, and played four or five days a week with Tom Burt. A sergeant, living with his wife below us, taught us to play bridge, and we would have bridge marathons. We played all weekend. We slept when we were dummy. The mechanics took us to the boxcar races where we'd dodge huge June bugs all night while watching the cars go round a big oval. Oh, yes, life was good.

The only negative was serving guard duty once a week. Tom showed me how to beat that, too. He told me to take a uniform to a seamstress, who tailored it to fit me perfectly. We bought a pair of Corcoran jump boots, then spit shined them to a gleam. Alexandra helped me memorize the ranges of all the howitzers in the military. I cleaned my M14, and practiced the parade maneuvers with the rifle. Guys hated it when they had to serve guard duty with me. If picked for soldier of the guard, I got to sleep on a cot outside the colonel's office receiving a three-day weekend pass. I had no competition for soldier of the guard, and racked up three-day weekends for months.

But, it all came to an end. Tom and I were getting ready for a "parts run" when one of the mechanics came up and said, "Hey App, I saw your name on the List." Most guys lived in the barracks on the base. Every week a list of new assignments was pinned to the bulletin board. It was called "the List." Most assignments were in Vietnam. I ran to the barracks, and couldn't believe my eyes when I saw next to my name "Vietnam." All those three-day weekends went down the drain.

In a panic, I ran to headquarters to talk to the colonel. He thought I was a good soldier and had chosen me for Soldier of the Month. The colonel called me in after talking with his clerk.

"What can I do for you, PFC?"

"Colonel, I made the List."

"Damn, Appenzeller, I'm sorry to hear that. You and Burt made a good team. Headed to 'Nam?"

"Yes, sir, I guess so. You know, the guy who recruited me told me I would be going to Germany."

"We're not at war in Europe, son. The Army needs you in Vietnam. We got a big push going there right now. When do you report for duty?"

"In a month, it says on the board. I have training in Oakland. I leave a week later."

"You got any leave coming?"

"I haven't used any."

"I'll push it through. You can leave in a few days. You're from California?"

"Yes, sir, I'm from Oxnard."

"By the Seabee Base?"

"Yes, sir!"

"Good luck Appenzeller, may God watch over you."

"Thank you, sir. I appreciate that."

I went to the NCO club, and saw Alexandra sitting by the pool in the tall lifeguard chair with a green and yellow umbrella over her head. She had a beautiful tan and looked sexy in her white bathing suit. She had her prescription dark glasses on and was focused on children of NCOs who were playing in the pool. My fatigues looked out of place. Usually I came in civilian clothes, so they wouldn't know I wasn't an NCO. When she looked down on me, she knew something was wrong. "Uh-oh, Robbie, what is it?"

"I made the List."

"What list?"

"I got orders to report to Oakland in a month for combat training."

"What?" she looked down from her chair, struggling to focus on me and the kids in the pool.

"I'm going to Vietnam, Alexandra."

Her attention now focused completely on me.

"I report to Oakland in a month. I leave a week later." I paused to let that sink in. "The colonel says we can leave in a few days. We're going home, babe."

I couldn't see her eyes through her dark glasses, but in a few seconds tears were running down her tanned high cheekbones as she slowly turned her head back to the kids in the pool.

Chapter 6
God is on Our Side

Alexandra and I packed our stuff into her blue VW bug and made the long sad haul back to Oxnard. We stopped in Vegas to relive our honeymoon and made love to each other with a renewed passion, as if we both realized that it could be one of the last times we would be in bed together. The next morning we drove quietly, our bewildered minds on a future impossible to imagine.

A pall hung over us like dark, ominous clouds the entire leave. Not only was I the first of my friends to get married, now I was the first to go to war. Time flew by, but as each day passed, the overwhelming weight of going to war grew heavier and gloomier. Everyone's sad eyes looked at me like I was already dead.

My dad felt there was never any justification for war and this one made him especially angry. "Son, I can see no reason for us to be in Vietnam. Old Cornpone has no idea how to fight this thing. I don't think I could stand it if you don't return. Please take care of yourself and come back in one piece." He spoke with tears in his eyes, and hugged me so hard and long I thought he might never let me go.

Dad was a Democrat. That was because he had only two choices. He disagreed with Republicans and that gave him only one party to support. He believed Republicans supported the rich and corporations. As a public school educator, he believed that social mobility was important and could only be accomplished through free, well-funded public education. The GI Bill allowed him to go to any university for which he was qualified, and the government paid for the books and tuition. He believed that everyone should have that right. While he knew the Democratic Party was equally beholden to the corporations that helped fund it, Democrats wanted to insure the blessings of liberty for many more people than the Republicans.

As Democrats and Catholics, we rallied around Kennedy in 1960. I went door to door passing out literature. His speeches were spellbinding. "Ask not what your country can do for you; ask what you can do for your country," made me want to rush out to join his Peace Corps. I felt proud to be an American when he stood in front of the masses in Berlin saying, *"Ich bin ein Berliner."* The roar of the crowd sent goosebumps down my back.

His assassination put a huge hole in my heart. I grieved along with the nation, and was stunned as I watched Jack Ruby move in front of reporters and policemen to shoot Lee Harvey Oswald live on TV. The black-and-white images of the funeral march, the black horse with the boots backwards in the stirrups, followed by the slow lowering of the casket with little John John's sad salute, brought me to tears and would be an image I'd never forget.

In high school in the early sixties, I had no idea the country had anything to do with Vietnam, or even where Vietnam was. I didn't watch the news. The national broadcast was only fifteen minutes long, and I was a long way from twenty-one when I would have a say in the matter through voting. I sang anti-war songs at our school hootenannies, like *Where Have All the Flowers Gone, If I Had a Hammer* and *With Guns and Drums*, but only mouthed the words not really focused on their meaning. I was focused on getting a starting spot on the football and baseball teams, catching waves with my surf buds, and wondering which girl was going to give me a chance to caress her breasts. Being cool was a priority, and I was not aware of any military buildup in Southeast Asia.

I did watch the news when I was on leave. Walter Cronkite was grim-faced and solemn when he described the battles. Black-and-white images of bleeding soldiers being carried off the battlefield made me shudder and gulp. *That could be me,* I thought, and felt like a dead man walking.

In the blink of an eye, I was on a bus to Oakland, and could still feel my dad's hug, and Alexandra's sweet sad kiss on my lips. A mental fog surrounded me with everything spinning quickly out of my control.

After arriving in Oakland, I moved into what looked to be a prison compound with lots of barbed wire and guards. I guess they were afraid we might want to bolt at the last minute. The sergeants sent me to a forest camp during the day to learn jungle combat maneuvers. I learned to load an M60 machine gun, easing behind the big gun, pulling the trigger, watching as it tore a huge hole in the target shaped like a Vietcong. I wondered if I could do that to a real human being. The sergeants called the Vietnamese "gooks" and "slope heads." They told us not to trust any of them, not the old men, women, nor children. They were all the enemy.

The night before we left, at the evening muster, a Catholic priest in fatigues with a purple sash around his neck asked if anybody wanted to confess their sins. I looked around. Several hands were in the air. I raised mine. We followed his lead to a tiny wooden chapel close by with about ten wooden pews and an austere alter with a simple cross.

I hadn't been to confession in a long time. Once out of school I rarely went to mass. Alexandra had to convert for us to be married in the church, but she did so somewhat reluctantly. She went along with it because she loved me. It was not a life changing event for her.

I recalled going to Father O'Sullivan, the priest I had known all my life, and asked him to marry us. Father O'Sullivan was from Ireland and still had his brogue. He'd been my confessor, and knew my thoughts had often been impure. With a concerned look he said, "Oh dear boy, is it that you have to, Robbie?"

It relieved him when I answered, "Oh, no, Father! I love the girl. I want to marry her." When I told him she would go to classes to convert, he smiled with delight.

The base priest, a middle aged stocky man with a crew cut and dark brown sleepy looking eyes, sat us down in the pews. Twenty of us had followed him. He raised his hand making the sign of the cross, then said, "Repeat after me: Bless me, Father, for I have sinned." We did. "Now I don't have to listen to all of your sins, men. I just need you to think of them right now. Think hard, men, God is listening."

I had difficulty thinking about all that I had done since the last time I confessed my sins, which was before Alexandra and I got married. We had to take communion at the wedding mass. My main sin had always been impure thoughts, like being in bed with girls in my class or movie stars. Being married, I felt like I could have all of the impure thoughts I wanted as long as they involved Alexandra. My main grievance was missing mass so many times. I thought hard about that one — the dark cloud of guilt hanging over me. The priest gave us five minutes for thinking and confessing.

"Now, men, on your knees." We put down the cushioned kneeler. "Let's all say a fervent act of contrition. Think about the words as you say them." Together we said, *"O my God, I am heartily sorry for having offended Thee, and I detest all of my sins because of Thy just punishment, but most of all because I have offended Thee my God, Who is all good and deserving of all my love. I firmly resolve, with the help of Thy grace, to sin no more, and to avoid the near occasion of sin. Amen!"*

"Now let's all say three Hail Marys and three Our Fathers." After we'd said each three times, he blessed us with the sign of the cross. "Your sins are forgiven, men," he said, with joy in his voice. "Now I'll conduct a mass, and you can all receive the sacrament of communion. Would anyone like to serve as an altar boy?"

I had done that so many times at Santa Clara Church with Father O'Sullivan. I raised my hand. "I know the Latin responses, Father."

"Then please come and join me," he said, nodding at me and smiling. "We both put on our sacred vestments before he started the mass. He smiled at me when he turned and said in a loud voice, "Dominus vobiscum" and I answered back loudly "Et cum spriritu tuo." I watched in awe as the priest raised the host and the chalice, changing the unleavened bread and wine into the actual body and blood of Christ, the miracle of the transubstantiation.

At one point in the mass the priest turned to the soldiers in front of him, saying, "I'll not give you a long sermon, men. In most wars, both sides believe that the will of God is on their side. Abraham Lincoln said it beautifully about the Civil War. That is not the case in this War. The enemy you fight does not believe in God; they believe in the ideology of Karl Marx. They're godless communists who have worked for years to destroy the church in Vietnam. Our Holy Father firmly supports the government of South Vietnam. In this war, God is truly on our side."

After the mass, he turned to us, and in a soft, solemn voice said, "Now, go with God, men. Your sins are forgiven. You have the body of Christ in you. May God watch over you, and protect you, and welcome you into heaven if you fall. May God continue to bless you, and may he continue to bless the United States of America."

I left feeling blessed. My sins forgiven, my soul pure, my heart filled with love for a God who had watched over me all my life. I was proud to be part of the body of Christ as a member of the Catholic Church.

We spent our final night sleeping on cots in a huge hangar surrounded by armed guards. The buses we would take in the morning waited in front of huge sliding doors. The soldiers sat around their cots, some played cards, others talked. My dad gave me a copy of John Steinbeck's *The Grapes of Wrath* to read during my long trip to Vietnam. I tried to read, but couldn't focus with so much on my mind. It was "lights out" by 10:00.

I slept little that night, already missing Alexandra so much that it hurt. They woke us before dawn, and we loaded onto the bus. We took little with us. They would give us jungle fatigues and jungle boots when we arrived "in-country," as they called it.

We drove to San Francisco International and boarded a brand new Boeing 737. I sat next to a window near the front of the plane. As we headed away from land, starting our long journey over the sea, I stared down at the water and the fading shore, and, in a whispered voice asked my self. *"Is this my last look at the country that I love?"*

PART TWO
THE GOLDEN BOY

Chapter 7
Vietnam

Looking out the small window at the big jet's engine, I imagined it in flames, even wished for it. Seated near an exit, getting out and swimming would be easy. I'd be rescued — a hero for fighting off sharks. Crashing now, with the possibility of surviving, seemed a lot better than the unknown fate ahead of me.

When we sighted land, my hopes were dashed. We banked right, flying high over the coast. Looking closer, I could see tiny helicopters moving along the shore. *Oh shit there really is a war!* We banked to the left over a mass of civilization below, and started our descent. Bouncing twice before the wheels engaged the tarmac, the plane slowly turned to the left and stopped. I was in Vietnam.

We quietly gathered our things, lost in our thoughts, waiting patiently for those ahead to file out. Slipping sideways into the aisle, I saw the door on the right, the sunshine illuminating it like the gates of hell. The humidity hit me like a wave when I took that last step through the gates. The smell was overwhelming. What was that smell? Was it cooked cabbage? Or was it death?

When I reluctantly walked down the stairs, I saw soldiers on our left in strange looking, dusty uniforms waiting for us to exit so they could board. They looked ragged with hair sticking out of their caps. One guy pointed at some of us like he was counting those who wouldn't come back.

We stayed in a line while tired looking soldiers moved us into a building. When they asked for our sizes, I no longer needed a large. The lightweight uniforms they gave us felt so much more comfortable than the tailored guard-duty outfit I wore. The pants were roomy with six large pockets. The tops, which hung like a suit coat, had two big pockets on each side. The boots had black leather on the tips and heels, green mesh over the ankles up to the calf. The most warlike thing they gave us were our helmets. When I put mine on, I imagined bullets bouncing off it.

There wasn't a lot of yelling. Those assisting weren't sergeants, and we were not recruits. They took our money, and exchanged it for what looked like Monopoly money. "What's this?" I asked.

"It is military script we call MPC," one of them said. "You can use it in the PX. You're not supposed to use it with the gooks."

They herded us toward large olive-green trucks where we threw our duffel bags to a soldier, then reached up, and pulled ourselves inside. The truck bed had no roof. Hard bench seats lined the two sides. Still lost in our thoughts, we sat next to and across from each other.

The trucks bounced along on rough roads — some paved, some dirt. With no one there to tell me not to, I stood and looked through the wooden slats at my first Vietnamese — a small woman in black silk pajamas with a large, wide, cone-shaped straw hat covering her head. She carried a bamboo stick across her shoulder with a bucket hanging on each end. As we passed, I flashed the peace sign, two fingers in the shape of a V. She didn't look up. This was not World War II. We weren't liberating France. This was Vietnam.

We bounced along for twenty minutes following other trucks, dust billowing behind. We went through a gate where armed guards ignored us. When we came to a stop, a sergeant ordered us out of the truck. We moved quickly to an open area.

"Get in formation!" he yelled, not to intimidate, but to be heard. We lined up, stuck out our left arms without being told and placed our duffel bags in front of us.

"This is 90th Relocation," the sergeant yelled. "You'll be here until you get your orders. You'll have a bunk, footlocker and wall locker. Don't unpack your stuff, you will not be here long. The mess hall will open three times a day. You have an hour to eat. The rest of your time you'll be on your own. Dismissed."

A corporal stood off to the side. "This way," he called. We followed him, each step raised dust that covered our new boots. He took us to huts, which were huge half-pipes of corrugated steel closed off at both ends with a steel door in the middle. "You're in Hooch 10," he said, pointing to a number over the door. "Grab a bunk. The mess hall opens at twelve hundred, it'll close at thirteen."

I took the first available cot — a standard army issue with a steel frame, metal meshing below a thin mattress. The top and bottom sheets were covered with a rough, green blanket, a small pillow at the head. Above the pillow a mosquito net hung from a hook on a thin steel pole with another pole and hook at the foot of the bed.

They had given us big pink pills which we were ordered to take three times a day for malaria. I'd taken one already. Malaria came from mosquitoes, which the net supposedly would prevent from biting us.

I hadn't slept much on the twenty-two-hour flight, so after stuffing my duffel bag into my wall locker, I pulled out the net, attached it to the hook, took off my new boots, crawled onto the bed, pulling the net over both sides of the bed. Though I felt like I was in a coffin, I closed my eyes.

From a deep sleep with no dreams a hand and voice jarred me to consciousness. The hand shook me, and the voice told me I had someplace to go. I couldn't recall where I was. The net over me freaked me out making me feel like I couldn't breathe. When I swung my legs around, they snagged in the net adding to my panic. I untangled my legs and swallowed a big gulp of air when my head was uncovered. When my memory returned, I knew where I was. Vietnam.

I laced my boots, left the net where it was, and glancing around the room saw the door we had come through. Stepping out into the afternoon sun, I saw green-clad soldiers moving in one direction. I followed them to the same open area where we'd met before. A sergeant stood in front with a clip board and started yelling names and assignments. Most sounded like infantry outfits. He did't call my name.

"Meet again tomorrow at 0900 The mess opens at 1630, closes at eighteen-hundred." My brain calculated the army time. We would meet again at 9:00 in the morning. Counting on my fingers I knew the mess hall would open at 4:30 in the afternoon. A glance at my watch indicated it was a little after 4:00. After I felt an uncomfortable rumbling in my stomach, I asked the guy next to me, "Where's the latrine?"

"That way." I started walking in the direction he'd pointed which turned to a jog because relieving myself became urgent. The latrines were ahead with many guys in line. Some looked to be dancing. I got in the shortest line, feeling like dancing myself, afraid I was going to crap my pants.

"It's the fucking pills," the guy in front of me said, gritting his teeth. "They give you the runs."

The guy first in line banged on the door. When it opened, a relieved soldier stepped out. "Hold your shit, man!" he yelled at the guy. He was ignored. The guy grabbed the wooden handle, swung the door open, entered, shutting it quickly. I was now two deep in the line with two more behind me. When my turn was next, I resisted banging on the door.

When the door opened, the stench almost knocked me out. It was dark inside. When my eyes focused, I glanced down at a hole in a wooden bench, fumbled with my brass belt buckle, undid the big green button, unzipped my fly, then pulled down my pants and boxers in a single move. Looking down at the contents below brought the few contents left in my stomach up in my throat. Trying not to gag, I looked away, sat on the hole, shit exploding from my ass. Overwhelming relief moved through my body. Knowing there were guys out-side with an urgent need, I grabbed a roll of toilet paper from the bench, cleaned up, quickly restoring my uni-form. The guy waiting outside almost knocked me over when I pushed the door open. How could I be angry when I could relate?

At the mess hall I found a guy who looked like he might know what was go-ing on. "What is this place?" I asked.

"This is 90th Relocation," he said, as he loaded his fork with mashed potatoes. "It's where we find out where we're going next. We meet at 0900 and 1600. Listen for your name. They'll tell you where you're going."

"I have a supply MOS, so they'll send me to a supply outfit, right?"

"I have no idea. I arrived yester-day late. In my two musters all I've heard are guys going to infantry. They'll send you wherever they need you. I guess the infantry has more holes to fill."

"No shit," I said with a shrug. *Oh, fucking shit*, I muttered to myself.

"Speaking of shit," I said, "what's up with those malaria pills? I don't think I've ever had to crap so bad in my life."

"I heard that nobody takes them. They give you the runs forever. People would rather get malaria than have to shit every half hour. I stopped taking 'em and felt better right away."

"No, shit!" I said, pun intended. Pun not detected.

We started filling our mouths with the overcooked meat, bland potatoes, and ugly looking wrinkled peas. He stopped, fork hanging over his plate. "I got an infantry MOS. I know what I'm doing. I bet I go tomorrow morning. Most guys don't last a day here. There's some kind of move we're doing in the field, I heard. They need infantry bad."

"Where you from?" I asked, a standard recruit question.

"Minnesota."

"I knew a guy in my last outfit from Minnesota. Tom Burt, ever heard of him?"

"Three million people live in Minnesota." He didn't seem like the talkative type. No one did. Too much on their minds to do much talking.

I went back to Hooch 10 to finish *The Grapes of Wrath*. Reading it, I learned to hate the landowners who used the cops to put the little people down. The only good guys were national government men who had camps for poor people like the Joads. I loved Tom for being willing to fight the owners and corporations who treated good honest people like dogs to make more money. While reading, I gained even more appreciation for my dad and mom. They had met Cesar Chavez, even ate dinner with him. We couldn't eat grapes for a year to protest how farm workers were being treated.

In the summer after my freshman year, my dad got me a job picking tomatoes with Mexican workers who lived in camps outside of Oxnard. They worked harder and faster than anyone I had ever seen for a dollar an hour. I couldn't keep up with them. "Hurry up, gringo," the few who could speak a little English would say at the end of the row of tomatoes. I still had fifty yards to go. They always said it with smiles on their faces. I lasted about two weeks and spent the rest of the summer surfing the waves at the Tank just outside Ventura. The next summer I got a job as a lifeguard at the Wagon Wheel Motel taking care of the owner's kid, teaching him how to swim. That job was much more my style.

I stayed two more days at 90th Relocation. Everyone I'd arrived with was gone, most to the infantry. On my seventh muster I finally heard my name called. "Appenzeller!" A bit of a pause, my fingers crossed. "448 S&S!" the sergeant yelled. "448 S&S," I kept saying to myself as I ran back to Hooch 10 to get my duffel bag. I liked the sound of that. It didn't sound threatening. It didn't sound infantry.

I threw my big green bag into the back of the M151 jeep waiting for me outside headquarters and jumped into the front seat. I asked the driver what

S&S stood for."What do you think, dumb shit? Supply and Support!" I wasn't offended. *Thank you, God*, was all I was thinking. *Supply and Support sounded much more like my style.*

Chapter 8
448 S & S

The bouncing jeep created a big dust trail behind us. I watched the young, blond haired driver grip the wheel as he steered around pot holes. He was a private first class, probably eighteen or so.

"So where are we going?" I asked.

"To headquarters," He didn't take his eyes off the road.

"Where's that?"

"Right here."

The jeep slid sideways into a screeching stop. Dust that chased the jeep flew over us in a cloud. When the driver hopped out, I reached back, grabbed my duffel bag and followed him into a corrugated steel building. A wooden sign above the door said 448 S&S Headquarters.

When he opened the door, I pulled my hat off and walked in behind him. "Just a second," he said over his shoulder. Behind the desk in the middle of the room were two doors. The one on the left had a sign that said Commanding Officer. Carrying a manila envelope, he walked in.

A nameplate on the desk said North, which I assumed was the driver. A few chairs were in front of the desk.

A minute later, when North came out of the door, I saw his name in black over his pocket.

"The lieutenant will see you now," North said without looking at me. He nodded toward the door as he sat at his desk.

When I walked through the open door, I stepped in front of the lieutenant's desk and stood at attention. "PFC Appenzeller reporting for duty, sir," I whipped up my right hand to my forehead in what I knew was a perfect salute, one practiced hundreds of times for Hostetler. My arm was at a forty-five-degree angle, hand straight, fingers and thumb together, my eyes looking somewhere over the COs head. His hand came up in a slow awkward movement. When he slowly lowered it, I brought mine down sharply to my side.

"At ease, Appenzeller."

I moved my feet about shoulder-length apart, my hands behind my back, eyes now fixed on him. He was a first lieutenant with one silver bar on his lapel. His uniform looked pressed. He was young probably in his mid twenties and had a large ring on his finger, most likely West Point. I saw his name was Walsh.

"Welcome to the 448, Appenzeller. Let me see what's in here." He read the contents of the folder. "Says here that you made E2 out of basic. Not that many do. Even got a notation from your drill instructor."

Good old Hostetler, I thought.

He kept reading. "You have an outstanding letter of recommendation from your battalion commander in Fort Sill. He indicates you were an excellent soldier." He kept reading. "You went to Fort Lee supply school, then worked in the motor pool at Fort Sill for a 105 Howitzer outfit. What did you do there?"

"I was the parts clerk, sir."

"You know a lot about cars, do you?"

"Not a thing, sir, but I know how to read a manual. I know how the army wants its parts ordered, handled, and stored. I know how to maintain a price load list. I know the mission, sir."

"And what is that?"

"Our mission is to keep the trucks running, sir. It's the drivers' mission, the mechanics' mission and my mission. I will do all I can to complete that mission and motivate those around me to complete that mission."

"You're pretty gung-ho there, Appenzeller." He narrowed his eyes and looked like he was pondering something. "Okay, I've heard from the colonel that we need help in the motor pool," he said slowly, then he yelled out the door. "North!"

North came to the door. "North, who's running the parts for the motor pool?"

North thought a few seconds. "Boehner, Lieutenant."

"Is he any good?"

"I don't know, sir. He isn't trained to do it. He's a mechanic by training. We stuck him in that spot because he wanted to get out from under the trucks. Nobody else had the training."

"Well, now we have someone who does. Move him back in with the mechanics. I think Appenzeller here can do a better job."

"He's not going to like that, sir."

"Well, tell him tough shit. Tell him that this order is coming from the CO."

"Okay, sir. Will do." North went out the door and returned to the gray swivel chair behind his desk.

"I'm not sure what's going on down there in the motor pool, Appenzeller. There's a warrant officer from the battalion who oversees that area. The 448 has only been here a month. They haven't finished building our barracks. The enlisted men are still in tents. North will tell you where to sleep and where to eat."

"Thank you, sir," I saluted.

He seemed to suddenly remember that he had to salute back, and casually threw his hand up, brought it back down, then looked at something else on his desk. I lowered my arm, did an about-face and marched out of his office aware that things may be more casual in the 448.

When I came out of Lieutenant Walsh's office, North looked up at me. "Boner isn't going to be happy about having to get grease on his hands again."

I nodded and noticed his pale skin that went with his light blond hair. He seemed serious like someone who didn't smile easily.

"I'll see if the top-kick wants to meet you."

The other door to the right of the CO's had "First Sergeant" printed above it." North knocked and a loud, deep "What?" came through the door. North stuck his head inside. "Top, we got a new PFC. CO says he's going to the motor pool. Says he's a parts guy. You wanna see him?"

I didn't hear a response, but North opened the door wide and I walked in.

A huge black man sat behind his desk. The nameplate on his desk and the name in black above his pocket said Johnson. On his sleeve he had three stripes above and three below with a diamond patch in the middle; he was a first sergeant, an E8 and could get only one more promotion. Few did.

I couldn't tell how tall he was sitting behind the desk — six four easily, he must have weighed two forty or two sixty. A huge man. He looked at me with dark eyes, the white parts beginning to yellow. North closed the door as he left.

"Where you from, PFC?" His deep voice resonated with a slight Southern accent.

"California, Sergeant."

"What part?"

"Oxnard."

"Where the fuck is that?"

"It's halfway between L.A. and Santa Barbara, Sergeant."

"You a beach boy?" he asked with a smile.

"Well, yes, I guess I am."

"Fucking beach boy gonna run the motor pool. Boner ain't gonna like that." He looked at me real hard, put both hands on his desk, and leaned forward. His smile disappeared, replaced by an intense glare that about knocked me over.

"Are you from CID?"

His size, along with the look he was giving me, was beyond intimidating. I had never heard of this CID.

"What is CID, sir, I mean, Sergeant?" I stammered.

"You better not be,"

Whatever or wherever CID was, I was glad I wasn't from there.

"Now, I hear it's pretty fucked up down at the motor pool. Can you straighten that shit out?" he asked, softening his tone a great deal.

"I'll do the best I can, sergeant," I said, relieved at his change in tone.

"You better, or the sergeant running the place will be on your ass."

"I'll get it done, Sergeant."

"Okay, what the hell is that name?" He squinted at the name patch above my pocket.

"Appenzeller, Sergeant."

"Apple what?"

"Appenzeller."

"North!" he yelled. North stuck his head around the door.

"Yeah, Top?"

"Show PFC Appen-whatever where he's sleeping."

When I turned to go Sergeant Johnson said, "Good luck, PFC. You're going to need it."

As I entered Norths office, he grabbed his hat, and started out the door. "Grab your shit and follow me."

I hoisted my duffel bag onto my shoulder and followed North.

When I caught up with him I asked, "What's a CID?"

"What did you say?" He stopped short, squinting at me.

"The sergeant asked if I was from CID. I have no idea what in the hell that is."

He looked me up and down. "Never mind. What you don't know can't hurt you. But I'll tell you this." He leaned closer, his intense eyes glaring. "If you are from CID, and the sarge finds out, you're gonna be dead. You got that?"

I was glad I was not from CI fucking D.

We started walking through a line of field tents until we came to one where North peeked through the flap. "Mills, you got a spare bed in here, don't you?" I heard a "Yeah" coming from the tent.

"Okay, this is your tent for now. Mills here will show you which bed is yours. He'll show you where the mess hall is. It'll be serving soon. Tomorrow, Mills can take you to the motor pool. You report to the chief warrant officer. Tell him that the CO wants you to be the new parts guy. You got that? Watch out for Boner. He's going to be pissed off."

"Yeah, so I've heard," I said, shrugging, then poked my head through the tent flap and saw a skinny guy with a couple of tattoos sitting on his bed with his shirt off. "Which bed is mine?" I asked.

"That'n over there," he said, pointing. His deep Southern accent sounded like some I had met hitching rides in the South.

I threw my duffel bag onto the bed. "This my wall locker?" I asked, pointing at the one next to my bed.

"Yeah, but, if'n I 'as you, I woon't take stuff out yo' bag. We gettin' hooches in a coupla days."

I put that sentence together in my head. "Where are you from, Mills?"

"Washin'ton,"

"D.C. or State?" I asked, surprised.

"Na', Joeja. 'Bout fiffy miles from 'Lanta."

"Really? I think I got a ride through there a couple of years ago." I remembered getting a ride with a couple of guys who I could barely understand. The only thing I did comprehend was that they were on a "nigger" hunt.

"Whar yo' from?" Mills asked.

"I'm from California--Oxnard, a beach town outside L.A."

"Yo' a beach boy?"

"Yeah, I guess I am."

"'Ell, I be damn." He looked at my name above my shirt pocket. "What's that name?"

"It's Appenzeller."

He narrowed his puzzled eyes as if he didn't comprehend.

"You can call me App."

"I sho' as hell will." He laughed as he grabbed his shirt. "I'll show yo' whar we eat."

On the way to mess, I asked what he did. He said he was a driver. He asked what I did. I told him I was the new parts guy. He said, "Yo' is? Uh-oh, Boner's gonna be pissed as hell!"

"That's what I understand," I said aware that I'd be facing anger.

The mess hall served the same drab army food as everywhere else, meat, potatoes, and overcooked vegetables. We finished, policed our area, then heading back to the tent, walking past more and more jungle-fatigue-clad soldiers getting off work making their way among the tents. I asked Mills where the latrines and showers were. When he took me to them, I showered the grime and dust off my body, then, feeling refreshed, put on clean underwear and a T-shirt, then my new fatigues over them.

When I got back to the tent, Mills had five guys crowded around his bunk. He introduced me around as "App." He said he had a poker game going, and asked if I played. I'd been in the poker club with the CAMF and knew the game. "What's the ante?"

"Only a buck," said one of the guys. I nodded, but my mind said, *A fucking buck*?

Back home we played what we called nickel-dime-quarter, with a nickel ante.

"You gonna play?" Mills asked again. I looked at the group. They didn't impress me as having had the best education or the highest IQs.

"Okay, I'll play. What do you guys play?"

The CAMF poker guys played all kinds of poker games, Stud, Chicago, Black Maria, Baseball with rules and wild cards galore in those games.

"We play poker," a black haired guy said, passing out the cards. "The pot's a buck shy."

I was dealt five cards. "Oh you must be playing Draw."

"What the fuck are you talking about?" the black haired guy said again.

"Never mind," I said, looking at my cards. I had two pairs, queens and fours. The dealer looked to his left at me.

"You bettin'?"

"Oh, yes, I'll bet a dollar." I reached into my wallet, and pulled out all the money I had. It was the play money I got when I arrived called MPC. I looked for two ones because I was the guy who was light. I threw them on the pile of ones.

Mills to my left threw in a five. "It'll cost yo' a bit mo, App."

"Well, it's gonna cost you a hell of a lot more than that," said the chubby guy next to Mills as he threw in a ten and a five.

I counted my money. It was fourteen more to me. I had twenty-five in my hand. I threw in the fourteen bucks, which left me with eleven. I asked for one card. It was a four. I had a full house — no way I could lose. When the dealer looked at me, I threw in my remaining ten.

Mills looked at me, laughing. "It'll cost yo' a hunnerd more, App."

A hundred dollars more? I didn't have a "hunnerd." The guy next to him raised Mills a hundred more. I looked at the guys around the bed. They all had hundreds of fake, but spendable, dollars in front of them.

I had a full house, but when the bet came to me I looked at Mills. "Mills, I don't have two hundred dollars!"

"Well, I guess y'all jus' have ta fold," said Mills, cracking a huge crooked toothed smile. I looked at him knowing he was right. Embarrassed, I threw in my cards, got off the bunk, stepped by the card players knowing I looked like a chump. As I lay on my bed, I glanced over at Mills. He looked at me with that yellow stained grin and said, "Welcome to the 448, App." Everybody laughed.

Chapter 9
Motorheads

I drifted off to sleep with questions swirling in my mind and woke with no answers. I dressed, had a mediocre breakfast of dry scrambled eggs and bitter coffee, found Mills, who took me on a long walk through the field tents that were situated beside nearly completed corrugated steel buildings. From there, we stepped onto a paved road and walked another fifty yards to a compound that was clearly the motor pool.

Five square wooden buildings with rusty zinc roofs covered with dust, double the size of the living quarters, stood side by side. Inside, trucks and jeeps were in various states of disrepair. Opposite these buildings, smaller steel or wooden structures held the offices. Two and half, and three quarter ton trucks, jeeps and fork lifts moved back and forth throughout the compound. Mills took me to one of the offices and introduced me. "Hey, Chief, this here's App. The CO wants him to be the new parts guy for the 448."

I didn't know whether to salute or not, but did. He gave a half-assed hand wave. "No need for salutes, Appenzeller. I'm Arnold, the chief warrant officer here." He read my name from above my pocket saying it slowly, then stuck out his hand for me to shake. Arnold, a middle-aged man with a Midwestern accent stood several inches taller than me, not huge by any standard. I couldn't see his belly under the baggy, jungle fatigues, but was pretty sure it hung out over his belt.

"You have any experience with parts supply?"

"Yes, I do, sir. I ran parts for a 105 Howitzer outfit at Fort Sill. I also had supply training at Fort Lee."

"Good, I haven't seen it done well by any of the mechanics who have taken on the job. The fucking inspectors have been on my ass about that since I was given this assignment. The colonel is pissed at me for that. Damn, I need a good parts guy. Let's find Sergeant Miller. I'll walk you to the 448 area. The 448 hasn't been here long. They were in Vung Tau."

"May I ask what the 448 does, sir?"

"You don't know?" His eyes widened in surprise.

"No, sir, the subject never came up with the CO and Top Kick."

"The 448 runs Class I, Appenzeller. They handle all the food for the Third Corps. I imagine they're feeding two to three hundred thousand soldiers. The Class I yard is huge, storing a million pounds of food. They run one convoy a day from Long Binh to

Saigon Harbor. Must be at least ten to twenty trucks in that convoy. That's a lot of trucks to keep on the road. You'll have a big job keeping those trucks running."

One question answered.

"These bays are for each of the classes of supply," he said, as we walked along. "The biggest and, maybe the most important, is class 1. 'An army runs on its belly,' as the saying goes. Hey, Miller!" he yelled.

A middle-aged, rough-looking staff sergeant in one of the bays yelled back. "What ya need, Chief?" He started a slow walk toward us, wiping his hands on a grease-stained rag.

"Sergeant Miller, this is PFC Appenzeller, from the 448. The 448 CO wants him to replace the parts guy in Class I. He actually has some experience, and was trained. Claims he knows what he's doing."

"Boner ain't gonna like that, Chief, he lobbied like hell to get that job." *Hmmm, New England accent,* I thought, *maybe New York.* Miller turned to Arnold, "Boner is a specialist fourth class, he ain't gonna like being replaced by a PFC. He only has a couple of months left in-country, you sure you want to replace him with this guy?" Before waiting for a reply, Miller turned to me asking with suspicion, "Where you from, Appenzeller?"

"California, Sergeant."

The sergeant looked at me through narrowed eyes. With his big hands, broad shoulders, and couple of scars on his cheeks, he had the demeanor of a boxer, reminding me of Hostetler.

When we came to the end of the line, I could see that this bay was by far in the worst condition. Five trucks were inside with soldiers under, over and around them. Most had their shirts off. Even at this early hour, they had grease all over their hands, arms, pants, and faces. Parts were every-where, most stacked along the walls. Compared with the bay Tom Burt ran at Fort Sill, this wasn't even close.

"Where's the parts room?" I asked.

"What parts room? We don't have no fucking parts room. The mechanics need a part, we give it to them. They keep the fucking trucks running. That's our job," Miller said defensively.

"We've talked about that, Ser-geant," Arnold said sternly. "We've flunked every inspection since I've been here. My ass is in a sling with the colonel. The inspectors are on his ass and mine. We've got to make some kind of attempt to do things SOP."

"Fuck the inspectors, Chief!" Miller shot back. "They don't know shit about the motor pool."

"I know that, Miller, and I agree with you. But, goddamn it, I have to get the colonel off my back. If we get another bad rating on our next inspection, he said he'll bust me back to enlisted. That's not going to happen. You understand that?"

They glared at each other. Sergeant Miller even looked threatening, but I knew as well as he did a sergeant can't hit an officer without doing major jail time with a bust back to private.

"Cool down, Miller. I'll introduce Appenzeller to the mechanics," Arnold said.

"Men!" he shouted, lifting his cupped hand to his mouth to help throw his voice.

A few guys looked up. Seeing the chief warrant officer, they reluctantly stopped what they were doing, got up, then ambled over to the front of the bay where we were standing. Most were wiping their hands with rags in futile attempts to clean them.

"This is PFC Appenzeller, men, the CO has made him the new parts guy."

They glared at me, then glanced back and forth at each other raising their eyes like I had failed their inspection. My clean, well pressed new fatigues made me feel self conscious as I stood there stiffly and swallowed.

Some of the mechanics were tall, others short, some with bellies, others like toothpicks. At least ten of them surrounded me — a grimy bunch, many had tattoos. The largest guy had the most tattoos, and couldn't keep his eyes off them. He'd stare at me, then look at his chest where he moved his tattoos on his pecs like a stripper I'd once seen in a San Diego burlesque theater. He appeared to be the mechanics' leader.

"You a Ford guy or a Chevy guy?"

"Fuck Fords!" said a guy down the line.

"And fuck your goddamn worthless Chevys!" tattoo-man yelled at the guy.

"Chevys rule!" shouted someone else.

"Chevys suck dog dicks!" another chimed in. Now half of them were screaming "FORDS" and the other half "CHEVYS." I thought they were going to come to blows.

The big Ford champion stared at me. "Well, what is it?" he demanded.

"I have a VW," I said, trying to be funny. By their disgusted scowls, I knew it didn't work.

"Fucking VWs are for pussies."

"Worse than fucking Chryslers!" another yelled.

"I like Mopar," one said weakly.

"FUCK YOU!" the Ford and Chevy camps yelled together.

"SHUT THE FUCK UP, YOU GODDAMN MO-TORHEADS!" yelled Sergeant Miller.

"Thank you, Sergeant," the Chief jumped in now that order was restored. "Men, things have got to change around here. We've flunked our last three inspections. We have another in a month and a half. Appenzeller has experience with motor pools stateside. I'm giving him the authority to make changes. You do what he tells you to do. Do you understand that?" Silence. They glanced at each other, grumbling, some making obscene gestures to each other.

"The chief asked you a question! Do you fucking understand?" shouted Sergeant Miller.

A few said, "Yeah, we heard him," a few mumbled, a few shook their heads.

"I fucking repeat, DO YOU UNDERSTAND?" Miller's eyes grew larger.

"Yes, Sergeant," they said, not quite in unison.

"Appenzeller, you have anything to say?" Arnold's eyes told me he expected me to say something. Blood rushed to my head. I didn't know what to say. I knew that I didn't have their attention nor their respect.

"Well," I began, clearing my throat. "Listen, you guys." Some looked up, but most still made gestures of disrespect. "Any changes that need to be made will be made by me. You have a mission to do, and that's to keep the trucks running. I can tell that you guys know that mission and do your jobs well." More of them were looking at me. I made sure to make eye contact with each one. "You just keep doing that mission. The Army has their SOP. We'll conform to that SOP. That will only concern you in a small way. You just keep those fucking trucks running whether they're Fords or Chevys." By then, most were looking at me, a few nodding like they understood.

The chief jumped in, "Dismissed men. Get back to work." The mechanics turned away and headed for the trucks. I heard a few comments, such as "Ford rules! Fuck Chevys!" and "Fuck Fords!"

I stood with the chief when an old beat-up three-quarter-ton truck came to a stop in front of us. A variety of parts lay in the bed of the truck. A tall guy with specialist E4 patches on both arms of his dusty uniform got out.

"Oh, good," said Arnold. "Boehner is here."

I gulped. I hadn't been looking forward to this confrontation.

"Boehner, we need to talk."

When he walked over, I saw he was about six-foot, thin, but strong looking with dark hair sticking out of this cap and dark, intense eyes. His thick black mustache made him look street tough.

"What can I do for you, chief?" he asked, guardedly with a New York City accent.

"Boehner, this is PFC Appenzeller. The CO has ordered me to replace you with him."

Boehner stiffened. "What did you say, Chief?"

"I said Appenzeller here is the new parts guy."

"What the fuck, Chief, he's a PFC! How can he replace me?"

"He can because the CO wants him to. He has experience, Boehner. He knows what the army wants."

"I know what I'm doing. The guys are getting their parts. The trucks are running. This ain't fair! God Damn it! What about the chain of command and all that?" He took a breath. "I ain't going back in that goddamn bay and getting under those goddamn trucks again! I hate being a damn grease monkey! You know that, Sarge!" His angry voice grew louder. The men had stopped their work. Most were standing, looking at us, listening to every word.

"Orders are orders, Boehner. You'll obey them or you'll be thrown in Long Binh Jail. You want that?" Miller yelled back.

"Welcome back to the bay, Boner," someone shouted from inside the building.

"Shut the fuck up, you assholes!" Boehner yelled.

"Settle down, Boehner!" ordered the chief.

"Sir," I broke in, speaking to Chief Arnold. "Can I have a word with you and Sergeant Miller?" They both shrugged. We walked several steps away.

"I'm going to need a lot of help organizing this operation. I'm going to need Boehner's cooperation. He obviously knows where and how to get parts.

I'm going to need help building a parts room with shelves and a front desk. I'll need places for the paperwork and I'll need more than Boehner. I'll need a builder if we have one. If it's okay with Boehner, maybe we can find a compromise that will be good for everyone."

Sergeant Miller called Boehner over. "Appenzeller has what might be a solution to this situation. Listen to what he has to say."

"Boehner," I started slowly, thinking about how my dad would handle this problem. I looked him in the eye and could tell I had his attention. "I know it's difficult for you having someone come in and take the position you have earned. I'd feel the same way if I was in your shoes. I know I'm an E3 and you're E4, that's supposed to count for something in the army. I'm not critical of the job you've done. You came to the job from being a mechanic. You know the trucks, you know the parts. I was trained at Fort Lee, and taught by a really smart guy who knew how to do things the army way. At the same time, he knew his main mission was keeping the trucks on the road. I'm going to need your help, Boehner. I can't do this alone. Could you consider being my partner in this effort? I think your practical knowledge of the vehicles, and my knowledge of army SOP, will make us a good team. What do you think?"

I could tell he was thinking pretty hard about what I'd said. "Well," he said eventually. "If it keeps me from under those damn trucks, I'll do it. I'm almost a short-timer. I just want to get by this last couple of months and get back home. Okay, I'll work with you. How do you say that last name?"

"Don't worry about it. Call me App. Deal?" I put out my hand. He grabbed it firmly, then went back to the three-quarter-ton truck to unload parts.

I walked a little distance with the chief warrant officer and the sergeant. I asked the chief, "Is that a satisfactory solution?"

"That was well said, Appenzeller. You calmed him down. Where did you learn that?"

"I had a great teacher, sir," I said, knowing my dad would be proud.

Boehner and I unloaded the truck. He showed me his organization. "We've got about thirty-some trucks in the 448, mostly deuce-and-a-halves. They're the ones the guys take to Saigon every day. You see this big pile here? That's the deuce-and-a-half pile. I keep that pretty loaded with parts. I worked on those trucks a lot. I know what tends to break down. Over here are the three-quarter-ton truck parts. We got a few of them. Over there are parts for the

M151 jeeps. North has one, so do some of the brass. These are parts for the forklifts that load and unload trucks to and from the Class I yard. This last one is for our specialty item. We have these airplane pullers in the Class I yard called a PSI X3-WT. Huge back tires, five hundred cubic engine, strong as a bitch. Pulls carts in the Class I yard. That thing can pull a 737. They say they can put twenty fully loaded carts behind the thing and it can pull 'em easy."

I looked at the mess. Boehner had inherited this system. "This is how the old parts guy ran things before he got short and left. I run it the same way."

"Do you have any idea of the numbers on how many parts you have?"

"Not a clue, half the stuff you see was here before I got the parts job. I just replace stuff as I go along. I've got to do the dispatching, too. That's the only paperwork I keep. Trucks go out, they got to go through me. I don't check 'em much. I figure they know where they're goin' and what they're doin'."

While we spoke we could hear the banter in the bay between the mechanics. It was all NASCAR, Sprint cars, and other auto racing stuff. Ford guys made their case; Chevy guys, theirs.

"How the fuck you Chevy guys can even talk about anything blows me away," said tattooed guy while reaching for a wrench.

"That's Thompson," Boehner whispered as we listened.

"Chevy only won one or two races all last year. I mean, come on! They ain't won but one this year."

"I don't care what you guys say. All of NASCAR the last two years has been dominated by Mopar. Plymouth is winning the most."

"Yeah, well, that's just 'cause they got Richard Petty. He could win in any vehicle he wanted. It ain't 'cause of that shitty Plymouth he drives. If he was driving a Ford he'd win every race!"

"Or a Chevy!"

"Fuck Chevys!"

"Fuck Fords!"

As we left the bay, Boehner shrugged. "See why I had to get out of the bay? That shit goes on all day and all night. Drives me nuts!"

Chapter 10
The Golden Boy

Boehner and I were a good team. He showed me how to get to the parts depot and introduced me to important allies. While he gathered the parts, I took care of the paperwork. I read the reports from the Army inspectors, who noted the chief infraction was the lack of a paper trail.

I found a builder, Johnny Fuentes, a fellow Californian from San Pedro. He was TDY (temporary duty) from Saigon and living with us until his next assignment. He'd been erecting office buildings at Tan Son Nhut Airport. He and I designed our new parts room. Fuentes knew where to find materials, and it was my job to fetch things for him, and hold boards while he sawed and hammered. Boehner handled getting the parts, using his old method.

We streamlined the dispatch system. Fuentes put in a large window that trucks could drive up to with dispatch orders, get them recorded, and move on. We built shelves for the parts, separating them into specific areas for each type of vehicle. We built a front counter where mechanics would order parts. I found manuals for each of the vehicles stacking them in order on the counter. Paperwork was in bins for each truck.

I set up the motor pool the same way Tom Burt had at Fort Sill. I found several empty transport containers, had forklifts bring them to the motor pool, storing them behind the 448 bay. I had Fuentes build a door in the back wall, so the mechanics could easily get to the containers.

Most of the time Fuentes and I talked about surf. He surfed Huntington Beach and Redondo, while I talked about South County Line, Leo Carrillo and the Rincon. The more we talked the bigger the waves got. Fuentes was a really cool guy who reminded me of some of the Chicano surfers I knew at my home break Silver Strand close to the Sea Bee Base. He had heard of Silver Strand and shuddered when I told him I surfed there.

"That's a totally locals only place, App, how'd you get to surf that spot."

"My folks rented a house at Silver Strand when I was a junior in high school, the homeboys considered me a local."

Meanwhile, I had Boehner identify parts, load them into a wheelbarrow, haul them to the containers, then organize them on shelves. He and I made labels for the parts bins and containers. We worked ten hours a day, six and a half days a week.

The 448 motor pool was ready for inspection in a month. The motor pool bay was cleared of all parts. The new parts were stored out front in the official parts room. Boehner organized the tools. It was time to have a meeting with the mechanics.

I knew the mechanics well by then; they were my buds. We swapped stories. They loved hearing about my tales of being a CAMF in a California beach town. I loved telling them stories about me surfing the big Pacific waves that hit the West coast. I exaggerated the size of the waves, but they listened spellbound. My favorite story and theirs was the Applefuck story. I loved acting the part of Hostetler. That story killed them. Most of them called me Applefuck or Apple after that. We were comrades-in-arms. We weren't fighting in the war, but we were working together to support those who were.

When we got close to the inspection I gathered them together for a meeting. "Men, I have a plan that I know will satisfy our paperwork obligations and help us pass our next inspection. Mechanics, you're excellent. You know how to repair trucks; that's your mission. Most of the parts are in the containers in back of the bay. Boehner has done an outstanding job of organizing those parts. What I need from you now is to start going to the parts hut in front of the bay. I need each of you to go to the counter and request Boehner or me to get you a part. We'll fill out the paperwork. It may take a little longer, but it'll give the inspectors a hard-on when they see the pile of paperwork. Is that cool with you guys?"

Later, I spoke to the drivers. "Drivers, you'll line up after you've loaded, drive to the dispatch office and give the dispatcher your log book. He'll record it and you'll carry out your orders. Check your oil and water before you crank your engine. Be aware of your vehicle's mileage for maintenance. Listen to the engine. If you hear something strange, report it right away. You don't want to break down on Highway 1."

"You got it, Applefuck!" one of them shouted. Everyone laughed, including me.

After we all laughed I continued. "I got some good news, men. We have two more PSI X3-WT airplane-pullers coming. You've kept the ones in the Class I yard running smoothly. Boehner will be leaving soon. I think we need to see him off in style. I say we unload those bastards, and have two groups of mechanics work on them, a Ford group and a Chevy group. You Mopar guys will have to choose which side you're on. That strip of road between here and the Class I yard will make a good drag strip. I say we trade for some cases of beer, cut an oil barrel in half, attach some legs, and make a grill. Let's get some of the general's steaks and have us a shit-kickin' going-away party for Boehner next Sunday afternoon."

A cheer came from the men. The Ford guys started yelling at the Chevy guys about how they were going to kick their butts. The Chevy guys yelled back insults about Fords. Neither team wanted the two guys who liked Mopar. It was all good-natured.

The afternoon I asked for the approval for the party, Chief Arnold thrilled me when he said, "I wouldn't have believed that you could have put this thing together so quickly, Appenzeller." Sergeant Miller stood next to him smiling and nodding his agreement.

"I was lucky to have found Fuentes, sir."

"I talked to the colonel, App, and he'll be here tomorrow. He wants to see what you've done. I've put you up for a promotion. Sergeant Miller agrees."

Miller shook his head, then said, "I don't see why you aren't running the parts for the entire motor pool. The chief and I will propose that to the colonel. It won't be a job for a private first class. We'll propose a field-level promotion. When we're at war, that becomes a possibility."

"Thank you, Sergeant."

"It might not happen for a while. It'll be temporary at first, but you can wear the patch and act the part.

We'll work on making it permanent over time. The colonel has power; General Westmoreland is his close friend. He'll push it through, you can count on that."

I was totally unaware of the power structure of the Quartermaster Corps. I didn't know which battalion we were with. I knew I was in the 448 S&S, and knew my CO and the Top. I knew our colonel was named Anderson and that the commanding general was Westmoreland. Long Binh had been a rubber plantation prior to the U.S. Army's absconding it to build the huge facility that became Long Binh Post. General Westmoreland lived in the Big House and, because Colonel Anderson and Westmoreland were friends, that made the colonel a powerful man.

The next afternoon, Colonel Anderson arrived in his clean new M151 Jeep with a colonel's flag attached. Chief Warrant Officer Arnold and Sergeant Miller were waiting for him in front of their office. They saluted smartly as the colonel stepped out of the jeep. He saluted smartly back. I watched from behind the counter of our new parts room. Boehner and I found some olive-green Army paint, and painted the outside of the counter, then stenciled 448 S&S in white paint across the front.

The colonel was talking with Arnold and Miller. He went into the office for a bit. I looked around our bay at the dirt floor that was kept clean with a rake and broom. We had several trucks in the bay that mechanics were busily working on. The bay looked clean and organized. Neat stacks of tires lined the back wall. The closed back door kept the secret parts containers hidden from view. The parts were wrapped and sat in bins in the parts room. Manuals in a large three-ring binder sat on the counter.

When the colonel came out of the office, he started a slow walk from the Class V bay, making comments to Arnold and Miller as they walked with him. He came to Class I and looked around. Sergeant Miller yelled "A-TEN-HUT!" The mechanics stopped what they were doing, moved quickly into a line, standing at attention. They wore green T-shirts with fatigue pants and boots. Their jungle fatigue tops were hanging neatly on hooks. They stood there, right arms at a 45-degree angle, hands straight just above their right eyes. I had never seen them salute.

The colonel saluted back, saying, "At ease, men." Looking around the bay, he moved to our new parts room. Boehner and I came out from behind the counter, and stood at attention. The colonel moved in front of us and looked at the freshly painted green counter with 448 S&S stenciled in white.

"Damn, Chief, you're right. It's a goddamn miracle." His deep, serious, no nonsense voice was now enthusiastic and he spoke with a smile.

"Thank you, sir," Arnold said, also smiling, proudly. "This is the young man I was talking about, PFC Appenzeller."

"Not a PFC for long. Where did you learn this, Appenzeller?"

"I was trained at Fort Lee, sir. I learned from an excellent soldier at Fort Sill."

"I was commandant of Fort Lee for a time. Good that we trained you well. But this took initiative, Appenzeller. This motor pool was an embarrassment to the Quartermaster Corps. We're at war, and army protocol can be lessened to some degree, but this place was a shithole. You've made an impact, soldier, and you'll be rewarded."

"I had the cooperation and support of the chief, Sergeant Miller, Specialist Boehner, and many other men, sir."

"I'm recommending a field-level promotion, Soldier. Chief Warrant Officer Arnold wants an administrative change. You will be the parts manager for the entire motor pool, and you'll have a rank that will support that. I'm also recommending you for Soldier of the Month. You'll have a three-day weekend in Vung Tau whenever you want."

Startled at this kind of praise from the colonel and not knowing how to respond, I made my best salute, saying, "Thank you, sir!"

He saluted back, did an about-face, and walked with the chief back to his jeep.

Boehner slapped me on the shoulders while the mechanics gathered around me. "Spec Five Applefuck has a nice ring to it!" one of the guys said and everyone laughed.

"Thanks, guys," I stood there beaming, my face glowing with pride.

Thompson, still glancing at the tattoos hidden by his T-shirt, looked up to say, "You deserve it, Apple. This place looks great."

I felt embarrassed, but happy that I was going to be promoted and excited about the three-day leave. I had put in for an R&R to Hawaii that was coming up in a couple of months. The promotion and R&R to Vung Tau would take longer than expected. The Vietnamese New Year celebration would be in a few weeks and that would change everything.

Chapter 11
REMFs

The 448 moved out of the field tents a couple of days after my arrival. The hooches we moved into were much like the barracks at 90th Relocation, large, corrugated-steel half-pipes screwed onto forty by twenty-four-foot cement slabs. On one end were two eight-by-eight foot rooms for sergeants or spec fives. The rest of the space was occupied by ten soldiers of lesser rank, five on each side, each having a bunk, footlocker and wall locker.

Two light sockets hung from the ceiling about six feet off the floor forcing a taller man to duck. Each socket had four electrical outlets which were used to plug in extension cords for the TVs and stereo equipment stretching from each footlocker like two octopuses with thin tentacles hanging down.

I bunked with a group of PFCs and spec fours, most serving as clerks somewhere in the battalion. North, now a spec four, had the bunk next to the sergeant's room on the left, while mine was in the middle of the row opposite North. On my right was a big guy named Peterson, a battalion clerk, who reminded me of Hoss Cartwright on "Bonanza" with his big head, big feet, big body, big everywhere, which he carried well. Despite his size, he spoke in a soft, kind voice, and surprisingly, was the only guy in the outfit who didn't smoke or drink.

On my left was another big guy from York, Pennsylvania named Albertson, a body-builder with bulging muscles on top of muscles. He walked on his hands from one end of the barracks to the other ten to twenty times a day. He had the annoying habit of reading porn books out loud he got from locals in exchange for cigarettes. When he lay in bed at night reading, I couldn't help but listen. One night when I was trying to write a letter to Alexandra, I lost it when he mumbled, "He reached down and touched her Virginia."

I jumped off my bed, grabbed the book and pointed to the words, "Goddamn it, Albertson! It's vagina, not Virginia, you idiot!"

He looked at me like there was no difference.

"Virginia is a state in the Union! A vagina is a pussy!" His eyebrows lifted, and he looked startled by my shouting, but he shrugged, and kept reading, his lips moving with every word.

Across from us in the middle bed was one of the few black guys outside of the Class I yard. Collins, a clerk at battalion headquarters, came from Chicago. According to him, affirmative action got him into an Ivy League school, but he dropped out a semester, which exposed him to the draft. Like me, he joined to avoid the infantry. He was taller than me, and thinner with milk chocolate colored skin. His eyes like deep black marbles gleamed when he spoke. He was the most intelligent, well-read person I had met in the enlisted ranks. He spoke clearly, articulating his thoughts well. I liked hanging with Collins and Peterson.

Most days after work the three of us met at a basketball court Class I guys built near their barracks. Class I guys, all blacks, lived in self-segregated living quarters ruled by an E7 sergeant named Bentley. We beat most of their three-man teams. I could shoot from outside, while Peterson could block out, rebound and set bone-crushing screens. Collins could shoot, and handle the ball. They called us Applefuck, the Hulk and Snowflake. There were some excellent basketball players in Class I. Though we didn't win every game, we won our share.

After showering and eating, we played chess. Because Peterson was learning, I'd take him on first, then Collins would beat the winner. By the end of the second game my motor pool buds Tom McNamara and his sidekick Larry Dunphy would insist that Collins and

I go with them to the club. Peterson, a committed Mormon, stayed behind to watch reruns of "Perry Mason" on the black-and-white TV he had on his foot-locker.

McNamara, which we called The Secretary after Secretary of Defense Robert McNamara, was shorter than me with green eyes, and a constant smile that showed off his perfect white teeth. He was from "Souty" which, he said, was the South side of Boston. This gave the Secretary a distinctive Boston accent. He was popular in the motor pool because he could do voices of famous people, especially news commentators like Walter Cronkite. He killed Collins and me with his routines.

Dunphy had to be one of the funniest looking guys I've ever seen with his hooked nose, freckled face, and dark close together eyes that were slightly off line. His main claim to fame was his false teeth. He'd pull them out, suck in his lips with his nose almost touching his chin, then blow out his lips like a party favor, which got us so hysterical, we'd fall on the floor laughing.

I tried to write to Alexandra as much as I could, and sent out at least one letter every other day. I would write them at work, or sitting on my bunk, but was disappointed that I wasn't getting any letters from her. Day after day became more painful than the day before. When I didn't get any letters for a month, I panicked and gave in to jealousy. I wrote a nasty accusatory letter filled with vile assertions that she was cheating on me. I sent it out the next morning.

That afternoon, North handed me about twenty letters wrapped together. "I got these today wrapped up like that. They must not have known where you were stationed."

Ohmygod! That fucking letter! I went over to North lying on his bed reading. "North, you didn't send that letter, did you?" I asked, hoping against hope that he hadn't.

"Out with the morning mail," he said casually.

"Any chance of getting it back?"

"Not a snowball's chance in hell."

Oh shit, I thought and composed a long apologetic letter begging for forgiveness.

Some nights a guy from Class I would come into the barracks. "Anybody want to serve guard duty for a hundred bucks?" We had to serve a guard duty, and do kitchen police, KP, once a week. A soldier could sell it, if he had the money. Class I guys had the money. I volunteered.

A guard had to walk his post in the Class I yard for about four hours with a shotgun. We walked between stacks of food containers with rows wide enough for a forklift. Lights shown at the end of the rows of containers, but in between, it was dark.

I made a fool of myself the first night I served guard duty. While walking my post composing letters to Alexandra in my head, I saw an animal in front of me I thought was a cat. I bent over to get a better look. When my eyes were fully focused, I realized it was a rat. When it made a hissing face, its mouth showing a lot of teeth, I pointed the shotgun, pulled the trigger, and blasted what was once a rat into a bloody spot with a little fur around it.

A jeep with a mounted M60 machine gun came flying around the corner. A GI jumped out with his M16. I stood with my hands up. He started yelling. "What the fuck is up? Why did you discharge your weapon?"

I pointed to the bloody spot. "It was a rat!"

"Goddamn, App, you can't be shooting at every rat you see. You're going to deny a gook his dinner." The three others laughed. "Hop in the jeep. Let me show you something."

They took me to a long line of back to back refrigerator units that must have stretched for two hundred yards. There was a space about a foot wide between the containers.

"Flash your light down that crack."

What I saw made my skin crawl. A hundred eyes were glowing in the light — some moved, others blinked. "You can't be freaked out about rats in Class I. We got millions of them."

The most frightening guard duty came every so often. I served it only once, and would pay almost any amount to get out of it. It was perimeter guard duty on the outside of the post. I checked in with the officer of the guard at the last guard house on the perimeter. He spoke in dire tones. "We have intel that Charlie is setting up mortar rounds in the trees outside the perimeter. You have to walk through the trees. If you run into them, take them out."

I carried an M14 with full clips in my pockets. I was issued my M14 the first week I arrived at the 448. North took us to a firing range to zero them in. They were kept in a container outside headquarters. With a sergeant in charge we set out after dark. "Stay quiet and stay low, you see something, shoot it; nothing is supposed to be out there."

The army had cleared a mile of forest around Long Binh. It was ragged land with huge piles of torn-up trees. We were inside the outer tree line. Every Sunday we heard rockets overhead. None hit the 448. They were aimed at the ammo dump a mile from us. This was a Saturday night.

I tried to position myself in the middle of the platoon, but was ordered near the front because I was a newbie. Short-timers got the middle. We walked slowly and quietly for hours, stopping every so often to take a drink from our canteens. At midnight we started circling back. My heart was beating hard the entire time. When any one of us stepped on a branch, I was ready to hit the ground. At dawn, when we returned with the sun rising I made a vow to never serve that guard duty again. After I made Spec five, much to my great joy, the Colonel made me exempt from guard duty and KP.

Another way to make some extra money came via Sergeant Bentley from the Class I yard, a black guy, not as big as Sergeant Johnson, but big, and more muscular and athletic than the Top. When he played basketball with Class I guys, he always won. He fouled like a son of a bitch, but I couldn't say a thing because he'd look at you with those intense black eyes, "Nice block, Sarge," was all I could say.

Bentley entered our barracks every so often with a box of stuff. "Who wants to make a hundred bucks?" he asked. One evening I raised my hand. He handed the package to me and said, "Here. Take this to the post office.

Send it to this place in Detroit. Fill your name in here."

I took the box. When Sergeant Bentley left, Collins, on his bunk, said, "I wouldn't do that if I were you."

"Why not, Collins? It's an easy hundred bucks."

"Contraband," he said, lifting it, "most likely liquor. I bet that address is a liquor store in Detroit. I've heard rumors about Bentley and Class I. There's something going on down there for sure. Those guys have money. They pass it around. How do you think they pay to get out of guard duty and KP? I think your Top down at 448 is in on it, too. Has some fancy jewelry, that guy, and he's best friends with Bentley."

I recalled my first meeting with the Top, and said to Collins, "When I first met him, Top asked if I knew anything about something called CID. He seemed real concerned that I might be CID. I still don't know what it is."

"CID is an army acronym for the Criminal Investigative Department. CID looks into criminal conduct by members of the army. If they're up to no good down in Class I, they don't want CID snooping around. The last place on earth you want to be is in Long Binh Jail. They kill people in there. It's a jungle. Nothing but deserters, murderers, and guys waiting to be shipped back to Leavenworth to be hanged. You

Page 137

don't want to end up in LBJ, App, no you don't." Listening to Collins, I was getting more and more answers to my many questions. When Dunphy arrived that night, I gave him Bentley's box and fifty bucks. He took it gladly and promised to send it the next day.

I invited Collins and Peterson to our going-away party for Boehner in the motor pool. We got two cases of steaks and a case of hamburgers from the Class I yard. We grilled them on the two barbecue pits we'd made from old oil barrels. We had cases of beer on ice in the bed of Boehner's truck. The Ford and Chevy teams had their vehicles primed and ready. The engines were so powerful they had to run them in reverse because if they gunned them forward the front end would lift up so drastically they almost flipped backwards. The Ford team beat the Chevy team two out of three, then they paraded around like they'd won the Daytona 500.

Chief Warrant Officer Arnold and Sergeant Miller were there drinking beers. "This is good for morale, App," said Arnold smiling. "We should do this every Sunday afternoon. This is the happiest I've ever seen the motor pool."

When the party was breaking up, Boehner pulled me aside. He'd been hanging all day with guys he knew from

New England. "Thanks for the party, App. This has been fun. The guys and I are going to the parts room to smoke some weed. You want to join us?"

I had only smoked marijuana once before. I heard from Boehner that you could exchange a carton of Salem cigarettes for a pack of marijuana. The locals delicately removed the tobacco from each cigarette and replaced it with pot. There were three brands, a Winston, a Paxton, which had a menthol filter and a Raleigh that we called a "three day weekend" because it was dipped in opium.

When we got to the parts room, Boehner took out a pack of Winston's from his upper left pocket. He pulled out a repacked cigarette, lit it, took a deep pull, held it, and let it out. He handed it to me. I took a long drag, held it in for a while as he had done, then let it out. I started coughing as the last bit left my lungs. He and his buds chuckled. "If you don't cough, you don't get off," one of them said.

They passed it around. When it got to me again, I took another hit, held it, and let it out. By the fourth pull, I felt light-headed, almost wobbly, my vision distorted. Sitting on the parts room counter, the floor looked a long way down.

"Here's my present to you and the motor pool, App," said Boehner, as he pulled some plastic off something hidden on a shelf in back. It was a turntable and stereo with good-sized speakers. "Listen to this shit, man. It'll blow your mind," he said, a Cheshire-cat grin on his face. He turned on the stereo, pulled an LP record out of a brightly colored album cover, setting it on the turntable. My stoned mind was slowing everything down. He lowered the needle, then turned around looking at me. His smile now seemed like a clown's. It made me laugh.

The sound coming from the speakers blew my mind like nothing I had ever heard. First, a guitar lead, then in a clear voice Jimi Hendrix started moaning about a purple haze that was in his brain. I could relate, the purple haze had taken over my brain as well.

Chapter 12
TET

A week after the goodbye party for Boehner, Peterson and I were playing chess on my bunk. Collins had guard duty. The only other person in the room was a new transfer named Smith. We called him the White Smith because there was a black guy in Class I also named Smith, we now called the Black Smith. The White Smith was a combat soldier recuperating from wounds and became addicted to morphine.

We were placed on Orange Alert for the Vietnamese New Year called Tet. The locals liked to celebrate by shooting off mortar rounds aimed at us. We heard them before, usually on Saturday nights and Sundays when the locals were off. Fortunately the shells never hit our area.

Though Peterson was learning the game, he was beating me consistently. After our third game, it was time for the "Perry Mason" reruns on the GI TV broadcast system. When Peterson moved toward the TV on his footlocker, we heard a loud sound that could only be one thing, an automatic weapon. It had to be either an M16 or the M60 we had mounted on jeeps for guard duty. Whatever it was, it sounded close. Peterson stopped, and looked at me with puzzled eyes. I shrugged, too startled to say anything. Then we heard it again, and this time it sounded like it was right outside the hooch.

Sirens started blaring, loud and often, shrill and ear piercing like British cop cars. "Oh, shit!" I said. "It's a Red Alert! We're under attack!" *Ohmygod! That's right!* I thought. *There's a war going on!* Being so wrapped up in the motor pool I'd forgotten we were in a combat zone.

Standing in my boxer shorts and T-shirt, I dashed to my locker and grabbed my fatigues. Out of the corner of my eye I saw Peterson doing the same. I struggled to get my stuff on, then grabbed my socks and boots just as Peterson hightailed it out of the door. Why was it taking forever to get dressed? Panicking, tying up my laces, a frantic soldier ran into the room yelling, "Lights out, Red alert!"

I guess he didn't see the "octopus" hanging in the middle of our room and ran right into it, causing the bulb to explode with a loud spark. I looked up and saw him go down. Thinking he'd been shot, I quickly crawled under my bed until the guy got to his feet and ran down the aisle. It got quiet again, real quiet. After a minute, I slowly risked rolling out from under my bed and finished lacing my boots. Suddenly, I heard rapid fire again. This time a long burst. Looking around, I realized I had no weapon. Our M14s were locked up in a container next to 448 Headquarters.

It got quiet again. I tiptoed down to the door opposite the room and stood with my back to the door, terrified to stick my head out in case Charlie was running around the area. I glanced at the White Smith, still sleeping in his morphine fog. Cautiously, I held my helmet outside the door, and when it didn't get shot, I stuck my head out, surprised to see a group of soldiers standing in a circle between our hooch and the next. They were stoners passing a Winston. Standing in the doorway, smelling the weed, I put my helmet on. "Hey, App! Ya wanna hit?" one of them asked.

"Guys, it's a Red Alert! We're under attack!"

"So, that's what all that noise is about!" another said. "Well, let's go get some guns."

At that moment, I heard a familiar sound, the loud whistle of a rocket then a scream from inside my hooch. "INCOMING!" I looked back and saw the White Smith rolling under his bed. Realizing what he was saying, I dove to the floor inside the hooch. The whistle turned into a screech, and the explosion that followed caused dirt, shrapnel, and debris to fly through the air outside the hooch with dust so thick it was impossible to see.

When, at last, it was quiet, I looked at the White Smith scrambling to get into his fatigues. I looked out the door through the settling dust to the guys on the ground covered in dirt and wood. When they got up, dusting themselves off, I couldn't see any blood on them.

We looked around and saw small flames and smoke coming from the stump of a tree not far away - a tree we called the Ralph Tree - a tree that guys who, sick with too much alcohol, went to when they needed to throw up. We killed that tree with the acid that comes up with vomit. The "stoners" loved that Ralph Tree. One of them realized what had happened. "They fucked up the Ralph Tree!"

Now angry, they hustled inside their hooch to get their helmets, then ran toward headquarters to get their weapons. I did the same, running more cautiously than they, darting from tree to tree, still not sure if Charlie was in the compound.

When I got to the container next to headquarters, I had to stand in line while an impatient White Smith showed up behind me. Finally, I got to the head of the line where the spec four inside asked for my weapon number, which I couldn't remember.

"Just give me a fucking gun, god-damn it!"

He looked at my name, made a cross reference, then handed me an M14. I looked at him. "BULLETS!" I yelled, feeling the fear bombarding me.

He had stacks of full clips. I started putting them into my pockets, then stepped away from the container and loaded my M14 with a clip. I drew back the handle locking in a bullet.

Soldiers stood there waiting to be told what to do. Top was there, huge in his fatigues. He didn't know what to tell them. I saw confusion and bewilderment in his black eyes, but then he yelled for the men to form up, and a few began cautiously to stick out their arms.

The White Smith had his weapon. He locked, loaded and pointed his M14 at Sergeant Johnson. "WHAT THE FUCK ARE YOU DOING? THE WHOLE COMPANY COULD GO DOWN WITH ONE ROCKET! GET THESE REMFS OUT BY HIGHWAY 1! THAT'S WHERE CHARLIE WILL TRY TO COME ACROSS! THAT'S WHY YOU BUILT THOSE DITCHES AND LAID THOSE SANDBAGS!" The White Smith started running in that direction.

Top stood there dumbfounded, but suddenly woke up and started yelling, "Follow Whitey, men! Fan out and get along that road!"

I started running. When I got past the ditches, standing with my back to a tree, I heard rapid fire, then looked back and saw soldiers jumping into the ditches, setting their M14s on the sandbags. I realized I was in front of them. Half of them were stoned; all of them out of their minds with fear like me. More afraid of them than I was of Charlie, I ran back, jumped into a ditch, put my back to the front sand-bags and looked at my comrades-in-arms. I didn't recognize many, there were many companies in the Quartermaster Corps, but I knew that none of them were combat soldiers.

My heart was pounding so hard I thought I could hear it. Blood throbbed through my temples. My head ached from it. I heard bullets screech by over-head. No way was I going to stick my head over the sandbags to see. Someone from our side shot up flares that lit the sky. It was almost beautiful.

After not hearing enemy fire for five minutes, a guy near me dared a look, then came back down. "A flare hit the brush on the other side and caught fire. I think Charlie's hightailing it."

We inched our way up to take a look. When I got my eyes just above the sandbags, I saw that indeed a fire was burning out of control. When I saw movement on the other side, I pulled up my M14; others did the same. Hearing firing from our side, suddenly we all started shooting. With my M14 on semi-automatic, every time I pulled the trigger the weapon kicked back into my shoulder. I pulled it in tight, like Hostetler instructed, aimed, and pulled the trigger, not sure what I was aiming at.

"Stop firing! Stop firing, goddamn it!" someone yelled. Who ever it was sounded like he knew what he was doing. It got deathly quiet. Gunpowder saturated the air. My nostrils stung from the pungent smell. No one moved, but we kept looking over the edge of the sandbags, waiting. No sound came from the other side of Highway 1. We waited, wondering how this was going to turn out. My breathing returned to normal. My heart rate slowed and I regained composure.

After fifteen minutes, we saw a figure stumbling down Highway 1 on the other side of the fence. He had his M14 strap over his shoulder holding the weapon waist-high. A flare went up. I saw that it was the Black Smith, stoned and loopy on reds. He looked back at us, yelling, "I got these motherfuckers!" He reached for the switch on his weapon, turning it from semi to fully automatic and pointed it at the other side of the road. When he pulled the trigger, the M14 started jerking out bullets at a rapid pace, the jolt caused the weapon to fly off to his left. By the time he finished, he was facing us. Afraid he would shoot us, we all dove for cover.

"Somebody's got to shoot the Black Smith!" someone yelled. We couldn't help but laugh.

I looked over again and saw he had taken out his spent clip. He didn't notice he was now facing us. As he reached for another clip, out of the corner of my eye, I saw an MP with a silver helmet running fast, lowering himself to make a lunging tackle. The Black Smith went down hard, his weapon and helmet flying down the road. Again, we couldn't stop laughing. Another MP ran over to help. They dragged the now inert Black Smith back to the gate.

We didn't hear a sound from the other side. The fire was dying out. While wondering what to do, we heard loud rumbling. It got louder and louder. Another flare went up. Off to our left we could see helicopter gunships with M60 machine guns sticking out of the open doors on the side. We knew gunners were behind the machine guns. As they approached, they opened fire. Every seventh bullet was a phosphorous tracer creating a fantastic light show. One after another they strafed the ground on the other side of Highway 1. Once one finished another followed. When the last one unloaded its machine gun, they moved on. A mouse couldn't have survived that firepower.

Once the loud noise stopped, we heard nothing but the ringing in our ears from our weapons and the cracking of the M60s. We waited and waited and waited some more. Some fell asleep. Others talked quietly. We were anticipating another attack that never came. Sergeants started releasing mess-hall staff to start breakfast. After another hour, others were told to go to the mess hall. Finally, those who ate came back. I got relieved as the sun peeked over the edge of Long Binh Post.

In the mess hall, I saw Collins, who said it was an amazing night to be on guard. He was the CQ of battalion headquarters on duty all night getting information, passing it to the colonel. He said that this was a major country-wide assault by the Vietcong and North Vietnamese Army. The U.S. Embassy in Saigon was nearly taken. The city of Hue in the North was in enemy hands. Other strategic areas were barely under control. Orders from Westmoreland were to prepare for another, even stronger, attack.

I finished breakfast and felt tired from the fear and lack of sleep. Walking back to the foxholes along Highway 1 to replace anyone who hadn't eaten, I saw The CO and first sergeant moving toward me. While raising my hand to salute, I was suddenly knocked to the ground, and my mind went black. Slowly emerging back into conscious-ness, I found myself lying on the ground unable to see the CO and Top. They had to be ten feet away, but I could see nothing, but terra-cotta colored dust. I tried getting to my feet to see if I could look over the dust. Standing there with my head throbbing, I covered my mouth with my fatigue top. Slowly the dust began to thin out. In a dusty tan haze, I could make out the CO and Top Kick getting their bearings. I staggered toward them.

"You okay, App?" The CO asked.

"I think so, sir."

"They must have hit the Class IV yard." The first sergeant muttered. Class IV was petroleum products. It wasn't that far from Class I and the motor pool.

"They're going to need water tankers down there. App, find as many drivers as you can. Get those water tankers rolling toward the Class IV yard."

I took off and ran toward Highway 1 and found Dunphy and the Secretary. I told them about Class IV needing water trucks. They ran to where the trucks were stored. I didn't know what else to do, so I ran to the motor pool to see if it was damaged because I could see black smoke coming from that direction. I ran into a few more drivers running to the truck depot. They said there had been a major hit at the ammo dump. Crates were on fire, the arsenal exploded, with bullets flying everywhere. They said it was out of control and asked for my help. I told them about

Class IV, but didn't follow them. In-stead I ran full blast to the motor pool now covered in dust but still standing. I breathed a deep sigh of re-lief that there was no fire.

I didn't know what to do. It was utter mayhem. Smoke and dust choked my lungs. Soldiers ran helter-skelter. Loud booms could be heard from the ammo dump. I found a dirty rag, covered my mouth and stumbled toward the hooches. Soldiers were running around there too, not knowing what to do. I made my way into our hooch, and saw my bed with the chess set still on it. The White Smith was on his bed again, crashed out. I brushed off the chessboard, the pieces flying on the floor, flopped onto the bed, closed my eyes, and fell into a long, dreamless sleep.

Chapter 13
Dazed and Confused

"App, App, App! Wake up!"

Someone shaking me spoke in a voice I could vaguely hear. It grew louder as I crossed the threshold into consciousness. My eyes were sealed shut, my head pounding, my ears ringing. As if waking from a horrible nightmare, through the blur, I saw the concerned face of the person calling my name and shaking me, Everything came back in a flash. It wasn't a nightmare. This was real.

Sitting on the bunk next to me, my friend, John Peterson asked. "You okay?"

Struggling to sit up, my mind vaguely recalled the chaos of the last moments before falling into sleep: the fires out of control, the Class IV bombing, the ammo dump erupting. I knew I wasn't the only soldier feeling this bad. Many others felt worse.

"What time is it?" I struggled to ask. "Or maybe what day is it? How long was I out?"

"I don't know, I found you here when I got to the hooch last night."

"What's going on? Have they stopped the fires? Is Class IV totally gone?"

"They've been working nonstop. Both fires are out. They're anticipating another attack. You're up next. Let's go get something to eat. We have eight-hour watches now."

I changed out of my dusty, smoke-scented fatigues, and pulled on a fresh set, laced my boots, then walked with Peterson to the mess hall. Everyone seemed to be walking slowly, heads down, lost in thought. Four days earlier we were drinking beer, eating steak, and smoking weed. The mechanics were taking victory laps around the motor pool. Now there was a gloom in the air like the dust that covered everything.

After getting back to the hooch from breakfast, I cleaned my M14 and went to the foxholes to give someone a break. This was war. Before we were support and supply. Now we dodged bullets, shot our weapons, and watched choppers clear an area. We had survived bombs and rockets. We moved back and forth between the road and the mess hall, waiting with maddening anxiety for the next attack. When it didn't arrive, eventually we went back to work.

The motor pool was a dusty mess. Boehner was gone. He'd left just after the chaos stopped, glad he'd gotten out alive. With my R&R less than a month away, I couldn't wait to fall into Alexandra's arms and stay in bed with her for the whole five days we'd be together.

After being given my temporary spec five patches, I took command of the parts for all the supply classes. The Colonel gave me an office. Fuentes returned from Saigon and erected structures similar to ones at 448. I started training a parts person for each of the five classes, passing on my concept of only doing some transactions with paperwork, reminding them that keeping the trucks on the road was our main mission. They had pushed back the inspection by a couple weeks due to Tet. I was confident we'd be ready.

I was able to hire locals to do the more menial tasks, but felt sorry for most of them because we paid them so little. They had to do horrible jobs. Going by the latrines when the mama-sans pulled out the huge buckets of waste, setting fire to the contents with diesel, made me sick. They had to keep turning the shit with a big stick, then burn it again. I couldn't imagine having to do such awful work.

One old Vietnamese man, we called "Papa-san," was helping clean the Class III bay. He had a French-to-English dictionary in his back pocket. When he turned to look at me, I saw a spark in his eyes that radiated wisdom. I asked if he spoke English. He answered, "Beaucoup, non," which I knew was French for not a lot. I thought by his manner and French response, he was being a bit coy. We agreed that he would come to work for me in my office. TET had made me curious about Vietnam, and I wanted to know what the Vietnamese were thinking about us and the war. His job would be easy. All he had to do was sweep and dust my office. When he was done, his job was to look in his dictionary to answer some questions. If an officer or sergeant walked in, he should act busy and start sweeping.

I had many questions about Vietnam now that I had seen the other side of war. I had no idea why we were here. Listening to President Johnson, who my dad called Old Cornpone, as he tried to explain it, didn't ring true. I knew about the Cold War, that the United States and Western Europe were in a competition with the Soviet Union for the hearts and minds of the third-world countries. I saw the TV shows when I was a kid about communist spies who stole our secrets about the atomic bomb.

That bomb scared me. I knew we came close to war with the USSR because they put missiles in Cuba. Kennedy, staring into the camera, saying that he would use "all means necessary" to keep the Soviets from activating those missiles, scared the crap out of me. My dad told me he meant nuclear weapons, weapons of mass destruction that could end life on earth as we know it.

One of my favorite films was Dr. Strangelove because it showed how one crazy man in the wrong position could start a holocaust. Now that I had experienced war, I wanted to know why we would risk the lives of so many good men.

In the hooch, now that I was an acting spec five, I was hoping to get my own room. It hadn't happened yet, but I was patient and enjoyed Peterson and Collins. I told them about the old man, and my plan for letting him write down answers to my questions.

"Well, I can tell you a lot of the history," said Collins, while Peterson and I were battling it out on the chess board.

"We're listening," I said, as I moved a pawn.

"Did you know that the leader of North Vietnam Ho Chi Minh and the U.S. worked together during World War II?"

"Really?"

"Yes, the U.S. gave him supplies that he used to help kick the Japanese out of Southeast Asia. Once the Japanese were gone he declared this a free and independent country called the Democratic Republic of Vietnam. This area used to be called French Indochina. During the colonial period the French navy and army defeated the local rulers, claiming the area for the French Republic and the Catholic Church, who ruled the area much like the British in India and other colonial powers throughout Asia and Africa. With World War II over, de Gaulle wanted Indochina back. In response to the French sending their army to Indochina, Ho Chi Minh created an army of insurgents called the Vietminh. They fought a long war with the French, finally defeating them at a place called Dien Bien Phu in 1954. The French were forced to leave. This time Ho Chi Minh declared the area the People's Republic of Vietnam. Are you with me so far?"

We had actually stopped playing and listened to Collins.

"With the urging of the U.S., French and Vietnamese officials met in Geneva, and signed an agreement that artificially divided the country in half at what we call the DMZ, the Demilitarized Zone. Ho Chi Minh could have the North, while the South would be ruled by the old French collaborator Bao Dai, who gave way to a family supported by the U.S. called the Diems. The Geneva Agreement promised a free and open election for unification in 1956. Still with me?"

We nodded yes, our eyes fixed on him.

"Well, this, of course, was at the end of the Red Scare. Joseph McCarthy was looking for Communist infiltrators. He maintained there were thousands, especially in the U.S. Army. He could only come up with a few, but he got a lot of publicity.

"Our president, at the time was the former commanding general of the European Theater in World War II, Dwight Eisenhower. He had two brothers working for him, named John Foster and Allen Dulles. The former was the secretary of state, the other was head of the CIA. These brothers knew Ho Chi Minh was a communist and they believed landowners were leaving North Vietnam because he was redistributing the land. The CIA took a poll of Vietnamese citizens, that determined Minh was beloved by both the North and the South because of his leadership against the Japanese and the French. The Diems weren't loved by either.

"The Diems were Catholic. One brother Ngo Dinh was the president, another the head of the secret police, and a third was the bishop of the city of Hue. The people of Vietnam, north and south, are primarily Buddhists. Diem wasn't going to win in a free and open election. So with the support of the U.S., the Diems canceled the elections. Clear, so far?"

Again we nodded yes. Collins was a good storyteller.

"When North Vietnam brought the issue up again in 1957, Diem refused to allow an election with the backing of the U.S. By this time Ho Chi Minh gave up on the Geneva Agreement reconstituting his Vietminh army of black pajama-clad peasants. He now called them the Vietcong. They started taking over villages, and much of the landscape outside of Saigon.

"The army of South Vietnam wasn't well organized and found it difficult to get troops to fight for their cause. The Buddhists began showing how much they disliked the Diems. They're peace-loving, so they showed their dislike through passive resistance, mainly in the form of self-immolation."

"What's that?" both Peterson and I asked.

"Self-immolation is the act of suicide as a sacrifice, most often by setting oneself on fire. Vietnamese monks in their orange robes would cover themselves with gasoline then strike a match. It's horrible to witness, but it does get people's attention."

Collins stopped, took a deep breath, and looked at both of us to see the horror on our faces, then continued.

"In 1960 the U.S. elected John Kennedy as the new president. Eisenhower left office warning Americans about the Military Industrial Complex. While President, he had kept troops out of Vietnam. Congress limited the amount of money paid to the Vietnamese government. Kennedy did the opposite. He asked Congress to help fund the South Vietnamese government and its army.

"He also started sending advisers. Several thousand at first, but that kept growing. The President controls foreign affairs and is the commander in chief of the U.S. Armed Forces. Congress has control of the money, and they can declare war, but this was only advisers. We didn't want to give up South Vietnam to the communists.

"Even with Kennedy's money and advisers, the Diems were losing the battle for the hearts and minds of the people. More monks were immolating themselves, and the world was turning against the Diems. In 1963, President Diem and his brother were assassinated with help from the CIA.

"Really, the CIA helped with the assassination?" I asked.

"Right, App." Collins said, nodding then continued.

"There was military rule for the next few years until this year when General Nguyen Van Thieu became the President of South Vietnam with Nguyen Cao Ky as Prime Minister in what most in the world agree was a rigged election.

I interrupted, "So the good old U.S., the world's great democratic government, has done all they can in Vietnam to stop democracy?"

"Yes, App, I'm afraid so. As my favorite professor at Princeton used to say, the U.S. likes democracy, but loves capitalism. This war isn't about democracy. It's about markets. Colonialism was about establishing markets, markets for the goods that we make in exchange for the natural resources to make those products. Great Britain was the best at it. At one time they were the world's biggest drug dealers. They took the raw material in Burma which made opium. They traded the opium to the Chinese, who had millions of addicts, and in exchange, the Brits got silk and tea from the Chinese. The French, Dutch, Spanish and Portuguese did the same kind of thing. The main trade for them was my ancestors. They traded rum for slaves."

Peterson stopped him. "Collins, you're not painting a very positive picture of America or Western civilization."

"Sorry, Pete, it is what it is. If you can find any evidence that paints a different picture, please show me. We Americans are the great defenders of the free enterprise system. That system runs on free markets. We don't want to give up any territory to anyone who doesn't support that system. It's a system that rewards greed and cheats labor. What we're defending here are the corporations, whose only god is profit, and the banks who own the capital. The banks' goals are getting you and countries into debt. Once you have that debt, they own you."

My head was spinning. Some of this I'd heard from my father. I started to wonder if I might be fighting on the wrong side by fighting for greed against labor, against democracy, against the ideals that I thought America stood for. Not knowing what to think, I sat there in disillusionment, dazed and confused.

I was relieved when the Secretary and Dunphy showed up. I needed a drink.

"Good evening, this is the evening news on NBC, I'm Chet Huntley and this is today's news," stated the Secretary.

Dunphy patted me on the back and said in his Arkansas accent, "Good ol' Apple, let's tie one on tonight, whaddaya say?"

"Great idea, Dunphy, that's a really great idea."

Chapter 14
Inspection

Back to being zeroed in on the motor pool with the inspection in a week, I supervised construction of the parts rooms, made sure parts were exchanged with paperwork, checked dispatch logs and gathered parts orders. All afternoon I made sure I collected what was on my list from each of the parts guys. I ordered far ahead for what I knew we would need and returned in the evening to distribute the parts to the different bays. These were long tiring days.

I didn't have any time for basketball. I showered, ate a meal at the mess, and sat on my bed writing letters to Alexandra. I would play chess with Peterson while Collins read on his bed waiting to beat the winner. Their time was growing short, and they would be gone soon. Damn, I'd hate seeing them go. They were the most rational guys in the compound.

We avoided conversations about politics and history. Collins and I knew Peterson was struggling to hold on to his beliefs about America. Though I had my serious doubts, Collins didn't. He made it clear that it was immoral to be fighting so that corporations and munitions makers could expand their markets and increase their profits.

He had another year to pull in the army, like I did if I finished my tour of duty. He would serve out his time, go back to Princeton, then join the antiwar movement. Colleges were being shut down, and rioting in the streets grew more intense. I had no idea what my future would be. I knew I had Alexandra who was smart and had a job. I was going crazy wanting to see her, touch her and hold her. I figured I'd go back to college on the GI Bill, but that was almost two years down the road. My total focus now was to pass the inspection, earn my permanent E5 rank, and save the extra money I'd be making.

I intensified efforts by the parts guys the last two days before inspection. We found paint to cover the wood, and, after cleaning the bays, stored the wrapped parts in the bins. We stacked tires, brought in water tankers to wash the dust from everything. On the day of inspection the place sparkled and never looked better. Lucky to have gone through Tet with no damage, we were a shining light in a dilapidated Long Binh.

At last, Colonel Anderson arrived with the inspectors in his spotless jeep. He had a wide smile as he looked around the yard. I told the water tanker guys to spray the dirt so it looked like the infield at Dodger Stadium and told the parts guys to be out front to represent each bay. The mechanics worked on the vehicles wearing their green T-shirts and fatigue pants, while their jungle-fatigue shirts were hanging neatly on hooks.

Standing with Chief Warrant Officer Arnold and Sergeant Miller in front of the motor pool headquarters, we saluted as the colonel approached. The inspectors followed like tails on a comet. He saluted us as we stood at attention.

"Ready for inspection, sir." Arnold said, crisply.

"I can see that, Chief. Let's see if the inspectors agree."

They walked to the first bay. The parts guy standing there was a big curly haired Russian named Romanasky. His first name was John, but we called him JR. His guys loved him, and were motivated. He had a stack of parts out back of his bay, and another container filled with items that he gathered for trade - generators, water pumps, a few air conditioners. He'd hold on to anything that might be of value. JR saluted smartly, completely serious, then brought out his paperwork in new binders. The inspectors looked them over, turned pages, and nodded. The colonel, his face serious, but his eyes smiling, glanced our way.

When the inspectors moved from bay to bay, the parts guys behaved professionally. Their parts rooms were freshly painted. Romanasky had binders for all of them. Though it cost him a generator, he got a boxful of them. The inspectors checked their dispatch logs looking for errors, then checked parts orders and parts receipts. They finished at 448 where I had given my job to Tom McNamara. Aside from his ability to do impersonations, he was smart and, like all the rest, his stuff was ready.

The inspectors seemed impressed. Colonel Anderson looked beyond satisfied, almost proud. The chief inspector met with his people, and stood in a circle talking. The colonel, Arnold, Miller and I stood together to the side as the chief inspector, wearing the gold leaf of a major, approached us.

"I must commend you, Chief Arnold, for the improved condition of this facility. It's remarkable what you've been able to accomplish. We came here expecting to see some improvement from what we saw last time, but this is far beyond our expectations. We have many motor pools at Long Binh. This one may get our highest rating. If you don't mind, Colonel, can I send other warrant officers to this motor pool to see how one should be run?"

"Absolutely, Major! The Quartermaster Corps is here to support and serve wherever and however we can!"

The inspectors walked toward their jeep. The colonel turned toward us with a big smile. "Chief Arnold, meet me tonight in the officer's club, I owe you a drink or two. In this difficult period, you and your men have done a remarkable job." He looked at Miller. "Sergeant Miller, you should celebrate your hard work with a party at the NCO club. You deserve it." He started to walk away, then stopped, and looked back at me. "Appenzeller, you're still up for Soldier of the Month, that in-country R&R will be there for you to take whenever you can fit it in. I know you had a hand in this."

"Thank you, sir! I leave for R&R in Hawaii in two days. My wife is meeting me there."

"You must be looking forward to that!" He laughed, looking at the others who were laughing, too. "I'll have my driver take you to Tan Son Nhut."

"Thank you, sir!" I said, surprised at the offer, then saluted sharply.

Arnold and Miller did likewise.

Colonel Anderson saluted back. "Job well done men. Very well done!" He lowered his arm, did an about-face, marched to his jeep, and pulled himself into the back seat.

As the jeep left the compound, we turned to see the men moving out of the bays toward us. When they got closer, one of them yelled, "How'd we do?"

Miller yelled back "Whaddaya think? We kicked ass! That's how we did!" A cheer went up from the guys. "Big party tonight at the NCO club!" Sergeant Miller announced in a loud voice. "I'll make sure you all get in. Drinks are on me. They got a gook band tonight, but they ain't all that bad." Another loud cheer followed. "All right, we'll celebrate tonight. Now, get your asses back to work." Miller said gruffly, but with a big smile.

Miller moved toward one of the bays, leaving Arnold and me in the middle of the motor pool. "Good job, App, I appreciate what you've done. I was worried about my job for a while. I didn't know all that much about running a motor pool. I came from pure supply. Sergeant Miller didn't care all that much for protocol, and the previous colonel didn't either. Colonel Anderson does, and wants to be a general. He's on track to making it. You helped save my butt and his. He'll remember that, and so will I."

He had his hand out to shake, and when I grabbed it he said. "So, you're going to see the wife in a couple of days. Must be looking forward to that, young man."

"You got that, Chief. Worst case of blue balls ever!" We both laughed.

"You got anybody in mind to take your place while you're gone?"

"I'm gonna talk to Romanasky about it, sir. He's one hell of a parts guy. Knows his shit and can trade like a son of a bitch." We laughed again.

When he walked away toward his office, I headed for Romanasky's bay where I saw him talking with some of the mechanics in class V. He was tall--about six foot two or three with curly blond hair and mustache. He looked like he could be a football tight end with big hands and muscular build. He had bright blue eyes that I can only describe as laughing. He always seemed on the edge of laughing whenever he talked.

"J.R., can I have a word with you?"

"Sure, App, what's up?"

"Day after tomorrow I'm going to Hawaii to spend five days with the wife."

"I heard, you lucky bastard!" He laughed.

"You mind handling the parts run for me while I'm gone? I'll show you where it is this afternoon."

"Sure, App, I know where it is, but I'll go with you. And yeah, I can do your job while you're gone."

"Cool, J.R., I think this could be the beginning of a beautiful friendship," I said, trying to imitate Bogart in Casablanca.

I went back to my office. The old Papa-san heard me coming, and leaped to his feet sweeping. "Good job, Pop! You look real busy," I said, almost laughing. He looked up at me, puzzled with no clue about my humor. "Have you worked on any of my questions?"

Shrugging, he pulled out a wrinkled piece of paper. I eagerly waited for the answer to my first question - "What do the Vietnamese think of Americans?"

"French better," was first.

"French live here," was followed by, "French know Vietnam people. French like Vietnam people."

Under that, he'd written, "Americans don't know Vietnam people."

"Americans don't like Vietnam people."

"Americans have own music."

"Americans have own culture."

"Americans don't like Vietnam culture."

"Americans are war people."

"They kill Vietnam people."

"Wow, Pop. That doesn't sound very good. Do you think most Vietnamese feel this way?" I asked this slowly, apprehensively, sensing an upsetting answer.

He shrugged and nodded yes, but his sad eyes said more than his words.

"I can see why you would believe that. We don't treat you with much kindness."

He nodded again, causing me to take a deep, painful sigh.

Collins, Peterson and a few others were the only ones who didn't use words like gooks or slope-heads, or other negative terms when referring to the Vietnamese people. Some GIs were the world's worst diplomats; they were more the prototype "Ugly Americans."

"I'm sorry we're not kind, Pop. I want to be your friend. I want you to trust me."

He wrote something down on the paper then showed it to me. "Name not Pop," it said. I was no better than any other GI.

"I'm so sorry." I almost said Pop again. I looked into his dark brown eyes. "What is your name?"

He wrote it down. "Nguyen."

"May I ask how to pronounce this?"

"Win," he said, adding an N at the beginning.

Win, I repeated to myself. Win-Nguyen. "May I call you Mr. Nguyen?"

He nodded with a slight smile.

"Thank you, Mr. Nguyen, for teaching me about the Vietnamese people," I bowed my head a bit. Looking at me with his soft intelligent eyes, he bowed, too.

I saw Collins and Peterson that night after showering and eating the crappy food in the mess hall. "We passed the inspection, guys. Sergeant Miller is throwing us a party at the club. Why don't you join us? It should be fun. Got a band there and every-thing!"

Collins hopped up, ready to go. Peterson looked like he was going to stay. "Come on, Pete, you have to come. I'm out of here after tomorrow. You and Collins will be back in the States in less than two months. Come on, they have Coke at the club!"

"Caffeine," he said.

"What the heck can you Mormons drink?" I laughed. "I'm sure they have water there."

Collins reached down and grabbed his hand. "Come on, Pete, we have to help App celebrate."

Reluctantly, he let himself be pulled up. We stuck on our hats and headed for the club.

It was a great party. We drank beer and scotch. The Secretary did his routines and Dunphy took out his teeth. Romanasky told some funny stories. I told more tales of my CAMF life. Several asked me to tell my Applefuck story. Many had heard it, but not Romanasky. He laughed hard at that story. He called me Applefuck from that day for-ward.

After the pall that had fallen on us after Tet, it was good to laugh again. We needed it. I felt happy being with good friends. We passed the in-spection, and I went from E3 to E5 in only three months. North told me that I would get one of the rooms when I got back from R&R. Soon, I would be with Alexandra. Damn, I couldn't wait to make love to her.

We were hungover the next morning as we walked to our various posts. Romanasky was with me all morning while I was went over his duties as my replacement. At noon when we stepped out of the office, I saw all the guys from the 448 standing in front of the bay.

"Hey, App," they called. Romanasky and I walked over. Thompson spoke for the group, still eyeballing his tattoos. "We know you're leaving tomorrow, you lucky son of a bitch, but you'll be back in a week. We wanted to say thanks, App, for what you did for the motor pool."

Guys from other bays were shuffling over. I heard a truck start up in the bay. "We didn't want you to have to use Boner's old three-quarter-ton truck. Romanasky found this one. We fixed it up, rebuilt the engine, and painted it. It ain't olive green, though; it's almost lime green."

Out rolled a truck that looked brand new. On the door was a white circle with big letters - 448 S&S, clear as could be.

"It's all yours, App. Army don't own it, you do."

It was the coolest looking three-quarter-ton truck on Long Binh.

"I got a camera, App. Let's get a picture with you standing next to it," Thomson said, his eyes off the tattoos.

Since Tet, we wore our helmets instead of our ball caps. I stood next to the truck with my sunglasses, helmet and a clean uniform. When I got back from R&R they gave me that picture - one of only a few that I have from my experience in Vietnam.

Chapter 15
Hawaii

The night before my R&R passionate images of Alexandra and me in the frenzy that dominated our sexual lives kept sleep at bay. Usually these thoughts led to some form of relief through masturbation, but I was determined to save all of myself for Alexandra, and somehow found the will power to resist.

When dawn finally arrived, I rechecked my packed duffel bag making sure my toiletries and civilian clothes were ready, then saw Collins and Peterson with their arms spread for a quick manly embrace. I made the long stroll to the mess hall to slap five with my Class 1 basketball buds, then to the motor pool to say goodbye to my colleagues, who wished me luck. A few minutes later, I shook hands with the Top and saluted the CO. Even North gave me a slight nod when I left headquarters. At battalion headquarters, Collins gave me another hug, then called the Colonel to come out of his office. Though I saluted, he casually waved back, wished me a safe trip, then ordered his driver to take me to Tan Son Nhut.

At the airport, I showed soldiers my orders, exchanged MPC for greenbacks, and smiled when they gave me a ticket. Fortunately, the colonel had arranged everything.

From my window seat in the middle of the 737, I saw the great expanse of the city of Saigon as we took off, then the jungle on the coast. Soon we were over the Indian Ocean. Next stop, the Philippines, then Hawaii, where at last I'd be in Alexandra's arms.

My seat mates did not speak English, which gave me time to think about my remarkable Vietnam experience. My rise in the motor pool to a position of major responsibility was aided by the personal traits I had developed as team player in high school as well as the unique training I received from the Army, especially my experience with Tom Burt.

That Colonel Andersen thought highly of me, and singled me out as soldier of the month, was not only personally satisfying, it also gave me a degree of power and freedom. How I'd use that power was yet to be seen, but exciting ideas were bouncing around my brain that I knew could make my Vietnam experience even more interesting.

Eventually my thoughts were overwhelmed again by the reality that soon I'd finally have an outlet for the sexual energy stored up after three months away from Alexandra - an energy that had dominated my life from the time I was twelve years old when my next door neighbor introduced me to the wonderful world of masturbation.

Up until that time my life was headed in a totally different direction. In second grade after revealing my admiration for my father's good friend, and our Principal at Santa Clara Elementary School Father O'Sullivan, the nun I told this to believed with great joy that I had received a calling from God. The love and kindness that she and the next five Sisters of St Joseph shared with me gave me a positive sense of self; however, that came to an abrupt end one afternoon when I spent the day drawing pictures of naked women with my next door neighbor, Donald, who was several years older than me. As the pictures began to resemble real women, my breathing grew rapid, and sensations I didn't recognize came over me. Similar feelings came from looking through the women's underwear section of the Sears Catalog. These images caused my penis to harden and my heart to race. Don could see my discomfort, and asked if I had ever jacked off. Jack off? I didn't know what he was talking about until he described it to me and wanted to show me, but suddenly a feeling of dread came over me. I asked to leave because I was feeling nauseous. The pukey feeling came from guilt, dread and fear.

When I returned to my house from Don's, I still felt guilt but, also, overwhelming sexual energy. My penis stayed stiff despite the guilty feelings. In my bathroom, I stroked my penis exactly how Don suggested. Damn, it felt so good. While staring at the half naked women in the bra section of the Sears catalog, my body went through an unbelievable transformation that was out of my control, and ended in an overwhelming ecstasy that made me so dizzy I thought I would faint with the pleasure.

Each week I confessed to Father O'Sullivan how impure thoughts invaded my brain and how horrible I felt for having them, but now I seemed to be encouraging them. This was followed by an enormous bombardment of guilt. Now, not only would I have to confess impure thoughts but an impure action. I was certain that the sin had moved from venial to mortal. Mortal sin was the death star of sins and meant an everlasting life in hell.

This moral terror struck me practically every day. Before I could sleep at night, I felt compelled to stroke myself to the images of sexy women in my brain. This was always followed by excruciating guilt and confusion, but then eventually I'd drift off to sleep.

In seventh grade I finally told the sisters that I could no longer be a priest. Their obvious disappointment showed in their sad eyes, and in their withdrawing of love. This caused my self-esteem to waiver and tumble. My grades began a steady downward trend. But now my thoughts could be totally unleashed. Being with girls, touching and kissing them, and eventually having sex with them, became an obsession.

These thoughts dominated my brain as we landed for refueling in Manila. They continued as I retraced each step forward in my sexual curiosity. I relived each girl who allowed me to touch her breasts while she played with my penis. These thoughts ended with Alexandra, who shared my love of sex. I was so happy to be her husband and relieved to no longer feel guilt about my sexual thoughts and actions. We were married, and I could have all the sex I wanted.

This three months had been the longest time I had gone without sex with Alexandra since we started dating. Relief seemed so close when the 737 finally taxied to a halt. My anguished impatience with the slowness of those in front of me made me tense as I walked down the aisle, then down the stairs to a lovely Hawaiian girl who put a lei around my neck. When I walked through the big glass door into the airport and saw Alexandra in a cute black short dress, I ran to her, dropped my bag, and hugged her with all my might. Kissing her, and feeling her hot body next to mine, caused my excited penis to harden as we pressed our bodies together in a passionate embrace.

We grabbed our bags, rushed outside, and hailed a taxi. In the back seat we started kissing wildly. We were grabbing and touching, lost in a sexual frenzy that we couldn't control.

When we reached our hotel, I couldn't fill out the hotel registration form, and gave Alexandra the pen. She scribbled down something, then grabbed the key, and we dashed to the elevator. Once inside that tiny ascending space alone, we were back at it, desperately kissing and moving our hands all over each other. When the door opened, we dashed down the hall looking for our room. I fumbled with the keys to the door, finally getting it open. After closing it, I grabbed her and had her dress off in a second. While I fumbled with her bra, she pulled down her panties. I started throwing my clothes across the room. Completely naked, she lay there with her smooth tan legs spread apart, waiting for me.

Still with my socks on, I dove between her legs, needing her more than I had ever needed anything in my life. My erect penis entered her warm welcoming wetness. We moved passionately. In seconds Alexandra came, and a minute later my hot seed was planted, but that didn't stop us. We kept moving together, thrusting harder and harder against each other. Her ecstatic moans and screams caused both of us to erupt again. Breathlessly, I collapsed on her, both of us now feeling intensely satisfied. Though we slowed down a bit, we weren't close to being finished. Now we could take our time.

When I rolled over onto my back, we gazed warmly into each others eyes and smiled. A moment later we hugged, and gently kissed, then cuddled, savoring our being together. We lay there for a long time.

"I'm kinda hungry," I whispered into her ear.

"Me, too, I'm starving. What time is it?"

I checked my watch, surprised that it was after ten. It was four when we arrived at the hotel. We hadn't separated for six hours.

"I gotta pee, too," she said, laughing.

We finally let each other go, took a wonderful shower together and made love one more time under the cascading water.

Later, holding hands, we strolled into the humid Hawaii air, as happy as we'd ever been. Luckily, we found a Chart House that was open late. While waiting to be seated I found myself doing routines that I did with the Secretary, talking in Jonathan Winters characters. Alexandra seemed not to mind and actually laughed at some of the jokes. I can't describe how different it felt being with a woman and not surrounded by men.

Once seated, we held hands and gazed at each other, then ordered two glasses of red wine, and placed our order with the waiter.

"So what's new back home," I asked, glad to have this relaxed time.

"Your family has moved out of Oxnard and are now renting in Camarillo while the house they purchased is being built." Alexandra sipped on her red wine.

"Really? Isn't that the second time they've moved? What's going on?"

"Lots. You know your family with eight kids, it's drama after drama. I think Tina is officially getting married to Ken McDonald."

"They've been going together for a couple of years, good for them."

"Katie is the star of another play at Oxnard High. Some kind of Greek tragedy called *Medea*."

"Really, she was so good as Mammy Yokum in *Li'l Abner*. Katie can hold your attention when she is on stage. Mom must love it. How are mom and Dad?"

"They're so worried about you. You send them reassuring letters, but they're both worriers. When they read that Long Bihn was attacked during Tet, they were beside themselves." Alexandra took a sip of wine and a deep breath. I could feel her concern. "So how was it during Tet?"

"I'd almost forgotten that I was in a war zone because I was so busy rebuilding the motor pool. We heard automatic weapons and ran out to defend Highway one. Charlie was just on the other side shooting at us. I tried to stay as safe as I could, but I was really scared. My heart was beating so fast. Luckily it's been really calm since then. I think that Ho Chi Minh did all he could and doesn't have much left. More and more troops keep arriving. I think we are over five hundred thousand."

"I was so worried too, Robbie." She reached out and clutched my hands, tears welling in her eyes. "We all were. It's hell not knowing what's going on and seeing all the death and destruction on TV."

When I saw tears falling down her cheeks, I squeezed her hand. "Don't worry, Babe. I am safe in Long Bihn. I'm getting more and more responsibility, and they jumped me up two ranks. The Colonel likes me. He made me soldier of the month. I get to go to some place called Vung Tau for an in-country R&R. I will not take any chances. My life is just beginning with you."

"I love you so much, Robbie."

"I love you too, Alexandra, I am so happy we are here."

We leaned across the table and gave each other a lovely long kiss that was broken up by the smiling waiter who arrived with our steaks.

After a long luxurious dinner, we walked hand in hand back to the hotel ecstatic that we were together again. We made love again when we returned to our room, our pace now slower, more sensual and tender, more focused on each others pleasure. We slept until noon, made passionate love again, then ordered room service breakfast staying in bed all afternoon, cuddling, kissing, sharing each blissful minute.

Later, we ventured out for a walk in downtown Honolulu, held hands, looking in windows and sneaking kisses. Even though I tried to stop with the Jonathan Winters, Alexandra didn't seem disturbed and actually laughed at some of my silliness. We were having fun - something I needed after months in Vietnam.

We ate another fabulous dinner at an expensive seafood restaurant. We took hours eating slowly, drinking Mai Tais, continuing our talk about what we'd been doing the last four months. I told her about the Bob Hope Christmas Show with Rachel Welsh I had seen at an amphitheater in Long Binh.

She filled me in on politics, telling me how much she admired Bobby Kennedy. "He will end this war, Robbie. I just know he will."

"This is one of the most delightful dinners I've ever eaten, my love."

"Me, too, it was perfect." Her radiant smile melted my heart.

After strolling back to the hotel, we made slow, leisurely love, and slept in each others arms.

We woke again at noon, and after a leisurely brunch, I shared my need to surf the waves at Waikiki. We hailed a taxi to the beach. Seeing the beautiful blue water with soft waves breaking out on the reef, the Diamondhead crater glowing in the sunlight, the pure white sand in front, made my heart swell at the beauty surrounding us.

We searched for a stand that rented boards. When I saw the size and shape of most of the boards in the surf rack I thought I might be in the wrong place. They were seven-foot long at most with pointed noses that looked nothing like the boards I had surfed a little more than a year before. I looked at the guy renting the boards. "You can't surf on that," I stated, as if it was a fact.

"Where've you been, man, that's all anybody's riding. They're shortboards. Everyone's ripping the waves with these boards."

When I asked if he had a nine-two, like the board I used to ride, he said. "Yeah, dude, I got one somewhere in the back - kinda old, though. You sure you don't want to try a shortboard?"

"Nah, I can't ride that. Get me a longboard."

He brought out an old yellow Dewey Weber that was starting to delaminate. While I waxed it up, my heart started to pound with the anticipation of once again riding the waves. There's nothing like the surf stoke. It's the only thing that can come close to the joy of good sex.

The board was so wide, my arms could barely get around it. My muscle memory kicked in while starting the long paddle to the outside reef.

Approaching the surfers sitting beyond the reef, I saw guys taking off, making radical turns at the top of the waves, then even more radical turns at the bottom. They did this back and forth all the way down the line. I had never seen anything like it.

I got to the line-up, sitting tall on my longboard compared to those around me, who sat a few inches in the water. A wave on the horizon moved in my direction, so I paddled toward the peak. The others let me have it. I used my best sprint paddle to match the speed of the wave, felt the tug as the wave took control of the board, then muscle memory again took hold as I pushed myself up drawing my feet under me, feeling a bit wobbly, but on my feet. I started the dance on the board, and positioned myself for maximum speed. That speed seemed slow compared to the guys using shortboards, but the exhilarating feeling told me I was surfing again.

After I caught a few more waves, I paddled back to shore with tired arms and aching ribs. When I found Alexandra in her yellow bathing suit lying on a towel, she looked so sexy, I felt myself getting excited again, then quickly sat next to her.

"How did surfing change so fast?" I asked.

She shrugged. "I don't know, I haven't followed it."

"It's a totally different game. I don't know what to think about it!"

"Well, don't think about it. Think about this." She spread her legs wide apart like an invitation to a wild party.

"You're right. Let's get a taxi back to the hotel."

We made love, this time including things that we had never done before. I remembered how my imagination worked every night prior to sleeping in the hootches fantasizing sexual adventures with Alexandra that ended in masturbation. Now I could actually experience these acts, and share mutually exhilarating orgasms, which were hugely more satisfying than fantasizing.

We woke late. I wanted to surf one more time, so we went to Waikiki and the surfboard rental stand. This time I rented a seven-foot shortboard, which I could barely paddle out to the line-up. My ribs and arms were sore. I tried taking off a few times, but couldn't catch a wave with the smaller board. I tried to get one late, but when I got to my feet, the board was too loose, and shot out from under me. I fell backwards, barely surviving the washing machine. Bummed, I found Alexandra tanning on her towel. I was pretty sure my surfing days were over if my only option was the new shortboards.

The next day would be our last. We were both feeling sad. I would be going back to Vietnam; she, to California. Neither of us wanted this to end. We stayed in bed all day, ordering room service. We made love, we talked, we made love some more. We stayed up late talking about what we might do when I finally came home for good. We knew I had another year to do. When we drifted off to sleep in each others arms, neither of us wanted the next day to dawn.

But it did, and we both had planes to catch. We took a taxi to the airport, hugged one last time, never wanting to let each other go.

"I love you so much, Robbie. Please be careful and please come back in one piece."

"I love you, so much too, Alexandra. I'll be safe. We have our whole lives ahead of us."

We hugged, and kissed passionately one more time, then finally let each

other go. Knowing she would be waiting
for me when I got home, gave me
strength to finally say goodbye.

PART THREE
King of the REMFs

Chapter 16
Restructure

I reported to North at 448 Head-quarters after my long return flight from my blissful five days with Alexandra in Hawaii. He told me that the sergeant who had occupied the room on the right of our hooch had been deployed back to the States and asked if I still wanted the room. "Hell, yes" I replied. Glancing at the new patch on his arm I said, "Congratulations on making spec five. How'd you get that?"

"How did you get yours?" he asked back.

North was a tight-lipped son of a bitch who had little to say to me or anybody else. I thought we could be best friends if he wasn't so reserved.

"You want to meet the new CO?"

Not waiting for an answer, he knocked on the door, and stuck his head in. "Spec Five Appenzeller is back from R&R. You want to see him, sir? "He opened the door all the way, nodded toward the inside, indicating I should enter, then sat back down in his comfortable swivel chair.

When I stood in front of the desk, I saluted. "Spec Five Appenzeller reporting for duty, sir!"

"At ease, specialist. How was your R&R?"

"Too short, sir. Beyond that, it was the best five days of my life."

"Where'd you go?"

"Hawaii, sir, my wife met me there. We had a fantastic time. I'm dying to go back."

"Too bad we only get one of those things."

"You're right about that, sir. Seven and a half months seems like a long time to be away from my wife. Not much we can do about that."

"I'm married, too, Appenzeller. I can relate." He looked away, and bit his lip as if thinking about his wife.

I saw he was a first lieutenant and judging from his accent another Southerner. He was clean-shaven with close-cut blondish hair. He had the name Williams printed over his pocket and a big gold ring on his finger.

"Oh, yes," he said, coming out of his thoughts with a slight sigh. "I recall that the colonel spoke highly of you. Jumped you up in rank so you could have authority in the motor pool. So how'd you manage that?"

"Good training, sir, I was lucky to have been stationed in a motor pool at Fort Sill with a smart parts guy. Showed me how a motor pool should be run. I applied that to the motor pool here."

"North says that you're getting the room next to him."

So North got the other room, I thought.

"Yes, sir, I'm looking forward to having my own room."

"You might have to share it eventually. There's a big push right now. After the Tet fiasco, General Westmoreland has asked for another hundred thousand troops. They've started to arrive. Almost all our space in Long Binh is filled with field tents."

"I didn't watch much news when I was in Hawaii. I was pretty focused on the wife," I said, smiling.

He laughed. "I would be too, Appenzeller, I would be too. You're dismissed. Check out your room, then report to the motor pool."

I saluted, turned, and walked by North. "Lieutenant Williams said you got the other room, North. Nice move."

He looked up, shrugged, but didn't say anything, then went back to work.

When I walked to the hooch with my duffel bag to see my new room, I could see that the door was closed, and it didn't have a lock. When I looked inside, a standard issue U.S. Army bunk bed, a footlocker and a wall locker made up the small, bare room. I checked out the footlocker, happy to see the stuff I'd left behind was still in there. My wall locker also showed nothing missing - clean uniforms hanging, helmet on the top shelf. I opened my duffel bag, separating stuff that needed to be washed, and stored the rest in the wall locker or footlocker. While looking around the room, my mind started imagining how to jazz it up and make this place livable.

Walking the three-hundred-yards to the motor pool, I passed hooch after hooch for over a hundred yards, then a paved road that led to Westmoreland's mansion. Now many field tents filled what used to be open space. Down the road to the left was the motor pool.

"Look who's back!" a voice yelled as I got closer to the office. "Hey, App! How was it?" A few guys hollered.

"Great" I yelled back. "I'll be over in a minute, guys. Gotta check in,"

Chief Warrant Officer Arnold sat behind his desk, his head down concentrating on some paperwork. When he looked up he smiled, then came out from behind his desk with his hand out. "Welcome back, App, good to see you."

"So, did the place fall apart while I was gone?" I asked, laughing.

"Not really, things are running smoothly. Sergeant Miller is short now. I'm wondering if we have to replace him. The way things are set up now, I don't see the need."

"How did Romanasky do?"

"No complaints, he seems to know his way around the parts depot. Comes back with a lot of stuff. The parts rooms seem well stocked."

"Is he here right now?"

"I don't think so. He's been using your new truck. I don't see it near your office. He must be on a parts run."

"Okay, Chief. I'm going to check out the bays, then head to my office. How much longer do you have on your tour?"

"Under two months, I'm almost short. I'll be glad to get home to the wife and kids. I miss them so much. Damn, App! I haven't asked about the R&R. How was it? How's the wife?"

"It was fantastic, Chief. And so was she. I could have stayed forever. Time went by way too fast."

He smiled shaking his head like he could relate.

"Well, I'm going to check things out," I said, then drifted out to the Class I bay.

The guys greeted me warmly asking about Hawaii, Alexandra and the surf. It felt good to be talking to them about something happy and positive. The Secretary joined us breaking into some of his new routines. He assured me that Romanasky did an outstanding job as my replacement. We agreed to meet that night in the club.

When I walked into my office, I saw Mr. Nguyen sweeping. "Nice to see you, Mr. Nguyen. The place looks good,"

I said, looking around at the plywood walls and floor. I glanced at a couple of shelves filled with manuals, and the standard gray file cabinets, then took my seat behind the desk in the middle of the room.

"Have you been answering any more questions for me? That's your main job, you know." I said smiling. He pulled out some sheets of paper and a booklet that he handed to me.

"Wow, you have been working! Okay, let me have a look at them."

"Why are America and North Vietnam at war?" was the next question. His short, neatly written message shocked me. "POPE PIUS XII." I mumbled the words out loud, bewildered.

"Why do you think this of Pope Pius XII?"

This Pope had been the leader of the Catholic Church for most of my childhood, his picture hung in every room at our school. As head of the Catholic Church, he was infallible, incapable of error, because he spoke for God on earth. When I looked at Mr. Nguyen, I didn't know what to say. He gazed hard into my eyes.

Slowly he pointed to the small pamphlet in my hand written in Vietnamese. I could see that Mr. Nguyen had written an English translation beneath the Vietnamese words that said, "History of Catholic Church in Vietnam." I looked at him.

"Read book," he said.

I started reading the first page, but his small printing made it slow reading. Intrigued from the beginning I realized that this was a history I had never heard of and wondered if Collins knew anything about it. He'd be going back to the States soon where he could find supporting or refuting evidence.

I set the pamphlet down and noticed Mr. Nguyen looking at me intently. "Mr. Nguyen, what did you do before the war?"

He looked at me with his dark, intelligent eyes. "I was teacher."

"You must be my teacher now, Mr. Nguyen. Thank you for this gift." I bowed to him. He smiled and bowed back.

As I continued reading I realized with horror that much of my childhood was a lie. I read things that I found impossible to believe, but they resonated with the ring of truth. While totally lost in thought, Romanasky barged through the door, startling me.

"Applefuck! How was Hawaii? How was the wife? It's good to have you back. I hate doing all that paperwork!"

When I put the pamphlet aside and stood up, the big Russian gave me a hug, jarring me out of my thoughts.

"Now that you're back I have a few ideas I've been thinking about, Apple. There are some markets out there to explore." His eyebrows went up in a gesture that suggested these markets might not be totally on the up-and-up.

"I've been thinking about some restructuring in the motor pool too, J.R., I talked to the chief, and I think he'll agree. He's getting short. He'll go along with most anything as long as it keeps him out of trouble. How's your replacement doing at your old job?"

"He's all right. I check on him. He's getting the job done. Why? What are you thinking?"

"Well, Miller is real short, out-of-country next week. I'm proposing we do away with his job. The way we have it set up now, the chief and I don't think we need another sergeant. The mechanics do their work, the parts guys take care of the paperwork, store and issue parts. Everyone is answerable to the chief. That leaves you and me. I'm gonna suggest to the chief that you be the full-time parts guy. I'll look after the paperwork here in the office and out in the bay. If I get caught up, we both can take the truck on the parts run. If we have time, we might visit a few clubs on our way back!" I said with a big smile.

"Goddamn, Apple! Great minds think alike!" Romanasky patted me hard on the back. "That's almost exactly what I was thinking. I got it wired at the parts depot. I've been greasing the wheels down there with a few deals. I got our parts ordered for months ahead. We're top priority with those guys. I've also been doing a little club-hopping. Been talking with some of the sergeants who run 'em about maybe expanding into the restaurant business. Guys would pay good money not to eat that shitty mess-hall food. You got contacts with the black guys down in Class I. We could work a deal with them. Whaddaya think?"

"Damn, J.R. great minds do think alike. That's exactly what I was thinking. I'll run all this by the chief. Well, not the club business; that will be our little secret. I'm sure he'll go for it. I saved his ass with the restructuring of the motor pool. I told you JR, "This could be the beginning of a beautiful friendship." I said the last bit in my best, but I'm sure awful, Bogart. We both started laughing.

Mr. Nguyen kept dusting and sweeping while watching and listening to our conversation. Romanasky took me aside. "What's with Papa-san, Apple? This place doesn't need a full-time maid."

"I got him doing some research for me, J.R. You just let him be. He's a smart guy. Used to be a teacher. I'm finding out some shit you wouldn't believe from Mr. Nguyen. Do me a favor call him that from now on, will ya?"

"Sure, Apple, can do. Hey, I heard you got a room to yourself. Damn, you lucky bastard."

"After work, cruise on down there and take a look, J.R. I think with your trading ability and my sense of style we could make it into a pretty cool hangout."

"Damn right!" he said, moving toward the door. "I gotta go distribute the parts to the bays. I'll bring back the paperwork."

As he left, he looked at Mr. Nguyen sitting on his stool in the corner. "Goodbye, Mr. Nguyen," he said, bowing slightly. Mr. Nguyen bowed slightly back, then looked over at me making a much bigger bow. After bowing back, I eagerly grabbed his book, found the spot where I'd left off, aware, but frightened how this book was shattering my entire world.

Chapter 17
Pete and the Mormons

Sometimes when Class I guys were deployed back to the States they'd come into the hooch and throw piasters around like they were at a ticker tape parade. Believe me, I had no problem gathering the abandoned money. So, I normally had a nice wad of the Vietnamese cash in my pocket. Today when I sent Mr. Nguyen home, I gave him some piasters, and he gave me a big bow with praying hands.

When finished with organizing the paperwork that Romanasky left me, I walked back to my hooch hoping to see Collins and Peterson. Both were getting short. I knew they wanted news about my R&R. When I stepped into the bay, Peterson was on his bunk reading.

"Hey there, Pete! What's up?"

He jumped up, happy to see me, and wrapped me in his huge body. "Wow, App! Back so soon? How was it?"

"Amazing, Pete. Five days of connubial bliss, I've never had a better time!"

"The wife is Alexandra, right?"

I nodded yes.

"She doing well?"

"Fantastic! It was the hardest thing in the world walking away from her in that Honolulu airport."

"Man, App, I can't wait to get home. My wife will be waiting for me. We're sealed for life." His smile and beaming eyes revealed his joy.

"You're out once you get to the States, right? What are your plans?"

"I'll enroll at Bringham Young and finish my final two years. I told you before that I did my church mission in South America. The army called me after I finished. Not sure what I will major in yet. I'm waiting for a sign."

"You'll be returning to your Mormon world, right, Pete?"

"Can't wait." He spoke enthusiastically. "You have no idea how I can't wait."

"You know, Pete, I don't know a darn thing about the Mormon religion. When I was traveling in the South, I met a Protestant preacher, and realized that I didn't know much about the Bible. I know a lot of prayers, and the whole Latin mass, but that guy could quote chapter and verse, and could defend his beliefs with the 'Word of God,' as he called it. I had little to say to him. He was in rapture with it."

"I'm not surprised. The evangelicals do know their bible. Mormons do, too. That and the Book of Mormon - that's where we got our name."

"Really? I don't know a thing about any of that."

"We prefer our religion to be called The Church of Jesus Christ Latter-Day Saints."

"That's a mouthful, I've heard a few stories about the Mormons. What's the church's history?"

"You really want to hear it, App?"

"Yeah, I do, Pete. I'm curious about religions."

"Well, the story goes like this. In 1820 the founder of our religion, Joseph Smith, was directed by an angel to a place where he found golden plates that had been buried a long time. These plates told the story of an ancient tribe of Israelites who eventually became indigenous people in America. They believed that Jesus Petet was the son of God.

"Over the next three months, he dictated over five hundred pages of the Book of Mormon to Oliver Cowdery, insisting that it was revealed to him in an ancient language that he translated from the gift and power of God. Smith had a vision of Jesus Christ and God, the Father. They were separate, that's a major difference between Mormons and other religions. We don't believe in the Trinity of God, the Father, Son, and Holy Spirit, being one. We believe they're separate. We call it a Godhead. Smith saw them as individuals. We call it 'The First Vision.'

"Smith had many visions with visitations by angels. They told him that all other religions were wrong. It was up to him to establish the true religion based on the Book of Mormon. His followers then, and we Mormons now, see Joseph Smith as a prophet, guided by God, to establish the one true Church of Christ."

He stopped and looked at my face for a reaction, but I chose to listen stoically, my mind swirling with doubt and questions.

Finally I asked. "How is your church different from, let's say, the Catholic Church?"

"We share a lot with the Catholic Church. We believe Jesus was the son of God, that God has a plan for us on earth. We believe that repenting of sin and transgression is essential to salvation. We believe you must be baptized by an authorized representative of God. We believe in the gift of the Holy Ghost by the laying of hands. We believe that Jesus is the redeemer of the world, if you follow his path you'll live forever in heaven."

Halfway through Pete's explanation Collins arrived. When he saw we were in deep conversation, he patted me on the back, sat next to me, and listened. When Peterson finished his last thought, Collins broke in. "Hey there, App. How was it, man? How's the wife?"

"It was unreal, Collins, I've never had a better time. It was hard to leave. But I'm back now, and you two are short, you lucky sons of bitches." I gave an apologetic nod to Peterson, who never cursed or took the Lord's name in vain. "Pete here was explaining his Mormon religion to me; fascinating stuff."

Collins rolled his cynical eyes. "I took a Comparative Religion class at Princeton, and, I must say, Pete, Mormonism may have been the most difficult for me to believe. Not a lot of evidence. No golden plates, no book with a strange language that Joe Smith supposedly used to dictate the Book of Mormon. There was some other pretty weird stuff, too, like baptizing the dead and polygamy. How many wives did Brigham Young have, Pete? Over sixty, I read."

"The Church ended polygamy back in 1890, Collins." His voice grew tense and he stiffened defensively, as if he sensed he was going to be attacked.

"Well, that was because the U.S. Army was going to invade Utah territory if they didn't end the practice. Ending polygamy was the only way Utah could become a state."

Now Peterson shrugged, then shook his head from side to side, rejecting the comment.

Collins went on. "What about 'continuous revelation' that God continues to reveal secrets to the living prophets, especially the one selected prophet who's invincible."

"Kind of like the Pope?" I asked.

"Yeah, App, like your Pope. You know I like the Constitution of the U.S., App, but Mormons believe it's a divinely inspired document. Right, Pete?"

Pete reluctantly nodded agreement. Obviously, he had dealt with doubters before.

"There are so many weird things you Mormons believe that it makes my head spin. You believe in the spirit world. That you can get folks out of Hell by baptizing their spirits. I heard you're baptizing Jews who died in the Holocaust. Get this, App; if a Mormon atones for his sins, and follows the life of Christ, he doesn't just go to heaven, he becomes a god himself with his own earth to rule over. Am I right, Pete?"

Scowling, Pete stared at Collins.

"And what about my people, Pete? We have 'the Curse of Ham.' God has singled us out, painted us black, making us unworthy of becoming one of your priests. Hell, we can't even go into one of your temples. Your Joseph Smith is like Muhammad. They both found mythical texts dictated to them by what they said was the word of God. Joe Smith had a vision where he talked to Jesus and God the Father. Muhammad sat on a winged horse, flew to heaven, and had a chat with Moses, Jesus and Allah. I hate to tell you, Pete and App, but it's all ridiculous. None of that shit happened. It couldn't have happened. There's not a shred of evidence for any of it. All we've discovered in the last century points us in a totally different direction." Collins swallowed a deep breath before continuing.

"The world was created by a big bang. Life was an accident created by volcanos, climate, earthquakes and other natural phenomena. Life evolved. It was destroyed, and it evolved again. We're accidents of evolution. There's no evidence supporting any other explanation of life. Don't you see, defending this childish view of the origins of the earth is what is responsible for most wars and most horrible events in our history. Until we abandon these nonscientific notions we're doomed to their ideas of how the world will end. Now we have the means to do it. The bomb in the hands of a believer in the Rapture is the most dangerous thing on the planet!"

Peterson stared at him for a moment before speaking. "But, Collins, what if I'm right and you're wrong?" He took a deep disgusted breath, slowly stood up, glared at both of us, and stormed out of the hooch.

Collins looked back at me, shaking his head. "Sorry for the rant, App, I hope I didn't offend you too badly. I just get so worked up about this stupid religious bullshit that has no evidence whatsoever to justify its existence, yet ninety percent of the humans on earth believe in it. It drives me fucking nuts."

"You know what, Collins? My mind may be moving in your direction. I was raised Catholic and told it was the one true church with a direct connection to Jesus Christ through his apostle, Peter. 'Upon this rock I will build my Church,' Christ says in the Catholic bible. But after reading just a little of what I was given today by the old man who keeps my office clean, I have serious doubts about the church I've believed in all my life. I'll let you read it when I'm finished. It might fill in any blanks you might have about why we're here in Vietnam. It's another war over religion that's been kept from the American people. When you read it, it'll blow your mind."

"Damn, App, what the hell could be in that book?"

"It's more like a booklet, or pamphlet. Let me finish it tonight. We can talk about it tomorrow. All I need to say is that it's having a big impact on me"

As I was starting to head to my room, in walked Romanasky, the Secretary, and Dunphy. *Oh, shit*, I thought, *there'll be no reading tonight.*

"Hey, Applefuck! Look who's back!" Romanasky said, grinning. From around the corner came Johnny Fuentes, the builder, back from Tan Son Nhut.

"Johnny! My home boy from San Pedro! *Que paso, mi amigo*?"

"Short is what I am, App! In a week I'm back to the land of Latinas and tacos. The guys told me you got back from R&R in Hawaii with the old lady. How was it, man? Did you surf?"

"It was all-time great, Johnny, best time ever. Surfed at Waikiki. Dude, you should see the boards they're surfing now; short, pointy fuckers. I couldn't even get up on one. Did okay on the nine-two Dewey Weber."

"Ah, the new shortboards, I saw a few before I got in the army. They've taken over, is that it?"

"No shit! They were doing some moves with those boards that didn't even look like surfing. You'll see soon enough, you lucky bastard!"

"Come on, App. Let's check out your new room. E5 motherfucker now, big-time money."

As soon as we entered my room and looked around, Romanasky turned to Fuentes "We could make this into the sweetest room on Long Binh, right? Let me see. Got to get an air conditioner. It's fucking hot in here with you bastards," JR said, laughing as always. "I can get a refrigerator. I got a line on a two-burner stove. These bunk beds

suck. I plan on crashing here sometimes, so we got to get some better
beds. Fuentes, you can build some
shelves before you go, can't you?"

"Sure, J.R. Hell, let's get rid of
the wall locker and footlocker. I'll
build some nice cabinets. I'll build a
bar on that side over the fridge and
stove. You gotta get a good stereo,
App. We gonna want to play some Hendrix."

"I got the latest Cream album,"
added the Secretary. "That Clapton is a
god, I tell you."

"Sounds like we got a plan, boys,"
I said. "Let's get to the club and have
a few."

"But first let's have some hits
from this Paxton I got," said Fuentes.
"Menthol-tasting weed; the home boys
won't believe that shit when I get
back."

We went outside the hooch, looked
around for officers or NCOs, then stood
in a circle so we could see all around.
When we finished, and we stumbled toward the NCO club, Dunphy took out his
teeth, showed us his gummy mouth and
got us laughing our asses off.

Funny how weed works. Halfway to
the club we saw the first sergeant with
some other NCOs walking toward us. I
thought for sure I was totally out of
control, but when they got closer, the
Top said, "Hey, App! Back from R&R! How
was it?"

"Outstanding, Top! Totally out-standing!" I said in a clear, un-stoned voice.

They laughed as we passed. If they thought we were stoned, they didn't say a thing. Now that I think about it, they were most likely stoned them-selves. Bentley was with him, and I heard he chain-smoked Winstons all day long.

Collins came to the club after a while and joined the fun. There was a band of Vietnamese musicians who didn't know a word of English singing a Jef-ferson Airplane song *Give Me A Ticket For an Airplane,* about a guy who wanted a ticket on an airplane to see his girl friend. Because they would be going home in a few days, Fuentes and Collins sang it louder than all of us, the lucky motherfuckers.

Chapter 18

Mr. Nguyen and Buddhism

I woke up with a horrible taste in my mouth, my head feeling a couple of sizes larger, especially around the temples, where my blood seemed to swell with every beat of my heart. When my eyes opened, I discovered I was on the top bunk in my room. My eyes focused on a large spider that had built an intricate pattern of silk in the corner about three feet from my head. It had many bags of small bugs wrapped throughout the web. I decided to leave him be, since he was the best anti-mosquito system available. I greeted him as my first guest to my new room. That spider would be in the corner of my room the rest of my tour of duty.

He wasn't my only guest. Somebody was snoring below me. A look at the lower bunk revealed the snorer - Johnny Fuentes. I didn't remember inviting him; in fact I couldn't remember much past the fifth or sixth shot of Chivas Regal.

I looked forward to the two-burner stove Romanasky was on the lookout for. I'd love to just make some coffee right here and avoid the hundred-and-fifty-yard walk to the mess hall. My stomach began growling. I checked my watch. Fuck, it was after eight o'clock, and I had to get rolling. When I opened my wall locker to check for some clean fatigues, the metal door made a racket.

"Goddamn it, App! You gotta bang that thing this early in the morning?"

"It isn't early, Johnny, it's after eight. I'm going to the mess hall, then on to the motor pool. What have you got going, you short son of a bitch?"

"No shit, App. Three more days and I'm in Latina heaven. I'm tired of banging the locals. That band was pretty good though, man. How many times did we get them to play that song? Me and Collins were ripping that song."

"I could go without hearing it again for the rest of my life."

"I'll get started on the room, App, as soon as I really wake up."

He lay back down. As I walked down the aisle in the hooch I could hear him sing the song from last night in his horrible off key voice.

When I walked into my office Mr. Nguyen had the yellow broom and was moving dust from one side of the room to the other. "Good morning, Mr. Nguyen, I want to thank you again for giving me that book. I'll try to find time to read it again this morning. You know, Mr. Nguyen, I was raised a Catholic. I went to Catholic schools all my life. In every room in school was a picture of Pius XII. He was loved by my teachers who were Sisters of Saint Joseph. There's no way they would have told me the things I've been reading so far about Pius XII. To them he was the spokesman for God on earth, incapable of error. Yet, it seems to me now, he supported some of the worst causes in this century."

He shrugged, his narrow dark eyes looking into my blue eyes and nodded in agreement.

"I take it, Mr. Nguyen, that you're not Catholic."

He nodded an emphatic, "No."

"Then what do you believe in, Mr. Nguyen?"

"I follow teachings of Buddha; I am Buddhist." He spoke softly looking into my eyes.

"Well, this must be my week to learn about religions. I have no idea what Buddhists believe. Can you explain that to me, Mr. Nguyen?"

Thinking, he sat silently for a moment, then finally took a deep breath and spoke. "Buddha was Prince Siddhartha Gautama. He leave palace. He sees sick man, old man, dead man and monk. He understands that even a prince will suffer. He follows the monk. He lives holy life. He asks questions; why must man suffer? What causes suffering? He spends many years meditating, praying, and fasting. He discovers the Basic Truths of Life."

"You're kidding me. What did he mean by 'basic truths?"

"There are three Universal Truths of Life and four Noble Truths of Life."

"Really? And what are they, Mr. Nguyen?"

He took another deep breath through his nose, held it, then exhaled through his mouth. He did this slowly three times with his eyes closed, then opened them, looked at me and handed me another small pamphlet he had translated. "Read to me the Universal Truths of the Buddha."

I took the book, cleared my voice and started reading aloud. "The Universal Truths are: everything in life is impermanent and ever-changing. Since nothing is permanent, a life based on possessing things or persons does not make you happy. There no eternal unchanging soul. 'Self' is just a collection of changing characteristics and attributes."

I looked up at him after reading and tried to grasp the meaning of the words. I read them over several times, and concluded they seemed to describe the world that I lived. My life had gone through so many changes over the last couple of years indicating that life wasn't permanent. I understood how things I once owned didn't really make me happy. My concept of myself was in a constant state of flux from early elementary to middle school to high school. My life and thoughts were dramatically changing constantly, I knew it was changing at this moment.

"I think I understand them, Mr. Nguyen. They make sense to me; they fit the world I have seen. What are the four Noble Truths?"

He pointed to the next section of the pamphlet. "Please read and let me hear it."

I started reading again. "The Noble Truths are: human life has a lot of suffering. The cause of suffering is greed. There is an end to suffering. The way to end suffering is to follow the Eight Fold Path."

"So, Mr. Nguyen, what is this Eightfold Path?"

While waiting for him to speak, I thought about the suffering caused by greed, and how the war we were fighting was caused by greed. I looked at Mr. Nguyen with his eyes closed meditating on something. He opened his eyes and saw me waiting for him to speak.

"Eightfold path not living life of luxury, and not too much fasting," he said. "You must follow the Eightfold Path." He looked at the pamphlet. "Read Eightfold Path."

Again, I looked down at Mr. Nguyen's translation and read out loud. "The Eightfold Path: Right understanding and viewpoint, based on the four Noble Truths. Right values and attitude, compassion rather than selfishness. Right speech, don't tell lies, avoid harsh, abusive speech, avoid gossip."

I read slowly, thinking about each word. "Right action, help others, live honestly, don't harm living things, take care of the environment."

I paused in my reading, thinking about the words then continued.

"Right work, do something useful, avoid jobs that harm others. Right effort, encourage good, helpful thoughts; discourage unwholesome, destructive thoughts. Right mindfulness, be aware of what you feel, think, and do. Right meditation, calm mind, practice meditation which leads to nirvana."

I looked up from the pamphlet, the words resonating with thoughtfulness. I couldn't help but compare them to the Ten Commandments with all of the "Thou shalt nots." Compassion over selfishness, help others, live honestly, do something useful, encourage helpful thoughts, have a calm mind. If we could follow this wonderful path, there would be universal peace and well-being.

From what I had read in his other pamphlet, my church, the Catholic Church, was doing all it could to prevent these peaceful people from following this path. Anger rose in me toward my church, and I suddenly realized that anger is the child of unwholesome destructive thoughts. This thought made me realize that while all that Mr. Nguyen said made sense, putting it into practice would require changing much of the way that I had learned to think.

"Mr. Nguyen, this is a way of thinking and behaving that I was not aware of. I would dearly love to learn how to think this way. The end of this right meditation, this calm mind, is nirvana. Tell me, what is this nirvana that you're seeking?"

He repeated the word nirvana and I could see him look away as if looking inside, thinking. "Not easy to tell. It is freedom - freedom from suffering. It is being alive, living in the moment.

Through meditation you can get to stillness of mind, then enlightenment." He stopped again, and with his eyes closed, took a deep breath through his nose, held it, then let it out slowly. He seemed to be at peace, then spoke.

"Mr. App, you must accept the universal truths and the noble truths. Follow the Eightfold Path and you, too, can reach peace of mind, enlightenment and nirvana."

I had nothing more to say to Mr. Nguyen, and he seemed to understand my silence. He continued to breathe deeply and think. Or maybe not think. My mind wasn't at peace. Though these ideas made sense to me, they were so different from the way I had been thinking all of my life. These revelations brought a disturbing restlessness to my spirit.

"Thank you so much, Mr. Nguyen, for this gift. I've never heard of this way of thinking. It makes sense to me. I see it as a hope for mankind. If everyone thought this way I wouldn't be here disturbing the lives of a people who think this way. I'm sorry, Mr. Nguyen, that my country is driven by greed and not compassion."

Mr. Nguyen bowed and made prayer hands then looked into my eyes with profound kindness.

Just then, we heard someone on our porch. Mr. Nguyen quickly stood, grabbed the broom, and began sweeping dust from one end of the office to the other. Romanasky opened the door and poked his head around the corner.

"You okay in here? Seems awful quiet. Hi there, Mr. Nguyen, how are you doing?"

Mr. Nguyen nodded.

"Apple, let's stop by Class I and see if we can get a case of steaks or burgers. Let's get started on our little plan, whaddaya say?"

"Great idea, J.R. I'll finish up this paperwork. We can go after lunch."

When Romanasky left, I looked at Mr. Nguyen and knew my life would never be the same; that I could no longer follow a religion that wasn't based on the Universal and Noble truths and didn't follow the Eightfold Path. I desperately wanted to be on a path to enlightenment by doing useful work and having thoughts that were accepting and loving. I felt reborn.

Chapter 19

Kings of Long Binh

J.R. came by with the 448 three-quarter-ton truck — now more his than mine — which was okay with me. His keeping the parts rooms full, and the trucks running, while I was focused on the paperwork, and contemplating what I was learning from Mr. Nguyen, amazed me. We were a great team.

When we went to the Class I yard, where I knew a bunch of guys from my basketball days prior to Tet, a guy named Green came over. We shook hands, and talked a little NBA. I liked the Lakers, he liked Detroit's Pistons. We also rapped about the James Brown show we saw last week. "Was that a great show or what, App?"

"Hardest working man in show business! That was a great event, my man!" Again we slapped some five, then bumped fists. "Listen, Green, can I get a case of steaks and hamburgers. I got a deal going."

"I'll check what we got."

He went in the back for a couple of minutes, then returned with two cardboard boxes, and handed them to Romanasky with a wink. "I'll just put 'Lost in shipment' on this here piece of paper. By the way, we still got the hoops going, App. I think we could beat you, the Hulk, and Snowflake even without Bentley cheatin'." We laughed at that.

At the parts depot J.R. had many friends who were solid contacts, which meant we had a top priority. He always had things to pass out to them - scrounged objects, or stuff he had traded for. With his gregarious personality, he made them laugh. I was just along for the ride. They knew and liked me, but J.R. had stolen their hearts.

With our truck loaded with parts, we headed to Club 9. J.R. said he had talked to the sergeant there, and he was ready to make a deal.

"So what deal do you want to make, J.R.? I know we can get away with a few lost-in-shipment cases of steaks and burgers, but what kind of deal are you thinking about?"

"I'm not sure. We could get a cut of the proceeds on the restaurant side of the business. I can haggle that deal. What are you thinking?"

"Well, J.R., if we start a money trail, when the shit hits the fan, we could go down with the sergeants. I'm not sure I want to go down that road.

Last place I want to do any time is in Long Binh Jail. We have to do these deals without money being exchanged." I paused thinking. "How about if we say that we'll bring them some steaks and burgers, but we don't want money, all we want is to be the 'Kings of the Clubs.' We get free drinks and free food. You tell him to keep a bottle of Chivas Regal on the shelf behind the bar for me and a bottle of Jack Daniels for you. They take them down when we show up and give us some glasses of ice. Everything is on the house. We get to eat all we want. Hell, you'll eat way more than any money they gave us could buy. I know they're getting the booze almost free so they'll make that deal."

"I don't know, Apple, seems like we ought to make some money out of this thing."

"I agree, J.R., but here's something else I've been thinking about. I've heard a lot of guys talking about how pissed they are that they don't have any guns to defend themselves in any kind of emergency like what happened during Tet. You remember how it was, having to stand in line to get our M14s. They want guns, J.R.. I think I have an idea of how we might be able to get them some."

"Shit, Applefuck! Now you're talking about some dangerous shit. Gun dealing is worse than selling steaks."

"That may be true, but it depends. Let's say we meet some guys from the Screaming Eagles at Club 5. We give them a couple of free shots of Chivas. We tell them that the next time they're deployed to find as many captured weapons as they can. We tell them if they fill up a footlocker full of them, we'll throw their outfit a huge party with steaks, burgers and beer, just like we do on Sundays at the motor pool. If we get a couple of footlockers full of guns, we'll have some major trading material, J.R. What do you think?"

"I like the idea of being the Kings of the Club, App. I like getting our drinks and food for free. I think the sergeants will go for that idea. And I'll punish them, too. You know how much I can eat. The gun deal might work, too. They give officers 45s, and there's no law saying you can't carry a gun here, it's a goddamn war zone! With all the shit that's going down now, and all the new outfits, there's no way they're going to be looking at us. I say if the sergeants go for that deal, let's do it. If we meet the right guy from an infantry outfit we can trust, let's do that, too. We're here to defend the Constitution of the United States of America. Nobody's going to mind if we fill a market to help our soldiers practice their second-amendment right to bear arms. Let's go for it!"

"Well put, J.R., you should go to law school when we get back," I said laughing.

When we brought our case of steaks to Club 9, J.R. and I talked to the sergeant running the place. "Sounds cool" he said and took the deal. A minute later, he took out the bottle of Chivas for me, and a Jack Daniels for J.R., and wrote our names on them. We drank a few on ice, the way we liked it, and gave him a couple, too. We made that same deal with five of the clubs that were close to infantry battalions including the local one. We'd hit each one once a week.

It was great being the Kings of the Clubs. We'd arrive in my cool lime-green 448 truck. The sergeant gave us our bottles and glasses. If a soldier sat near, we'd offer him a drink. He rarely said no, then we'd find out what outfit he was with, where and when he might be deployed next. If we thought he was a person we could trust, we would tell him about our deal. We laid the groundwork for a few deals, not sure if the GIs would follow through.

Meanwhile, J.R. found some Hollywood bunk beds for my room, a refrigerator, and that two-burner stove top. He even bargained for a new air conditioner. I got him the steaks, he made the trades. I bought a new stereo with big speakers and a turntable at the PX. They had a color TV there, too, so I bought that as well. With all that, along with the cabinets and bar that Johnny Fuentes had installed, my place became the hangout after work. It was the coolest place on Long Binh.

J.R. crashed there most nights, but was bummed when a new spec five got assigned to my room, a guy named Chaves. He'd been in the army about six months, went to some special school and came out a spec five. He was stoned from the first hour he got in-country. With all the shit around Long Binh, he was stoned all the time. He wasn't a bad guy, just "young and dumb," as we used to say. After all, I was twenty-one and J.R. and the Secretary were twenty. Dunphy was in his thirties.

We asked Dunphy how come he was even in the army. The draft was for guys from eighteen to twenty-six. He told us stories about how he was married and had some kids. Said he would go out to buy milk, then show up a couple days later. His wife had about as much of him as she could take, so he joined the army.

One day he pulled out a picture of the wife and kids and I knew why he joined up. She was about the ugliest woman, and the kids were definitely the homeliest kids, I'd ever seen.

Several days later, when I was caught up on work, Dunphy asked me to join him on a convoy to Saigon. "Bring yer hat wid the 448 on it. I'll get ya a shotgun," he said. We wore distinctive 448 metal pins on the front of our hats.

I found J.R. and I told him what I was doing. "Don't get a dose of the clap," he said, laughing.

The convoy planned to organize along Highway 1 at ten o'clock. Dunphy left the base at nine. "I gotta see the li'l honey," he said, smiling. We went about a mile out of the gate on Highway 1, then turned onto a side road. About three hundred yards in, Dunphy stopped in front of a small village of hastily constructed shabby plywood huts all leaning haphazardly this way and that with GIs moving from building to building.

"You can pick one out if ya want, Apple" Dunphy smiled with his false teeth firmly in place; it wasn't the hilarious grin.

When we got out of the deuce-and-a-half, we started walking past the six-by eight-foot huts made of cracked and partially rotted plywood nailed to rough two-by-fours with a zinc roof tilted to one side. Dirty rag-like sheets nailed to openings served as doors. Dunphy pulled back a sheet and looked inside.

"Well, looky here, App."

When I did, I saw a PFC sitting on an old dirty mattress with his pants down getting a blowjob.

Walking from hut to hut Dunphy pulled back the sheets where various states of sex were going on. If not, the smiling girl inside would wave us in. "Me so horny, GI, me boom boom long time, me sucky sucky."

"Ya want that 'un, Apple?" Dunphy said, holding the sheet back while I looked at the young, partially dressed girl.

"No thanks," I said emphatically.

I made a promise to myself not to break my wedding vows and didn't want Alexandra to. It was as simple as that.

"Here we are," Dunphy said when we got to the hut he was looking for. Inside, an older lady with slightly graying hair sat on the bed and looked up with a big toothless smile obviously excited to see Dunphy. Greeting her, he quickly sat next to her, wrapped his arms around her, then looked up at me with that silly grin, "Ain't she purdy, Apple?"

I didn't know what to say.

"She's got a great smile, don't ya, sweetheart?"

All I saw was her tongue and gums. I smiled back and thought, *what a perfect match for Dunphy.*

"I won't be long, Apple. Check out the other huts. Ya'll find a purdy 'un."

I had no interest in going into another hut and went back to the truck, took out my pack of Tareytons, stuck the cigarette in my mouth, lit one up, and through the smoke I exhaled thought about the life we created for the Vietnamese people — the old ladies cleaning the shit barrels, the whores in these huts, and Mr. Nguyen. I thought about the three Universal Truths, the four Noble Truth, and realized with horror we weren't doing good work here. We were causing suffering. Suddenly, a deep, profound sadness came over me like a dark, ominous cloud. Shuddering, it was all I could do to hold back anguished tears.

Dunphy showed up about thirty minutes later, still grinning. After starting the truck, we rolled down the dirt road to Highway 1 and took our place behind a line of waiting trucks, smoke and exhaust fumes rising. A half hour later, the convoy started moving.

We moved quickly down the highway. Much of the landscape was green open land with many streams and ponds. We passed small villages where people went about their lives hauling water, gathering wood for fires, gardening, mothers carrying babies. As we entered Saigon the roads were clogged with hundreds of colorful motorbikes. Many had to scramble to get out of the way because the military vehicles, like bullies, weren't going to stop for them. When we almost hit a guy on a moped I yelled, "Damn, Dunphy, be careful! You almost hit that guy!"

"They's only gooks, App, whadda we care?" He looked at me with his shit-eating grin.

I looked away and sighed. No use arguing with Dunphy. He was an idiot.

Motorbikes and people walking back and forth, filled the crowded, noisy streets. Ducks hung by their necks from brightly colored buildings. Food-stands with delicious aromas were everywhere. Dunphy pulled over in front of a bar with GIs standing around outside talking to girls. Inside, it was crowded with GIs and Vietnamese women in lovely long dresses or tight short-shorts.

"Take off your helmet and put on your hat, Apple. Ya brought some piasters like I told ya?"

"Yes, Dunphy, I brought them. What's the big deal with the hat?"

"Ya'll find out soon," he said with that horrid grin. "I'll be back in an hour or two to pick ya up."

I got out, slamming the door behind me and felt the humid hot air. I looked around and stood in the blinding, hot sunlight, then slowly entered the crowded bar. Just as I was beginning to see clearly, a woman yelled, "448! 448! 448!" Suddenly, women of all shapes and sizes were jostling each other to get a hand on my arm.

"Buy me drink, GI! Buy me drink!"

Girls, who had been paying attention to soldiers dressed in fatigues or civilian clothes, were now gathered around me. Though startled by the attention, I knew I'd better choose one quickly, or there'd be a riot. I picked a cute young girl in red short-shorts. She grabbed my arm and winked at her girlfriends like she had won a prize.

I took her to the bar, and ordered a Chivas Regal on ice, while she had a pink-colored drink that cost twice as much as my Chivas. I paid with piasters given to me by several black guys from the Class I yard on the day they left. I had a pretty good wad of them.

A soldier with a girl next to me said, "Damn, man, what was that with you and the girls?"

"I have no idea. My outfit has money. The girls must know it. According to my buds, they get the same reaction everywhere they go."

He looked at the pin on my hat. "448, you know, I've heard of that company. I'm short now. I was stationed most of the time at the base in Vung Tau. The 448 used to be there. There was a big CID bust. Lots of guys went to jail. That must have been about seven months ago. How long have you been with them?"

"Almost six months," I said.

"Well, the 448 still has a reputation with the locals. They were all over you like you were a king."

Yeah, I thought, *King of the Clubs and now King of Saigon. Long live the King.*

I tried to talk to the girl next to me. She only knew a few English words and my Vietnamese was even more limited. I bought her a couple more drinks and hoped she was getting a cut of the money I was paying for her pink ginger ale. I had another Chivas while starting to inventory in my head the many questions I'd had on my arrival at the 448. Most of them had been answered. One big one remained. Where was all that money coming from?

Dunphy honked out front. I gave the girl some of my remaining piasters. She bowed, gave me the praying hands, and I bowed back. When I climbed into the truck Dunphy smiled, "Did ya get that one, App?" I just shrugged, indicating he should put the truck into gear and get us home. I wasn't so amused by Dunphy anymore.

I knew he was like so many of my fellow American soldiers. He wasn't raised to be empathetic or culturally accepting, but was the victim of a culture that believed we were somehow superior to others because we had the largest economy in the world. My mind was turning against everything I saw us doing in this country. We had no right or business being here. Dunphy was too ignorant to understand that. He didn't really mean harm, and with those teeth sitting beside him on the seat, he was still goddamn funny-looking.

"That was a good time, right, Apple? Yer a good ol' boy. Let's have a drink in the club when we get back." He blew out his lips making me laugh whether I wanted to or not.

Chapter 20

Martin Luther King

It was sunset when Dunphy and I got back from Saigon. Bright orange and dazzling red clouds glowed in the deep purple sky. Though beautiful, my heart ached from realizing that Dunphy, like so many GIs, had no understanding of the peace-loving ways of the people around them. They didn't see them as people looking for the Middle Path - simple people, who were trying to live lives of compassion, good thoughts, and quiet meditation. To him, and to many like him, they were gooks.

Dunphy dropped me off at the motor pool. Chief Warrant Officer Arnold and another warrant officer were out front. As I walked toward them, I could see that Arnold was upset.

"Have you heard the news?" he shouted as I approached.

"What news, Chief?"

"Somebody shot and killed Martin Luther King."

"Oh, no! You have got to be kidding me! How'd you find that out?"

"It was broadcast over Armed Forces Radio. He was in Memphis, Tennessee to support a strike of some kind. There are riots in every city in America. I wouldn't go to the Class I yard if I were you. The black guys are really pissed off. Your Top is down there trying to get them under control."

"Christ, Chief! I have to find my friend Collins. He's Stateside in three days. He's got to be angry as hell." *What kind of America would he be returning to.*

"By the way, App, this is my replacement. I'm out of here soon. This is Warrant Officer Gabriel."

When I saluted, he saluted back, then stuck out his hand. "Nice to meet you, Appenzeller. The chief has good things to say about you. I'll be relying on you to keep me squared away on how things are run around here."

"Thank you, sir. You're filling some big shoes. Chief Arnold has been a great leader for the motor pool." I finished shaking his hand. "If you don't mind, sir, one of my closest friends is a black guy who works at battalion headquarters. He's got to be shook up about Dr. King being killed. I have to find him."

"Go ahead, App. I've met Collins. He seems like a bright young man. Go find him."

I dashed out of the motor pool and ran as fast as I could down the paved road, crossed over to the barracks, then galloped the next hundred and fifty yards to our hooch, and breathlessly darted inside. Peterson was on his bunk busy packing. He'd be out-of-country tomorrow, and Collins would be joining him in three days. Still gasping for air, I asked, "Have you seen Collins, Pete?"

"No, App, he hasn't been here. I took the day off to get my stuff together. I found out a couple of hours ago about the assassination. Don't go near the Class I hooch. Man, they're really angry and should be. I feel just awful for Collins. I know he believed in the nonviolent movement that Dr. King led. This could be bad, App, real bad, I heard there's rioting and destruction in every major U.S. City. We don't have a big black population in Salt Lake City, but I hope the families there are okay." His deep sigh, closed sad eyes, and the slow shaking of his head revealed his compassion and anguish.

Suddenly, his eyes widened and looked behind me. He quickly got off his bed. I turned to see Collins storming into the room. His face looked grim, his bloodshot eyes were swollen from tears and rage. I tried to find words to comfort him, but could only say, "Come on, Collins. Let's go to my room. Let's have a drink. I know I need one. I'm sure you do too."

Peterson followed us into my room and closed the door. Collins collapsed onto the bottom bunk and pounded the bed with hard karate chops.

"Go ahead, Collins. Beat the shit out of that bed. Get it all out," I yelled, then grabbed my bottle of Chivas Regal from the bar, filled two glasses with the light brown liquid and waited until he was exhausted. When he turned around worn out, I handed him his glass, then took a healthy sip from my own and felt it burn my throat. Collins drank some of his and shook his head as he swallowed.

"Goddamn it, App, why King? Why the man of nonviolence? I don't know if I'll ever trust America again. They killed the voice of reason."

He took another swallow, setting down the glass, then pounded his fist into the mattress again harder than before. "I don't know what I'm going to do, App. I can't stay in this fucking army when they're killing the best and brightest of my people. He was our leader, loved by the world. He won the Nobel Peace Prize, for God's sake. God damn America!" he screamed. "God damn America!"

Witnessing this deep anguish from someone who had always shown so little emotion hurt. The empathy I learned from my father swelled in me. This was pain. This was suffering. I didn't know what to say other than, "I'm so sorry, Collins. Dr. King was one of my heroes, too. I stayed home to watch the march on Washington. His 'I Had a Dream' speech is one of the greatest in history. I'm so sorry." I grabbed his glass when he finished, and poured him another inch.

Though quiet, Peterson's concerned eyes were focused on Collins. They had been together longer than me. Though they differed on many things, they shared mutual respect for each other's character. He waited until Collins got off the bed and embraced him. Collins leaned on him for a long soothing time, and I could see by their embrace how close they had become despite their differences. He pulled away, took another swallow of Chivas, then looked at me. "Chicago's in flames, App, what a homecoming that'll be."

Finally Pete spoke in a low, soft voice. "I'm sorry for your loss, Collins. I feel like we lost an important member of the human family. I know you don't think it will do any good, but I'll be praying for you, praying that you'll recover from this darkness and regain your spirit. I'll pray that your people's anger will subside, and that they don't destroy their own communities. You're a good man, Collins. Don't let this make you any less of the good man that you are."

I knew Collins did not believe in praying, but we both felt the warmth of Peterson's sincerity.

In my left upper pocket I had a pack of Winstons. I knocked one out and fired it up, then turned on the air conditioner full blast. "Take a hit, Collins. Let's listen to some Hendrix." I handed him the joint. Without judgment, Peterson opened the door, quietly slipped out and shut it. We passed the weed back and forth listened to the weeping guitar, both deep in thought. Five minutes later, I climbed onto the top bunk and spaced out. Hopefully Collins did the same.

While lying there, visions started moving through my head. Visions of the America I saw hitchhiking through the South. Visions of nice ladies proudly pulling out pictures of their father standing by a black man hanging from a tree, his neck broken, his feet bare, other white faces grinning into the camera. Guys, who could barely speak English, laughing, while casually asking if I wanted to go on a "nigger" hunt, like it was a game of basketball. I remembered my godfather being carried into the room by a black man, ranting and raving about the worthlessness of the people he exploited by charging them higher prices because they were black, and my grandfather sitting there grinning and nodding in agreement. This was my family; this was my America.

I thought about Collins and hoped he was falling asleep and forgetting for a while about this horror that had struck his people. Collins was the most intelligent and best educated person in the entire battalion, yet Mills and Dunphy could never see it; they were blinded by prejudice, blinded by their personal histories, blinded by those around them who supported their ugly distorted views. It could have been any one of them who pulled the trigger to kill Dr. King.

I admired Martin Luther King for many reasons. He eloquently pointed out the inequality that his people suffered. He hoped to lead his people to the Promised Land. Now that gentle voice was silenced. America should be ashamed.

I had memorized much of Dr. King's "I Had a Dream" speech. I recited it in my history class at Santa Clara. My mother helped me with it. His words, "I had a dream" resonated in my head as I drifted off to sleep. The last thing I recalled saying were the inspiring words: *"one day this nation will rise up and live out the true meaning of its creed: 'We hold these truths to be self-evident, that all men are created equal…"*

Chapter 21

Losing my Religion

A dream was fading away while my fuzzy consciousness was slowly returning. As my brain cycles increased their speed, I dared a blurred peek through my eyelids, and saw my old spider friend with his eight legs splayed out waiting for his next prey. *Good morning, my friend*, the voice in my head said. My eyes closed again, and my mind tried to focus on what had happened last night.

Ohmygod! Dr. King is dead, the horror screamed in my brain. Leaning over I saw Collins in the bottom bunk laying curled in a fetal position. Looking around the room, I knew that Chaves must have arrived late, saw the situation, and let Collins lay passed out.

I glanced at my watch and saw it was after eight. Sitting up, I slid to the floor as quietly as possible not wanting to disturb Collins. Seeing no one in the hootch, I went next door, and found a mechanic returning from the mess hall who said he would tell the chief I was with Collins.

Back in the room, I made coffee, then checked the refrigerator for eggs and milk. Collins and I didn't have to go anywhere. It felt great being the King. When the aroma of fresh coffee filled the air, Collins started to stir. He rolled onto his back, and his eyes flickered open "Damn that smells good, App. You got it made in this room, man."

At first, his eyes were bright as he looked at me, then a cloud darkened them as he remembered yesterday's news. He lay his head back down, closed his eyes, and clenching his fist, pounded the bed a few times and shouted, "Fuck, fuck, fuck!"

I poured us two cups of coffee into hard plastic cups and handed one to Collins as he sat up. Lost in thought, he grasped his cup with both hands and slowly sipped.

"Two more days in this hell-hole, Collins, you lucky bastard. Two more days and you're back to the world. I wish it was under different circumstances. Who do you have waiting for you at home?"

"Both my mom and dad will be there. Dad works for the city, Mom is an elementary school teacher. I have a couple of sisters in high school. I bet they're out there raising hell after what's happened."

"My dad was a high school teacher; now he's a guidance counselor. I know he's upset about this, too. He and my mom loved Dr. King. My dad actually knew Cesar Chavez, the leader of the United Farm Workers. I was too focused on getting laid and making the sports teams to see much around me. It wasn't until I hitchhiked across the South that I had any real education. I had a Catholic education. I didn't know how distorted that was until I read that book Mr. Nguyen gave me."

"You were going to let me read that book, App. You still have it?"

"Yeah, I do. You might not be shocked by what's in it, but given my education and upbringing, it took me by surprise. I don't think I'll ever call myself a Catholic again."

"Why not, App? What's in there that could have changed your mind so drastically?"

"Well, Collins, when I was in elementary school, I loved and admired the principal of our school, Father O'Sullivan. He was also my dad's good friend. He was kind and loving and I wanted to be like him. I told that to the nuns, which brought great joy to them because they thought I had God's calling. From second to sixth grade I got straight A's because the nuns loved me so much. I took it seriously. I studied my catechism, learned my prayers, took my first communion, and served mass each morning as an altar boy. I was a whole hog believer."

"No shit, App, I had a public school education. I went to the school where my mom taught. I loved that school. The teachers were excellent. They treated me well. I think they loved my mom more than me, but I didn't care at the time. I was getting good grades. They made me feel smart."

"I felt the same way, Collins. The nuns loved me because they thought we shared the calling. The point I want to make is that in every classroom there was a picture of the Holy Father, Pope Pius XII. He wore glasses and looked saintly. The sisters would make the sign of the cross each day in front of his picture. Every year my classmates and I would go to the auditorium to watch a film called *The Miracle of Our Lady of Fatima*. It was about a girl and her two cousins who saw a cloud with a lady in it who the girl said was the Virgin Mary, the mother of Jesus. The Virgin told them to return every month on the 13th.

"The parish priest and the girl's mother tried to stop them, but they returned as the Virgin told them to. There were sixty people there waiting for them. She said she saw the Virgin again. Every month more and more people came to the area to see this miracle. The crowd couldn't see the Virgin, but they believed that the children could. The children said that the Virgin Mary told them that there would be another world war if people didn't stop sinning, and if Russia wasn't converted to Catholicism.

"In the movie, the local authorities arrested the children, accusing them of lying. They told the oldest one, who is the only one who actually saw the Virgin, that they'd killed the other children and would kill her, too, if she didn't recant her story. She refused, willing to die for the Virgin. She told them that the Virgin Mary would show them a miracle that would prove that the girl was telling the truth. Forty-thousand people showed up in a driving rainstorm to witness the miracle. The rain stopped, the sun peeked through a rainbow, then suddenly started to drop to the earth in a zigzag pattern, causing people to panic. Those who came with diseases or afflictions were suddenly cured. It was called the 'Miracle of the Sun.'

"Collins, I saw that movie every year from third grade to eighth. It solidified my belief in a God who could do miracles, who could heal the sick. I had no doubts at all that the event happened the way it was portrayed in the movie."

"Okay, App. I never saw that movie. Kids are gullible. What's the point of all of this? How does it relate to Pius XII and Vietnam?"

"Sorry, Collins, I know this is a long story, but it all ties in at the end, I promise."

"Okay. Pour another cup of coffee, finish beating those eggs, and I'll try to hang with you."

I broke the eggs into a cup, added some milk, mixing them together, threw them into the sizzling skillet. In a few minutes, I handed him plate of scrambled eggs and another cup of coffee. I started again.

"Now, according to the book Mr. Nguyen translated for me, Pius XII was a big believer in this Miracle of Fatima. He had a statue made of the Virgin, had a crown made worth millions of dollars. It was made of solid gold with hundreds of pearls and thousands of diamonds.

"He was also a rabid anti-communist. Before he became pope, he was Monseigneur Pacelli, chief adviser to

Pope Pius XI. His fear of communism was so great that he and the Pope backed Mussolini in Italy and Hitler in Germany. Pius XI called Mussolini 'the man sent by Providence.' They seemed satisfied with fascism as long as it fulfilled the predictions of the Miracle of Fatima. He sent the statue from country to country causing a religious fervor that became the 'Cult of Fatima.'

"When Pacelli became Pope Pius XII, he urged the fascists to invade Soviet Russia and was overjoyed when Hitler did so, and called it 'Divine Providence.' He encouraged Catholics from all over the world to join with Hitler to bring about the predictions of Fatima so that he, as The Holy Father, could consecrate Russia to the Virgin's immaculate heart."

"You're kidding me, App! The Pope and the Catholic Church were behind Hitler and Mussolini?"

"According to Mr. Nguyen's book they would have backed anyone who would fulfill the Virgin's predictions at Fatima. Ending communism in Russia was the only way Pius XII could do that."

"Okay, I'll check on all this when I get back to school. So again, what does all this have to do with Vietnam?"

"Sorry, Collins, I know it's a convoluted story but I think you'll see the connections in the end."

"Okay, App. Continue."

"Pius XII was disappointed in the outcome of World War II. The godless, communistic Soviet Union emerged as the world's second-greatest superpower. So he turned his attention to the world's greatest superpower, the United States.

"He had several powerful political allies there. First was his confidant Cardinal Spellman in New York City; second was the Catholic lobby, led by powerful Catholic families like the Kennedys; and third were the anticommunist crusaders, the Dulles brothers, John Foster and Allan.

"He sent the statue of Our Lady of Fatima to America. The Knights of Columbus paraded the statue in major cities, reminding Catholics of the Virgin's prediction of the conversion of Russia. The Catholic lobby supported the Catholic senator from Wisconsin, Joe McCarthy, in his anti-communist crusade. They helped put important Catholics in power in the U.S. government; James Forrestal was secretary of defense, Francis Matthews became Secretary of the Navy under Truman; Eisenhower selected John Foster Dulles for secretary of state, and his brother

Alan as head of the CIA. They were not Catholics, but they shared the Pope's hatred of communism.

"Pius XII supported a policy of a preemptive nuclear attack on the Soviet Union. Secretary Mathews gave a speech in Boston in 1950 supporting this idea. When President Truman didn't follow the advice of Secretary Matthews, Pius XII's focus became Southeast Asia. He and Cardinal Spellman, using the Catholic lobby, supported France when they tried to take back Indochina after World War II. Eighty percent of the financing for the French effort came from the U.S. government.

"Pius XII was disappointed when France was defeated by Ho Chi Minh. He was further disappointed with the Geneva agreement that gave Ho Chi Minh North Vietnam. There were more Catholics living in the North than the South. Ho Chi Minh was not anti-Catholic. One of his advisers was a Catholic bishop. He had Catholics in his administration, but he had been to Russia and believed in Marxism, so he was seen as an enemy by Pope Pius XII, Cardinal Spellman, the Catholic lobby and the United States of America.

"All of them worked to get Ngo Dinh Diem appointed president of South Vietnam. Diem had been groomed for years by the Vatican. He lived in one

Catholic monastery after another in Europe and the U.S. His brother became the archbishop of the sacred Buddhist City of Hue because of Pius XII. Diem selected his younger brother to head the secret police to spy on Buddhist activities.

I paused to take a sip of coffee which was getting cold, and took a deep disgusted breath, then continued. "As you know, they refused to allow the elections stipulated in the Geneva Agreement in 1956. It was then that Pius XII made one huge effort to establish a Catholic South Vietnam. He sent the Lady of Fatima to North Vietnam. There were more than a million Catholics in the North. Many came to see the Virgin. Then the Virgin was taken to the South. The Church with the help of the CIA dropped millions of leaflets over North Vietnam saying that the Lady of Fatima and her son Jesus Christ had left North Vietnam. North Vietnamese Catholics must join the Lady in South Vietnam. A million of them did. Can you believe that! A million of them. Meanwhile, Dulles told the press that they were being forced out of North Vietnam by Ho Chi Minh.

"Diem had a much stronger base, but still not strong enough to defeat Ho Chi Minh in an election, so they continued to defy the Geneva Agreement.

So you see, it was the Catholic Church, led by Pope Pius XII and his allies in the U.S. that brought about these hostilities. One of the main spokesmen for the Catholic Lobby was John F. Kennedy. When he became President, as you know, the U.S. government took a much stronger role in Vietnam.

"Today, South Vietnam has a Catholic president, a majority of Catholics in the administration, and many Catholics in control of the military. That's not the only reason the U.S. is in Vietnam, but it's one of the main reasons."

"Wow, App, that's an amazing story. I've never heard anything like it. I'll be back in the States the day after tomorrow, you can bet I'll try to verify that history. But it doesn't surprise me that the Catholic Church was willing to drop a bomb on a million nonbelievers. It's consistent with the history of the church, which will do anything to continue to expand its power. The Crusades in the eleventh through thirteenth centuries, the Conquistadors in the sixteenth century and the Inquisition are all horror stories of torture and death."

"I know, Collins! This is a life-changing story for me."

I looked down at my half finished plate of eggs and drank down the last of my cold coffee, then sat back.

Collins nodded. "I can imagine how hard learning this must have been."

"It was, but Mr. Nguyen has shared with me the basic beliefs of Buddhism, and they sound so reasonable. They believe that suffering comes from greed. To escape suffering, you have to take the middle path, which means not a lot of luxury nor too much poverty. You get to this path by choosing compassion over selfishness, mild speaking over harsh speaking, doing good work, and not hurting people. That all sounds like a good idea to me. Yet here we are killing these gentle people in the name of the U.S., but with the huge shadow of the Catholic Church behind it. I don't know what to think anymore."

"Follow your heart, App. You can see what's good and what's bad. We'll survive this. I know I will. I'm leaving tomorrow. I'll play Army for as long as I have to, but when I'm out, I'll do all I can to educate the public, and end this fucking war."

"I'll do the same. I can say this, I'm no longer a member of the Catholic Church. I can't be a part of the killing of so many kind compassionate people in the name of free markets and economic principles."

"Shit, App, you're sounding like a Buddhist, my friend," He laughed.

"I don't know what to think. I like that there's no mention of God in what Mr. Nguyen explained to me, just the conclusions drawn after many years of contemplation by the first Buddha, Siddhartha. Those conclusions make sense to me right now."

Collins smiled. "They make a hell of a lot more sense than any of the religions I've read and studied, that's for sure. Hey, thanks, App, for taking my mind off the horrible thing that happened yesterday. I'll try to have a more peaceful mind about it."

"Thanks for listening, Collins. Not too many around here would have." I paused. "Let's say goodbye to Peterson."

We squared away the room, then went into the hooch. We found Peterson packed, sitting on his bed. "I thought you guys would never wake up," Peterson said, smiling. "North is taking me to 90th Relocation in a couple of minutes. I was ready to go pound on your door." He stood and gave each of us a bear hug. "You're the only two that made this thing tolerable. Thanks for hanging around with me and including me in all of the things we did. I'll remember you guys."

"I'll remember you too, Pete. You have a big heart, my man. It's been a pleasure having you for a friend," said Collins.

"Same for me, Pete," I said. "I don't know what I'll do without you two around here. You were the only ones who would listen to my bullshit. Pardon the expression, Pete."

"I know what you'll do. You'll party with your pals, App. You have a lot of friends here, man," said Collins, patting me on the back. "In fact, I hope we party big time tonight on my last night in-country. Your buds sure do know how to do that, App."

"Well, I have to go," Pete said. "Thanks again for the basketball, the games of chess, and the conversations. You two guys were great." He gave each of us one more big, heartfelt hug, and stepped out the door.

I knew I'd never see him again.

Chapter 22

Wellington

We did party big time that night in the local club. Another Vietnamese band was playing American pop tunes, mangling the lyrics, but we didn't care. We sang along, getting drunker as the night went on. When drunk, I would sometimes express my evolving view of the war, explaining to anyone who would listen what I had learned. Some started calling me Radical Rob; most still called me Applefuck.

Collins came by my office at the motor pool on the day he left. We hugged, saying we would keep in touch, knowing we probably wouldn't. Before we said our final goodbyes, Collins told me, "App, your story connects with what I had learned before about this war. I think your Mr. Nguyen is right; we don't have the hearts and minds of the people. In the office with the colonel I've heard we're using chemical weapons against the Vietnamese people and their villages. We're destroying forests and burning whole communities. We're doing a horrible thing here." He looked tired as he went on, "I don't know if I'll be able to serve out my term. Chicago is going to be a red-hot place soon, App.

The Democratic Convention is there this summer, I don't think I can sit on the sidelines. There's much I can confirm about this war that's only whispered about. America is doing evil here, they've been doing evil with my people from the beginning. I can't stand with evil anymore, App."

"Come on, Collins. I can't even imagine going there, my man. It means jail time. You'll be classified a deserter. You'll be hunted down." I put my arm on his shoulder. "You have your whole life in front of you. You'll have a month of leave time to think about it. Your mom and dad will help. Tell people the truth, but don't let this war ruin your life."

We hugged, then I stood back looking at my friend. "You know, Collins, I've known you for seven months. I don't even know your first name. What is it?"

"It's Demetrius, App. I just learned yours last night, Rob. Short for Robert, right?" I nodded. "Well, Radical Rob, you keep working on these guys. They're the pawns here, you've made yourself a King. Use that power, use your knowledge, spread the word. Stay out of trouble, but don't let the lie they're telling be the final word. You've been a great friend, App. Stay cool, man!"

"You, too, Demetrius, I've learned a lot from you, my brother. Let them know what's going on here. Do your time, keep whatever freedom you still have, then join the movement." We hugged each other hard, not wanting to let go.

Romanasky walked in soon after Demetrius left. "Got some parts that should be in at the depot, then heading to Club 11. Maybe somebody has taken us up on our offer of a party," he said, winking. "I know some guys who would want to trade for some of those items. It could be well worth our efforts."

"On it, J.R. They have those little tacos you like at 11. Good use of the burgers we've supplied. Where did you get those taco shells?"

"Found a mama-san in Bien Hoa. They're not real tortillas like in California; they're made out of rice. But they look like little flour tortillas. Damn, Apple, let's get going. I'm hungry already."

J.R. had cases of beer and soda and an assortment of items in the back of the 448 truck to trade with the parts depot guys. I could tell by their smiles and happy eyes how delighted they were to see him when we pulled in. He passed out the cases and items to guys excited to get them, then started collecting the parts on his list. I signed the paperwork, then organized them in my folder. Romanasky said his goodbyes after writing down a few requests for things only he seemed able to get, then we drove the dusty road to Club 11.

Inside the dark club only a few soldiers sat at the twenty or so tables, while a few others hovered at the long wooden bar. I pulled out a stool and smiled at Sergeant Benson when he grabbed my bottle of Chivas Regal and placed it in front of me with a glass of ice.

"There was a corporal from the 25th Infantry looking for you, App. Said he might be in later today. A guy named Howard. He said you guys talked in here a couple of weeks ago."

"Thanks, Sarge. Romanasky and I will be here most of the afternoon. Send him my way if you see him."

Corporal Howard was one of the guys we'd talked to about filling a footlocker with guns.

Romanasky had been making the rounds bullshitting with guys at the tables. When he pulled up a stool next to me, I leaned forwarded, "Sarge said Corporal Howard from the 25th was looking for us. I think we might have to be throwing somebody a party soon."

"No shit. We'll have to check that out. See if he has anything worth a party."

"Ya know, J.R., I've been thinking that it might be easier to take a couple of deuce-and-a-halfs to their location, pick them up, then take them to our motor pool where we have the party most Sundays. We won't need to deliver the stuff, we can have the party right there."

"Excellent idea, Apple, it'll look like our every Sunday party, no questions asked. I'll run that by him when I check out his stock."

"Wait, is that him walking in?"

I waved to the sarge for another glass with ice as Corporal Howard pulled out the stool next to me. Romanasky moved to sit to his right.

"Did you find anything of value in your last deployment?" I asked while pouring him some Chivas over ice.

"Yeah, App, we raided a bunch of tunnels and found a lot of stuff you might be interested in."

"Like what?" Romanasky asked.

"We got some old Colts; some are Commanders. We have a bunch of M1917s that Charlie uses, plus a couple of Brownings, some Smith & Wesson 15s and

12s - also a couple of Hush Puppies. Come out and take a look. I got the box in the jeep outside."

"Take a look, J.R. I don't know shit about guns. Go see if they're worth it."

"Got it, App. I'll check this out. Okay, Howard, let's go see what ya got."

As they walked out the door, a big man entered forcing both Romanasky and Howard to quickly step aside. J.R. glanced back at me before he left. The guy looked familiar, like I'd seen his face before, but couldn't remember where. Checking out his rank I noticed something I'd never seen. He had three stripes up and three down like the Top, but unlike the Top, he had a star in the middle, making him a sergeant major. Now I recognized the face. It was Sergeant Major Wellington, the first person in the Army to ever wear that patch.

He stood there for a bit, looked around and squinted to adjust to the dark. His erect posture suggested a man in charge of the situation. When he looked in the direction of the bar, he saw Sergeant Benson grab a bar towel to wipe his hands dry. A second later, he moved down the bar and shook hands.

Wellington shook it firmly, looking Benson in the eyes.

While they stood there talking, Benson cleaned the bar with the rag. I tried to watch them without being obvious, but glanced in their direction every so often. I noticed Benson nodding in my direction. Wellington looked my way. I stopped staring, focused on the bottles of booze on the shelves behind the bar.

I sensed the sergeant major slowly moving towards me. When he stopped within a yard, I risked a glance at him. When he looked down at me, I couldn't think of anything to say, but felt I had to say something to acknowledge the great man. "Good afternoon, Sergeant Major," I said forcing a smile to hide my nervousness.

"Good afternoon, Specialist, I was just talking to Sergeant Benson about you. He tells me you're responsible for his business expanding into selling bar food." He glared at me.

"Yes, I suppose so, Sergeant Major."

"Suppose so? Is that a yes or no?" he asked in a deep commanding voice.

"Then that would be a yes, Sergeant Major," I answered, trying not to be intimidated, but knew my voice sounded anything but commanding. He waited several seconds, long enough for me to ask, "Would the Sergeant Major care for a drink?"

"I don't drink until after eighteen hundred hours, Specialist."

I glanced at my watch and saw it was 4:30, then took another sip of Chivas anyway.

"How is it that you're able to supply Sergeant Benson with these additional food items?"

"Through trades, Sergeant Major."

"Trades?"

"Yes, you know how the Quartermaster Corps works, things are done through trades. I'm trading to get the food items. I trade with Sergeant Benson."

"And what are you getting from Sergeant Benson?" his eyes narrowed with curiosity.

I paused before answering, wondering what his reaction would be when I responded.

"I only asked to be the King. Free whiskey and free food seems like a good enough deal to me."

Wellington nodded and smiled when he heard this, then he looked away for a bit, before facing me again.

"Did you know that these clubs were my idea?"

"I've heard that, yes."

While he spoke, out of the corner of my eye, I glanced at Romanasky walking in.

"I look at each one of these clubs as my enterprise, and make sure they're able to stand alone providing a service for the men who are fighting this war." He paused. I took another sip. "Do you know why we're fighting this war, son?"

Though I knew many reasons why we were fighting, I didn't feel comfortable telling him what I thought, then after a deep breath finally spoke. "I listened to the President. I also listened to a priest before I was deployed. We're fighting against communism, Sergeant Major."

He nodded. "Yes, but what are we fighting for Appenzeller?" he asked, glancing at my name above my left pocket.

Feeling on the spot, I shrugged. There was no way I wanted to get into a debate with the most highly ranked noncommissioned officer in the entire U.S. Army.

Finally he said, "We're fighting for the free enterprise system. Do you know what that is?"

Again I shrugged, pausing, "I don't know that much about economics. I assume it's the opposite of communism."

"It's more than that. It's the freedom they talk about in the Declaration of Independence. We're fighting for that freedom. The freedom to make something and sell it. The freedom to have an idea and sell it. It's the freedom to do business, to make business with little or no interference. The communists want to tell people how their lives and businesses should be run. We're fighting so that we can run our businesses ourselves with no government intervention. These clubs are a business, Appenzeller, they're my business." He paused and fixed his eyes on mine to make sure he had my attention.

He did.

"In America we should be free to make whatever profit we want. That's what we're fighting for. Our rights in America are individual rights. The individual is free to say what he wants, to publish what he wants, and to make as much money as he wants. We're fighting for the free enterprise system. You are part of my system now. I don't know that being the King is part of that system. It galls me that you don't want to make a profit. I don't believe it. You are doing something, Appenzeller, to make some kind of profit. It might not be here, but you have your finger in some kind of pie."

He paused, having a thought. "And I don't care, because we should have every right to participate in the system that we're here protecting and fighting for. Do you understand that?"

Realizing a shrug wouldn't be the right answer, I looked him in the eye and said, "I do, Sergeant Major. That was well said and has put things into perspective. I'm sure you're doing well in this enterprise. I know that the soldiers are much happier because you're providing this business for them. I thank you on behalf of all the soldiers who get to use this club."

Wellington smiled and seemed satisfied with my answer, then he slowly walked back to the end of the bar. Sergeant Benson just returned after delivering a huge plate load of tacos to Romanasky and Howard's table. After Wellington shook hands with Benson, he slowly walked toward the door, but before leaving, he gave me a slight smile and nod. I nodded and smiled back.

After he left, Romanasky waved me over. I grabbed my glass and the bottle to join them, but before I sat down, he said, "Tell Benson we're going to need a couple more plates of these little tacos, Apple. Have some; they're really good."

I went back to the bar where Benson stood with his towel. His scrunched eyebrows showed concern. "What was that all about with the sergeant major, App? He grilled me on where I was getting the food. He's one controlling son of a bitch. I had to tell him it was you."

"No problem, Sarge, he gave me a lecture about why we're fighting this war in Vietnam. Turns out we're fighting for his right to operate this little enterprise you guys have running here," I said laughing. "By the way, Romanasky wants a couple more plates of tacos, I think he's going for a record."

"Goddamn, App, I think I might be on the short end of the stick on the deal we made. Fucking Romanasky can eat like a horse."

"Oh well, you made the deal, Sarge. According to Wellington, our being able to make that deal is why we're fighting this war," I said before stuffing half a taco into my mouth.

I took the huge plate of tacos over to Romanasky and Howard. "So how's it look, J.R.? Do we have a deal?"

"He's got enough to qualify for a party. There's a Colt Commander I want for myself. Has a holster and everything. I'll be the baddest sumbitch on Long Binh," Romanasky said in a bad Southern drawl.

"Yeah, J.R. We be some bad sumbitches," I said in an equally bad drawl, while grabbing a taco, and pouring myself another Chivas Regal.

We loaded the footlocker filled with weapons onto my truck, then, after covering it with truck parts, returned to the motor pool, and hid the footlocker behind the 448 bay. After parking the truck, we walked back to my room.

JR was concerned about my long conversation with Sgt Major Wellington. I assured him that he was not a problem and gave us permission to supply steaks and burgers. McNamara and Dunphy showed up and we died laughing because Dunphy was out of Polident and was without his choppers. McNamara did some of his best Cronkite and Huntley making us laugh at Dunphy's ugly face. Chaves showed up, too, and the room was pretty crowded when our new Company Commander, Lieutenant Weber, walked in with North. He loved my room and wanted to know how to get an air conditioner. Suddenly inspired, I told him I could get him one if he could get me an emergency leave. When he asked why, I told him I had blue balls because I had been three months away from Alexandra, then I took a deep breath, gathered my nerve, and said he could find out how to get that leave if he talked to North. I knew North was pissed off at me for asking, but grimly said, "Yes I will show him how to get it done." Then he left scowling while the lieutenant looked happy about getting an air conditioner. After they left, the boys died laughing, slapping their thighs and my back at my blue balls line and saluted me as the King of the REMFs for finagling my seven day emergency leave. Afterward we got pretty drunk at the local club, and I returned to my room happy that I somehow had manipulated myself into living such a cool life in the middle of a war and soon I'd be in Hawaii making passionate love to my amazing wife.

PART FOUR

Losing Faith

Chapter 23

North

Major hangover the next morning. Pain around the temples, eyes not wanting to focus, and when they did, I saw that the little guy was still building his fort in the corner of my room capturing anything flying by. Though I loved that spider, when I saw a sac full of eggs in a section of his web, I was certain I didn't want hundreds of the little guys climbing on my bed. I would have to do something about that.

I leaned over, looked below, saw Chaves waking up, and hoped he would put on the coffee. I still had eggs. Romanasky said he had ordered a toaster from one of his many contacts. "Freddie, time to get up, my man. We got trucks going out in a half hour. They have to be dispatched, and guess what? You're the dispatcher. So haul yourself out of that bed!"

"You're cruel, App. My head hurts."

"I wonder why? Everybody who was in that club last night has to be hurting. Now let's get going." I said, and rolled out of my top bunk. I made my bed Army-tight, insisting that Chaves do the same. I brewed coffee and made some scrambled eggs. We ate quickly, dressed, and, when heading out the door, saw North standing in his doorway. He didn't look happy, but then again, he never looked happy.

"Hey there, North, sorry about yesterday, man. I didn't mean to put you on the spot with the new CO."

"I need to talk to you, App." He nodded his head toward his room inviting me to follow.

Oh, shit, I thought. *North is going to read me the riot act.* "Chaves, get on down to the motor pool and start dispatching those trucks. Tell the new warrant officer I'll be there in a few minutes."

When he took off, I followed North into his room. "Like I said, North, I'm sorry about what happened yesterday."

He looked at me with his cold blue eyes. "Don't sweat that, App. I'll get you your emergency leave. It may not be for a month, but I'll make sure the CO gets it done. I'll have him fill out the paperwork, so you can get him his air conditioner."

"Thanks, North, I can't wait to see the wife again," I said, looking around his room. Compared to my room, it was spartan: standard issue bed, footlocker and wall locker. Aside from a small bookshelf, his only frill was the air conditioner in the window, everything else was army issue. Because he kept his door closed with a padlock so no one could get in, this was my first time seeing his room.

"You like to read, don't you, App?" he said, pointing at the book-shelf. There were about twenty books, but five were tied together with twine. He grabbed that bundle, and started un-tying them. He looked at me with pierc-ing, serious eyes, slightly narrowed. "These are my favorites," he said toss-ing me one, a western by Louis L'Amour with a guy on a white horse on the cover.

"I've never read any Louis L'Amour, but I hear his books are pret-ty good."

"Look inside," North said, flatly, his eyes staring blankly at the book, then at me.

I thumbed through it and noticed that he had a green bookmark on almost every page. When I stopped and looked at one, I was startled to see that it was a crisp fifty-dollar bill. On an-other page was a hundred-dollar bill. I had only seen a few of them in my life. Looking further, the book was filled with fifties, hundreds, and twenties.

"All of the books in that bundle have the same bookmarks."North spoke, calmly.

"What the fuck, North? How did you get money like this? How did you get greenbacks? How much is in here?" These bewildered questions poured out of me.

"I'm gonna tell you something, App, that I've told to no one on this post. You can't tell a single person about it. If you do, I can't protect you. The two people I work with, the Top Kick and Bentley, will kill you if they think you're a rat."

Oh shit, I gulped, knowing those two were big treacherous men, and I had little doubt that North was telling the truth. I listened, unable to believe what I was hearing, while North continued.

"I arrived in-country three months before you. The 448 was in Vung Tau running Class I from Saigon Harbor. Trucks would pick up Class I products like they do now on Long Binh. Class I was run by a staff sergeant. He had three sergeants under him. They were dealing with the local black market in Vung Tau. They were making money, but stupid about it; way too obvious.

"The Top and Bentley arrived at the same time as me. They found out what was going on and could see that those sergeants were going to get popped. Sure enough, CID came down in a storm early one morning and everyone was detained. The sergeants were arrested. They ratted on everyone involved. Thirty guys went to Long Binh Jail. Some are still in there. The sergeants are in Leavenworth."

I gulped again. I was getting the answer to my final question. It wasn't something I wanted to hear. North went on.

"When we arrived in Long Binh, Bentley took over Class I. Top hadn't been connected to the guys in Vung Tau, so he escaped the shit-storm. We laid low for a while. I did some research in Bien Hoa and Saigon. I looked for some secure connections and found a group in Bien Hoa who would pay top dollar for items in Class I. They were trustworthy - ran street markets in Bien Hoa and Saigon and had police protection. They were smart business guys." He paused again, looking at me to make sure I was following his story. I was; but I also wondered why he was telling me this.

"I got with Bentley and we worked on a plan that would be foolproof, that wouldn't raise suspicion. Bentley recruited black guys for his yard. He could trust them. They wouldn't be rats. He told them not to make any small time deals. Green almost got the shit kicked out of him for dealing with you and Romanasky. Bentley let it slide. He knew Wellington had his part covered. So we let Green make those deals."

Again I gulped, shaking my head at what I heard, then asked. "So Bentley and Top both know about my set-up with the clubs?"

"Of course they do. Green would be dead right now if he didn't have permission. They kind of liked the idea. Bentley likes you. Says you can hit an outside jumper."

"No shit. So, I'm kind of wrapped up in this deal?"

"You're on the list, App, and now you know it, which means you have to keep your shit on low profile. We can't do anything to bring in CID. The last guys did, and now they're doing hard time in LBJ."

Holy fucking shit! I thought.

North continued. "We started doing small deliveries, looking over our shoulders to see if anyone was watching. Our only problem was the guys in Class I who were throwing piasters around. Bentley has tried to keep control of that. We watch any new guy in the outfit closely. If there was any hint they might be CID, they're shipped out, or there would be an accident." He paused again to make sure I understood his meaning and saw by my attentive eyes that I did.

"We watch the COs. I keep close tabs on them. If they get at all suspicious, out they go. I have contacts in General Westmorland's office. If they want their steaks and lobsters, they call me to see that they are not lost in shipment. We pay one of the clerks big money to be our eyes and ears."

When he paused, I reached into my right pocket for my pack of Tareytons and flicked out a cigarette offering it to North. He took it. Grabbing another, I pulled out my lighter, and noticing my hand shaking a bit, gave us both some flame. North took a big drag, blew some smoke out through his nose and continued his conversation.

"After Tet, we started expanding our operation. With all the new companies there was no way to keep tabs on which truck was delivering to which outfit. We started doing bigger deals. Truckloads with two pallets of stuff. Then two to three trucks. We did one delivery using ten trucks. That was a bit risky, but Bentley and I split thirty-five thousand in Piasters and MPC on that deal."

"What are you selling?" I asked, suddenly realizing the size of the operation, and the consequences of knowing about it made me tremble, and my mouth go dry. *This isn't good. This is dangerous.* "Most anything that we have in Class 1 is salable on the black market - canned fruit, canned vegetables, canned meat, even Spam has its own market. Raisins are huge, a handful in a baggie goes for ten piasters on the Saigon black market. We store them in number ten cans, ten cans in a case, twenty-four cases on a pallet, two pallets on a deuce-and-a-half. That deal alone gets eighteen thousand in piasters and MPC. There's a huge demand for food in Saigon and Bien Hoa, and App, we have the supply."

"Where did you get the greenbacks?" I asked, without thinking.

"Now that's my little secret, not even Top or Bentley knows about the greenbacks. I found a guy in Saigon who does black market money. He drives a hard bargain. He knows the money is dirty, but he has cover and protection. It costs me over sixty cents on the dollar, but it's worth it. You can only declare ten thousand bucks when you leave. Any more could get you arrested. I have a plan for getting the money back to Gary, Indiana where I live. That's why I took my leave in the

Philippines. It'll work; I have it covered."

"So why are you telling me this? It's not something I need to know about."

"I'm getting short, App. Out of here in two months. I'm tired of taking the risk, even though I have everything covered. I need to pass the business on to someone. I've looked at everyone in the company. You're the only one who's smart enough and has a job that could make a good cover for going back and forth to Bien Hoa to make the deals and collect the money. I want to turn this over to you, App. It's foolproof. We've kept under the radar. You can make a shitload of money."

Dumbfounded, my dazed head spinning from North telling me about the thirty guys in LBJ and Leavenworth, then he tells me that he's the head of the new cartel, and next, he offers to pass the operation on to me? *Holy shit!* Was all I could think.

North kept staring at me with that grim, determined look that seemed tattooed on his face, waiting for an answer I didn't have.

"Who are these guys you trade with in Bien Hoa?" I asked, trying to waste time so I could think.

"I told you that, App. They're guys who are running the Saigon and Bien Hoa black markets."

"But, North, are you sure of that? Could the food be going to the VC?"

He stared at me, blue eyes deep, black pupils tiny. "We can't be sure of anything in life, App." He paused. "I know this, they pay me, and they pay me well. I'm going back to Gary, Indiana a rich nineteen-year-old man. I'll prosper, get married and have kids, have a house and a business. I'm offering you the same deal, App. This is the American dream. It's your chance to make that dream come true."

Pictures were jumping in and out of my brain. Alexandra and me in our own house with lots of money to spend. I wanted to be rich. I wanted the American dream. I also saw myself in a cell in Long Binh Jail with murderers and thugs, getting the shit kicked out of me every day. I saw the shame of being called a traitor for selling food to the enemy. I did not like this war, in fact, I hated it, but I was not a traitor. No matter what North said the risk was too high.

"Well, App, you have to decide. Are you going to take this once-in-a-lifetime opportunity? It's foolproof, I tell ya. No way to get caught. I have over a hundred thousand bucks in those books. That could be yours, too."

I thought of my dad, mom, and Alexandra. As much as North said it was foolproof, it was a huge risk. Even more than that, it wasn't good. It stinks! It could be selling to the enemy. I could be considered a traitor to my country. I was disgusted by what my country was doing in Vietnam, but I wasn't a traitor.

Finally I said, "I can't do this, North. I appreciate your thinking I'm smart enough to do it, but I can't take that risk. I just want to finish my time here. I want an honorable discharge so I can go back to school and have a family. I just can't take such a huge risk."

North stared at me for a long time and sensed that my mind was made up. Nothing he said would bring about a different answer.

"Well," he said, after a deep sigh. "That's disappointing, App, I told you that I've told this story to no one. I thought I could trust you. I thought you had the smarts to run this thing. I guess I was wrong."

"You can trust me, North. I won't tell a soul… not a soul."

"In my position I can't trust any-body. Do you understand what that means?" The menacing bitter tone of his voice and his cold aggressive eyes staring at me made me wonder if I was going to fight him right here, right now. My emotions turned from fear and apprehension to anger.

"I told you that you can trust me. I'm a man of my word. "I paused, grit-ting my teeth, to think some more. "You can trust me, North. You said that I was already on your list, whatever and wherever that list is. Now that I think about it, you've been using my trucks for your black market business. I want my cut of that business. Give me a hun-dred bucks in an envelope for every truck that goes out. That way, you'll know I won't ever rat on you. Is that a deal?" I spoke in a determined, aggres-sive tone that surprised me: a voice I hoped would surprise and shock North as well.

North grabbed the book out of my hand, put it with the others, and retied the twine. "I think you're turn-ing down the best opportunity in your life to make big money, App. I'll give you your money for your trucks. You'll be on the list - not as a King, but as a pawn."

After putting the books back on the shelf, he opened the door. I stepped out into what seemed like the freshest air I had ever breathed, and watched him lock up his room with all that money inside. He gazed coldly into my eyes one more time, I saw the bitter frustration of a man used to getting what he wanted. Without another word, he walked away in one direction, while I went in the other.

Chapter 24

Cognitive Dissonance

After my confrontation with North, I made the long dusty walk to the motor pool with a heavy, anguished heart, my mind spinning with confused, complex emotions. I now knew that the 448 was a criminal enterprise, and I was a part of the ugly picture. I was on the list. Thirty people had been arrested in Vung Tau, and I was part of the new thirty. These thoughts filled me with over-whelming dread that made me tremble. It seemed inevitable that I'd be caught trading guns, or getting paid for dis-patching black market trucks.

These activities were against everything I believed in. I believed I was an ethical person able to choose right over wrong. I was choosing wrong. Somewhere along the line I had fallen into an ethical trap. I had the guns hidden in a container behind the 448 mechanics' bay. Soon piasters and MPC would arrive in envelopes with my name on it.

I had thoughts that frightened me even more. Thoughts about what I should be doing. *You should report this,* a voice in my head lectured me. It was the Irish voice of Father O'Sullivan. *This is a crime, Robbie. These people are stealing Army food and trading it to people who may be working with the enemy. This is treason. You're aiding and abetting the enemy!*

The idea of doing the right thing brought up the real and immediate threat of Top and Bentley. They had eyes and ears in Abrams' office. If word got around that I was a rat, I wouldn't get to see how long I could last in LBJ. I'd be dead. Mom, Dad, and Alexandra would get a letter about how I was accidentally killed in the line of duty.

Entering the motor pool, I no longer felt the pride and joy I'd felt for having made this place something more than it was. The colonel gave me a combat advancement in rank because of the work I'd done here. I looked at the parts rooms as I did every day; neat and organized, everything in its place. The mechanics were busy doing their work, gabbing to each other about this and that, mainly the ins and outs of how to keep the vehicles running. They were the workhorses. They wouldn't make Soldier of the Month, get an R&R to Vung Tau or go on an emergency leave to Hawaii. I would. Once proud of that, now I was a guilty participant in a criminal enterprise.

I stepped onto the porch in front of my office, and turned to look at the motor pool that once filled me with pride, but now filled me with guilt and paranoia. Who out there was CID? Who was watching me? I was such an open book. Everyone knew Romanasky and I could trade for anything. Surely the word was out about the guns. They knew about the black market, but not like I did. Still they knew it was going on. The Class I guys were too obvious, and not only were they destined to go down, I would go down with them.

When I stepped into my office, Mr. Nguyen was sweeping dust around. He stared at me intently for a few seconds with his dark, narrow eyes that radiated intelligence.

"What wrong, Mr. App?"

He wasn't quite five feet tall with his long, white hair, a wispy bit of a white mustache, and a long, braided white beard that extended from his chin to his chest. His English had improved over the last four months he'd been moving dust in my office. We could have conversations.

"I don't know, Mr. Nguyen, but my mind isn't at rest. I have many conflicting thoughts; difficult thoughts, troubling thoughts. Thoughts that are making me feel bad."

His soft brown eyes reflected compassion. Compassion for me, and gratitude for helping him provide for his family with a few extra piasters.

"If you don't like thoughts, change them," he said thoughtfully. "Choose better thoughts, thoughts that make you feel good, not bad."

It sounded so easy coming from this wise old man.

"But that's hard, Mr. Nguyen, I've found out about things that could change my life in an awful way. I'm having a difficult time choosing the right thing to do. I don't have a moral compass anymore. I'm no longer Catholic, no longer Christian. Without a religion to guide me, I don't know where I'm going. Do you understand that?"

He looked at me with a caring expression in his narrow dark eyes "To change mind not too hard, Mr. App. No one but you control mind. Your thoughts are yours to choose. Don't think about bad things until they happen. It is waste of time, only makes you feel bad. You can understand this; you are smart man."

"I wish it was that easy, Mr. Nguyen. I really do."

"Control thoughts, Mr. App. Choose peace of mind. Bad things happen, bad things not happen. Your thoughts not make things happen, or not happen. Choose good thoughts, Mr. App. You are good man."

He spoke with such conviction and sincerity that I was moved by his words. Hearing that I was a good man from this thoughtful man, helped me realize he was right. I was making myself feel bad about something that may never happen. I was learning a new way of thinking from Mr. Nguyen.

"Thank you for these words of wisdom, Mr. Nguyen. I've lost my religion. I believe the middle path is a good way for people to behave. I'll work on having wholesome thought and doing good work. That's difficult when I realize the horror that my country has brought down on your people. America is not doing good work here. It breaks my heart to be a part of that."

"America wrong for being here, for killing Vietnam people, and not letting Vietnam people choose leader." He shook his head from side to side revealing his disapproval. He spoke harshly, bitterly and his dark eyes looked fierce and darker. This was the first angry face he allowed me to see.

"Who would you choose, Mr. Nguyen?"

He pondered the question, or was it my reaction to his answer. He took the risk. "Ho Chi Minh good man, Mr. App. He only want good things for Vietnam people. He want freedom for Vietnam people. He want life to be more fair for all Vietnam people. He want only that America leave us alone. Ho not like China. China too big, China has bad history with Vietnam people. Ho Chi Minh follows middle path. He's not Buddhist, but not against Buddhism or Christians. He thinks right for people to decide what to believe."

"Do most South Vietnamese people feel the same as you, Mr. Nguyen?"

"There is only one Vietnam; no South, no North just one Vietnam. America want South Vietnam. Catholic Church want South Vietnam. Vietnam people want one Vietnam with Ho Chi Minh as leader."

I could see the truth in this. The DMZ wasn't Ho Chi Minh's idea. He was told there would be a free election. It was the idea of John Foster Dulles and his Catholic American allies. Ho Chi Minh defeated the Japanese and the French. He was determined to defeat the world's greatest superpower, the United States.

Still holding his broom, Mr. Nguyen continued. "Most of world want U.S. to stop this war. You must read New Year letter from Ho Chi Minh to people who support Vietnam. He is good man, wants Vietnam to be free." He pulled out a piece of paper. His block printing in English was under the Vietnamese words. "Read out loud, Mr. App. I love words of Ho Chi Minh."

I read: *"On the occasion of 1968 New Year, I wish you a Happy New Year. As you know there are no Vietnamese coming to make trouble in the United States. Yet there are over half a million U. S. GIs coming to South Vietnam along with 70,000 puppet and allied troops to massacre Vietnamese people, to burn and destroy Vietnamese villages and cities.*

In North Vietnam, thousands of U.S. planes have dropped over 800,000 tons of bombs, destroying schools, churches, hospitals, dikes, and populated areas.

The U.S. government forces thousands and thousands of American youth to die and be wounded uselessly on battlefields in Vietnam.

For its war in Vietnam, the U.S. government wastes each year tens of billions dollars, the money of American people's sweat and tears.

In brief, the U.S. aggressors not only do crime against Vietnam, but also cause death and harm as well as dishonor of the U.S.

You are striving to struggle to demand that the U.S. stop its aggressive war in Vietnam, both to protect and thus you are defending the just cause and supporting us.

For the independence, freedom, and unification of our motherland, for our aspirations to live peacefully with all the nations of the world, including the U.S., the whole Vietnamese people are unanimously determined to fight against the U.S. imperialists. We are supported by friends all over the world.

Our victory is certain, and yours is, too.

Thank you all for supporting Vietnam.

Best Wishes,

Ho Chi Minh."

I read the words slowly aloud, then I read them again to myself trying to absorb the thoughts expressed by Ho Chi Minh. I looked over at Mr. Nguyen. He had tears in his eyes.

"Ho Chi Minh good man," he stated in a low, sincere voice that expressed his reverence and touched me deeply.

How could I disagree?

Chapter 25

Losing Faith in My Country

I told Romanasky I had some work to do when he asked me to go on a parts run. I accomplished it in silence, still lost in the many thoughts competing for time in my head. As much as I wanted to choose my thoughts as Mr. Nguyen suggested, some frightened, worried thoughts managed to dominate my thinking. By mid-afternoon I was a total wreck about being on the list, ending up in LBJ, when Mr. Nguyen spoke.

"Mr. App, you still look like your thoughts are hurting you."

"Sorry, Mr. Nguyen, I just can't get these thoughts out of my head. I'm from a family of worriers. I've seen my mom and dad worry about things. It's natural for me to be worried, to think about horrible things that might happen. It's hard for me not to worry."

"Not say it easy, Mr. App. Must rest mind, learn to think about nothing. That is meditation. Must do something to take mind away from thoughts. Mr. App, you have eaten Vietnam food?"

"No, Mr, Nguyen, I haven't. I haven't had a chance to try it. I've only been to Saigon once and Bien Hoa a few times. So, no, I haven't tasted Vietnamese food."

"Vietnam food good, you must come with me to my house to eat Vietnam food. You come tonight."

"I would love to do that, Mr. Nguyen. I'm free this evening. I can give you a ride home. Where do you live?"

"I live Bien Hoa." He hesitated before asking, "Mr. App, you have other clothes?"

"Yes, Mr. Nguyen, I have some civilian clothes. Why?"

"Uniform will frighten children."

"I didn't know you had children, Mr. Nguyen."

"Not children, grandchildren."

"Okay. Romanasky should be back in an hour or so. I'll change out of my uniform, come back and pick you up."

Though he didn't smile, I loved the light twinkle in his eyes.

After taking a shower and dressing in a pair of khaki pants and madras shirt, I walked back to the motor pool trying to keep my penny loafers from getting too dusty. Romanasky and the Class IV parts clerk were taking things out, organizing them.

"J.R., when the truck is unloaded, I need to use it, okay?"

"Of course, Apple, it's your truck," he said laughing.

J.R. always seemed ready to laugh at most anything, which is why so many people liked him. "What ya got going?"

"I'm giving Mr. Nguyen a ride home. We're going to have dinner together."

"Really? Well, have a good time. That Mr. Nguyen doesn't look like a party animal to me," he said laughing again.

"It should be a cool cultural experience, J.R. Can you be finished in a half hour or so?"

"No problem, Apple, I'll park it in front of the office when I'm done."

In my office, Mr. Nguyen set his broom in the corner while I went to my desk.

"The truck will be ready in a couple minutes, Mr. Nguyen,"

He nodded with a slight bow.

I put a few papers in their correct folders, then filed them in the cabinets. Soon the 448 truck came to a stop in front of the office, and seconds later, Romanasky tossed me the keys. "Now you two don't party too hearty!" he said with a big smile.

We left the office and rode in silence to the gate where a MP I knew from the club stood with his M16 at his side.

"What's up with the civvies, App?"

"I'm going with my friend Mr. Nguyen, Jenson. We're having dinner at his place."

His eyes narrowed, and he cocked his head to the side at the words. "my friend."

"You be careful out there, App!" he said, as he waved us through.

Once outside the gate, Mr. Nguyen motioned with his right hand that I should turn right onto Highway One.

It had been four months since the Tet Offensive. We anticipated a full-on charge by the North Vietnamese army and heard they had a secret road through Cambodia bringing men and supplies. We had five hundred thousand troops in-country waiting for the attack, which never came. In fact, we'd had four months of relative quiet. Our troops were still on maneuvers destroying Vietcong held villages, using napalm and Agent Orange to destroy forests and rice paddies, but no counterattack ever came. I felt secure driving with Mr. Nguyen to his house.

Bien Hoa looked like a thriving community as we drove past two and three-story buildings standing close to each other, many sharing a common wall. Most had a business on the lower floor. Tiny tables and chairs were set out in front of small restaurants. They looked like they were for children, but adults sat in them, knees bent, spread apart, hands holding chopsticks.

We found a place to park in front of a building with caskets displayed out front, and many more stacked on top of each other in the back. Beautiful caskets made of shiny wood, some with ornate designs, sat out in the open. I stood by the truck while Mr. Nguyen crossed the street and disappeared inside a small shop where there were baskets of fruit and vegetables out front.

Looking more closely into the casket shop, I saw an old lady in a dark corner squatting by a small table with what appeared to be light brown dried herbs. Moving closer, I noticed she was taking tobacco out of a pack of Winstons and piling it on the table. The carton was off to the side. Beside her sat a duffel bag filled with weed that I could smell from yards away.

After Mr. Nguyen returned with a bag of groceries, he led the way to a narrow wooden staircase where we walked up two flights of stairs, then stopped in front of a door with a small Buddhist icon nailed to it. He kicked off his sandals then glanced down at my shoes. When I saw a pile of sandals to the right of the door in all shapes and sizes, I tossed my penny loafers into the pile.

He opened the door into a deep gloom. I realized it was darker than it should be, because I still had on my Ray-Bans. When I took them off, I saw a sofa on the right with two children who looked to be six or seven. A large round table sat in front of a window facing another building in back of the house. The table was set with six wooden chairs surrounding it.

Prominently placed along the back wall was a shrine with a large-bellied smiling Buddha carved from dark brown wood in the center. Red, yellow and purple flowers were draped around him. The sweet aroma of incense and candles filled the room with its wonderful sweet fragrance. Small plates of food were placed in front of him along with cups of brightly colored tea. Above the

Buddha was a picture of a serious young man with an intense determined look.

I eased closer to the little altar, and saw the young man resembled Mr. Nguyen, who now stood beside me looking at the photograph with his brow wrinkled and sad, narrow eyes. He had given the bag of groceries to the young woman standing with a nine or ten-year-old girl next to her.

"Who is that, Mr. Nguyen?"

"He my son, Mr. App. He was soldier for Vietcong. He killed by U.S two years." He bowed his head, and so did I. After a minute or so of silence, he took a long match and lit another candle. I swallowed the anguished pain that I felt rising. I was a U.S. soldier, my people had killed his son, the young woman's husband, and the father of these children. *Holy shit*, I muttered to myself.

We turned around, and speaking in Vietnamese, he called his family together. They bowed their heads in agreement at whatever he was saying. He introduced each child using names that I couldn't pronounce and would soon forget. They each stepped forward when introduced, put their prayer hands under their chins bowing respectfully. I bowed to the little boy who looked intently into my eyes. I smiled and also made prayer hands, then turned to the little girl whose brown eyes stared deep into my blue eyes as if peering into my soul. Puzzled, I looked at Mr. Nguyen.

"It is the eyes, Mr. App. They are blue. They have not seen blue eyes." I bowed to them, and, smiling, opened my eyes wide, so they could see them even better.

We moved toward the table. The young woman pulled out a chair for me to the right of Mr. Nguyen. She placed a bowl of soup in front of me with noodles and bits of fish in the broth, and leaves that gave off a delightful aroma. When we all had soup in front of us, Mr. Nguyen very formally switched his bowl with mine. In that bowl was a fish head with dead eyes looking at me. I figured this was a form of respect. I bowed to Mr. Nguyen making prayer hands. He did the same, while the whole family nodded with smiles of approval.

I glanced at the children, noting they used chopsticks to pull the noodles out of the broth, while using big spoons to sip the soup. I picked up the chopsticks beside my plate. Peeking at me, the kids were ready to laugh at my attempt to use chopsticks for the first time. Fortunately, I had given lessons to patrons on how to use chopsticks when I was a busboy at the Trade Winds restaurant.

I prepared the chopsticks by moving the wooden sticks quickly back and forth as if sharpening them, placing them on my middle finger and pointer with my thumb holding them tightly. I bounced the tips on the table to make sure they were equal. Using all the dexterity learned at the Trade Winds, I gouged the fish eye out, squeezed it, and pulled it out of the broth, letting it hang above the soup bowl. All were watching as I slowly lowered my head bringing the eye up to my mouth, sucked it in, and, moving it with my tongue to my back molars, crushed it with one big bite. Suddenly, an oozing jelly like substance exploded into my mouth that tasted like fish, but didn't feel like fish.

Everyone in the family smiled. Mr. Nguyen bobbed his head up and down as if I had passed some kind of test. I stuffed noodles, and vegetables into my mouth, laboriously scraping meat off the fish's head. I gouged the second eye out, confidently reaching for it with my chopsticks, pulling it out of the broth. Again all eyes were on me. While lifting it toward my mouth, the eye suddenly slipped out from between the sticks and flew halfway across the table, causing the children to laugh.

Their mother tried to smother her laugh, but the children were delighted with the flying eye. Mr. Nguyen looked at them sternly, but when I started laughing too, he broke into a big smile.

We followed the soup with a course of lightly cooked vegetables served over rice with a tangy sauce. Pieces of grilled chicken were added to the vegetables. It was a wonderfully delicious meal with so many spices that left a delightful aftertaste in my mouth. We drank refreshing water out of metal cups. I was a bit worried about that water having been warned not to drink it, but there was no way I would insult Mr. Nguyen.

The family spoke in quiet tones during dinner. Everyone had a clean plate when they were done. I asked Mr. Nguyen if I could smoke one of my Tareytons. He nodded. I tapped out a cigarette using my lighter. I stood, looking at the clean spartan room more closely, and imagined that the bottom of my socks were still white. The few posters on the wall were mostly political posters featuring Ho Chi Minh. A few framed letters were also on the wall. I pointed to one written in English. "What is this, Mr. Nguyen?"

"It letter from Chairman of World Peace Council."

I leaned closer to read it.

Napalm and toxic gas have been used on the South Vietnam population. The peoples of the world note with repugnance the U.S. government's violation of all principles of international law. They demand an end be put to these barbarous acts. Such an aggression is threatening Southeast Asia as a whole, and peace all over the world. I read the signatures on the bottom, the first one being "Professor J. Bernal, Chairman of the World Peace Council March 1965."

After reading it, I swallowed a deep breath, sickened by the horror we were causing these people. I looked at the happy smiling children helping their mom clean up. That a person like me had taken their father's life with no care for who he had shot awoke in me horrid shameful thoughts that forced me to turn away from the children and their mother. Taking a deep breath, I was glad I was wearing a checkered madras shirt and light tan pants. I would have felt like an ogre if I'd been wearing my uniform.

Several more framed documents hung on the wall. Because the last one was so devastating, I was hesitant to ask their content, but I was curious. A short one under the World Peace Council document caught my attention.

To initiate a war of aggression is not only an international crime, it is the supreme international crime, differing only from other war crimes in that it contains within itself the accumulated evil of the whole.

I knew this Vietnam War was one of aggression. Ho Chi Minh had been promised an election, but instead, the U.S. started this war of aggression against the insurgent army of the Vietcong. I looked below the statement to see who had written this decree. It read: *The judgment of the Nuremberg International Military Tribunal passed on September 30, October 1, 1945, unanimously adopted along with the Nuremberg Charter by the United Nations General Assembly on December 11, 1946"*

I shook my head, ashamed. Here was more confirmation that we were fighting for greed against a country that wanted democracy and equal prosperity. We were fighting a war of aggression, and, to my horror, the world knew it.

I glanced once more at the small altar in front of the picture of Mr. Nguyen's son. Next to the candles and incense burning I saw two little human figurines on the shrine.

"Who do those figurines represent, Mr. Nguyen?"

He looked at them, then back at me. "They American heroes for Vietnam," he said reverently.

I saw little name tags under each. Bending closer, I read the names Norman Morrison and Roger LaPorte. I thought long and hard, but couldn't place these names to any history of the U. S. that I could recall. "I've never heard of these people, Mr. Nguyen. Who are they?"

"They heroes, they burn self to protest war against Vietnam people"

I remembered that someone had used self-immolation in front of Defense Secretary McNamara's window at the Pentagon, but had no idea what his name was, yet here in Vietnam, he and one other were considered heroes, their statues worthy of a place in front of the Buddha.

It had turned dark while we'd been dining and looking around the room at all that was displayed. I thanked Mr. Nguyen and his son's wife for the wonderful meal, then pulled out piasters to give some to the children, who seemed delighted. The rest went to the wife, who at first refused to accept them. I insisted. It was the least I could do. She took them reluctantly. They bowed graciously with prayer hands. I bowed back, hoping I didn't look foolish.

As I drove back weaving in and out of bicycles and motorbikes, I was again flooded with guilt and remorse. How could I have not known about these atrocities that we were doing to these people? How could I stay here and live with myself? Then the usual mental suspects forced their way into my brain: the fear of being arrested for being on the black market list and the gun trading.

The only ray of hope was that I would be seeing Alexandra again. I would be in Hawaii, away from this hellhole. I was having thoughts much like those of my friend Collins. I wasn't sure I could stand coming back to this nightmare America had created.

When I got back to the hooch I lit up a Winston. The guilt and fear took on new intensity. Marijuana can do that. Thoughts became hallucinations. My mind's eye could see the big evil men in Long Bihn jail. My heart swelled with overwhelming fear and distress that made me shudder. I was a mess.

Thankfully, while my anguished mind was out of control, Chaves crept in. I slowly made my way back to consciousness, my beating heart slowed down again, and I realized there was no need to run and hide right now. All that was in the future, or not. It would or would not happen. My rational brain was taking back control, when I looked over at Chaves.

"You still awake, App?"

"Yeah, Chaves, I'm awake. I don't want to be, but I'm awake."

"Why not, Apple? What's the problem?"

"I guarantee that you don't want to know, Chaves. Let's just say I'm looking forward to my emergency leave."

"Yeah, I bet you are. Hey, I forgot, the orders for your next assignment came in today. North gave them to me to give to you. Take a look. Where ya going?"

He handed me an envelope with my name on it. I opened it, and saw next to my name, Fort Leonard Wood, Missouri, "Fuck that" burst from me. I didn't mean to shout it out loud.

"So where ya headed?" asked Chaves again.

"It says here Fort Leonard Wood, Missouri, but that is not going to happen. I have a lot of stuff, Freddie. I'll trade most of it for a new assignment. I liked Fort Ord, it's nice in Northern Cal. Monterey, Carmel, Big Sur

- that's where I'm going, Chaves. You can be sure of that."

"You seem to get what you want, App. You'll find out how to get your orders changed. You want a hit off this Paxton?"

"No, thanks, that shit makes me think too much. I know it makes you sleep like a baby, but it keeps me up all night with wild thoughts that turn out to be stupid. I'll pass."

"Oh yeah, App, there are two envelopes in the dispatch office that have your name on 'em."

"I'll get them tomorrow, Chaves. Just hold on to them for me, will ya?"

"Sure, App, no problem,"

For you, maybe not, Chaves, I thought. *For me, a big problem, now I'm a paid member of the 448 black market.*

.

Chapter 26

Fort Ord

I did everything I could over the next couple weeks to prepare for my emergency leave. Romanasky was confident he could manage the operation. I was sure he could; it was a finely tuned machine, and J.R. had the charisma to keep it running. The soldiers liked him; he was one of them. I grilled him on the paperwork. We had another inspection scheduled soon, most likely while I was gone. He promised to keep them SOP.

I talked to Warrant Officer Gabriel, who said he was happy with the productivity of the motor pool. He got along well with J.R., and knew the motor pool was running smoothly. He appreciated that trucks not only got in and out quickly, but easily passed any inspections. He knew that I took care of the paperwork and stats, while J.R. had nurtured relationships that gave us highest priority at the parts depot. He never mentioned anything about our parts runs. We were the least of his worries.

On Sunday, Romanasky and I picked up Corporal Howard's platoon, who were living in field tents in the middle of Long Binh. We took them to the 448 Sunday drag races, fed them steaks or burgers with all the beer they could drink. Lots of 448 money changed hands with the boys from the 25th Infantry. Ford won again, two out of three. The platoon drank, ate, rooted for either Ford or Chevy, and shot the shit for four hours. While we were taking them back to their tents, Howard told me it was the best time they'd ever had in-country.

The day after I got the news from Chaves about my new assignment I went to 448 Headquarters and saw North at his desk. I pulled one of the wooden chairs next to the desk and leaned close so no one could hear our conversation.

"Listen, North, I got my new assignment." I checked to make sure no one was coming into the office. "It's Fort Leonard Wood, Missouri." I looked him in the eyes. "There's no way I want to spend a year that far from the ocean. Is there any chance you can get those orders changed?"

North looked at me with the same cold, impenetrable eyes he showed everyone. I sensed he was calculating if he needed, or wanted, to help me. We hadn't talked since our conversation about the black market.

"Why do you think I could get your assignment changed?" he asked.

"Because you have contacts at Westmoreland's office. You can pull a few strings. I know it can be done. They have access to everyone's records. They've got to be able to switch my assignment with a dead guy's assignment or something like that. I know they can do something. I have things to trade, North. You just check on it, okay?"

"Have you thought about my offer?" he asked, his eyes locked on mine.

"No, North, I haven't changed my mind. I want to be close to home in my next assignment. Fort Ord would be great. Work on that. I'm serious, I don't want to live a year of my life in Missouri."

"I'll check on it."

"Thanks, North," I said, then I remembered to ask, "Have the official orders for my emergency leave come back from the colonel?"

"Not yet, but their clerk is working on it."

"I'd love to get the new assignment before I go on leave. I have guys at Tan Son Nhut looking for a seat on any plane over the next couple weeks. I just need the orders."

"It'll cost you, App. The guys in Westmoreland's office don't come cheap."

"You know my inventory. Let them know that they have their choice of whatever we have."

"Like I said, I'll check on it."

"Cool, you do that." I nodded goodbye, then walked out.

The next two weeks were routine - going to the office, checking on paper-work, inspecting the parts rooms. J.R. and I would go on a parts run, hitting a couple of clubs in the afternoon, then come back to hang around my room, get high on a Winston, and listen to the Doors, Cream, or Hendrix.

We might go to the club later. If I was stoned, I'd dance by myself to the loud music played by the Vietnamese band. I hadn't danced in a while. Some of the black guys joined me, and showed me some cool moves that I'd try. They laughed till I got it right.

I staggered home most nights, barely able to get into my top bunk, and in minutes fell asleep. Alcohol was a good way not to worry about being in Long Binh Jail. I'd wake up with a hangover, feeling horrible, but I slept, which was a good thing. The hangover could be helped with a cup of coffee and a Herbert Tareyton.

A rumor got started that Bobby Kennedy had been shot. It seemed so unbelievable so soon after Dr. King's assassination. I was with Romanasky outside the 448 bay when we tuned into Armed Forces Radio, and heard the horrible news.

Alexandra had written that Eugene McCarthy was doing well in the primaries. I knew he was supported by those who wanted to end the war. Hearing that Lyndon Johnson wasn't going to run for reelection surprised me. Shortly after that, Bobby Kennedy entered the race, also vowing to end the war if elected. Even though I was skeptical of the Kennedy family after my conversation with Mr. Nguyen, I was for Bobby Kennedy, believing he had a better chance than Eugene McCarthy to win the nomination, and maybe the Presidency. He was our biggest anti-war hope.

I was crushed when we got the news he'd been killed after winning the California primary. Alexandra wrote about her fascination with Bobby Kennedy, but her next several letters were sad. She had seen Bobby Kennedy two days prior to his killing at a United Farm Worker's rally with Cesar Chavez and was so hopeful after Kennedy and Chavez spoke. After staying up to watch the victory speech, the assassination devastated her.

The few of us who knew anything about politics drank many shots of Chivas Regal that night at the club. Several of the black guys from Class I joined us. They could relate; they'd lost a leader in the same way only a few months earlier.

A couple of weeks after our conversation, North stopped me when I came out of my room. He looked at me in the deadpan way he always did. "I talked to some people. It can be done. They need to see the stock. They mentioned they can get you out weeks earlier using the new orders."

"You're kidding me, North! That's so cool! What's it gonna cost me?"

"The guy wants to see what you got."

"Send him by the motor pool. I'll show him my inventory."

"He's coming this afternoon. Be there. He'll have the papers with him." He went on, "Oh yeah, the colonel signed your orders. You leave in five days."

"Outstanding, North! This is my lucky day! I'll start pressing my guys at Tan Son Nhut to find me a seat on a plane heading to Hawaii. This is total-ly bitching, North. I owe you."

"Yes, you do, App. There may come a time when I might need you and your inventory for something."

"Anything I've got is yours, North. You just name it."

He nodded, then walked toward 448 headquarters.

I hadn't skipped since I was a kid, but I found my self skipping to-ward the motor pool. *I got Fort Ord! I'm getting out early! I'll be in Hawaii in five days.* My ecstatic thoughts swirled in my mind like a mer-ry-go-round.

I greeted Mr. Nguyen happily when I got to the office. He could see my joy, but didn't say anything. The visit to his house and meeting his family left little more for us to say. It was something I would never forget. I knew what he thought about the war and agreed with it. He wasn't the kind of person to talk about nothing, and with little more to say, we were quiet. He did a lot of sitting and meditating.

Using the key for the right front drawer of my desk, I unlocked it, then removed the twenty envelopes with my name on them. Opening each one with an eye on the door and Mr. Nguyen, I counted and separated the money into piasters and MPC. It came to two thousand to go along with the three or four thousand hidden in my room. Fuentes had made me a secret compartment in one of the cabinets. I'd be taking about four or five thousand dollars with me to Hawaii, which was fun to contemplate.

Romanasky barged into the room. "Going on a run, App, Club 4 needs some steaks. Can you work that deal?"

"Not today, J.R. I got a guy coming who needs to see our inventory. If he likes what we have, he can get me out of Fort Fucking Leonard Wood and into Fort Fucking Ord."

"You've got to be shitting me! That's so cool."

"Keep it to yourself, J. R. I don't need anybody but you knowing about this. If it goes down the way I want it to, I might even be home a couple of weeks early. So don't say anything to anybody, you got that J. R.? This can make or break my whole next year."

"No sweat, Apple, I don't know nothin' about nothin'. I hope it does happen. Fort Ord isn't far from Sacramento. We can get together and laugh about all this shit when I get back to the world."

"No shit, J.R. That would be cool." I paused. "Oh yeah, I finally got my orders. I'm out of here in five days. I'm getting off a letter to the wife. It might not arrive in time, so I might have to call her from Hawaii, but, do I care?" I pulled out the money fanning it in front of my beaming face.

J. R. laughed, "You'll be living high on the hog, Applefuck, you lucky dog. We got a lot to celebrate. The Secretary and Dunphy are officially short. I hope someone hides Dunphy's Polident so he can put on a show. He and the Secretary can make me laugh."

"A lot of things make you laugh, J. R. That's one of the things people like about you."

"Thanks, Apple. I'll tell Club 4 that they'll get their delivery tomorrow. Don't give everything away. I still have time to do," he said laughing, as he walked out the door.

I worked in the afternoon with the Secretary, who was training his replacement, Private First Class Gardner, another mechanic tired of getting his hands greasy. We were going over the books, when I saw a new jeep drive up, a waving flag with four stars rising from the back of it. This was the new Commanding General Creighton Abrams' jeep.

The speck four getting out of the jeep wore a crisp new uniform. He was over six feet with a square jaw - a guy girls might swoon over. He wore black rimmed Ray-Ban sunglasses that reflected the sun, when he looked around after getting out of the jeep. I approached him drying my hands on my fatigues. When I got closer he asked, "You Appenzeller?"

"Yeah, I'm Appenzeller. You can call me App."

"My name's Sawyer," he said, shaking my hand. "North said you had some things I might want to look at."

"I just might. Follow me."

We slipped through the 448 bay, out the door to the parts containers hidden behind a wall of tires. I unlocked one of them, pulled the door open, stepped inside and urged Sawyer to do the same. He squinted when he entered until his eyes adjusted. What he saw was handguns hung from their trigger protectors, organized according to brands and models.

"Where did you get this stuff?" he asked, pulling a few weapons off their hooks, looking them over.

"Not your concern, Sawyer. Let's just say we have access; one of the perks for being in the Quartermaster Corps."

"No shit, you have some pretty cool guns here, man." He grabbed a Colt Commander, put it in his right hand looking down the barrel. "You know I'm sticking my neck out to get you where you want to go," he said, grabbing another Colt. "I had to use a lot of white-out to get your name in there. You might have a different Military Occupational Specialty on that document, but what do you care? You'll be stateside and close to home," he laughed.

"So what's it going to cost me, Sawyer? Pick out three or four, and let's call it a deal."

"I got five friends in the office who need to keep quiet about this. I'm going to need one each."

"Pick out your five, man, I'll take that deal," I said, reaching for an ammo carrier to put the guns into. "Does that include the two-week early out?"

He started laughing. "Yeah, that exit date is on the new document. I'm throwing that in for free," he said as he put the last gun into the ammo container. "I have a copy of your new orders in the jeep. The copy looks better than the original. Present the one I give you to the headquarters of the outfit you're assigned to in, drum roll, FORT ORD, Motherfucker!" We both laughed. I started dancing, showing off some of the steps the black guys showed me.

As soon as we got to the jeep, Sawyer reached for the folder on the seat and handed it to me. I opened it quickly, and there it was: Robert Lee Appenzeller in bold letters, and next to it, Fort Ord, California. I stared at it to make sure it was really me, and I'd be out of here. I smiled like I had received a bucket of gold and placed the papers back in the folder. I shook Sawyer's hand with a firm hand-shake looking into his eyes with warm appreciation.

"Thanks, Sawyer. I didn't want to spend the next year of my life in Fort Leonard Wood, Missouri,"

"I can dig that. They say if the U. S. was shaped like a person, Leonard Wood would be the asshole."

We both laughed as he climbed back into the driver's seat, nodded at me, then took off in a cloud of dust. Back in the office, I unlocked the top right drawer and placed my new orders inside.

I looked over at Mr. Nguyen and smiled.

"You much happy now, Mr. App, you have good thoughts," he said returning my smile.

"Yes, Mr. Nguyen, I'm much happier. I'll see my wife soon. I'll get to rest and not think. I'll even try meditation when I'm in Hawaii."

"Meditation good, Mr. App," His smile grew even wider.

I swelled with happiness for the first time since North and I had had our discussion in his room. I couldn't believe I was going back to Hawaii with lots of money, and I'd be with Alexandra again. I had my new assignment. I knew she'd be happy to be staying in California. As a spec five I'd get base housing. Life was looking up.

We celebrated that night at the local club. The band was passable and they got better the more we drank. They started playing an Animals hit *We Gotta Get Out of This Place* and as we sang along my voice got louder when I sang how there's a better life for me and you, which were perfect lyrics for the moment.

I got on a rant with a couple of new guys from the 448, explaining in detail the history and immorality of the war. I even implied that I might not come back from my emergency leave. They laughed calling me Radical Rob.

Some had seen the riots after Dr. King's death. Some had been around college campuses that had daily protests. They described the crowds and the anti-war taunts. "You'll fit right in, Radical Rob. They believe the same things you do."

"Damn right they do, 'cause they're smart. They can see what's real, not what the government's selling them. It's all bullshit, we don't belong here, it's not our war," I said in a pretty drunk voice.

They shook their heads and kind of waved me off. I stopped my rant and I let them go. It was useless. They didn't want to know the truth. They couldn't handle the truth.

I went outside to take a couple of hits on a Winston. When I came back, I moved to the dance floor with the black guys. I loved dancing with those guys when I was stoned. I felt uninhibited, trying some more of their moves. They thought I was cool and so did I.

Chapter 27

Tan Son Nhut

I awoke drenched in sweat from a dream filled with frightening images of men in prison, me being one of them. The memory of the gruesome dream faded, but the disturbing feeling of fear lingered.

Looking at my spider friend in the corner of my room, I remembered that I hadn't wiped out her future generations. That would happen now. While reaching into the web, the spider grabbed hold of the silky strands, alert, ready to pounce, I took the egg sac between my middle finger and thumb, took a deep breath, and squished, and pulled it out of the web. Fumbling around, I found my lighter, flicked, and watched the silk sac shrivel in the flame in a half second.

After making some coffee, I woke Chaves with a shake or two. "Time to get up, Chaves." His eyes made an attempt at opening while he got to his elbows. "Listen, Freddie, take care of the room while I'm gone. My leave is getting close. I have two more days and I'm out of here."

"Can do, App." He sat up and put his feet on the ground.

I was already packed, waiting anxiously for some of Fuentes' contacts at Tan Son Nhut to call. There may not be a seat available for my entire leave - the price paid when flying standby, getting a seat would be the luck of the draw. I ate some Corn Flakes I'd bought at the PX, and finished my second cup of coffee. Chaves and I cleaned up before starting the long walk to the motor pool.

When I strolled through the dusty opening of the motor pool, Warrant Officer Gabriel stood out front and called me over. "What can I do for you, Chief?"

"I got a call from some guy at Tan Son Nhut who said he needed to talk to you pronto." Gabriel had the only phone in the motor pool in his office.

We walked into his neat, well organized room. "I wrote his number on that pad next to the phone."

"Thanks, Chief, I've been waiting for this call."

I dialed the number. "PFC Zellenburg, Tan Son Nhut Airbase," a voice said.

"Zellenburg, this is Appenzeller from 448, a friend of Fuentes. What have ya got for me?"

"I got a seat going to the Philippines on to Hawaii. Leaves at 14:00 this afternoon."

"Damn, that's two days early. You got any tomorrow or the next?"

"Not that I can see, App. This could be your only chance."

I thought about it. I didn't want to risk not going. "Put my name on the ticket, Zellenburg. When do I have to be there?"

"About an hour before, around 13:00 should be in plenty of time."

"Thanks, I owe you."

"Yes, you do, App. From what Fuentes says you've got just about everything a guy might need."

"Yeah," I said, before setting the phone back into its cradle. *Does everyone in Vietnam know about my business?* I wondered. Thoughts like those always produced a cascade of chemicals that made me flushed with worry I'd be caught. After a deep sigh, and remembering Mr. Nguyen's teaching, the feeling went away.

"I'm leaving for Hawaii this afternoon, chief. They got me a seat on a civilian airline."

"I thought your leave didn't start for another two days, App."

"Well, yes, technically it might, but I don't know when the next seat will be available. I'm going to get on that plane if it's the last thing I do. Is it okay if Romanasky gives me a ride?"

"Don't know why not. Have a great time in Hawaii," he said, smiling, extending his hand.

"Thanks, Chief".

I went out into the yard looking for Romanasky. I saw him in the Class III bay talking to the parts clerk and rushed over to him. "J.R., I need a big favor. I got a seat reserved for me at Tan Son Nhut. I need a ride. The chief said it was okay."

"Damn, Apple. I thought you still had two more days."

"Well, I do, but fuck that. I got a seat today and might not in two days. I'm going back to the hooch to put on my civvies and grab my duffel bag. I'm hoping the CO doesn't notice the date."

"He'll be pissed when he finds out."

"I'll deal with that when I get back," then added with a wink, "if I get back." I thought it was cool being Radical Rob, and started spreading the rumor that I might not come back.

"You'll be back, Applefuck. You're not that stupid."

"We'll see, J.R. We'll see."

I went to the office, opened my desk drawer, and removing my orders, looked at Mr. Nguyen. "I'm leaving today, Mr. Nguyen. Thanks for all that you've taught me."

"You not come back?" His questioning eyes narrowed.

"Most likely I will, Mr. Nguyen. I still have more to learn from you."

He smiled, bowing his head with his chin touching his prayer hands. I did the same, and when a warm, tingling glow rose and swelled through my body, I knew he was someone I'd never forget.

I walked quickly from the motor pool to my room. After going through my duffel bag one more time, I threw in my shaving kit and toiletries, then opened my secret compartment removing over four thousand dollars in MPC, the money left after converting my remaining piasters. I lost money doing it, but I didn't care, the army wouldn't exchange Piasters for greenbacks.

I ambled over to 448 headquarters, and puffed with positive energy, walked through the door. "I got a seat for this afternoon on a commercial flight to Hawaii, North. My leave begins today." I threw my orders onto his desk. He glanced at them, then narrowed his eyes as he looked up at me. He knew what it said. He knew my leave didn't start today.

Seeing the door to the CO's office open, I walked over and stood in the door way. The CO looked up from some papers. I saluted and he saluted back.

"I got a seat on a commercial jet to Hawaii, sir. It leaves at 2:00 this afternoon."

"Really, Appenzeller? I didn't realize your leave starts today."

I nodded enthusiastically, at his surprised eyes, not wanting to tell an outright lie, but felt relieved and delighted when he didn't say anything more.

"Well, have a great time with your wife, App. Take care of those blue balls."

We both laughed. "Thank you, sir. This leave means everything to me." I saluted again. He waved back as I left his office.

I glanced at North, while taking my orders off his desk. I signed my name on the dispatch clipboard. "He's gonna be pissed when he finds out," he said.

"I'll deal with that later. Hey, man, thanks again for all the stuff you've been doing for me. None of this would have happened without your help."

He looked up at me, shrugged indifferently, and went back to the papers on his desk. I grabbed my duffel bag, stepped out the door, and headed for the motor pool.

Romanasky and I left Long Binh before noon. Traffic was light. We drove through small towns with lots of open green space that looked to be farmland, much of it not being used. Cattle dotted the green fields. People in the villages seemed to be living normal lives. Many small businesses were open, motorbike repair shops, restaurants and convenience-type stores with basic living supplies. This area was not war-torn. The airport was on the other side of Saigon. Getting through the city traffic was always a pain. Traffic lights were rare and ignored. Motorbikes and bicycles were everywhere. Romanasky used his horn as much as the gas pedal. It took over an hour. It was 1:15 when we arrived at Tan Son Nhut.

We said fast goodbyes with quick hugs. I was in a panic to get to the plane. I asked around for PFC Zellenburg. They directed me to his desk.

"It's about time, App. You've got to hustle to change your money and get on that plane." He gave me the ticket. I showed him my orders.

"Oh, shit," he said. "Your leave doesn't start for another two days." He shook his head and wrinkled his brow. "I don't think they'll check these orders though. This is a commercial flight and you're not in uniform. When you get off the plane in Hawaii, wait a couple of days then check in at Fort DeRussy."

"Where's that?" I asked.

"It's right on the beach at Waikiki. You can get rooms, cheap, right there on the beach."

"Cool. Where do I go to change my money?"

He pointed down the hall, "They'll do it at that counter."

I walked over to a PFC behind the counter, took out my wad of MPCs and started counting them. He looked at me suspiciously. "I've been saving for this trip," I said, looking at him with a big gloating smile. He started counting, his eyes bulging at the piles, then he reached into his drawer and pulled out hundred-dollar bills. When he handed me over four thousand in greenbacks, I smiled my thanks.

Wearing my Indian madras short-sleeved shirt with light brown cotton pants and penny loafers, I boarded the plane, no questions asked. I smiled at the stewardess with her long blond hair and crisp blue uniform - the first Caucasian woman I'd seen since my last R&R to Hawaii. "Welcome aboard," she said, smiling, then glancing at my ticket for the row number, and pointed toward the back. After fastening my seat belt, a business-type guy with horn rimmed glasses sat next to me.

When we were settled in our seats, the plane started to move. The stewardess came walking down the aisle. I tensed, sure she was coming to get me, but sighed a breath of relief when she passed our row and found her seat farther back. The plane taxied to the end of the runway, then made a slow turn. The mile of concrete was now in front of us. The engines revved, the jet started moving down the runway, picking up speed as we went. My heart thumped faster like it always does during take-offs, but this time there was more to it. I had made it. I was out early. The CO would be pissed when he found out, but I didn't give a fuck. I was on my

way. Soon I'd see Alexandra and we'd
get lost in each other. I needed to be
lost.

..

Chapter 28

AWOL

My thoughts were different on this trip to Hawaii. The last time my focus was on sex. Recollecting every sexual experience I'd ever had put me in a frenzy by the time I got off the plane and found Alexandra. Realizing she wouldn't be there when I arrived, lowered my sex drive somewhat. I told her about the leave, but couldn't give her exact dates. I would call as soon as we landed.

My thoughts this time were of the mess that I created for myself at the 448. How did I get involved in any of that? I could have been just a parts clerk going about my business, serving out my time. Instead, I had to be the best parts clerk, so I could impress the colonel. That had been my MO for my life so far. In sports especially, doing anything to stand out was important to me. Being recognized by the colonel replaced being recognized by the coach. Working for recognition, however, did not explain my motivations and actions with the clubs and the black market. That was the result of another need. The need to be cool.

I've always wanted to be considered a cool guy. We wore uniforms at Santa Clara Elementary, which meant showing my coolness through my shoes and haircut. When white bucks were popular, I had to have them. When ducktails and waterfalls were worn by the cool kids at Oxnard High, I would change my hair after leaving the house into a ducktail with a waterfall down the middle of my forehead. I had my fifth-grade picture taken with the waterfall. My mom almost had a heart attack.

In high school I wore Indian madras shirts, tight jeans and black-and-white saddle shoes. I sun-bleached my hair, growing it long, letting it fall in my face so I could flick it back with my head. It was the newest look, the surfer look. It was cool.

When I went to college my look turned preppy: button-down shirts, nice slacks with penny loafers, hair perfectly cut like James Bond. Being seen by others as cool was important to me. I was a CAMF, a cool assed motherfucker, who drank Chivas Regal and smoked Herbert Tareytons.

When I made the deals with the club sergeants, it was so I would be the coolest guy in the club with everything on the house. Those deals led North to offer me the top spot in the black market cartel. That conversation was a life-changer. I was in the cartel, responsible for dispatching trucks used for black market deliveries.

Recently, I had become Radical Rob, sporting a brown mustache, longer hair, arguing with everyone. Why? It was cool being Radical Rob. I wondered about this need to be cool, realizing that it was this need that led me to a situation where my life was in jeopardy.

It seemed that no matter how hard I tried, I couldn't keep the dark thoughts about being caught, convicted, and thrown into jail with murderers and brutes out of my consciousness. Those thoughts would creep in, starting a cascade of hormones and adrenaline, causing my heart to beat faster and my blood pressure to rise. "Controlling the mind isn't easy, Mr. App," Mr. Nguyen had said many times. I knew that for a fact. I fought those dark anguished thoughts for most of the flight.

When I stepped out into the glare of the bright sun and walked carefully down the steps to the tarmac, my legs were like rubber after sitting for eight hours. A lovely dark-skinned girl with a grass skirt put a fragrant flower lei over my head that smelled so sweet. I couldn't help but smile.

I walked inside the airport nervously looking for someone in uniform, petrified the CO might have called ahead to have me arrested. What a relief not seeing anyone except a few sailors searching for their loved ones. When my duffel bag came around on the baggage cart, I grabbed it, ventured outside, where a taxi driver stood by his cab with the door open. He threw my duffel bag onto the backseat and invited me to sit down beside it.

"Where to, buddy?" he asked, glancing back at me.

"What's the best hotel in Honolulu?"

"Most people say the Hilton."

"Take me to the Hilton."

Walking into the huge reception area of the Hilton Waikiki Beach Hotel with its marble columns holding up the ornate ceiling was like walking into a luxurious palace. The lobby was filled with white wicker furniture placed perfectly among the indoor palms. When I saw the long counter with people waiting in line to check in, I hoped they had a room for me. It was late July, not the high season for Hawaii.

Finally, it was my turn, and the young, tanned woman in a flowery dress behind the counter asked if I had a reservation. I told her I was on leave, waiting for my wife to arrive. She smiled and looked at a large sheet of paper with boxes that represented rooms. She put her finger on one, then tapped the shoulder of a guy in a similar flowery shirt next to her and pointed to the square. He nodded yes. She smiled at me with gleaming white teeth. "Yes, we have a lovely room."

I filled out the paperwork, signed on the bottom line without reading the information, then pulled out my wad of bills peeling off a few hundred to pay for a week. Ping went the bell on the counter, which brought a bellhop to my side. He looked to be a native with dark skin against the white flowery shirt he wore over white Bermuda shorts. He picked up my duffel bag, and I happily followed him to the elevator.

After watching the numbers chime by, we stopped on the twelfth floor. He led the way to room 1245, opened the door, and allowed me to go in first. The first thing I saw was the king-size bed with a nice yellow and green bed cover and a simple wooden headboard. It faced a long polished wooden cabinet with many drawers. A big Zenith color TV sat on top of the cabinet. I'd never seen one so big. After turning on the air conditioner, the bellhop showed me how to use the Zenith remote control.

Though I'd never seen one, it wasn't difficult to learn about the on and off buttons and how to change the channel or volume with other buttons.

He then went over to the pale green drapes and pulled them open with two small plastic poles. Sliding glass doors opened onto a balcony where, in the distance, I saw Diamondhead. It seemed real close. Stepping onto the balcony, I gazed out at the blue Pacific, rimmed by the sands of Waikiki, the waves breaking beyond the reef. The breathtaking view made me giddy with happiness.

After I tipped the bellhop a couple of bucks, he left with a big satisfied grin. I jumped on the bed with the remote control and hit the ON switch. Nothing happened for half a minute, then a small circle began to fill the screen with the colorful NBC peacock - every color bright and clear. I switched around and found four stations.

A few minutes later, I jumped off the bed and danced to the balcony. Being afraid of heights, I approached the rail slowly, cautiously, almost breathlessly, my heart quickening. Gazing out at the blue green sea, the clear blue sky, and the jungle covered mountain in the distance, calmed me. I sat in a green wicker chair that matched the table, lit a Herbert Tareyton, breathed in the tobacco smoke, and let it out with a contented sigh. Was this really me in this fabulous hotel? The ecstasy of being away from Vietnam made me dizzy with happiness, the exciting thought of seeing Alexandra swept through me like a tornado, then, wow, I suddenly remembered I hadn't called her yet.

Using the phone in the room, I asked if I could call long distance to California. "Yes, sir, we'll put the charges on your bill."

I dialed Alexandra's number. Since she was living with her parents, working and going to school, her mom answered the phone. When I said, "Hi, Mom, it's Robbie," I heard, "Oh, my God!" then yelling, "Ralph, it's Robbie! Go get Alexandra!"

Dottie asked if I was okay. I told her I was fine, that I got an early start on my leave and was already in the Hilton Hotel in Honolulu. Then I heard Alexandra yanking the phone from her mom and her excited voice. "Robbie, is that you?"

"Yes, babe, it's me. I got an early start on my leave. I'm at the Hilton. Wait 'till you see this place! It's amazing! You've got to catch the next flight. I'm dying to see you."

I heard her pleading with her parents to take her the next day to Los Angeles to catch the first plane to Hawaii. "I'm so excited! I told them at work that I needed a week off. I'm sure they'll let me off tomorrow. I just have to see you. I miss you so much."

"Me too, Alexandra, it's killing me that you're not here right now in this big beautiful king-size bed. I need you."

"It's late now, almost nine. No airlines stay open this late. I'll call first thing in the morning and try to get an afternoon plane. I just have to be with you. Is everything okay? I keep watching the news. It doesn't sound like there's been too much action since Tet."

"I'm fine, Alexandra. I was lucky to get this emergency leave, but it won't start until you get here, so get here as fast as you can!"

"You know I will. I love you so much, Robbie."

"I love you, too. I'm so ready to see you. Hurry as fast as you can."

"This call is costing you a fortune, so I'll hang up. I love you, Robbie,"

"I love you, too, Alexandra, see you soon!"

After the click at the other end, still wanting to hear her voice, I reluctantly hung up.

While taking out some things from my duffel bag, I realized I didn't have anything cool. The spiffy outfits the hotel personnel wore impressed me. I had money. I needed to go shopping.

I checked out the pool area to see what swim suits people wore. When I saw a pair on a guy that would look cool on me, I rushed out of the hotel, headed to Kalakaua Avenue where numerous shops had stylish clothes on display. In one window, I saw the dark blue swimsuit that I'd liked. When I went inside, the salesman looked at me with raised eyebrows like I didn't belong. I look young for my age with just a wispy mustache and not much of a beard.

Pointing to the suit in the window, he brought a pair out for me to try on. I glanced at the expensive price, then shrugged no big deal. I bought two pair of Hawaiian-style shorts, three flowery shirts, two swimsuits and some cool-looking sandals with rubber tire treads for soles. Pulling out my wad of hundreds brought a wide eyed gleam to the salesman's astonished face. The bill barely dented the wad.

I changed into a new outfit, putting my old stuff into the shopping bag. Gazing at my image in the window, I saw my longer hair, the Ray-Ban aviator sunglasses and thought, *Man you look so cool.* Hopefully Alexandra would agree.

I couldn't wait for Alexandra to arrive but had a whole day. How could I make the time go faster?

After stopping in a restaurant that had a view of the beach, I ordered a hamburger, fries, and a beer to go with it. I looked around, amazed at the spectacle that was Waikiki: the white sand next to the pale-blue sea glistening in the sun, the blue sky with puffy white clouds being pushed by the soft breeze. Waves of warm feelings washed over me like the waves rolling onto the beach.

After lunch, I walked barefoot across the beach, watching families with kids playing in the water and surfers riding waves on the outside reefs. I stopped by the surfboard rental, and reserved a longboard for the next morning, figuring Alexandra wouldn't be here until tomorrow afternoon.

I bought a bottle of Chivas Regal on the way back to the hotel. When I sat on the bed to watch TV, I poured a bit into a water glass, sipped, and savored how smooth it went down.

The next morning I anxiously called Alexandra's house. The phone rang and rang, until Alexandra's sister Sylvia picked it up. She said her mom and dad were taking Alexandra to L.A. to catch a 2:00 plane that would arrive in Honolulu at around 2:00 Hawaiian time.

After the buffet breakfast that came with my package, I saw it was only eight in the morning. Six hours seemed like an eternity, so I asked one of the hotel staff about Fort DeRussy and he gave me directions. It was over a mile away. After a long walk in the warm humid air, I found a square box of a building, probably erected in the 40s, that stood out for its ugliness compared to the new stylish hotels built around it. I walked down the cement walkway with freshly cut lawn on both sides, and located the office on the right of the dreary lobby.

When the spec four asked to see my papers, I told him they were at the Hilton. With my new clothes and hearing the Hilton, he sized me up and told me about the rooms at Fort DeRussy. He added that there was a waiting list. I told him to put me on it. I pulled out a card from the Hilton, wrote my name and room number and gave it to him. "I'll call you if there is an opening," he said. I gave him five bucks as we shook hands.

I walked back to the surfboard rental stand and got a nine-foot Ole, which I waxed up before taking it into the water. Paddling to the reef, I saw that most guys were on the new short-boards. I had learned from my R&R that if I sat deeper with the longboard, I could catch the wave before the short boarders took off. They didn't like it, but it turned out to be a good strategy. I got some good ones.

When I got to shore, I had plenty of time to grab my stuff and walk back to the Hilton. I took a quick swim in the pool, went to my room, showered, shaved, selected my best new ensemble, rode the elevator to the lobby, then asked the valet out front to get me a taxi. He flagged one down. I gave him a dollar before jumping into the back seat.

The driver, a local, dropped me off at the airport entrance. My watch said it was near 1:30. Inside the terminal checking flights from L.A., I saw one was due, on time, at 2:00. I headed for Gate 11. Arriving at 1:40, the next twenty minutes were the longest in history. Many planes landed, but none taxied towards Gate 11. I kept glancing at my watch. At 2:04, at last, a plane approached Gate 11. After coming to a stop, two guys moved portable stairs toward the door. People filed out, walking down the stairs to the lovely tanned girls waiting with leis.

Where was she? I was losing hope, then I saw a girl with dark hair, cut in a pageboy-style, standing in the plane's doorway wearing a sleeveless white blouse with a black leather miniskirt. The effect was so sexy I instantaneously felt a bulge in my pants. I moved past other greeters waiting until Alexandra stepped inside the terminal. When she crossed the threshold, I ran to her and we hugged like we would never let each other go.

After I picked up her bags, we headed for the exit and hailed a taxi. "Hilton Waikiki Beach!" I said with a huge smile. He smiled back, grabbed Alexandra's luggage, and put them in the trunk. We sat in the back seat kissing passionately until the taxi driver coughed loudly a few times, and we saw we were in front of the hotel. I paid him, pulled Alexandra's bags out of the trunk, and led her through the tropical landscaping to the front doors. Before entering, Alexandra's wide eyes looked at the Hilton in awe.

We stepped into the lobby with its lovely furniture and pillars. In the elevator, we rode in a long continuous embrace, then holding hands, ran down the hallway to our room. I almost bent the key trying to open the door. Alexandra ran inside, checking out the room, then went to the balcony to gaze at the view. Having already seen the view, the only view I wanted now was of her naked body.

I unzipped her black skirt and pulled it down along with her white silky panties. With her skirt puddled on the floor, I fumbled with my belt and moved her toward the bed where, kissing her, our tongues swirling, our bodies growing hotter, I entered her bushy, wet, opening, for the beginning of two hours of absolute bliss.

The first two days we never left the Hilton. We loved the room where we made passionate, sweet love over and over. We ate at the hotel's excellent restaurants, or ordered room service. We walked around the hotel and swam in the pool. Though we knew a world out-side the hotel existed, we didn't want to be too far from our king-size bed and the room with the fabulous view.

We went to Waikiki on day three where I rented another longboard, and staying outside, catching the waves early. Alexandra lay on a towel tanning an already brown body. Seeing her lying there in her blue two piece bathing suit only made me want to take her back to the Hilton.

During breaks in the sex and eating, we talked. I decided I wasn't going to tell her about my being part of the black market, but told her some of North's conversation with me. I avoided telling her about dispatching black market trucks. Why cause worry when the outcome was not decided. Still in the back of my mind, thoughts of my involvement haunted me.

She told me how depressed she was over the assassination of Bobby Kennedy and described seeing him two days before his death when he spoke at a rally in Oxnard. She hoped he would end the war and knew Eugene McCarthy wouldn't win the nomination. She didn't trust Hubert Humphrey because he had been vice president under Lyndon Johnson. She hated Johnson for expanding the war and had marched in several protests. Her involvement made me love her even more.

I told her some of what I had learned from Mr. Nguyen about the Catholic Church. She did not seem all that surprised. Her conversion to the church was only because she loved me. She did not identify herself as a Catholic and seemed somewhat relieved that I no longer did. I described my dinner with Mr. Nguyen and his family. We laughed at the flying eye as I described it. I revealed to her some of the things I saw in his house that proved that the church and the US were on the wrong side of history and morality. I also introduced her to some of my thoughts about Buddhism, describing it as a positive way to live a life and raise children.

On the fourth day, we were awakened by a call from the spec four from Fort DeRussy. He said he'd have rooms in two days. I asked how much. Compared to the Hilton, they were cheap. I told him to pencil us in. When I told Alexandra I was two days early on the leave, so we could stay at least nine days, her excitement bubbled over into big hugs.

We decided to rent a car for a day to see more of the island, and drove to the North Shore, Sunset Beach, Waimea Bay, and the Banzai Pipeline. We went swimming at Sandy Beach where waves break hard on the sand. Alexandra got pulled over the falls by one which filled her suit with sand. I was worried for a second, but knew Alexandra was an excellent swimmer. Later, we drove the car back to Honolulu, ate a fantastic meal, and made mad, passionate love all night.

Day six would be our last night at the Hilton and we knew it would be difficult to leave after such a fantastic experience. We took a taxi to Fort DeRussy to see the rooms, which weren't bad; it wasn't the Hilton, but it was right on the beach. I booked us seven days, even though I actually only had two days left on my leave, but by now I didn't want to go back. I was certain CID had raided the 448 and would be looking for everyone on the list, including me. I still had lots of money. I didn't have a plan other than hanging at the beach during the day, and making love to Alexandra at night. I could think of no good reason to stop doing that.

On day nine, the day I was supposed to leave, I took a bus to Schofield Barracks/Fort Shafter to find out how to book a flight back to Vietnam. The guy there looked at my orders and asked if I had gotten shots before I went. I told him I wasn't sure. He said I had to get some. When I asked him how, he shrugged, saying he didn't know. After asking around, I learned I needed to go to the clinic on the base. I went back to Fort DeRussy instead, because in my mind I was living in an Army compound, which meant I wasn't Absent WithOut Leave (AWOL).

Alexandra and I stayed all seven days. They were glorious days on the beach, surfing, eating good food, making love every night.

Being with Alexandra helped me forget the troubles that would be awaiting me upon my return to the 448, but, eventually the money ran low, and Alexandra had to get back to work, so with great reluctance we booked her return flight to California.

When I went back to the base to get my shots at the clinic, I ran into a friend from Oxnard, someone I'd almost joined the Army with on the buddy system, Joey Cohen. He was a clerk in the clinic. With a wink he said that I had to wait a few days for the shots.

When I took Alexandra to the airport, we realized that it wouldn't be too long now before we lived out my active duty at Fort Ord. We had been together for two glorious weeks and felt like a couple again. When we held each other at the airport, it was hard to let her go. It almost broke my heart watching her board the plane for California.

I went back to Fort DeRussy to check out. I had Cohen's number and called him to see if he had a bunk for me to sleep in, which he did.

At Schofield Barracks I hung around for another six days, each day checking on the shots, and for a flight out. With the answers to both being no, Cohen let me take his VW Bug to Sandy Beach, where I got pounded every day, body surfing. Damn, I loved every minute of it.

After three days with Cohen, they gave me my shots. I made sure they gave me the paperwork. Now I only had to check one thing in the morning. If there was no flight out, I was off to the beach.

On day six they told me they had a spot on a Hercules C 130. I had two hours to get packed, tell Cohen "adios," and get to the C 130, which was a four-engine propeller-driven plane. Three guys and I had seats on the bulkhead, looking at all kinds of Army equipment strapped down with thick nets. The journey was cold and loud. They gave us headphones to protect our ears and rough Army blankets. I had plenty of time to think.

I had spent twenty-one days in Hawaii and knew I would be in hot water when I returned to the 448. The CO would be pissed because I'd left early, and double pissed because I'd stayed an extra fourteen days. I sat stuck to that cold bulkhead debating with myself about scenarios to tell the CO. I had the shot card. No way would they let me leave without my shots. I was on stand-by with no planes leaving, what the fuck was I supposed to do? They were flimsy excuses, but I didn't care. Those fourteen days with Alexandra had boosted my spirits. If I could somehow manage to not be arrested, I would return to her in three months. All I needed was a good story.

I settled on one line of thinking when we landed in Clark Air Force Base in the Philippines. I worked out the details from Manila to Tan Son Nhut. I had an explanation that the Army would understand - a snafu. It wasn't my fault. I'd done all I could to get back. Yes, it was a typical Army snafu, which stood for Situation Normal - All Fucked Up. Snafus happened all the time in the Army. I had a snafu story that just might work.

.

Chapter 29

SNAFU

I arrived mid morning at Tan Son Nhut still in civilian clothes. Zellenburg seemed surprised to see me. "Wow, Appenzeller! Where the fuck you been, man? I got a call from your warrant officer at the motor pool. He said everyone was looking for you. You've been AWOL for fourteen days. He said your CO at the 448 was ready to send you to jail. What the hell happened?"

I thought I would test-drive my story. "It was a typical Army snafu, Zellenburg. I put in for standby at Schofield Barracks, but no planes out had an available seat. When one eventually did, they wouldn't let me on because I needed shots. It took a couple days to get the shots. Then I waited around Fort Shafter for a seat on anything. Finally they put me on a Hercules C 160. I was miserable as hell on that plane. It was loud and cold. It was no picnic."

He chuckled with a skeptical squint. "I hope your CO buys that story. From what I hear he's really pissed off."

"Well, it's my story and I'm sticking with it," I smiled. "So, what's the best way to get from here to Long Binh?

"I'll check to see if anyone from around here is heading in that direction." He got on the phone. I sat down, pleased with the story, relieved that Zellenburg seemed to buy it.

When he hung up, he looked at me. "I got a jeep heading to Long Binh with paperwork. The driver will take you." He sat back in his chair and grinned. "So you turned a seven-day emergency leave into twenty-one. How was the surf?"

"Outstanding! Surfed Waikiki several times. I body-whomped Sandy Beach. I ate a lot of sand, but I do love bodysurfing."

"You spend that entire wad?"

"Yeah, stayed at the Hilton for a week, then moved on to Fort DeRussy for a week. Spent the last days with a bud from Oxnard who was stationed at Schofield Barracks. Had a blast, man. Hated coming back, but I ran out of money."

"Twenty-one days, you're a motherfucker, App. I hope you get away with it."

"Well, what did you think about the story I told you?"

He started laughing. "You're too tanned to be arguing that you were anywhere but the beach."

"It was hot at Schofield sitting in the hot sun waiting for a seat. It was boring, Zellenburg. Boring and hot, day after day waiting for my plane." I winked, "What do ya think?"

"Throw in a few tears and maybe they'll buy it. Twenty-one fucking days on the beach in Hawaii while a war is going on. That's a classic, App, I'll tell that story. I hope there's a happy ending."

"Me, too, Zellenburg, me, too!"

I found a chair to sit in while waiting for my ride. A PFC walked in gathering some papers. When he got to Zellenburg's desk they talked, then Zellenburg looked over at me. "This is Sanders, App. He'll be giving you a ride to Long Binh." I got up to shake his hand.

"So you're the guy who went AWOL in Hawaii for twenty-one days," he said with a sense of awe in his voice. "How did they finally find you?"

"It's a long story, Sanders, with a couple of versions. I'll tell you both on the ride to Long Binh." En route, I told Sanders the real story and the cover-up story. He laughed at both. By the time I was done we were in front of 448 headquarters.

"That was a cool story, man. I hope you get away with it," Sanders said as we shook hands.

A Class I mechanic leaving the office when I arrived looked at me with wide shocked eyes. "How was Czechoslovakia, App? How'd they catch you?"

"Czechoslovakia?" I asked, bewildered.

"Yeah, when you didn't show up, the rumor went around that you were in Czechoslovakia helping some rebels fight the Soviets. So how was it?"

"I'll tell you later, Jones. Tell the Chief and Romanasky that I'm back, will ya?"

"Sure, App, I hope they don't bust you too bad. That was a lot of AWOL time." He left after patting me on the back.

When I walked into the office, North sat behind his desk. His wide surprised eyes stared as if in shock. "Man, you got a shit-storm to face in there. The CO was pissed you left early, then he heard that you weren't coming back. He was going to initiate an investigation today. Looks like he won't have to."

North knocked on the door, waited, then stuck his head in. "Someone to see you, sir." When he pulled the door wide open, I walked through and stood in front of the CO's desk. He was looking at papers in a folder, but when he glanced up, his startled eyes widened as if he'd seen a ghost.

"Spec Five Appenzeller reporting for duty, sir!" I said bringing my hand up in a salute.

He pushed his chair back, narrowed his eyes, his mouth grim, then stood stiffly and didn't return my salute, leaving me standing there with my hand over my eye. He slowly reached to his side, unsnapped his holster, pulled out his Colt and pointed it at me.

"Appenzeller, you're under arrest. You've been officially AWOL for fourteen days. You will be confined to quarters until I issue your punishment. This will be at least an Article 15. I'll check with the colonel for how far down I can bust you or how long you'll spend in LBJ. Is that clear, Appenzeller? You have disappointed me. You have disappointed the colonel. You have totally fucked up here, boy."

I stood there feeling like an idiot with my hand still at my forehead in a salute, staring at the gun. Without removing my hand, I asked, "Permission to speak, Lieutenant."

I waited for a reply which didn't come, then he spoke in a stern voice. "What have you got to say?"

I lowered my hand slowly, then standing in an at-ease position looked him directly in the eyes. "This is a total Army snafu, Lieutenant. I met my wife in Honolulu, sir. We stayed at the Hilton. We had a wonderful time. When my leave was up, I went to Schofield Barracks to get a hop back to Vietnam. They said I would have to fly standby. My wife and I checked in to Fort DeRussy. Every day we went to Schofield sitting there waiting for a ride. There were no seats. They called on the eleventh day informing me they had a seat. The wife went with me to say goodbye. They asked me for my shot card. I showed it to them. They said there were new shots I needed in order to return to Vietnam. They canceled my seat. I had to find a place to get the shots. It took days, sir. My wife finally had to go home. I checked into Schofield Barracks, got the shots and waited some more. I finally got a seat on a Hercules C 160. It took forever. The plane was loud, slow and cold. I had a little seat on the bulkhead. It was no vacation, sir. I did all I could to get back on time. It was just an Army snafu."

He stood there wavering, nodding. I could tell that he had at least listened to the story.

"Sir, when my leave time was up, I was either at Fort DeRussy or Schofield Barracks. I have the receipt from DeRussy, and my shot card from Schofield. I'm sorry I angered the lieutenant by leaving early. I was desperate to see the wife. I was not sure there would be another seat available and had to grab it. Look what happened when I tried to get back. It took forever. I hope the lieutenant can understand that all of this was an Army snafu of the highest order. I really tried to get back in time."

He slowly put his gun back into his holster, but looked at me with daggers in his eyes. He didn't believe a word of what I'd said, but I had evidence to make it a believable story. "You're dismissed, Appenzeller. You're confined to quarters until I talk to the colonel. I'll tell him your story. I don't believe a word of it. You may have to explain it all to him."

"I'd be glad to, sir." I saluted again, waiting for him to do the same, which he reluctantly did. When I left his office and closed the door, I smiled at North.

"You arrested?"

"No. Confined to quarters. The lieutenant needs to check my story."

"Will it check out?"

"No way for them to check. I have evidence. It's a compelling story."

"Is it true?"

I shrugged with a slight smile, grabbed my duffel bag then changed the topic. "Have things been cool while I was gone?"

North shrugged, but didn't answer.

My room looked okay when I arrived. Chaves's bed was a little sloppy. I pulled stuff out of my duffel bag and put everything into the cabinets, then went to the bar, poured a finger of Chivas Regal, and sipped it slowly, savoring the warm relief as I swallowed. I climbed onto the top bunk, glad to be in my own bed and fell into a deep sleep.

Hours later, a hand shook me awake. "Apple! App! Wake up, man! The colonel wants to talk to you!"

It was Chaves. I checked my watch and saw it was 5:00. "He sent word to the motor pool. They sent me to get you. You okay, App? How was Czechoslovakia?"

"What the hell is with Czechoslovakia?" I asked, trying to come to complete consciousness.

"Everyone heard you say you weren't coming back. When you didn't, the word just spread that Radical Rob was in Czechoslovakia."

"Why the fuck Czechoslovakia?"

"There's some kind of uprising there right now. Soviet tanks have invaded. All the world is watching Czechoslovakia. We figured that's where you might have gone."

"No shit? That's fucking crazy."

I slid off the top bunk and reached for my boots and hat. After lacing my boots, I checked myself in the door mirror. This was an important meeting. I straightened out my uniform, buffed up the toes of my boots, then started the long walk to battalion headquarters.

Battalion headquarters was twice as big as 448's. Three clerks out front, five doors to offices with a name on each door. I told a PFC who I was. Knowing the colonel was waiting for me, he beeped from the intercom, and told him I was waiting.

"Send him in," came the colonel's rough voice. After knocking, I marched in, stood at attention in front of his desk, making my best salute. "Spec Five Appenzeller reporting as ordered, sir."

He saluted back taking the cigar he had been chomping out of his mouth. "Goddamn it, Appenzeller! What the hell happened to you in Hawaii? Your CO at 448 is pissed off. He thinks you're trying to bullshit him. What's your story?"

"I'm sorry, Colonel, for you to be involved. It's a case of an Army snafu at its worst." I told him how there were no seats available and how I sat frustrated in the waiting room at Schofield Barracks every day waiting for a flight. Then told him how they finally stuck me on a C 160, and I had to ride on a tiny seat on the bulkhead. I told him how it took forever and was loud, really cold and slow. The 448 CO had heard ridiculous rumors about Czechoslovakia that were not true. I finished my story with a hopefully final point.

"If the colonel would like to check, please write my father-in-law. He just retired from the Navy. His name is Commander David Johnson and lives in Port Hueneme by the Sea Bee base. He will back up my story. I'm sorry about this snafu, sir. Not much else I could have done."

I stood there waiting. He took out a lighter put a flame to his cigar, puffing it until it was red on the tip. He let out a huge plume of smoke. "God-damn it, App, I'll take your word for it. You may have to take those days off your leave time, but I'll order your CO to back off. While you were gone we did well again on the motor pool inspec-tion. I like the new warrant officer Gabriel. He gives you a lot of credit."

"He's a good man, sir. There are many good men in the motor pool."

"Have you taken that R&R to Vung Tau yet? I'm short now. You'd better take it before I'm gone."

"Will do, sir! Thank you, sir." I raised my arm again in a salute. He saluted back. I walked out of his of-fice. Once outside, giddy with happi-ness, I found myself childishly skip-ping toward the motor pool again think-ing, *I'd done it! I'd turned a seven day leave into twenty-one, and gotten away with it. No punishment, not even a slap on the wrist. Talk about cool. Dude, I was cool.*

When I got back to the motor pool, the guys spotted me and started whoop-ing and hollering. Walking towards me, the mechanics cleaning their hands with old rags, laughed. "So how was it, Apple? How did they catch you?"

A happy crowd formed around me. "I'd say it was great to be back, but that would be a lie." They laughed. "All the rumors you heard aren't true. I didn't even know about any uprising in Czechoslovakia. I'm amazed you knuckleheads can even pronounce it!" They laughed again. "I spent the whole time in Hawaii with my wife, Alexandra. We stayed at the Hilton and Fort DeRussy right on the beach. I went surfing almost every day. There was a big snafu about me needing shots. There weren't any planes leaving for Vietnam. This place isn't on the Club Med tour." Laughter again. "I finally got a ride on a Hercules C 160; what a pain in the ass that was. But I'm back, with less than three more months to do. Soon I'm going on an R&R for being Soldier of the Month." Another roar. "So remember, if anyone asks you, I had a miserable time waiting around for a transport from Schofield Barracks to Vietnam. Got that?"

"We got it."

"Now it's almost quitting time. I heard you guys kicked ass on the last inspection while I was gone. You don't even need me anymore." They smiled, slapped me on the back, then went back to work.

I saw Warrant Officer Gabriel smoking a cigarette on the porch outside his office. When I walked over to him he turned to me. "So there's no truth to the rumor that you were in Czechoslovakia?" he asked smiling. "I figured that was bullshit. So how was it? What took you so long?"

"It was great, Chief. I've never had a better time. Stayed a week at the Hilton Waikiki Beach Hotel. It was amazing. There was a snafu with me getting a plane back, but I didn't complain cause my wife stayed with me at Fort DeRussy. But get this when I walked into the CO's office he pulled his gun on me."

"You're kidding me. He came here pissed off one day asking about why you'd left early. He came again a couple of days ago, saying he was going to throw you into Long Binh Jail."

"Yeah, he didn't buy my story, but what matters is that the colonel did. He said he'd order him to back off. So I'm back. The colonel spoke highly of you, Chief. I guess you guys did well on the last inspection."

"Just following your game plan, App. This thing runs smoothly, especially with Romanasky. That guy is good at getting the parts we need." He looked behind me. "Here he is now."

The 448 truck come around the corner. Romanasky came sliding to a dusty stop in front of us causing us to jump out of the way. J.R. got out of the truck with a huge smile on his face. "So how was Czechoslovakia, Applefuck?" he asked laughing.

"Don't tell me you fell for that bullshit rumor, too. What the fuck would I be doing in Czechoslovakia when I had a beautiful wife and excellent waves in Hawaii?"

"I knew it was bullshit. So how was it?"

We started walking toward my office. I told him the whole story and how after Alexandra left I stayed with my friend Joey Cohen. "It was great, J.R. Twenty-one days in Hawaii in the middle of a war. Is that cool or what?"

"Goddamn, Applefuck. As I've said before you are one cool-ass motherfucker. Let's go to your room to celebrate. You still got oysters?"

.

Chapter 30

CID

Romanasky and I celebrated my return with Chivas Regal and Jack Daniels. Many of my friends were gone. I missed them. Collins and Peterson were great friends, the Secretary was amazingly talented, and Dunphy was just plain funny-looking. I missed all those guys. J.R. and I were joined by Chaves, who had weed. We smoked some outside and had a rambling conversation, but, being tired after the travel I went right to bed.

I woke up, made some coffee with scrambled eggs, then walked with Chaves to the motor pool. Noticing that Mr. Nguyen wasn't there, I went to Warrant Officer Gabriel's office. "Where is the papa-san who was keeping my office clean, Chief?"

"Sorry, App, I couldn't justify keeping him on. He might be working around here somewhere."

"Damn, chief. I liked that guy. You're not sure where he is?"

"Not a clue, App, I had to let him go."

I walked back to the office, wondering what to do about finding Mr. Nguyen, hoping that someone might know where he was. I looked in my drawer, seeing a nice pile of envelopes, that brought a smile, but also a feeling of concern and guilt. After a few minutes, I went back to the chief's office and told him I had to go talk to some personnel people about taking fourteen days off my leave.

After I found the right office and waited my turn, a spec four called me in. He died laughing when I told him my story. Thought it was the coolest thing he'd ever heard.

"This story needs a totally happy ending, Appenzeller. Here it is, I'm not going to add it to your leave time, too much of a pain in the ass. You're free and clear, my man." He slapped his thigh and laughed. "I can't wait to tell that story. Twenty-one days surfing in Hawaii in the middle of a war, that's the coolest, man, that's just the coolest."

I left glowing from feeling so cool and got back to the motor pool in time to join Romanasky on a parts run. When we stopped at Club 5, Romanasky told everyone my Hawaii story. One guy said, "Got away with it, App! That's so cool, man." The other guys applauded while I beamed.

After our run, we went to the local club. I wasn't so eager to tell the guys in 448 about my exploits and told Romanasky to be cool about it. I didn't want my story to get back to the CO. That night I went to bed feeling like the coolest guy in the world, but the next morning, woke up feeling like I was totally fucked.

I was awaken from a dead sleep when I heard a shrill whistle blowing. My eyes felt like they were glued shut. Another loud whistle and shouting voices invaded the quiet. A guy opened my door yelling at us to get up. I looked down at Chaves trying to wake up. "What the fuck is this, App?" he growled, then yawned and stretched.

"Got me, Freddie. Could be we're under attack."

An MP with a silver helmet stood in the doorway. "You'll get in formation in front of your headquarters in five minutes. You're under arrest. CID has surrounded the Class I compound and the Class I living quarters." He walked down the aisle of our hooch.

"Oh shit! The fucking list."

My heart pounded. Blood rushed to my head. Dizzy, I almost passed out, but held onto my bunk. I anticipated this. Dreaded it. They would read the list and my name was on it.

"You okay, App?" Chaves asked.

"I'm fine, Freddie." I lied, lightheaded. "I'm still tired from the travel."

We got dressed, then, apprehensively, marched to 448 headquarters. I saw the Class I guys and was surprised to see that they didn't look worried. The first sergeant had been gone for over three weeks. I hadn't met the new Top. I didn't see North or Bentley. A portly major with a thin mustache stood in front of us while we stood at attention. He said, "We have information that you've been running a black market in goods from the Class I yard. You're confined to quarters while we search for evidence. Dismissed."

While we walked back to our room, my mind swirling, Chaves faced me. "What's going on, App? You know anything about a black market?"

"I don't know anything, Freddie. It doesn't concern us. We just work in the motor pool, you got that?"

"Yeah, sure, App, no problem, we don't know nothin' from nothin'."

"You got that right, Freddie."

Back in our room, I made some coffee. We put on Cream and listened to Clapton while I waited to be arrested. Finally a loud knock on the door made me shudder. When the door opened, an MP with a stiff backed lieutenant entered. "I'm from CID." He spoke with a controlled, but stern voice. "We know there's a criminal network working in this outfit." He stared at me then Chaves. "You'll tell us everything you know about the Class I yard, then we'll inspect this room for evidence. Is that clear?"

"Yes, sir!" we both said.

I knew the MP from the club. He looked under our beds, in the fridge and cabinets. The CID lieutenant asked for our names and jobs. "I'm Spec Five Appenzeller, sir. I'm the parts guy for the motor pool. This is Spec Five Chaves, the dispatcher."

"Where'd you get this stuff, Appenzeller?" he asked, looking around the room at the cabinet, the bar, the stereo.

"I got a lot from the PX, sir. Made trades for the rest. All aboveboard, I can explain where I got everything."

The MP found my secret place where I kept my money. It was empty. I had spent it all in Hawaii. They found nothing in my room. As they were leaving the lieutenant asked, "Have you seen Spec Five North? He's reported missing. Were either of you friends with him?"

"Not really, sir, North didn't have many friends."

I looked out my door and saw North's lock had been broken, his room torn apart and the bundle of books was gone. The MP and lieutenant stormed out of my room and rushed down the aisle where the rest of the men were lying on bunks. They jumped to attention when they saw the officer, while the MP started going through the footlockers and wall lockers.

Despite Mr. Nguyen's advice, I couldn't stop worrying that my name was on a list somewhere. I spent the day nervously waiting to be arrested. At the end of the day we had another formation in front of headquarters. The CID major asked us one more time if we knew where Spec Five North and Sergeant Bentley were. An MP came out of the office carrying a clipboard. He rushed over to the major and pointed at something on the board.

"What, Soldier? That's impossible!" the major yelled, and looked at the clip board again. "Does anyone know why Spec Five North and Sergeant Bentley's names are on the dispatch list?" He glanced at the CO, who shrugged. When I looked at the

Class I guys, they were smiling at each other.

"I repeat, is there anyone who knows where Spec Five North and Sergeant Bentley are?" No one said a thing.

It dawned on me. North had eyes and ears in Westmoreland's office. They got advance warning. Travel orders were arranged, now North and Bentley were on a plane heading home. I knew North had a plan to send the books when he got to the Philippines. The rest of the Class I guys knew what was up, and their money was stashed where no one could find it. Without the money, the CID had no evidence. No one in Class I was a rat, and there was no way I was going to say a damn thing. I felt like the luckiest guy in the world, and hoped they wouldn't search my office in the motor pool, where I had a bunch of envelopes with my name on them.

Finally we were dismissed and could go get chow. We were no longer under arrest. I was sure there was a big party in the Class I hooch. I didn't go, but was with them in spirit. Walking back to our room, I breathed a huge sigh of relief. Chaves turned to me and asked. "What was that all about, Apple? Do you know anything about that black market stuff?"

"Freddie, you don't want to know, my friend."

A huge weight was lifted from my shoulders and for the first time in months, I felt light as a feather on a breeze. I'd get the money out of the envelopes, find Mr. Nguyen, give him the piasters and save the MPC for when I went home. With my my monthly checks that I had not yet cashed, I knew I'd have a pretty nice pile.

Now I was free to look forward to my R&R in the coolest place in Vietnam - Vung Tau. Nice beaches with waves every so often. I know I was just back from my leave with Alexandra, but need-ed to relax after this stressful day.

I had a few drinks with Chaves then we shared a Winston. It felt great to lay down and, for the first time in a long time, I wasn't thinking thoughts of Long Binh Jail. I wondered how North and Bentley were doing. I pictured them being taken into custody in Hawaii, neither with more than a hundred bucks on them; North's books were on the way to Gary, Indiana, Bentley had stores filled with contraband in Detroit. It was a good ending for a bad business.

.

Chapter 31

Davey

We were in our fourth day of non-stop rain. Planks were laid out between hooches. The motor pool became a quagmire. I hoped my R&R to Vung Tau for the coming weekend would have better weather than Long Binh's.

I hated being in the office alone without Mr. Nguyen. I thought about him a lot, especially when I heard that Ho Chi Minh had died. No Vietnamese showed up for work that day. We heard rockets over head most of the day. Most bound for the ammo dump. I still had the new years letter Ho Chi Ming wrote and wondered how Mr. Nguyen was doing. I read the letter again and felt bad that my efforts to locate Mr. Nguyen on the post were not successful.

After my return from Hawaii, there wasn't much to do in the motor pool, so I investigated the best way to get to Vung Tau. I didn't have access to maps of the region, but heard that it was a peninsula some sixty miles from Saigon, even further from Bien Hoa. Because we were close to the 24th Evac Hospital, there was a constant flow of Hueys bringing in wounded soldiers. I had heard that 24th Evac could be my best bet for a quick ride to Vung Tau.

I had been to 24th Evac only once. Back in my first month in the hooch, I'd found a forty-five inch industrial fan that I set on my footlocker to keep the mosquitoes away. One night, Albertson, the walking-on-hands bodybuilder, turned it so it was facing him. I woke up sweating with mosquitoes buzzing around me. When I got up to move the fan, my thumb slipped through the screen encasing the blades slicing it deeply. I was so damn furious, I pounded him with my bloody hand while he was wrapped in his blanket.

After recovering from my fury, he walked with me to 24th Evac where a nurse with short curly hair gave me some morphine for the pain and stitched me up. She rolled her eyes when I asked if this qualified me for a Purple Heart.

In the afternoon I walked to the helipad at 24th Evac to ask about Hueys going to Vung Tau and found out they went every so often. My R&R was a day away, I thought it might be worth a shot. I'd return on Friday to get a ride. While walking out of 24th Evac, I saw a guy sitting behind the wheel of a jeep. He looked familiar. The amazing look of recognition came over us at the same time.

"Appie!" he shouted.

"Davey!" I yelled, unable to believe that I was running into my bud from back home - Davey Manfrino, the fire chief's son, halfway around the world in a war zone. He jumped out of the jeep, and, wow, did we ever hug each other.

It turns out Davey, a medic with the 4th Infantry Division, was driving a doctor from his combat outfit to the hospital. I told him he had to check out my living quarters in the 448. He ran inside to square it with the doctor, then came out saying that he had an hour.

Thankfully, it had stopped raining, so we walked on the paved road until we came to the 448, then walked on the planks covering the mud until we got to my hooch. I opened the door. Davey's eyes practically bulged out of his head when he saw my room. "You rear-echelon motherfucker, Appie. What the hell is this place?"

"This is my room, Davey. I have access to lots of things through being a parts clerk in the motor pool. I poured him a glass of Chivas Regal, which he downed in one gulp.

"No shit, I've never seen anything like this. We live in fucking tents."

Davey looked much older than when I saw him last at our final physical before basic training. I remembered Davey being the funniest guy I had ever met. His jokes and funny observations were the main part of his lively personality, but now his eyes no longer had that spark. I wondered what happened to him.

"So what have you been doing, Davey?"

"You don't want to know. It's been fucked up being a medic in the fucking 4th. We've been in Tay Ninh and Pleiku almost to the fucking Cambodian border. We've seen some shit, man."

I saw his empty glass and refilled it.

"What the fuck have you been doing? You've been here your whole tour? Motherfucking REMFs; I hate to tell you, Appie, but you guys make me sick."

I shrugged. "I was lucky to get this assignment. I knew how to run a motor pool, so they gave me a combat promotion to E5 so I could run it. A month ago I stayed with Alexandra in Hawaii for fourteen days, then moved in with Joey Cohen for another week. They arrested me when I got back, but I talked my way out of it. Didn't even get leave time taken away."

He just looked at me real hard, then sighed. Obviously, he didn't think that was as funny as my REMF friends did. I doubted anything seemed funny to Davey Manfrino anymore. He took another long swallow of Chivas, and I filled his glass again.

"So how was fucking Cohen?" he asked.

"Lucky bastard has been in Hawaii for his whole tour. Medical clerk in the clinic at Schofield Barracks. I almost went in with him on the buddy system. Would have spent my whole tour in Hawaii. What a cool place that is, Davey. Where'd you spend your R&R?"

"Went to Bangkok to bang some whores. It reminded me of Saigon. It was okay. Fast fucking seven days."

I didn't want him to think it had been all fun and games during my tour, so I told him how we got attacked during Tet. "We sat in foxholes and had to shoot across the road. Saw the Air Cal put on a show. It was hairy during Tet."

He just looked at me perplexed, like angry dark thoughts were rising. When I filled his glass again, he said, "I won a Silver-fucking-Star during

Tet. I had to stack up wounded guys to protect less wounded guys from enemy fire. We were out in the open waiting for a Huey. You could hear the bullets smash into the guys. We saved ten, lost twenty."

I saw that this memory, mixed with the booze, was making him angry. Looking around my room, made him angrier still.

"You motherfucking REMFs, livin good while guys are dying; what a bunch of shit."

"This war is nothing but shit, Davey. We don't belong here; it's not our war."

"Fuck you, Appie. My guys didn't die for nothing. Don't tell me that."

I had nothing more to say. He had seen friends die. He'd had to sacrifice some to save others. It was impossible for him to think that it had all been for nothing. For him, it was personal. I wasn't going to argue with him, so I changed the subject. "How much longer do you have, Davey?"

"I'm short, I got less than a month. I'm not going out there again. I'm out when I get home. I'll try to forget the whole motherfucking thing." He looked at his watch. "I gotta go,

Appie. The doc should be done soon. When do you get back?"

"I'm about a month out. I got a two-week early out. My next assignment is at Fort Ord. Alexandra will come up there to live with me. I got a whole year more in this fucking Army."

He took one more scornful look around my room before he left. "Fucking REMFs!" he said bitterly, as we stomped out of my room. Outside, by the road, we stood there for a few seconds - me in my new fatigues with polished boots, Davey in his dusty, worn fatigues stained with what I knew was blood. While we shook hands, it broke my heart that he was no longer the funny friend I knew a year ago. When he walked towards the hospital, a bit on the wobbly side, I heard his bitter voice yell out one more time, "FUCKING REMFs!"

.

Chapter 32

The South China Sea
Surf Club

I woke early on Friday ready for my R&R. Hearing nothing pounding on the metal roof, I realized it had stopped raining. I dressed in one of my Hawaii outfits: tan linen shorts, white and tan flowered shirt, my penny loafers with no socks. In Hawaii I bought a light brown leather bag a little bigger than a briefcase and stuffed the other clothes I'd bought in Honolulu into the bag. I threw in a pair of low-top black Converse tennis shoes with a pair of socks. At the last minute, I decided to bring the Colt Commander I'd been carrying lately, and wedged it next to my toiletries. That was it.

As I was leaving for my three days, Chaves threw a small light yellow box at me with a picture in front of a bearded guy wearing a cool hat with a feather. Written in red was Raleigh.

"You have a three-day weekend, App. Smoke 'em if you got 'em," Chaves said, smiling.

Inside, there were ten brown filter tips with light brown paper that had been soaked in opium. Happily, I opened my little suitcase and tucked them into one of my Converse shoes.

When I walked to the helipad outside the 24th Evac Hospital, the dispatcher said I was on standby and needed to wait. Fortunately several Agatha Christie novels had been moving around the 448, I brought one with me and started on it, somehow, ignoring the continuous beating blades of the Bell UH 1 Iroquois, popularly called a Huey. By ten o'clock the dispatcher alerted me that a Huey was going to Vung Tau. Excited, I grabbed my bag, ran under the blades, my hair and cloths blowing from whirling wind as I climbed into the open cab.

A rush swept through me and my heart was in my mouth as the Lycoming T53-L-13 engine thrust us straight up into the air, flying forward across Long Binh. I feared high places, and here I was definitely in a high place. Strapped in, leaning against the back bulkhead, I saw on my left a big M60 machine gun with a lean, young corporal sitting behind it.

The loud engine rang in my ears, and the strong wind rushed by while my queasy stomach quivered. We flew over open territory, farms and small villages passed under us. In the distance, I saw the blue green ocean. We were flying over a thousand yards high and soon the peninsula with the small town of Vung Tau got closer. The pilot circled over the base on the outside of town, then landed on the heliport. After jumping out, the corporal threw me my bag.

When I asked where I should go to show my R&R orders, a PFC pointed to a headquarters building, where I checked in and asked where to spend the night. The Spec Four behind the counter said, "You have all day to play, but you need to be off the streets by ten. There are some hotels downtown, get secured in one of them."

"I heard that Charlie gets to party after ten. Is that true or bullshit?"

"That's a rumor, but you have to be off the streets by ten. The Australians run the town, and they'll bust you if you're walking around past the curfew. You got that?"

"Got it. How do you get to the beach from here?"

"Grab a Lambretta. Tell the driver you want to go to the beach."

I stepped outside, then walked down a paved road to a gate where an MP sat. Being in civilian clothes, I kept my orders with me and some ID. I showed him my papers and asked about the beach when he handed them back. He pointed to a Lambretta, an Italian three-wheeled vehicle two can ride in comfortably with the driver up front.

"Take me to the beach," I asked the tiny Vietnamese driver.

We bounced through the town of Vung Tau, which was much like Bien Hoa with bright colored buildings of two to three stories jammed together on narrow streets. Bikes, motorbikes, and Lambrettas could move easily along, but cars and military vehicles slowed everything down.

Many Vietnamese crowded the streets, or sat in front of their businesses chatting in small groups. I saw motorbike repair shops, tailors from Hong Kong and India, many restaurants and bars. Some bars looked more shabby or sordid than others. In front of several Australian bars a bunch of guys stood with beers in their hands wearing light khaki uniforms and bush hats buttoned up on one side. Other bars had GIs with women in assorted outfits, most being a long slim dress with a slit up the side to just below the armpit and flowing matching pants underneath. Vung Tau appeared to have a booming economy untouched by war.

The Lambretta drove out of town onto bumpy dirt roads between sand dunes and brush. We came to a long stretch of beach with a white building in the center. Tables, chairs, and a bar appeared with several guys lounging around in swimsuits. At some of the tables soldiers on R&R sat with pretty Vietnamese women.

I paid the driver and looked for a bathroom where I could change into my swimsuit. I noticed a couple of old longboards leaning against the building near the bathroom. I was stoked to see some white water hitting the beach.

On the sand about halfway to the water was a small tower with a guy sitting under a light green umbrella. After changing into my swimsuit, I walked across the hot sand with my leather briefcase, then asked the lifeguard if I could use a board. Tanned, with bleached-blond hair, he asked where I was from. I told him Oxnard. He smiled and said he had surfed Rincon and California Street in Ventura. When I told him I lived at Silver Strand, his eyes widened.

"Dude, I heard Silver Strand is gnarly. My bud's car got fucked up there. It's totally a locals only place."

"It is, man. My folks rented a house there the summer of my junior year in high school. I got to know the locals. The toughest were Mexican surfers who weren't cool with anyone outside their group. I was lucky to become friends with a few of them, so they let me in the lineup."

"You going to take out one of the longboards?"

"Yeah, I'd like to. I just got back from Hawaii. I was there for twenty-one days."

"How in the fuck did you do that?"

"Long story, but I got away with it. Now I'm here in Vung Tau hoping to get a wave or two."

"Welcome to the South China Sea Surf Club, my friend. You should get one of these downtown." He turned so I could see a rough tattoo on his shoulder of a longboard crossed with an M16 rifle. South China Sea was written above the graphic, Surf Club below.

"Grab a board, man. We rarely have anything to surf, but there's a little swell today. You can leave your stuff here. I'll watch it for you."

I put my leather bag under his tower, went back to grab a board, then looked around for some wax. I asked a few Australians who laughed, having heard the question many times. The surface of the board was pretty rough, so I scratched it up some more with sand.

It wasn't much of a wave - just a one to two foot beach breach break with few, if any, peaks. They were so small that all I could do was catch the break, pop up, and ride the whitewater. It was barely surfing, but it was surfing nonetheless. After an hour or so, I took the board back to the lifeguard stand. He gave me a thumbs up as I grabbed my bag. After putting the board back along the wall of the R&R center, I went to the bar under the zinc roof and ordered a beer. Like many government clubs, they featured Schlitz.

An Australian standing at the bar nearby said, "These are shitty little beers." He opened both sides to his can, threw back his head, downing most of the Schlitz in one swig.

I stepped away from the bar and looked for a spot at a table. That's when I remembered the Raleighs. Rummaging through my bag I found the pack, pulled out a light brown Raleigh, stepped outside the R&R center, moved toward the sand dunes, where, hidden from view, I took two healthy tokes, felt the effects, then, after two more bigger hits, man, was I stoned. I snuffed out the joint in the sand and stuffed it back into the pack.

My body was floating when I got back to the R&R center, where I ordered another Schlitz, pulled out a chair, and sat at a table in the blazing sun. Listening to a DJ playing records, the music now seemed louder and vibrated. The blue sea gleamed, and white waves sparkled as they crashed on the beach. Above, big white clouds drifted in various shapes. Stoned and realizing I was burning in the sun, I found a place under the zinc roof, pulled my chair up, laid my head on the table for just a second, and, not realizing it, I dozed off.

Somewhere in my foggy brain, I heard, "Dude! Hey, Silver Strand guy!"

Someone slapped me on the shoulder. I recognized the lifeguard. "You've been sitting here all afternoon, dude. It's seven-thirty, they're closing up the place. You have to *de de mow.*"

Not knowing exactly what *de de mow* meant in Vietnamese, I figured it meant I had to go. My neck hurt from being in the same position for such a long time. I felt slobber on my hand where my head had been. Still groggy, I gazed up at him, "What do I do now, man?"

"You've got to find a place to stay. There are some hotels, but most of them are booked by now. You have to be off the streets by ten or the Aussie MPs will arrest you for breaking curfew. Grab a Lambretta, have the driver take you to town to check out hotels."

There was only one Lambretta by the R&R center, so the lifeguard rode with me part way. Apparently he had a girl friend outside of town. When we arrived at his stop, he told the Lambretta driver to find me a room. We bounced around on the muddy roads until we got to town. We stopped at a few hotels, but all were completely booked.

Famished after, surfing and sleeping, I had the driver drop me off at an Australian bar - an old wooden building with a well stocked bar and ten to fifteen tables. After ordering a burger, I asked the Australian bartender where I could get a room. He pointed to a bar across the street. "There are lots of girls in that bar. A few will take you home for the right price," he said in his Australian accent. The burger with fries was excellent along with the Australian beer. After paying, I started across the street to the bar.

A red neon sign out front blinked the club's name *Su Secret* on and off. Also, in flashing neon was a sexy girl with a leg in the air, her head thrown back facing the sky. Opening the door, I strained to see anything in the dim light. The first clear thing I saw was the bar, which also had red neon lights around a big mirror. From behind the bar, an older Vietnamese woman stood smiling at me. To my right were several tall tables; one with two GIs and a couple of Vietnamese women, at another table sat five women looking at me trying to make eye contact.

I walked to the bar, and after checking out the bottles on the shelves in front of the mirror, asked for a Chivas Regal. The attractive, older Vietnamese lady picked up a glass and polished it with a small rag. After taking down the bottle of Chivas, she poured a finger full into the glass, she glanced at the girls, nodding with her head for them to move in my direction. She then smiled at me. It wasn't easy to focus on them in the dim light, but as they got closer, I saw that some were clearly as old as the bartender, others younger.

"You want to buy drink for pretty girl?" the bartender asked.

In the pocket of my shorts was a nice wad of piasters, the last of my earnings from the 448 black market. After quickly assessing the women surrounding me, I pointed to a short young woman with a pretty face, and a slight enticing smile on her red lips. She wore a long pink dress split down one side with long white pants underneath.

When the others drifted away, she came over and stood beside me.

Her raven black hair hung halfway down her back, and her smile revealed sparkling white teeth. She was lovely, but her age could have been any where from sixteen to thirty. When she put her hand on my arm and moved closer to me, I looked into her dark black eyes and asked her name in English. She looked confused and glanced over to the bartender.

"She new girl, she not speak English. Her name Lan,"

Pointing at her I said, "Lan?" She smiled eagerly nodding up and down. I pointed at myself, "Robbie". She looked at me and said, "Lobby." Knowing how difficult it was for Vietnamese to pronounce the letter R I just nodded. She leaned a little closer, smiling, and I smelled her sweet fragrance.

The bartender brought her a drink. We clicked glasses taking sips while looking into each other's eyes. She was so cute, in fact after several drinks, very cute. I looked at her with so many emotions fighting for dominance. Her hand on my arm brought a tingling to my loins. It had been well over a month since I had last had any sex. The manly part of me wanted to have sex with this lovely person. The last person I had sex with was Alexandra, my wife, who I loved. Lan could be a real challenge to my wedding vows.

A glance at my watch showed that it was well after nine, which increased my anxiety. I had less than an hour to be off the streets of Vung Tau. I signaled the bartender, while she served one of the other men. When she came over to me and Lan, I said, "I'm on R&R from Long Binh. I don't have a place to stay the night. I need to find a room. Do you have one here?"

"No, GI, we don't have room. But you can go with Lan. You must pay bar fee, you must pay for long time stay." She looked at Lan and spoke in rapid Vietnamese. Lan nodded, but asked a few questions, which left me wondering what they were saying. Lan looked shyly at me, and nodding with a sweet but very suggestive smile, gripped my arm firmly, letting me know I would be staying with her.

Relieved, but in turmoil, I ordered another drink for the two of us and gazed closely at Lan's lovely face. Though she was in high-heeled shoes, I imagined she was well under five feet tall. She had small, delicate hands, one still squeezing my arm, the other gripping her drink. Looking deeply into each others eyes, my heart melting at the intensity building between us. I suddenly remembered the time, and, glancing at my watch, panicked when I saw it after nine-thirty.

I asked the bartender how much for the bar tab plus the bar fee for Lan. She scribbled some numbers on a piece of paper and with a big smile handed it to me. I pulled out my wad of piasters, counted the money, giving her a nice tip. She smiled even more broadly, then glanced and nodded at Lan. I grabbed my bag and left *Su Secret* with Lan on my arm.

The town was busier than when I had entered the bar. The outdoor restaurants were full and lively. Little markets had ducks hanging by their necks alongside plates of exotic Vietnamese food. The fragrance of cooked meat coming from grills in front of the restaurants was intoxicating. Seeing many more Vietnamese men walking around in the street, the thought they may be Viet Cong caused a slight tremble.

Holding my hand and weaving our way through the foot traffic, we crossed several streets, dodging motorbikes, then turned down a dark side alley less than two yards wide. She stopped in front of a wooden door with a Buddhist icon nailed to it. She kicked off her high heels. After I slipped out of my penny loafers, I realized I stood over a head taller than her.

She opened the door to a little hallway with a shrine to the fat Buddha smiling into space, then bowed while lighting a candle. I bowed, too, prayer hands touching my nose, then mimed that I would like to light a candle. Smiling sweetly, she handed me the still burning match. I lit one of the candles, and looking at the Buddha, asked for his help in the excruciating decision I faced. Lan looked up and smiled at me with more affection as I showed my respect for the Buddha. She blew out the match and placed it in a small dish with other spent matches.

She tiptoed up the stairs to the right of the Buddha. Glancing back, she waved at me to follow. My heart thumped hard, blood rushed into my brain. My sexual desire was at an all time high. My attraction to her, and her affection to me, as well as her petite, sexy body, had me struggling desperately with my arousal.

When we rounded a corner into a living room, an entire family was waiting for her. A mother stood in the kitchen preparing what looked to be a large meal. Four children watched something on a black-and-white TV, while her father sat in a comfortable green chair in one corner, reading a book, his head surrounded by smoke from the long pipe in his mouth.

I stood there in the doorway startled by this turn of events. Lan looked back at me and smiled, then walked over to her father, and bowing, spoke in a hushed tone. He nodded. She moved to her mother and also spoke quietly to her. When her mother looked at me, I made prayer hands and bowed. She did the same, smiling. The children took their eyes off the TV to ponder who their sister had brought home. They smiled, while speaking to each other, a few breaking into giggles.

Relieved that I may not have to break my wedding vows, I suddenly felt comfortable with this family in the same way I did with Mr. Nguyen's. I saw they had a table set for dinner. Lan's mom found an extra stool, put it with the others, then efficiently moved the settings around, placing a white plate with a set of chopsticks on the table. Her father closed his book, stood, and walked toward me. Barely five feet tall, he stood in front of me and bowed. I bowed back. He motioned for me to set my bag down by the wall and come sit at the table. When I did, I noticed his dark hair combed neatly back and his clean shaven face.

Lan sat to my right, her father to my left. Her mother's slightly graying hair was tied in a bun, and she was dressed in traditional Vietnamese clothing. When she placed bowls in front of us, mouthwatering aromas rose with the steaming orange colored soup with green leaves floating on top. Noodles with bits of chicken added to the delicious appearance. Having eaten only a few hours before, I thought I was not hungry, but the delightful aroma from the kitchen encouraged my appetite.

The children stared at me as I picked up my chopsticks, reached into the soup, and pulled out a large steaming bundle of noodles. They looked disappointed, ready to laugh at my inept attempt at using chopsticks. When I stuffed the noodles into my mouth my eyes started to water. As soon as I swallowed the noodles, I reached for the glass of water. Now the children got a chance to laugh as I frantically waved my hand at my mouth.

When we were finished with the soup, Lan and her mother picked up our bowls and placed them into the small sink in the kitchen. Lan came back with a bowl of steaming rice and using a large spoon, put a big scoop of rice onto the plates her mother had placed in front of us. This was followed by big bowls of food filled with vegetables mixed with meat or seafood. Each had its own delightful aroma. Her father took the first bowl, using a big spoon he placed the food beside his rice. He passed it to me. When I did the same, I passed it to Lan, who glanced at me shyly and we smiled affectionately at each other. There were four dishes, each with its own special set of spices and smells. It was wonderful sharing this meal with these kind people. The meal lasted over an hour with much discussion between family members. They ate slowly, talking and laughing between bites.

When I could eat no more, I placed my napkin onto my plate and leaned away from the table. Soon, the others did the same. The children, ranging in age between seven and twelve, began moving around the table gathering plates and bowls.

Lan's father walked over to an open window, indicating that I should follow. He brought out his pipe, cleaned it with a thin metal wire, stuffed tobacco into the bowl and lit it. Big puffs of smoke billowed around us. The tobacco smell had a sweet fragrance. I took out my pack of Tareytons and raised my eyebrows to him as a way of asking permission.

After several nods from him, I tapped one out of the pack, lit it with my lighter, took a deep drag, letting a big puff of smoke drift out the window.

I loved standing there smoking with him while the family cleaned up.

Once the family had finished cleaning the kitchen, the children moved over to the couch to watch TV. Lan came over to me while cleaning her hands on a towel. She put her hand on my arm then leaned on me. If the father noticed this, he didn't seem concerned. Lan pointed to an opening in the living room into a hallway with two doors on one side and one on the other. The father walked with Lan and me down the hallway. He showed me the bathroom at the end of the hall. It had a small toilet with a chain hanging from a tank above it. He motioned toward the shower and sink making it clear that I could use them.

He opened one of the doors along the hallway. When I saw the small bed, I understood that this was where he wanted me to sleep. I nodded, doing prayer hands to show my gratitude. I didn't know if I should pay him now or before I left. He walked away, leaving Lan and me standing outside the room. She went into the living area bringing back my leather bag. She gave it to me then nodded toward the bathroom.

I used the toilet, shaved, crammed myself into the shower, washed myself under the soothing warm water, then dried off with a small towel. Feeling clean for the first time all day, I put on a pair of shorts and a shirt that I would wear tomorrow. Lan walked me down the hallway to where the family was now watching TV, then used the empty bathroom. I bowed my thanks to the family. They smiled, bowed, then turned their attention back to the TV. I went into the bedroom and closed the door.

The bed was so small, my feet hung over the edge. Having slept for several hours at the beach, sleep seemed out of the question. The question was what to do if Lan joined me. I heard a light knock on the door. Lan slipped in wearing a light silk slip. She looked down at me and smiled. In the light coming from the hall the thin slip could not hide the body underneath.

After closing the door, she went to the small window. When she opened it, a little light and fresh air came into the small room. She stood by the window, her face framed by the light. She smiled, reached down, gathered the edges of her slip, then slowly pulled it over her head. Her long black hair flowed over her shoulders cascading down her back. Though tiny, her breasts were full with small dark nipples. Her hips were wider than I'd imagined and she had a silver jewel in her belly button. The dark bush at the top of her legs was trimmed into a slight V shape.

I swallowed at her beauty and knew this was going to be the biggest test ever for my wedding vows.

I lay on the bed in my boxers and gazed at her sweet, almost innocent smile, her dark intense eyes penetrating me. She inched closer to the bed, then laying down, forced me to move next to the wall. With her back pressed against my chest, she reached behind her with her hand, grabbed my left hand, and pulled it to her breast. She moved closer to me, pressing her soft round ass against me in a most enticing way. Despite a wave of guilt, I pulled down my boxers, my vows quickly fading with the rising desire possessing me. How could I disappoint this luscious, lovely, sexy young woman, and me? My guilt was submerged by the overwhelming force of passion, erupting in exquisite orgasms that, for those wonderful moments, took my mind away from the horrible reality that I had broken my vows.

.

Chapter 33

MIA

I didn't sleep well with Lan. The small bed made it difficult to stretch out and get into a good sleeping position, but more than that, my quilt washed over me like a crashing wave. With my passionate lust satisfied, my vows broken, the horror of imagining Alexandra breaking hers, cheating, making love to another man, overwhelmed me with painful, jealous thoughts. A dark cloud hovered over me and made the small bed like a cage. *My God, what have I done?*

I think I dozed for a while, but never went into a deep sleep. Next to me, Lan slept peacefully, rarely moving. I checked on her breathing a few times, she was that still.

Eventually, as the sun lightened the room, Lan began to stir. She opened her eyes, recognized me, smiled while wiggling her bottom closer. I put my arm around her and felt her soft warmth.

Soon we heard movement in the hallway and knew the family was up. Lan moved away and sat up. When I stood and stretched, gazing down at her lovely nude body, I started getting an erection. I turned away letting my wavering conscience guide me reluctantly to get dressed.

Lan picked up her slip from the floor, and pulled it over her head. She took my hand, giving it an affectionate squeeze, then opened the door. Seeing the bathroom door was closed, we went into the family room where the children were sitting at the table. Rice and leftovers from the night before were in little white bowls on the table. Their mom was boiling water for tea. The father came out of the bathroom and took his seat at the head of the table. We smiled, and bowed a greeting to each other as I went to the bathroom to freshen up.

I sat next to Lan at the table. Not used to rice first thing in the morning, I picked at it and the leftover food. I looked around, apparently there would be no coffee. Bumping Lan's shoulder with mine to get her attention, I pantomimed the act of paying. She understood, giving me a lovely smile. Pulling out the wad of piasters from my pocket, I placed some in front of her. She went through them, selecting several and seemed satisfied with the transaction. I moved the wad over in front of her father. He selected a few more. I took the remainder, walked around the table, giving piasters to each of the children and their mom. Their smiling eyes told me how happy they were to receive the money. Lan came over to me, giving me an affectionate hug. I bowed to each member of the family with prayer hands, and they reverently bowed back.

After getting my bag, Lan and I walked down the stairs to the Buddha statue. When I asked if I could light a candle, she gave me a delighted nod. I lit a candle and bowed deeply to the Buddha with prayer hands. When we bowed to each other, Lan had a radiant sweet smile on her lovely, innocent face. When I walked outside into the morning sunshine, a warm glowing feeling rose in me for the family I had spent a lovely night with, but nothing could take away the darkness of my broken vows to Alexandra.

Strolling through the streets of Vung Tau, I eventually found the Australian bar and a much needed cup of coffee. I started a conversation with the owner, a stout, jovial man, and found out he'd been stationed in Vung Tau a few years before, returning to run this bar with his Vietnamese wife, who was cleaning tables and helping the cook. He seemed content with his life.

I left the bar, found a Lambretta, instructing the driver to take me back to the beach. It was the only thing I could think of to do. It had rained in the night, and the streets were wet and muddy. The Lambretta weaved through the crowded streets of Vung Tau, and finally reached the beach. In the sunlight just breaking through thick gray clouds, I was happy to see a wave breaking about twenty yards out.

Setting up his stand, the lifeguard unfolded his umbrella, then applied some lotion to his shoulders from a brown plastic bottle. I pushed through the warming sand to the tower and asked if I could use a board. "Absolutely, dude, no problem."

Curious, I asked where he was from. When he said Malibu, we talked about surfing at South County Line and Leo Carrillo. He described other secret spots he and his buds surfed in the Malibu area. I asked how he got this job, and he told me, "Right place at the right time." I told him I could relate.

I told him about my twenty-one days in Hawaii, describing how I got away with it with no punishment. He laughed, astonished, saying, "Man, that's the coolest, fucking, story I ever heard."

After talking, I took out the board again and surfed the whitewater, caught a few faces on some waves, but not many. When I got out of the water, my ribs were sore, my back was burnt, but I was happy I still had the muscle memory and strength to ride the waves.

The bar restaurant had a grill, so I ordered a burger with a Schlitz. Following a second beer and a Tareyton, I took out the half-burned Raleigh, went behind the dunes for a few tokes, came back, found some shade, lay down, and fell into a deep sleep.

I was awakened this time by the feel of the warm sun on my face. It was late afternoon and the sun had moved a long way toward the West. I was hungry and still tired since I didn't sleep well with Lan. I changed out of my bathing suit into my black shorts and polo shirt and put on my black Converse tennis shoes.

I found a Lambretta and pantomimed sleeping to the driver, so he would take me to a hotel. We bounced along the dirt road away from the beach. He made a turn to the right at a spot in the road that surprised me, I thought town was straight ahead, but I figured he knew where he was going. The road was muddy and little used, and seemed to me to be heading away from town. It went on for several miles, and I noticed the terrain was now populated with different species of trees and thick overgrown brush with few open spaces. There was no sign of civilization. I wondered where in the hell he was taking me. Soon we came around a corner where in the distance I could see a dilapidated house. As we approached, I saw some movement around the house.

The Lambretta slowed as we came closer. The movement turned out to be soldiers in jungle fatigues with M16s at their sides, bandoliers of bullets around their shoulders. The closest soldier started running to the Lambretta, locking and loading his weapon. He pointed it at me yelling in a deep southern accent, "Who in the fuck are you? What the fuck are you doing here? Get out of that goddamn Lambretta."

He was a big black guy and appeared to be both scared and angry. Startled and trembling, I got out of the Lambretta with my hands up.

"Bryant, come over here and check this guy out."

Another black soldier approached, his uniform showed no rank. I looked at the first black guy, and saw his patches had also been ripped off his fatigues. The guy called Bryant patted me down, then began tying my hands behind my back.

"What's going on here, guys?"

"Who the fuck are you? We're MIAs. We ain't going back to no motherfucking army."

Holy shit! I had to do some fast talking. "I'm with you guys on that!" I blurted out.

"What do you mean?" the leader asked.

"Bro, I've been on the run now for days. I almost got away in Hawaii." I started slowly, making it up as I went along. "I stayed twenty-one days. They finally caught me and brought me back. They were processing me for being AWOL when I got away. I'm looking for a place to stay until I can get my head straight and figure out a way to get to Laos or Cambodia. I'm done with this fucking war, man. What the fuck are you guys doing?"

I looked the leader in the eye, my heart beating madly, hoping he would believe me.

Bryant let go of my hands, pulled the rope away and I continued. "Listen, bro, I ain't bullshitting you. Check out my briefcase, you'll find nothing but Hawaiian clothes and a Colt Commander. I'm on the run same as you. I'm glad I found you."

Bryant checked out my bag and pulled out the Colt, aimed it at a tree, pulled the trigger, and when it went off, the loud shot rang in my ears, making my heart leap, and my head dizzy.

"Motherfucker works," said Bryant, with a smile, admiring the pistol in his hand.

Three other black guys came running around the corner, M16s pulled tight under their arms. "What the fuck is going on?" one of them yelled.

"Got us another deserter," Bryant said laughing. He tucked my Colt under his belt. All five now glared at me. I stood my ground, but dressed in my spiffy civilian cloths, knew I didn't fit the image of a deserter.

One of them yelled, "What's your name, deserter?"

"It's Appenzeller. People call me App."

"Where you from, App?"

"Oxnard, California. Where you guys from?"

"I'm from fucking Texas," Bryant said. "Jones is from Alabama, Thomson's from Georgia, Wilson's from North Carolina and our leader Snowden is from Mississippi. We're Southern blacks who have had enough of this white man's war."

"You got that fucking right, Bryant," Snowden said, then faced me. "You got any money, App?"

"Yeah, I was with the 448 in Long Binh. We're Class I. We got busted a month back by CID. I had some money hidden away." I pulled out the piasters to show what I had.

"Cool, man. Let's send Yu to Vung Tau for some booze and shit. Hey,Yu!" he yelled at the Lambretta driver. Yu came running. "I don't know why you brought this motherfucker here, but it turned out okay. Don't bring anyone again, sabe?" The frightened Lambretta driver nodded. Snowden turned to Wilson, "Have him take Mim with him. Give her the money. We can trust her."

Near the run-down house, I saw several Vietnamese women hanging back. When Wilson yelled at them in Vietnamese, a small, young, black haired woman came over. She nodded, then smiled as Wilson spoke Vietnamese to her. A second later, she took the money, climbed into the Lambretta, and Yu and Mim slowly took off in the direction of the setting sun.

"Check out what we got going here, man," said Jones as we walked along an old dirt path toward the house. "This is the best place we've had since we took off five months ago. This here is the kitchen."

They had piled up rocks to support a makeshift grill that used to be a fan cover. Embers smoldered under it with a thin spire of smoke rising straight up. A couple of old pots and pans were scattered next to a pile of kindling.

"We sleep inside, and we got girls with us." He pointed at Wilson. "Wilson speaks Vietnamese. The girls talk to him all the time. I'm getting better at it." They had some logs to sit on around the fire. "Goddamn it!" Jones said, slapping his leg. "We should have told Mim to get us some cigarettes. I need a smoke, man."

I pulled out my pack of Tareytons, grabbed one for myself, and tossed the pack to Jones. Thanking me, he took a couple, and passed the pack on to Bryant. By now all of them were sitting around the fire, a woman at the side of each guy. I flipped the lighter to Jones after lighting my cigarette. "So what the fuck happened to you guys? Why are you on the run?"

"We lost it when King got shot, right guys?" Snowden spoke and the others nodded, agreeing. "It was bad enough being in this white man's army fighting in a stupid war for no good reason, but when they killed King, that was the end for us. None of us wanted to go back to no USA anyway. The Vietnamese treat us better than the redneck assholes back home." While listening, scenes from my travels through the South and my grandfather's house flashed through my mind. "What's it with you, App? Why'd you leave?"

"Similar reason, I knew when they shot Bobby Kennedy they were never going to end this war. It's a fucked-up war, man. I found out the real reason we're here and it changed my life, bro'. With all the shit that went down in Chicago, Nixon is going to win this election. He's in a whole other classification of assholes. He's the king of the assholes. I know, he's from California, even my mom and dad hate his ass."

"It's fucked up for sure, App. So what's your story about the real reason we're here?"

"It's a long story, but I'll tell you the short version. First, ask the ladies what they think about Ho Chi Minh. I bet they'll tell you that they would have voted for him in a heartbeat if they had a chance. That was supposed to happen in 1956, but the U.S. and the Catholic Church worked together to stop the election."

"The Catholic Church? You've got to be kidding me, man."

"No, the Pope hated communism. It's godless, and that's bad for business. They worked with the Nazis and Fascists to destroy the godless Soviet Union. They were disappointed with World War II. The Soviets came out of the war a huge superpower spreading the idea of a godless communism to the poor countries of the world." I leaned forward and knew they were listening.

"They took a stand in Vietnam. The U.S. negotiated a peace agreement which forced Ho Chi Minh to allow Vietnam to be divided into north and south. They guaranteed Ho Chi Minh a unification election in '56. The Catholic lobby and the anti-communists worked together to make sure that didn't happen." I lit up another Tareyton.

"They put one Catholic family, the Diems, in charge of the government, the police and the Church in South Vietnam. The Pope wanted a Catholic nation of South Vietnam. So, we're here fighting for the Catholics and the corporations who hate communism, because it's bad for both businesses."

"Fuck, man. That's a wild story, App, Where did you hear that story, man?"

"I had an old papa-san named Mr. Nguyen tell me his version of why we were here. It makes sense if you understand that the U.S. is the defender of the free enterprise system and the Catholics want more and more converts. There's a whole other fucked up story about how the church fooled people into giving up their property in North Vietnam to move to the South. I used to be Catholic, but I'm not now. I used to love the U.S., but I don't now."

By now the sun had set into the South China Sea. The women began building a bigger fire. The Lambretta returned with Yu and Mim along with some food and cheap Vietnam whiskey. While the women went to work on dinner the guys started passing around the bottle. When it came to me I pretended to take a gulp. Though I felt connected to these guys, I knew I couldn't be with them. I was not a deserter. I didn't believe in this fucking war, but I'd serve my time, determined to get back to Alexandra.

"So you're with us now, right, App?" Wilson asked after taking a swig of the whiskey.

"Do or die, brother. Do or die."

"We've kept alive, App. We been on the run the whole time, but the people don't rat us out to the Army. We hope to last this thing out, get to Cambodia or Laos and live with the people."

"I love these people, my friends. I love their beliefs in Buddhism. It's peaceful. It's about finding the middle path. I want that middle path. I won't fight for greed and wealth against the common man."

"I hear that, App. I hear that!"

The women used whatever they had to make a good meal. They had rice, vegetables, and some meat. They found spices to liven it up. It was good, eating out under the stars.

I'd been in a panic since I arrived here. I had to think fast or die. These were desperate men. They wanted me to be desperate with them. I was, but my desperation was figuring out how to get away. They trusted me, I thought, but if I made like I was going, they would shoot me sure as shit.

I glanced at my watch, it was after nine. With the whiskey almost gone, the guys were getting up to go into the house to sleep with their girlfriends. I looked inside my bag and saw the tan colored box with the red label. "The Ralieghs!" I said out loud, not having meant to.

"What was that, App?" Jones asked.

"Guys, I forgot I have some excellent marijuana from Long Binh. You guys ever do a Raleigh?"

"We had some shitty-ass weed up in Pleiku," said Wilson.

"Well, dude, you're in for a treat. These Raleighs are excellent. Let's have one before we hit the hay." I tapped out a Raleigh and applied some flame. I didn't hold in any smoke, but pretended to, and hoped they didn't notice, then passed it to Jones. He took a long hit, held it, coughing when he breathed out. He passed it to Wilson, who did the same. It moved on to Thomson, Bryant and Snowden. When it got back to me I pretended to take another hit, even faked a cough. I passed it back to Jones. When it made five rounds, I knew I might have a chance at getting away.

I started stretching and yawning. So did the others. We slowly got up, and walked to the house. Snowden had an old mattress. The others had blankets. I found a place in the corner, took off my shoes and curled up to go to sleep.

I waited an hour before lifting my head to look around. I heard snoring and deep breathing. Wilson had the first guard duty, but was sitting by the door fast asleep with his woman lying next to him in deep sleep. I moved slowly into a sitting position with my back to the water-stained wall. This would be my one chance to get out. I couldn't take my bag or even put on my shoes. If they woke, I would tell them I was taking a leak.

I slowly stood up, my joints making a cracking sound, breathlessly waiting for anyone to move. When no one did, I took cautious steps forward, my socks making no noise. After a few more steps, I was a yard from Wilson, whose head was hanging to one side, slack-jawed, breathing deep and slow. The full moon threw enough light in the doorway for me to see where I was stepping. I slipped out the door by the snoozing Wilson, and took another slow step focused on the ground, not wanting to step on anything that would make a noise. After three more steps, I was away from the house.

At last, I found the dirt trail that would take me to the road. I walked faster down the path, breaking into a jog when I hit the dirt road, which had ruts and bumps, luckily my socks provided some protection. I didn't look back, but kept a steady pace until I eventually came to a fork in the road, and instantly made the decision to turn right. I slowed to a rapid walk, breathing deeply. It had been a long time since I'd done any running.

In the light of the moon, my watch said it was two. I realized that I'd left my money, suitcase, gun, book, and the Raleighs behind. I did have my empty wallet and my orders were in my front pocket.

I walked several more hours with more houses and shops appearing on the side of the road. Continuing to walk, more buildings came into view indicating I was on the outskirts of Vung Tau. Feeling safe, I walked through Vung Tau toward the Army base. The dawn sky was streaked in yellow, orange, and red clouds. Approaching the gate, the MP looked me over and saw that I had no shoes, wore dirty shorts and a dirtier shirt.

"Rough night?"

"You got that right."

He looked at my orders. "You got one more day here. You going to the beach?"

"Nah, man, I'm going to find a ride back to Long Binh. I'm done messing around. Which way to the airfield?"

He pointed. "Down that road. You can't miss it."

I started walking and came to the headquarters in front of the small airport. Inside, I recognized the guy behind the counter from when I'd arrived. "I need a ride back to Long Binh, my man," I said.

He pointed to a plane on the tarmac. "That one's leaving right now."

"Great," I said and dashed outside just as soldiers pulled up the stairs of the de Havilland C7 Caribou. What were left of my socks I trashed while running on the corrugated runway with holes the size of fifty-cent pieces. I yelled at the top of my lungs, but could not be heard over the propellers. I saw the plane speeding down the tarmac, then lifting into the air.

Oh fuck! I shouted and watched it take off, then limped back to the terminal. I asked when the next plane or chopper was leaving for Long Binh. The PFC wasn't sure. I sighed and asked, "Do you have anything to read?" He took out an Agatha Christie novel.

"That will do," I said.

Sitting there, I thought about what had just transpired before opening the book. I felt lucky I wasn't killed by the angry black MIAs. It was lucky, too, that Chaves gave me the Raleighs. It dawned on me that this would be the last thing I would do before leaving

Vietnam. Having survived this ordeal, I sat back happy to be free and alive with a great story to tell. I felt like a winner.

Chapter 34

Lessons Learned

Laying on a dusty floor with the Agatha Christie book under my head serving as a pillow, the dispatcher shook me."Hey, App! App! You got a Huey leaving in five minutes." I was lying on a dusty floor with the Agatha Christie book under my head serving as a pillow. I sat up seeing my torn black socks barely covering my feet, the mud spatters on my shirt and shorts. Not seeing my leather bag jolted my memory like a flashback. A shudder swept through me, followed by a gasp and a deep sigh of relief.

My joints made cracking noises when I slowly stood up. My legs were tired from my run to Vung Tau, and my sore feet ached. Stretching, I saw the dispatcher pointing to a Huey on the heliport urging me to hurry. Hobbling as fast as I could with my eyes fixed on the spinning propeller, my hair blowing in the wind, my hand reaching, my heart pounding, I grasped a corporal's hand and took a deep relieved breath when he pulled me aboard. While he strapped me onto the back bulkhead, I saw two guys strapped to gurneys in front of me.

The Huey took off with a huge noise and gust of wind. I closed my eyes, my heart thumping, my mind swirling with eagerness to get back to Long Binh. A plan for my last month in-country was developing. Convincing the new CO and Top to go along with it would be my next goal.

In less than fifteen minutes we were circling outside 24th Evac Hospital. The gunner helped me out of the Huey onto the tarmac, now wet from the rain. My feet were sore with bumps, bruises and blisters, but I managed to limp down the road toward 448 headquarters, and, at last, I was sitting on one of the wooden chairs in the office. North's replacement and new company clerk, Private First Class Henderson, did a double take when he saw me. "What the fuck happened to you, App?"

"Let's just say I had an interesting time in Vung Tau, Henderson. Is the new CO in? I need to talk to him."

He knocked on the CO's door and stuck his head inside. "Lieutenant, Spec Five Appenzeller is back from R&R in Vung Tau. He would like to speak with you." He opened the door wide allowing me to limp in.

"Jesus Christ, Appenzeller! What happened to you?" His eyes widened and his mouth hung open.

"Fell in with some bad people outside Vung Tau. I was lucky to get out alive."

"What kind of bad people, App? Who could have done this to you?"

"They were black soldiers on the run, sir. They held me captive for a while. I was able to slip away."

"You must report this, Appenzeller. The army needs to know about these guys."

"I would, sir, but it won't do any good. They'll move on when they discover I escaped. I couldn't tell you where they were staying. I was lucky to get away from them. I walked all night to the army post in Vung Tau. I don't know if I'll be able to walk on these feet for a while."

"How much time do you have left, Appenzeller?"

"A little over a month, sir," I said, then took a deep breath. "I have a proposal for you."

"What's that?" He cocked his head to the side and narrowed his eyes as if expecting an unwanted surprise.

"While I recuperate, I could be the CQ here in the office each night. Someone has to do it. I'll do it until my tour comes to an end. It would re-lieve others from that task."

"You want to be permanent CQ? What about your duties at the motor pool?"

"I've worked my way out of a posi-tion there. Talk to Warrant Officer Gabriel. They passed inspection when I was on my emergency leave in Hawaii. Spec Five Romanasky is doing my job there. I'm tired, lieutenant. My tour is close to being over. I've survived. I don't want to take any more risks. I'd like to walk from my room to the office, and back again for the remain-der of my tour."

"It's an unusual request, Appen-zeller. I'll talk to the Top about it and let you know. In the meantime, Hen-derson can take you to 24th Evac. Have them look at your feet."

"Thank you, sir. I hope this works out."

Henderson drove me to 24th Evac Hospital, where a charming black nurse cleaned my feet and bandaged the open sores. She asked how I got the abra-sions. I gave her the long version, en-joying this time with a woman who spoke English. She gave me an old pair of clean white socks and laughed when I asked if I was up for a Purple Heart. After that Henderson drove me as close to my room as possible. I limped the rest of the way.

Looking around my room, I felt at ease in this special place. It reminded me of my friends who helped me build it. Most were gone; only Chaves and Romanasky were still around. Climbing onto the top bunk, laying there with eyes gazing at my little friend still capturing flying insects, I soon drifted into a deep sleep.

Chaves opened the door and shuffled in with a PFC I didn't know. "You don't have to be quiet Freddy, I'm awake."

"Dude, what happened to you, Apple?" asked Chaves, looking at my bandaged feet.

"It's an unbelievable story, Freddie. I ended up with deserters in Vung Tau. I acted like I was in their gang. Thank you for giving me those Raleighs. They were my ticket out. I got them so fucked up they passed out. It was the only way I could get away. Otherwise, I'd still be with them. I'd be MIA, like they were, living a desperate life."

"No shit, Apple? Another amazing story! Oh, this is my friend Harry Leonard. Like me, he's from Ohio." I shook Leonard's hand.

"So you're the guy who took twenty-one days in Hawaii?" I just smiled. "Dude, you're a legend. Now you have this story to tell as well."

"Yeah, well, I'm done with messing around, Leonard. I just put in a request to be permanent CQ at 448 Headquarters. I don't want to go anywhere other than here to headquarters. No more partying for me, my man, I'll be up all night reading, sitting in the company clerk's nice swivel chair. My legendary days are over. I just want to get back home."

"I can dig that, App. We're heading to the club; you sticking around?"

"My feet are hurting, Freddie. I'll be in this room for the next couple of days. When you see Romanasky and the chief, let them know my plans."

As they were leaving, the big Russian appeared at the door, then saw my bandaged feet. "Goddamn it, Apple-fuck! What in the hell did you do this time?"

"In the wrong place at the wrong time, J.R. It's a hell of a story that no one will believe. I'm lucky to be alive."

"No shit? You've got to tell me what happened," he said reaching for the Jack Daniels.

"You want some Chivas?" he asked, pouring some Jack into his glass.

"Why not, J.R.? Make it a double."

I told him about the surf and my night with Lan. He thought that was pretty cool. I told him how the Lambretta took me to the deserters, and explained how I convinced them that I was a deserter, too, so they wouldn't shoot me then and there. "It was the pack of Raleighs that saved the day, J.R. It put them into a deep enough sleep for me to slip away." I described my long night's practically barefooted walk to Vung Tau from their hiding place.

"I'm done messing around, I put in to be permanent CQ for the remainder of my time here. I was lucky to escape Tet, lucky to get those twenty-one days in Hawaii, and really lucky to get away from the deserters. I don't want my luck to run out. I'm tired, J.R. I want to make sure I get back to Alexandra."

"No sweat, Apple, the chief and I have things squared away at the motor pool. Guys at the clubs ask about you. I'll have another cool story to tell them. You think they'll let you be permanent CQ?"

"I hope so, J.R. I don't see a reason why not. What else am I qualified to do here?"

"You ain't qualified to do shit, but you've managed do a lot in one tour of duty. Here's to you Applefuck, the King of the REMFs!" We clinked glasses and downed our drinks.

They did allow me to be permanent CQ. Reporting to 448 headquarters at 7:30 pm, I was there for twelve hours. I found every Agatha Christie book in the battalion. For some reason the challenge to discover the hidden clues that Mrs. Marple or Hercule Pierot would reveal in the end kept me awake.

I had a lot to think about when not reading. What a relief it was to no longer be living in fear of being busted by the CID. That was one lesson learned from my tour of duty. I lamented the wasted time worrying about things that never happened. Endless anxious hours imagining worst case scenarios, feeling horrible, causing my body to produce toxic chemicals and hormones that caused useless anxiety. Worrying was going to be a hard habit to break.

Worrying was tied to guilt, one of the outcomes of being raised Catholic. There were reasons for feeling guilty. When opportunities for making a little money or improving my living situation arose, I took it. I didn't weigh the moral ambiguities, and chose what would make me look cool. Yes, ever since high school being cool became my main motivation. After all, I was a CAMF, a cool assed motherfucker. How shallow was that as a purpose of life; how meaningless, stupid and dangerous.

So what was my purpose in life? I entered the army as a Catholic, and believed that as a member of the Catholic Church, I was a part of the Body of Christ on earth. I believed that Jesus Christ was the Son of God sent to earth to be a guide in how to conduct our lives so we could live with him for eternity. New knowledge about the complicity of my church in the lead-up to war in Vietnam created a cognitive dissonance, a moral dilemma. Learning the war was morally wrong, meant the Church and the United States were both on the wrong side of history and morality.

My conversations with Collins and Peterson about the Mormon Church, and the many difficult things that religion asked its followers to believe, led me to question my church and all religions. Religions required belief in things that science and common sense revealed to be nonsense, yet billions of people in the world don't question the veracity of the stories which are the foundations of their church. They're willing to die defending their beliefs which ultimately were empty superstitions that had caused wars throughout history.

I pondered the ideas about life that Mr. Nguyen shared with me. They were simple, but profound. Do good work, think positive thoughts, be kind, be compassionate, be honest, help others. I believed that if we all conducted ourselves this way, the world would be a better place. Shaving my head and walking around in an orange outfit spending my days meditating didn't seem like a viable option. I was going back to the real world. Adhering to these Buddhist ideals, however, would be a good way to live my life and raise a family.

I knew that my experience in Vietnam changed my life. I was no longer even close to being the shallow man I was before going to Vietnam. The world, too, had changed while I was in-country. Martin Luther King had been killed. His work to bring equality to black Americans would now take a more radical turn. The death of Robert Kennedy led to riots in the streets of Chicago during the Democratic Convention. The war in Vietnam demonstrated the futility of our efforts to force others to accept our democratic traditions and economic beliefs.

In the end I realized I had a story to tell - a story about my personal growth and development as a man, a story about taking advantage of situations that came my way as a way of being cool. I wasn't proud of what I had done, though I knew I would be treated like a hero when I returned home. Down deep I knew I wasn't one. I had heard that some returning vets were spat upon by those who hated the war, but I knew my parents, brothers, sisters and friends would treat me like a hero. Though it would make me uncomfortable, I would accept it, and tell the truth of my story, so that it would be a lesson.

Time moved slowly at 448 headquarters, but the end, for me anyway, was drawing near. A week before I was due to leave, it was announced that there would be a change in the MPC. We had to exchange our old money for new money that was printed in different colors featuring other people on the front and back of the currency.

I heard there were thousands of Vietnamese outside the gate begging GI's to exchange money for them. We had paid many of our workers in MPC. It was the money used in Bien Hoa and Saigon. Many Vietnamese woke up that day with pieces of paper that no longer had any value.

When relieved of duty in the morning, I wandered down to the gate and witnessed the hordes of crying people who were suddenly impoverished. Wanting to help them, but having no means of doing so, caused me great anguish and another realization of the horror of this war. There was a limit to the amount of money I could exchange.

A familiar face stood next to the fence. It was Mr. Nguyen. It broke my heart to see him with a fistful of MPC in his hand. I asked him to give me the money. I would do one more thing for him to hopefully pay him back for the profound affect he had on me. When he passed the money through the chain-link fence, others scrambled desperately to give me their money. I quickly moved away, went to the exchange booth, got new currency, and returned to see so many hands clutching old money outside the fence that it became difficult to find Mr. Nguyen. When I found him, he was patiently standing there waiting for me. We made the exchange quickly. After he stuffed the money into his pockets, we stood staring at each other for several seconds. All I could say was, "Thank you, Mr. Nguyen, for all that you've taught me." He bowed his head with his prayer hands under his chin, a tear in his eye slowly trickling down his face, while my throat ached unable to stop the tears running down my cheeks. Though sad, great joy swelled in me that I could help Mr. Nguyen and say goodbye to the dear sweet man who had changed my life.

A week later I said goodbye to Romanasky and Chaves. We decided to stay in my room for the final night. I was amazed that at the end of my tour there were so few people I knew. My friends were gone, friends I knew I'd never see again, but would always remember for being part of a significant period of my life.

That night we drank Chivas and Jack then smoked our last Paxton. We told stories and laughed our heads off. Once started with J.R., it was impossible to stop. His contagious laughter made us so hysterical tears poured down our faces. At the end we all hugged and promised to keep in touch. Unlike my other Army pals, I knew I'd stay in touch with J.R. It would not be the last time we laughed at the surrealistic world we experienced in 1968.

I left the next morning with little fanfare, and spent the night at 90th Relocation, then boarded a plane in the morning and read an entire Agatha Christie novel on the way to Los Angeles.

What a thrill it was to exit the plane and see Alexandra, my beautiful Alexandra in the window waving at me. She had been with me throughout this adventure in Hawaii and in the many letters we exchanged. I couldn't wait to make love to her, for us to start our family and a new life. We hugged, kissed, and felt ecstatic to be together, our Vietnam days behind us.

When we got to my parents' house I embraced my family long and hard. My family and friends treated me like a hero, just as I thought they would, forcing me to hide the truth that I was no hero, not even close.

I handed my dad an envelope that contained a certificate of achievement from now Brigadier General McD. Anderson Jr. USA Commanding. He had it delivered to me on my last day at 448 headquarters. Holding Alexandra's hand while standing next to my mom and the rest of my family and friends my dad read it aloud with tears welling in his eyes.

THE UNITED STATES ARMY SUPPORT COMMAND, SAIGON, CERTIFICATE OF ACHIEVEMENT IS PRESENTED TO SPECIALIST APPENZELLER FOR OUTSTANDING AND MERITORIOUS PERFORMANCE OF DUTY WHILE SERVING IN THE REPUBLIC OF VIETNAM DURING THE PERIOD NOVEMBER 1967 TO NOVEMBER 1968. AS A PLAN LOADING LIST SPECIALIST IN

THE 448TH SUPPLY AND SERVICE COMPANY, SPECIALIST APPENZELLER DISPLAYED KEEN AND PROFESSIONAL INSIGHT FAR BEYOND THAT EXPECTED OF A MAN OF HIS GRADE AND EXPERIENCE. THROUGH HIS ENERGETIC AND DILIGENT ACTIONS, HE OBTAINED SUPERB RESULTS AND EARNED FOR HIMSELF THE RESPECT AND ADMIRATION OF ALL OF HIS ASSOCIATES. HE PERFORMED HIS DUTIES IN A MANNER WHICH REFLECT GREAT CREDIT UPON HIMSELF, HIS UNIT AND THE UNITED STATES ARMY.

I stood there crimson faced listening to the words "outstanding and meritorious performance of duty" feeling suddenly great pride in myself. When my dad finished reading he looked at me with such love and admiration as my mom stood next to me smiling her huge smile, tears dripping from her chin. I felt Alexandra's hand squeeze mine tight and the pounding on my back by some of my friends. Tears were dripping down my cheeks as well. Tears of happiness that I was finally back home, that I had served my country and earned a certificate of achievement. But also tears of anguish for Mr. Nguyen and others who were left behind who had to endure living in a war torn region created by our country with little hope for it to end.

I knew deep in my heart that I was not the man every one was seeing. I had taken advantage of my meritorious performance of duty to create a relatively good life filled with booze and drugs. I had bullshitted my way to Hawaii and bullshitted my way out of trouble with the MIAs. I was surrounded by corruption and used that as justification to defy all that I thought was ethical and right just to be considered cool. I felt like a phony as I looked at the smiling proud faces of my family and friends hoping I would have the courage to tell the truth about how I had served. I knew I would eventually, but that would be for another time. Today, I was a hero and was glad to be home.

The End

Epilogue

For those who like to know how the story ends, here's a quick epilogue that tells what happened after my transformative year in Vietnam. Alexandra and I did my final year in the Army at Fort Ord, California. I was given an easy job moving supplies from Fort Ord to the decommissioned Camp Roberts and I only had to work about two or three days a week. Alexandra and I bought a fancy little Datsun 2000 and cruised back and forth to Carmel and Big Sur. In September of 69, our son Paul was born and then in November I received my Honorable Discharge and my three years as a soldier came to an end, but not my memories. I enrolled at San Diego City College where I had to get a 4.0 to make up for my horrible grades at Ventura College. I was accepted by San Diego State and eventually earned a degree in Social Science, but spent much of my time protesting the War in Vietnam as part of Vets Against the War. My degree qualified me for one thing — teaching, which fit with the Buddhist sensibility I had learned from Mr. Nguyen. Alexandra and I bought our first little house while we were going to college, and when I got a job teaching in La Mesa, we bought our dream house on the hill above La Mesa Middle school where I taught. In November of

74 our daughter Erica came into our lives. Alexandra worked at SDSU in administration and got her Masters degree and eventually her PHD. My first eight years I taught eight special education students — a wonderful opportunity to pass on my beliefs in the power of empathy, self-esteem and mindfulness. I also taught classes in music, science and English, but over time taught Social Science and was the advisor for the Associated Student Body. It was a charmed life with everything I could possibly want, but by the late seventies something happened with Alexandra and me. It is hard to recall all that went wrong, but it hurt to drift apart and in 79 we divorced. Single again, I set out on my next adventure — a transformative and challenging journey through Europe following my performance artist sister which is the subject of my next book called Angst.

About the Author

The author Robbie Appenzeller was a middle school teacher in La Mesa California and was part of the Partners in Education program with San Diego State. With his wife he raised his two children Paul and Erica. After retirement he eventually moved to the Isla Colon in the region of Bocas del Toro, Panama. For years he travelled throughout South and Central America and Mexico where he surfed some of the great waves in each region. He had an epiphany at sixty-nine and went to Southeast Asia to write his book Boomer War. At seventy-two he still surfs and is working on his second manuscript about his travel in 1979 with his avant-guard performance artist sister Katie Duck.

Acknowledgements

Thanks to all who gave me support during the writing process. Especially my Brother Dan who encouraged me to get started. The final edition came about with the help of my first editor Allene Blaker and then the professional editor Mike Garrett. A special thanks to my final editor the poet and writer Arnold Greenberg. A special shout out to the artist Julie Jorgensen who read the book and then designed the wonderful cover.